TEXIT

A STAR ALONE

GANPY NATARAJ

MOYGA BOOKS

MOYGA BOOKS

Copyright © 2023 by Ganpy Nataraj (Nataraj Ganapathy)

The Library of Congress has catalogued the Moyga Books edition as follows:
Names: Nataraj, Ganpy, author.

Title: *TEXIT – A Star Alone* / Ganpy Nataraj

Description: Novi: Moyga Books, 2023

Identifiers: LCCN:
Library of Congress Control Number: 2023918899
Moyga Books Trade Hardcover Edition ISBN: 979-8-9892435-0-1
Moyga Books Trade Paperback Edition ISBN: 979-8-9892435-1-8
eBook ISBN: 979-8-9892435-2-5

Cover and interior design by David Ter-Avanesyan/Ter33Design
Cover images by Shutterstock
Map image courtesy of *Moon Texas*, eighth edition from Moon Travel Guides

moygabooks.com

For my grandfather

CONTENTS

NEW MEXICO
Santa Fe
Albuquerque
Adrian
McLean
Sha
Amarillo
Hereford
Palo Duro Canyon State Park
Childress
Roswell
Lubbock
Dickens
Socorro
Brownfield
Alamogordo
Snyder
Carlsbad
Monahans Sandhills State Park
Odessa
Midland
TEXAS
Franklin Mountains State Park
El Paso
Guadalupe Mountains National Park
San Angelo
Juárez
Rio
MCDONALD OBSERVATORY
Fort Davis
Fort Stockton
Sonora
Grande
Marfa
Alpine
Seminole Canyon State Park
Big Bend National Park
Amistad Reservoir
Del Rio
Ciudad Acuña
Chihuahua
MEXICO
Ciudad Jiménez
Monclova
© AVALON TRAVEL

Fayetteville
Tulsa
Jonesboro
Oklahoma City
ARKANSAS
OKLAHOMA
Little Rock
Wichita Falls
Lake Village
MS
mour
Paris
Gainesville
Denton
FORT WORTH STOCKYARDS
Dallas
Sulphur Springs
Caddo Lake
Shreveport
Fort Worth
Tyler
Dinosaur Valley State Park
Corsicana
Red River
Toledo Bend Reservoir
LOUISIANA
Alexandria
Waco
Lufkin
Sam Rayburn Reservoir
Enchanted Rock State Natural Area
Bryan/ College Station
Woodville
Big Thicket National Preserve
Lafayette
Fredericksburg
Austin
Orange
Lake Charles
NATURAL BRIDGE CAVERNS
Houston
Beaumont
Port Arthur
San Antonio
Galveston Bay
Galveston
Victoria
Matagorda Bay
Corpus Christi
Laredo
Kingsville
Parde Island National Seashore
Falcon Reservoir
Santa Ana National Wildlife Refuge
Brownsville
Matamoros
River
Lake Texoma
do
TEXIT
A STAR ALONE
0   50 mi
0   50 km

PREFACE

Despite its controversial premise, this book is a work of fiction born in 2021 largely due to events that started disturbing me.

I witnessed a few fringe bills being brought for legislative discussions across a few different states here in the USA. The disparity between reality and what was once thought impossible was quite wide back then, but this was the spark that began my journey towards writing these pages.

Characters that you will meet in this book are drawn from life's experiences and not based on any one person or persons. They embody those who we may know or are surrounded by every day.

While this book is primarily written for entertainment purposes, my true intent does not seek political awareness or inculcate fear—although it may manifest in either form regardless.

And if it does, they merely serve as a reminder: That which seems unimaginable today could well become our tomorrow.

The Author
November 2023

CHAPTER 1

THE DAY AFTER ELECTION

istory makers are a rare breed. Such a person possesses the drive and determination to manufacture their own opportunities and thereby leave their mark on the world. When these individuals are blessed with power, they become unstoppable forces with the potential to effect great change. Either for better or for worse.

Derek Fisher was sitting in his recently inaugurated office, looking around at all the unfamiliar and formal trappings. He allowed himself a moment to reflect on the strange journey that had taken him here—from a self-made businessman to an aspiring politician with a vision for change, and finally to being elected as the highest representative of public office within this great state of Texas. Sure, success did not come fully without cost or sacrifice; there had been plenty of long nights spent away from home preparing speeches, answering questions, and creating the political phenomenon and persona he had become. But now he looked around his new surroundings, proudly knowing it was all worth it.

As the governor stood alone in his office on the second floor of the Capitol, he stared out the window at the vast expanse beyond. He thought about all the promises he had made during his campaign for office—promises to make improvements to public education, women's health, and the state's sovereign independence. Promises that seemed so audacious and not achievable only a few months ago. Now he wondered how far the people of Texas would allow him to go. He was not worried if he could deliver on his promises, but how soon. If not during his first term, he thought he could accomplish most of them in his second term. Or even the third, since Texas had no gubernatorial term limits.

His eyes searched endlessly across the Capitol corners, as if searching for an answer.

"What could bring Texans together? What form of civic action would work now more than ever before?"

He was smart enough to know that these questions had no easy answers—but he believed it was within his reach to find them, since no one before him had ever tried reaching this far. He fully believed he was the new superstar conservative politician the state needed.

And that's why here today, surrounded by uncertainty, old furniture, and doubts, Derek Fisher began the first chapter of an historic term, fully determined to actualize his premier aspirations toward a brighter future collective that the people of Texas could enjoy.

A future independent Texas—freeing itself from the clutches of the Union.

Jason Greer was a bit nervous as he waited in the lounge. This was not his first interview, but he needed this one to be massive. He had left his career dreams in Washington, DC to move back to his home state just to follow what he sensed to be an historic and significant political shift in Texas. He wanted to be part of it. He wanted to play a role in shaping the future of Texas. He did not know if he had the power in him as a news reporter at *The Austin Star* to change people's minds, but that was not going to stop him from pursuing the truth.

"Do you know when this painting was brought in here?" Jason asked the secretary, who was busy typing something in her computer.

"No, sir. I have no idea." She was not very pleased to entertain Jason.

"Hmm. This looks like an historic moment being captured. Doesn't it? Do you mind if I walk over there to check it out?" Jason asked politely.

"Sure."

Jason knew he was the only one waiting in that room, so he left his bag on the chair. He got up, stretched his legs, and adjusted his black and gray plaid sports coat as he walked up to the painting.

"Ah! This is The Settlement of Austin's Colony, by Henry McCardle. 1875. Wow! 1875!" Jason read the description under the painting loud, then turned around to look at the secretary to see if she was paying attention.

"Wow indeed, sir," she said without making any eye contact with Jason.

He walked back to his chair. Before he sat down, he peered at her again.

"The governor should be seeing you in just a minute. You know the ground rules for the interview we had already shared with your team, Mr. Greer?" She looked back at him.

"Yes. Of course."

"Well. You have twenty minutes. Follow me this way, Mr. Greer."

Jason was ushered into a conference room with two tables. One was a long and an oval shaped table with ten chairs around it and the other one was a short one, meant for four people. The room was large enough to have enough space between these two tables. He looked around the light blue gray walls and noticed that there were no paintings here. The conference room was designed to have no distractions whatsoever. There was one spider web conference phone in the middle of the long table and some audio-visual equipment. He did not know where to sit. So he decided to stand in the space between the two tables.

Within a couple of minutes, Governor Derek Fisher walked in.

"Good morning, Mr. Greer! It is a nice day to be in Austin. Isn't it?" He approached Jason and gave him a very firm handshake.

"It sure is, governor. It's my honor to meet you. Thank you for your time, and good morning!" Jason shook the governor's cold hands and realized how weak his handshake was compared to his.

"Shall we begin, Mr. Greer?" Fisher pulled out a chair from the eastern end of the small table and gestured Jason to take his seat.

"Jason. Just call me Jason, sir." Jason pulled out the chair that was opposite to Fisher's.

Jason cleared his throat and placed his notebook on the table.

"I see you still do it old school. I like it." Fisher smiled.

"Yes. *Mostly,* yes. But it depends on whom I am interviewing, governor." Jason quickly realized that could lead to misinterpretation.

"I meant it depends on the nature of the interview. Not the person I am interviewing," he clarified with a nervous smile.

"Go on," the governor prompted him to start the interview.

"Let me start off with the most important question, governor. Do you really think that your referendum to secede from the Union will pass?" Jason fired his first salvo.

"Oh, yes. Absolutely. Willing to wager?"

"No. That's not my area of expertise, sir. But without getting into the constitutional viability and such, you do realize that this is setting up the state of Texas in a path of permanent chaos?"

"That's an abrasively presumptuous take, Jason. How can you say that? From what I have heard, you have spent the last ten years in DC. Clearly not in touch with what's going on here in Texas. Are you? Firstly, constitutional viability be damned. We are seceding. And that means the Constitution that binds the Union together no longer will apply to us. Will it? We are going to frame our own constitution after we become independent. Sure, this is going to involve many stages, and there are many parts to it before we can break away completely. And it is not going to be easy. I have never hidden these facts, Jason. The people know these facts. I have never said this is going to be a path full of roses. If we cross these bumps together as Texans, there ain't going to be no chaos," Fisher responded aggressively.

Jason was taking notes as the governor was speaking. He did not know shorthand but had developed his own codes, which only he could decipher later. Within these first three or four minutes, Jason felt how much he would have loved to have a recorder. But when one was interviewing the governor, one did not really have a choice to ask for exceptions from the ground rules set.

He continued.

"I want to clarify my previous question, governor. Since you just mentioned that this secession is going to me a multistage process, and no one really knows the timeline clearly, what I wanted to ask was how are you going to prepare

Texans to navigate this tumultuous period?"

"Um. I am the newly elected Governor of Texas, and I am here with a sixty-one percent mandate. I think that's reason enough to believe I can convince my people to stick with me till we cross the finish line," boasted Fisher.

"But governor, are you not worried how your controversial campaign promises to push for extreme conservative social values will affect the lives of so many people of Texas? And then you are throwing this secession into the mix. I want to …" Jason was no longer nervous. He was in a flow, and he could sense that his interview subject of the day liked to talk. He stopped looking at the time and just wanted to get in as many questions as he could. This was the highest profile interview he had ever done in his entire career.

"Again, you are being presumptuous, Jason. You are saying people's lives are going to be affected. You have no clue what you are talking about. So, DC and so out of touch." Fisher was showing his annoyance.

"Mr. Governor, I don't think I am being presumptuous. Even if the sixty-one percent stick with you, the other thirty-nine percent who did not vote for you, a good chunk of them, will say their lives are being affected by your policies. Do you sense that? My question is why throw this secession on top of all the changes? Why can't the referendum to secede wait for another year or more? Why now?" queried Jason.

"You don't get it, Jason. You just don't. I come from the business world. If I can take a big risk and invest in something today that will give me a bigger and long-term profit tomorrow, I would rather do that than keep picking those low hanging fruits for smaller profits today." Fisher got up from his chair and walked to the corner refrigerator to get himself a bottle of water.

"Water?"

"I'm good, sir. Thank you."

"Look at this label. You know who makes them?" the governor asked.

"No."

"I do. This is my brand. Well, technically not mine, since yesterday."

"That's interesting, governor."

"What's interesting? That a rookie reporter from *The Austin Star* gets to break the news that the new Governor of Texas sources his own brand of water for his office? Nah. I'll tell you what could be interesting, Jason. What do you think of TEXIT?" Fisher placed two bottles of water on the table and stared at Jason.

"I beg your pardon, sir."

"TEXIT. You get to be the first reporter to break the news, Jason. Go on. Run with it. We are calling this movement TEXIT. I am going to deliver on my promise and announce the TEXIT referendum soon. My administration is looking aggressively into locking the dates for referendum. It will be held statewide on the same day. It could be just a coincidence. The TEXIT referendum will be held exactly six months from today. You heard it here first!"

OFFICIAL BALLOT

Referendum on the Great State of Texas's status as a sovereign state under the Constitution of the United States of America and its status to continue using the Federal Government of United States of America as an agent for certain enumerated powers.	
Vote for not more than one	
Remain in the Union	⬭
Leave the Union	⬭

ARTICLE 49

1. Any member State of the Union of the United States of America may decide to secede from the Union in accordance with its own constitutional requirements.

2. A member State which decides to secede shall notify the United States Congress of its intention. In the light of the guidelines provided by the Constitution of the United States of America, the Union, led by the President, shall negotiate, and conclude an agreement with that State, setting out the arrangements for its withdrawal, taking account of the framework for its future relationship with the Union. It shall be concluded on behalf of the Union by the United States Congress, acting by a qualified majority, after obtaining the consent of the Senate. A qualified majority shall be defined as two-thirds vote in the Senate in accordance with the Constitution.

3. All privileges and treaties shall cease to apply to the State in question from the date of entry into force of the secession agreement unless the Union, in agreement with the State concerned, unanimously decides to extend this period.

4. The State concerned shall not engage in any negotiations or participate in discussions with any other member State or trade partner or any country outside the Union as a representative of the Union from the date of entry into force of then secession agreement.

5. If a State which has withdrawn from the Union asks to rejoin, its request shall be subject to the procedure referred to in Article 51.

CHAPTER 2

CURRENT DAY

There are varying degrees of hot weather. But summer in San Antonio was dictated by sweltering heat, sticky humidity, and a desire to stay cool. If one was stuck in the Sahara and they had access to an air conditioner, they would want to turn it on, wouldn't they? That's what Lisa Barkley wanted to do, because on this day in July, she felt like she was stuck in the Sahara, and the local weatherman had said that this heat wave could last for more than a week.

Lisa lived thirty-five miles to the east of San Antonio. A single mom with a two-year-old daughter—Lisa—did not have too many rooms to cool down in her small house. All she needed was the air conditioner in her bedroom to function as it once did three years ago. She had called one of the local electric contractors who had done some electric work for her in the previous year, and he had promised he would fix her air conditioner.

Gavin Forbes, a tall and bulky man in his forties, pulled his Ford F-150 in front of Lisa's house. He noticed that there was a red car parked somewhat crookedly in front of her house, and he knew it was not Lisa's car. It was not curiosity as much as anxiety that made Gavin quickly park his vehicle and jump out. He was certainly not a friend of hers, nor was he her well-wisher. But in a small suburb like this, one sort of looked out for each other almost instinctively.

Gavin's instinct at that moment told him that Lisa may be in trouble. So he did not want to make much noise announcing his arrival. He walked quietly to the side of the house where there was a flower patch and was hoping he could take a quick peek through the kitchen window. He breathed a quick sigh of relief as soon as he spotted Lisa sitting down on a chair in the kitchen. She didn't seem to have any visible physical injuries. From his vantage point, she seemed very much in control of the surroundings and did not appear to be under any threat. His eyes immediately shifted to the person she was animatedly talking to.

On top of a small barricade that separated her kitchen area from her living room, he spotted not one person, but two. A man and a woman. Lisa's face was angry one moment and frustrated the next, from what Gavin could tell. And soon, she cupped both her hands to cover her face, as if she was trying to control her crying. The woman got up from the barricade and rushed towards Lisa, hugging Lisa. At first, Lisa seemed to resist. Then she yielded. For the next few seconds, they hugged each other, and Gavin saw the woman comforting Lisa by patting on her back before they released themselves from each other's grips.

The man stepped forward, paused, and gave a quick hug to Lisa, too. Then he handed an envelope to her. Lisa seemed to acknowledge what the man was saying after receiving the envelope. The man and the woman waved goodbye, picked their backpack, and left.

American Airlines 1552 was on time. For a Friday morning, the Reagan International Airport wasn't quite busy. Perhaps business travel had slowed down a bit this week owing to summer and the holiday weekend. The coffee shops were busy, but the baristas were not terribly rushed, and those passengers trying to grab snacks from the airport stores didn't have to fight elbow traffic as they tried to maneuver their way through the narrow aisles.

Senator Ryan Dodson and Congressman Evan Williams were waiting at the gate. Those who had been following American politics over the past few months would have seen a lot of them on TV and yet they tried their best to appear low-key in their baseball hats, polo shirts, and blue denims, leaving aside their sports jackets. They tried to be as inconspicuous as they could be when they appeared in public because they knew every move of them could be watched by someone, no matter where they were. And at this moment in the airport, unbeknown to them, someone was trying to lip-read their conversations from a distance.

But this was a crucial time in the nation's history. A very crucial time in their own lives. The events leading up to this day and what they did right now in their capacity as elected representatives of forty-two million Texans in the Union would determine how history would be shaped. They had an opportunity to alter the future. So they had to continue doing what they were good at—no matter wherever they were. That was, to continue to play politics. A skill, an art, a game—whatever one calls it.

Dodson, a sixty-two-year-old Houston native, and the senior Senator of Texas had been a mentor for Williams for over two decades now. Williams, a representative of TX-02, was serving his second term in the US Congress. This historic moment he was getting to experience—a moment his grandfather would be proud that his grandson was part of—had changed him as a congressman, and as a politician.

All politicians must be opportunists. What differentiated a good politician from a bad one was how they used these opportunities. A good one would put their interests below those of others while a bad one didn't care, as they always placed their self-interests and ambitions above everything else.

"We have the final vote in two weeks, Evan," said Dodson. "And the last I heard, we are still fifteen short in the House. Is that right?"

"If you consider Adam from Michigan a no, then yes, we are indeed in need of fifteen more. But that's a long way from where we were two weeks ago, sir. This was going nowhere, remember? We needed thirty-six. We still got time. We can pull this off." Williams sounded very optimistic. This optimism was one of the main reasons why Dodson took Williams under his wing. He had spotted early on that Williams possessed an unfiltered arrogant attitude to get things done.

"But my worry is not what you can and cannot do, Evan. I am not sure what that son of a bitch is up to. He is spending this weekend in DC. Have asked my crew to check on him constantly and update me."

"You've always had your doubts about him, sir. Even before the referendum.

Your instincts were right."

"Damn right, son. It takes a rotten apple to know another one." Dodson guffawed.

"Listen, you and I have some important business to take care of back home. Let's try to deal with the nightmare scenario developing in Austin. Fisher is trying to fuck our dreams from the other end," he continued.

"About that, sir. I had a scoop I want to share. But perhaps this is not the right time. How about I send you an email and you can read it while you're on the plane? I'm sure it will keep you awake tonight. I know I'm going to stay up all night thinking about the next move."

"All right. Shoot that email now before we board. On that note…" Dodson pointed at the gate and let out a deep sigh to get up from his seat.

The gate agent was calling all first-class passengers to board. Senator Dodson and Congressman Williams were going to be sitting next to each other, and as far as their basic rules of engagement went, they never discussed business when they were inside a plane.

In another three weeks, the crops would be ready for harvest. Burl Fogg, the thirty-seven-year-old millennial farmer was getting started with his day in his peanut farm. Like most peanut farms in Texas, his farm was also in Lubbock County. Stansley, a small town of mostly farmlands, was where Burl was born. When his father passed away quite unexpectedly, he did not have many options left. He was surprised what a natural he was when it came to farming from the day he took over Fogg Farms. He and his sister had spent much of their younger years in the farm, helping their father, not really realizing how much they were learning. School was always secondary in his part of the world.

This had been a rough year. As much sustainable and low maintenance these peanut crops were, extreme droughts could make their lives miserable. Burl, with his buddy Dudley, had built an efficient irrigation system a couple of years ago, but this was the first year he was forced into a situation where he had to test the limits of the system. Not only Fogg Farms, but the entire farming community was under the never-before-experienced need to use their water very carefully.

If the drought continued for two more weeks, he knew that his crop would be only fifty percent of what the farm had last year. Even with the state government subsidies, he knew he would not be making much this year. He anticipated the drought a couple of months ahead of their planting season, so he decided to plant more Spanish and Valencia Peanuts this year as opposed to Valencia and Virginia that his father always grew in their farm.

"If you haven't eaten Valencia peanuts from Fogg Farms, you haven't lived a worthy life," his father would always comment during their sale negotiations with the food companies who purchased peanuts from him. Valencia was considered by many as the tastiest of peanuts, and those who enjoy boiled peanuts would never consider another variety if they tasted boiled Valencia Peanuts once in their lifetime. They were comparatively fast growing, maturing in ninety to 120 days. But they were slightly more drought intolerant. On the contrary, Spanish Peanuts were more resistant to droughts.

Burl, the first millennial peanut farmer in Lubbock County, was the youngest farmer to be invited for the annual Texas Department of Agriculture's summit where the commissioner specifically requested a twenty-minute private meeting with him. The commissioner wanted to know the challenges Burl was facing as a millennial farmer, and his thoughts on the future of farming in the state, given the latest political landscape shift and its potential ramifications.

Burl was prepared for the face-to-face meeting in Austin, and he had in fact collated many of his thoughts in a three-page document. When he met the commissioner at the appointed time inside a private office room in the hotel where the summit was being held, he handed over the letter to the commissioner.

The feds are evil.

That was the title on the first page.

When the commissioner smiled as soon as he opened his document, Burl instantly reacted.

"That's a sort of Fogg family philosophy, sir. My father never minced his words when it came to letting everyone who cared or did not care know how much he detested the DC politicians and the federal government. He never got a dime through all the supposed incentives the Federal Farm Act offered. You know, he always had a cold relationship with USDA. He often joked that if I ever took up farming, it would be over his dead body that I would be allowed to even talk to anyone who farted like an USDA employee." Burl smiled.

"Your father sure was a wise man, Mr. Fogg. Now if you may, Mr. Fogg, why do you say that state of Texas hasn't done enough for the farmers?"

"Sir, if I may be so blunt, I think the state has squandered the opportunity during the past twenty years or so to modernize our farming technologies and equipment. In fact, we are somewhat caught between the nostalgia of the past and the promises of an independent future that our state has missed out on many such opportunities in other areas, too. Not just in agriculture."

"Interesting, Mr. Fogg. Don't get me wrong, I absolutely hate your bluntness. I really do. Tell me, what would you do if you were in charge? In charge of the state agricultural department?"

"Sir, I wouldn't know squat about any other farming. I just know peanut farming. That's all we do at Fogg Farms. But the problems we all face are somewhat common. I have friends in Lubbock County whom I speak to. As much as I hate the Federal Agricultural Board myself, they seem to have some interesting ideas. At least on paper. From what I've read."

"Like what?"

"Sustainable farming."

"Can you elaborate Mr. Fogg?"

Burl really didn't have time to elaborate during that meeting. But he assured the commissioner that he would prepare a document on sustainable farming and share it with him within the next two weeks.

Burl despised the federal government as much as majority of Texans did. Yet he really thought that the USDA had some interesting and forward-thinking programs, assistance and relief programs, and other ideas to help farmers. With the Union being so large, he understood how the overall efficiencies of such programs tended to go down, as these programs worked their way down to all rural communities in all states. Which was why he was frustrated that the Texas Department of Agriculture failed to borrow ideas from the USDA. Now he was worried it may have been too late. As for the next few years, Burl and most farmers in Texas knew that they all would have to be prepared for plenty of uncertainties and bumpiness.

Burl did not choose to be a farmer. After he became a full-time farmer, he never wanted to think about what other career he would have chosen had the circumstances been different. For a young man who had spent all his life in a Texan rural community, Burl had a better worldview than most around him. He was a very self-aware individual. He had accepted that he got into one of the riskiest professions, one which he had been enjoying very much until now.

And three weeks ago, Burl did make a very important choice along with seventy point five percent of Texans. He just wished his father, Fogg, Sr., was alive to see this day.

"The day we break free, I tell ya, son. Promise me you will send a bag full of Valencia shells to the USDA assholes in DC with a polite note that says, *Please shove these up your asses,*" Burl remembered his father telling him with a smile and a tear, just before he passed away.

The thirty-sixth floor of the Lindas building was buzzing with activity, which was very unusual for the C-suite floor. There was nothing unusual about today. With the news coming out of Austin, and with the first quarter earnings report out, the company executives had decided to start their celebrations a bit early. The conference room had champagne and caviar, among other things.

It was a muggy day in Houston. The mood inside the large office suite of Steve Riggs was anything but. He was on the phone, while his secretary was patiently waiting for him to dismiss her before she could go on with her other daily tasks, such as ordering more food and drinks to keep the revelry going.

"Yes, senator. We can make that work, I think. How about I meet you in DC next week and let's hash these details out. Doable?" Riggs got up from his chair as he hung up his phone.

Steve Riggs was a tall and well-built man. He rarely raised his voice except when he was angry on the phone or in a celebratory mood. Today seemed like a day that had brought out that side of Riggs. He was quite cherubic as he got up from his chair. And then he realized that Amanda was waiting for his permission to leave.

He cleared his throat.

"Where was I?"

"Mr. Riggs, you were asking me to schedule a meeting with Mrs. Greenburg, our lobbyist in DC. You didn't tell me when," replied Amanda.

"Oh, yes. Can you pick a day, umm . . . maybe middle of the week, and see how my calendar looks. If you can find a morning time slot, that would be wonderful. Lizzy is a morning person. She can get cranky in the afternoons, and I want her to be in a good mood when she meets me."

"Anything else, Mr. Riggs?"

"We are done. Thank you, Amanda. See you in the conference room."

He had already done the math. He knew what GTO's quarterly earnings of four-point-two billion would mean for his personal fortune immediately. More importantly, he also knew what it would mean for the company's future. GTO was the seventh largest oil producer in Texas. They had an incredible clout in DC, and that was all largely due to Mrs. Greenburg. She had been a friend of Steve and the most influential oil lobbyist in town. Her success stories would never go public like most lobbyists', because those people never shared their trade secrets. That has always been by design.

Steve wanted Lizzy, a.k.a. Elizabeth Greenburg, to be his ally in Austin, and she had been playing hardball. With so much at stake in DC, she was not sure if she was ready to put her twenty-year-old career as an oil lobbyist in DC dealing with politicians and businessmen across the spectrum at rest, all in exchange for a fresh start at a volatile but promising environment. Steve knew he would be able to convince her if he spent an hour with her.

If Lizzy got onboard, Steve was confident that Derek Fisher could be made to dance to his and GTO's tunes. He just needed a handful of months to work his magic on Mrs. Greenburg.

He closed his office door and started walking to the conference room. His cellphone buzzed again, and he checked the caller ID to find out who it was.

The caller ID read *Derek Fisher.*

Speak of the devil. Why is he calling me now? he thought to himself, then walked to the conference room. He opened the door and popped his head in barely enough for others to be able to hear him.

"Why don't y'all get started? I really must take this call. I'll join y'all in a few minutes. All right?"

As he started walking towards his room, he could hear all the loud cheers and popping champagne bottles.

Governor Derek Fisher had summoned Senator Richard Harvey and Congresswoman Sima Daly for a Sunday brunch meeting at his residence. The smaller dining room in the governor's mansion in Austin, where the three were sitting, had an intimate and cozy décor. A few photos of Fisher from his very short acting career adorned the wall, with the one where he was in his cowboy costume from a spaghetti Western flick taking the center spot. In fact, that was the only change in décor that the governor and his wife Gloria had made in that room.

There was a serving table on the side where their brunch dishes were being placed. The three had their coffee cups in front of them and were indulged in an intense conversation. The mansion wait staff stood at the corner of the room after he brought in all the food, all the while pretending not to hear the conversation. The governor caught his eye and understood he was waiting for instructions to serve their food.

"Don't think we need help with serving our food. Do we?" the governor looked at his guests and continued without waiting for their response. "John, you may leave. We will take care of this. Will buzz the bell if I need anything."

"Yes, sir."

And with that, John quietly closed the door and left the room.

Sima, an ambitious politician, represented congressional district TX-43, outside of Corpus Christi. Her father was a politician who never ran for public office. He enjoyed an immense level of influence among his peers in the Corpus Christi area. Sima decided she didn't want to follow her father's political career trajectory. When her teacher at her elementary school asked her what she wanted to be when she grew up, she responded "Governor," and never changed her response every time someone asked her the same question until she graduated from high school.

When she thought she was ready to run for office, she had already been a favorite political mentee of Governor Fisher. Fisher, a novice himself when it came to politics, had taught her some of the basics of electoral politics.

"It is never about how likeable you are. Remember it's always about how unlikeable your opponent is."

This was the single best advice she had ever received from anyone, and for that she owed a great deal to Derek Fisher.

Senator Harvey, a young and charismatic senator from Austin was whom most politicians of his party would dismiss off as an elite. He was an Aggie, got his business degree from Texas A&M, worked on Wall Street for five years, returned to Austin to start a FinTech business, sold it off when his company valuation hit ten times, and then decided to channel his ambition towards politics. He had no guide or mentor among his family or friends. Richard was always driven by the next big thing. When he decided to run for office, he got help from some of his data analytics friends, put together a social media team, and just approached the primaries in a very methodical manner. His general election win surprised many, as TX-14, the state senate district he represented, usually went the other way. To this day, his party leadership, including Fisher, found it hard to believe that someone could pull this off. Something that had never happened before.

Senator Harvey was a bit of an odd man out in the room. For anyone would think that he would have been the last person to get onboard with this movement. And yet, here he was, after eloquently discussing the pros of this movement with his defiant Senate constituents, the majority of whom voted the other way in the referendum, and still managing to come out largely unscathed—that was if the latest Gallup polls were to be considered.

Governor Fisher knew that Sima's agenda and his own were the same. They had been in conversation almost every day for six months leading up to the referendum. But Harvey was an unexpected ally they got in the last few weeks before the referendum. Fisher hadn't been able to quite read Harvey's maneuvers. He was willing to give him a chance because Harvey was the kind of politician who could appear on TV and had the words, wit, and media smartness to make everyone in the country believe that all Texans did not carry semiautomatic weapons, beat their women, and spoke in incomprehensible and insulting drawls. The governor needed an ally who could speak the enemy language. Someone who was on his side but could understand and speak to the dark side. Someone who could connect with the rest of the Union.

"I am not worried about passing Article 49. I am worried about the effect of 49 on Dodson and Jackson. More on Dodson," said Fisher with his food still untouched.

Senator Harvey raised his right hand as if to say, "Just hold on a second while I finish chewing."

"Here's the thing, governor. They are going to do what they are going to do. In fact, they are already doing it. I bet Dodson will be asking for a meeting within a few days. I mean … he hasn't been holding his cards that close to his chest. Is he? We know what he wants. He wants your job."

"The reason I asked you two to join me this morning is exactly for that. Dodson's office reached out to me Friday evening. He wants to meet me tomorrow."

"Not surprising at all," commented Sima. "I can find out more from my sources. I bet Congressman Williams will be with Dodson in that meeting tomorrow."

"Williams? Evan Williams?" asked Fisher.

Sima nodded.

"There are two ways tomorrow's meeting could go."

"Short or long." Fisher got up from his chair. "And I ain't got a clue right now which would be better for us. Go dig into your sources, senator, and Sima, and please meet me in my office at 8:30 AM. I am meeting Dodson at 10:00."

Both the senator and congresswoman looked at each other as the governor left the room.

"This lox is so good. I am going to have some more. You should try." Harvey was eyeing the food table again.

"A friendly piece of advice, Ricky. Don't ever get caught serving lox on a bagel while you are in Texas. Could end your career." Sima smiled and walked away. Harvey decided to spend a few minutes alone in that room enjoying a warm toasted bagel before letting himself out of the governor's mansion.

They told her she would be spending the night in Carlsbad. Ava didn't know who was going to pick her up as she waited at a Texaco gas station in the middle of nowhere. She had one duffel bag and a small backpack that held her essential electronics such as her laptop computer, a few books, notebooks, et cetera. It was well past 9:00 PM. There were not too many people at the gas station at that time of the night. But whenever a customer pulled in to fill gas or walked into the small convenience store, Ava turned her head away, pretending to be talking to someone on the phone. She didn't want to make eye contact with anyone. Her friend who dropped her off at the gas station was in a hurry. She handed a piece of paper and asked Ava to read the instructions. There was nothing the friend could have done to make these instructions clearer for Ava, because during their entire two-and-a-half-hour drive from Midland, the friend and Ava didn't exchange a single word. That was because Ava was in the trunk trying hard not to make too much noise.

Ava Walters, a celebrity science teacher at Midland Middle School, was thirty-two years old. Her life revolved around her students, school, her husband Bradley, and their only daughter Eveline, who had just started elementary school. The Midland community she lived in used to be a very friendly one, and everyone in her neighborhood was very welcoming when they moved to Midland from Odessa. Somewhere in the last eighteen months, everything changed. Not just in Midland, but everywhere in Texas. Teachers like Ava, who had taken up this profession because of their sheer passion to teach children, were now being made to feel like criminals.

Ava Walters was now a fugitive and was wanted by Midland Police. She was on the run, and had just crossed the border to get into the neighboring state of New Mexico, where she had hoped she would get a temporary shelter, a shield of protection, and relief, as her crime could not be transferred to another state. So was her hope.

About six months ago, Governor Fisher signed a new bill. The bill banned all schools from teaching, lending, and even displaying any textbook or reference book that had any content that would have "anti-faith" content. Most educators were startled at the audacious phrasing. What the new bill really was attempting to do was to ban schools across the state from teaching the concept of evolution, in whatever obscure form. The war on education had reached the next stage in the state of Texas. After the governor had banned books that taught the Civil War, racism, and the progress the country had made since, his and his party's target next was science. Specifically, teachers or books that had any reference to evolution or homosexuality. The latest bill went one step further by criminalizing the conduct. The state legislature, with the help of local police departments across the state, had taken this as a priority and had been successfully able to enforce these new laws aggressively. There were parents, neighbors, and even a few teachers who had been using the tipping hotline and letting the law enforcement officials know of suspicious activity in their schools.

As of that day, there were 142 teachers, thirty-six school librarians, six school principals, and two school district superintendents in prison. Their crimes ranged from showing defiance in the form of protesting outside the Capitol to teaching the banned content in the classroom. Public school teachers, by and large, were expecting things to get worse after the referendum should the pro-movement party get enough votes. Governor Fisher, who was already emboldened by the success of his first two bans, did not want to wait until after the referendum. This was the moment he and his faith leaning colleagues had been waiting for.

"The merger of church and state must begin at schools. Today, I sign a bill that bans all forms of evolutionary teaching at public schools. God's creation is pure, and anyone who sows a doubt in it has been possessed by Satan. They do not deserve a place in our community. I have complete trust in our law enforcement, and I am sure they will do what is needed to punish those who defy this new law. May God bless this beautiful nation of Texas," Governor

Fisher said in his brief address before signing the bill into law.

Ava Walters knew the ban was coming. But she was a science teacher, after all. She was not going to cheat on her own conscience. Ava had been planning for days in advance. For more than a week, she spent an hour every evening going through all the books in her school. She made notes. At the end of the tenth day, she had a list of about seventy-nine books that she anticipated would be affected by the new ban. She checked online bookstores to find out how much these books would cost. She discussed with Bradley if he was open to her plan. He was very scared for her.

"I feel this could change your life, Ava," he had said multiple times to her. "But I know this is the right thing to do. Someone must do it. And I am glad it's you. Eveline and I will be fine. We are proud of you. Go ahead."

Soon, Ava had received all the seventy-nine books in her mailbox, ordered in seven or eight batches, during the course of the next two weeks. Her plan involved using the help of her school librarian to make 200 copies of each these books—one for each child in the school. That was the easier part. The more challenging step, which was to come next, was finding a way to give access to all these books to the children.

Ava and the librarian planned for that, too. They set up a make-shift library in Ava's house, which was really Eveline's room. They made a schedule of sorts for the students, which they were going to implement if and when the governor signed the bill. It was an elaborate plan. One that involved cooperation from students primarily. Because if even one student slipped and shared this stealthy learning program that their science teacher was employing with their parents, then all these efforts would produce nothing. And that would risk Ava's life.

Ava had thought of a fallback plan, too. During the first week after the ban, she had made a list of about 140 students whom she had complete confidence in and believed that they would never let slip the information, but would show committed interest in learning. So she had already made individual boxes of books for each one of them and had instructed the librarian to drop them off at the respective students' homes. There were about sixty students about whom Ava was not sure of. They would come to Ava's house according to the published schedule and would borrow the books they wanted to read and had their names on them, take them home, and bring them back in two days if they thought their parents were not going to be supportive. On the other hand, if they felt comfortable enough, they could request for the whole collection, which Ava would then ask the librarian to deliver. This was a risky plan, but she trusted her students, and she believed in this cause. It was her responsibility to teach these students. She was enraged that a politician was dictating what she should teach and what she should not.

Eventually, after the bill was signed into a law, it was not any of the students who slipped, but the school custodian. He whiffed this stealthy book program within a couple of days of Ava starting it, followed one of the students one evening to put things together and to connect the dots, and then ratted Ava out to the local police department.

Fortunately for Ava, she was not home when the local sheriff showed up at her house with a search warrant. She was alerted by one of the students through a text message.

Cops at your house, ma'am! said the message.

Ava knew Bradley had taken Eveline to a local park while Ava went grocery shopping. She had already checked out when she saw the message and was carrying a large paper bag with all the groceries she had bought in a shopping cart. When she saw the message from her student, she didn't panic. Her first thoughts were about Bradley and Eveline. She told herself that irrespective of what happened to her, she would not put them in the harm's way. She rushed back inside and left the shopping cart in a corner, ran outside to her car with the grocery bag, and called her friend Rosaline.

"Water broke. I am at the grocery store. The usual," was all Ava said to Rosaline.

"Stay calm! Will be there soon," Rosaline responded.

Within twenty-five minutes, her friend was at the parking lot.

Meanwhile, Ava texted Bradley and asked him to stay calm. She specifically asked him not to come looking for her. She knew Bradley would be equally guilty in the police's eyes if they could even establish a remote coconspirator motive. She kept telling herself that Eveline needed Bradley, now more than ever. She wanted to keep Bradley as far away as she could from the situation she had just found herself in. Rosaline had packed some of her own clothes and essentials for Eva in a duffel bag and brought them with her. Ava had her backpack which she usually carried to school already with her. As much as she had mentally prepared for this moment, Ava was still in a state of shock and restlessness, when Rosaline asked Ava to jump into the trunk with her bags.

Ava looked at Rosaline as if to ask, "Are you kidding? Am I going to fit in?" There were not too many words spoken in the parking lot. Rosaline and Ava looked around to make sure they were far away from the crowd in the lot and farther away from any closed-circuit cameras the store may have had installed. Then Ava jumped into the trunk and crawled into a fetal position. She took a deep breath and smiled at Rosaline just before she closed the trunk. Ava found herself in darkness and realized she did not have much room to wriggle around. She managed to reach her pocket to reach for her phone and turned it off.

A five-seven woman could slip into a sedan trunk just like that? I must be in such a good physical shape. She amused herself with the fleeting thought of self-appreciation.

A car pulled in front of her at the Texaco gas station.

"Ava?"

"Yes."

"Get in. Now!" the voice from inside said quite firmly.

Jason Greer never drank coffee at lunch. He always said it kept him awake at night. On this Sunday though, he was having coffee after a carb-heavy Thai lunch. Through the window of the café, he could see the happenings on 3rd and Main. He did not have his cameraman with him, so should there be a need, he was ready to shoot videos and photos from his mobile phone. The café was busy, and the afternoon crowd was mostly moving in and out. Only a handful of customers like Jason were using the café to wait, watch, write, or observe. While his focus was really to observe what was happening outside, he kept scanning the café every few minutes as a matter of habit.

He had received some reliable information from his source that there would be a planned skirmish during the protest march scheduled anytime now, which would be made to appear spontaneous. The purpose of the skirmish was to arrest a couple of targeted prominent activists in the state. Jason did not know who these activists could be. He looked at his watch, quickly took a last sip of his espresso, closed his tablet, and cleared his table. The march could start any moment, and Jason was ready to cover what he believed to be a huge story.

The closest spot to the Capitol that the Austin police gave permission for the protest march to start from was 3rd and Main. The march organizers had done everything they could to ensure those protesters were fully educated of these rules. This was the not the first protest that the organization March for Texas had called for in recent months. But this was the first time they were working together with the Texas Women's Rights Advocacy and the Freedom of Press, two other organizations who also wanted to let the politicians and the government in Austin know of their concerns about the recent draconian and authoritarian laws introduced in the state.

In March of this year, the governor had signed a specific law that made the job of reporters like Jason Greer harder. The Fake News Protection Act of Texas gave sweeping powers to citizens of Texas to deny permission to the press, question them, and even take legal action against them if they found any of their behavior suspicious or offensive. In other words, reporters and journalists could be charged criminally very easily under the new law. This also meant that any public office building, including the Capitol, could simply deny access to media outlets they didn't find acceptable. And citizens had also been given extraordinary powers to report reporters and journalists whom they suspected to be engaging in criminal activities under the new act.

Jason Greer was working for *The Austin Star*, a news publication. *The Austin Star* was not a progressive magazine by any stretch, but their coverage of the referendum in general in recent months and their overall negative tone in how they covered the results made many in the Fisher Administration consider Jason's outlet an adversary of the state. Jason rose to prominence after getting to interview the new governor on his first day in the office. He was also the first to break the news about the referendum date. In his stint at *The Austin Star* thus far, today was the first day Jason had been given a political field assignment, which he was very much looking forward to.

He started walking towards the Walgreen's at the intersection of 3rd and Main when his mobile phone buzzed.

Russell and Emily, the text message read.

Instantly, Jason understood the magnitude of the day's events.

Meanwhile, about 200 meters away, at the Regent's Park, the activists had gathered in a large circle. In an open space in the middle were the leaders of the three organizations that had called for today's march. There were speeches interjected with emotional sloganeering. There was a small group of anti-protesters who were trying to sabotage the rally. Some of them stood rubbing shoulders with the march goers. And some were carrying placards, while some walked around carrying firearms in full display. After all, this was Texas.

Russell Weston spoke.

"Don't think we have lost control just because we lost the referendum. There is still a long way to go. And we have time to fight. We need to keep fighting. Keep fighting every draconian law that Fisher signs. I am not going anywhere until Article 49 is defeated. Please assure me y'all will keep fighting for Texas."

Then it was Emily Chase's turn.

"We met a young woman this week. A single mom. She is carrying a baby from marital rape. She has health issues that will prevent her from delivering a healthy baby, and even if she manages to deliver a healthy baby and somehow survives the child delivery, she knows she can't afford to raise a second child. But she also knows she doesn't have a choice in Texas. Unacceptable. Enraging. She actually wrote a suicide note. Somehow, she had the presence of mind to send that note to us before she did anything tragic. We met her and gave her words of comfort. We have given her some hope. I want to fight for all the Lisas in the beautiful state of Texas. We should fight for our rights to choose. Don't you agree?" Emily's voice began to break a bit.

"Right to choose!" she yelled.

The crowd joined. The slogans ranged from "right to education" to "no ban on books" to "democracy dies when free press dies," and in general they avoided any reference to Fisher, his government, or anything to do with the referendum.

"Are you ready? Are you ready to show the world what we are fighting for?" asked the rally leader.

"Yes!"

"Let's go!"

The rally began. It was a hot Austin Sunday, but the sun hadn't quite come out in its full glory. The marchers were going to walk just half a mile till they reached 3rd and Main, where there would gather, give speeches, and raise organized slogans before dispersing. The police had given them just an hour for all of this. The march leader was keeping an eye on his watch.

Russell and Emily were out in the front, holding huge banners that carried TWRA on them—Texas Women's Rights Advocacy. When the group of marchers was about a block away from its destination, a bicyclist rode towards them out of nowhere, from the eastern side of Madden Street. He crashed into the crowd and fell. There was a bit of commotion in the crowd. Russell's right arm was hurt, as the bicycle made direct bodily contact with him and he was in visible pain. The bicyclist seemed to be wounded, too. The cops who were standing at the intersection started walking towards the march goers.

Someone from the crowd pelted a glass Coke bottle, aimed in the general direction of the cops, who were walking towards them. It landed on the asphalt road, inches away from one of the police, and splintered into pieces. One of the cops yelled and pulled his gun out. Another took out his gun and shot in the air. Yet another started charging towards the crowd, pointing his gun at them.

That was the moment the rally leader knew he had lost control of the march. He stood there helpless. So did Russell and Emily.

Jason Greer saw the events unfold from Walgreen's. He turned the camera on and started shooting the scene as he kept running towards the 3rd and Madden intersection. He maneuvered his way through the agitated crowd as fast as he could and started to slow down immediately after he saw a cop pull out a pair of cuffs. It all happened within a couple of minutes, and Jason's attempt to capture the arrest on his phone was in vain.

Russell and Emily were being escorted to the sheriff vehicle while Jason could witness the rally organizer animatedly pleading with the cops. Jason decided he wasn't going to go anywhere near the scene.

The reporter's instincts kicked in, and he quickly sent a text to his supervisor.

They got' em. R and E in custody. Will be there in 15 minutes to put together a draft.

"Sir, Congressman Williams is here."

"Send him in." Dodson lifted his head to look at his secretary. He removed his reading glasses and left them on the coffee table.

"Morning, senator! Hope I am not too early."

"Top of the morning, Evan. Let's get down to our business right away. Shall we?"

"Yes, sir. As you please. You're the boss." Evan smiled.

Both Williams and Dodson had originally planned on meeting only later that week, to be precise, on Tuesday. But the email that Williams sent before they left DC on Friday prompted Dodson to call for a Monday morning meeting.

"About that email, Evan," Dodson began. He had always treated Evan Williams as his student and sometimes as his own son without all the endearing attachments. He would take the liberty to call him out even when he made inadvertent errors.

"Sir, there have been further developments on that front. My sources tell me that Harvey is onboard."

"Who? Ricky? That Yankee Ricky?" Dodson was surprised.

"Yes."

"So tell me now. What are they cooking?"

For the next few minutes Congressman Williams laid out what he thought were Derek Fisher's plans as soon as Article 49 was passed in the state legislature. According to Williams's sources, Fisher was prepared to directly confront Senator Dodson and challenge him in the elections if it came to that. Adding Richard Harvey as his ally was part of his grand plan to smoothen his electoral prospects.

"Son of a gun!" Dodson reacted as he banged the table gently with his right fist.

Senator Dodson was perhaps the senior most politician in the party from Texas, and a veteran one at that. But when it came to connecting with the people of Texas, Fisher found himself in a uniquely advantageous position, especially in the recent months. The campaign for the referendum, the new restrictive policies on education, press freedom, and women's rights, all of which he touted to the people of Texas as faith-based policies, had given him constant media coverage, and an overall perception to his team that his popularity ratings were soaring. On the other hand, Dodson was carrying a DC label that was not going to be easy to erase.

Both Dodson and Williams had spent weeks carefully working on their strategy before the referendum. They made sure they worked together with Fisher and his team to ensure that they drummed up support for the referendum. The most important goal was to position Dodson as a strong advocate of the pro-movement who had as much vested interests in the future of Texas as Fisher did, and not as some distant DC politician. So, many campaign rallies, fundraisers, and dinner with donors notwithstanding, as soon the referendum was passed in their favor, Dodson had started to feel that Fisher was after all a dense wool made from a different sheep. He had reached out to Fisher's office on Friday after he boarded the plane from DC. He had specifically wanted to meet in person with Fisher that Monday morning. Needless to say, the email Evan had sent before they boarded the plane prompted Dodson to set this meeting up with Fisher.

"What about Daly? What's she up to?" Dodson asked.

"Well, for now, sir, it is no surprise that Sima Daly is on Team Fisher."

"I am meeting Fisher in a couple hours."

"What? Did you ask for the meeting or did he?"

"I did. Didn't tell you Friday, cause I didn't know if he was going to accept my meeting request. He did accept it Friday evening."

Dodson got up from his seat. He stretched his arms up. The crisply ironed blue shirt showed no signs of fatigue. He grabbed a notepad and pen from his table and walked back to the couch where they both were sitting. He threw the notepad in front of Evan on the coffee table.

"Now, tell me, Evan. What do I tell Fisher? I'm thinking I'm going to be direct. We don't have much time to bullshit around, do we? He needs to hear from me that I am going to fight like hell to become the first president of this nation. And he better not fuck around with my ambitions, because I've been dreaming of this longer than he has."

Evan nodded.

"Agreed, sir. He should hear directly from you."

"Do you have any ideas?"

"Give me a couple of minutes, sir."

Evan grabbed the notepad and signaled towards the senator, asking for the pen he had in his hand. Dodson threw it towards him. After spending approximately five minutes, Evan tore a sheet of paper from the pad. The sheet of paper had some quickly scribbled notes. He gave it to Dodson and dropped the pad on the table.

He told Dodson that he should go through the notes before his meeting with Fisher. There were only a handful of things Fisher really enjoyed as much as someone stoking his ego. Evan had written on the paper how Derek had always embraced the idea of compassionate conservatism and why that mattered to Dodson a lot. He suggested Dodson should try to find ways to praise him for Fisher's compassionate conservative leadership style. The congressman went on to elaborate a few more points he had written on that piece of paper.

"Remind him that although everyone remembers Washington as the first president of the country, not many remember what exactly he did as the president. Because he was just laying the foundation. But people do know more about the presidencies of more impactful presidents who came later and who built on that foundation. Tell him you could offer your experience to him and be the political guide Fisher needs at this historical moment of the founding of a new nation. Tell him how Fisher could forever cement his legacy as the most impactful future President of Texas, perhaps as the second president, building on the foundation you are going to lay."

Dodson seemed very satisfied with Williams's suggestions.

When Williams left the room after that brief meeting, he turned back and gave a thumbs-up to Dodson. As he turned back, he noticed the door sign that read *Senator Dodson*.

He reimagined that label to read *President Dodson*.

President Dodson had a nice ring to it, he thought to himself, and continued to walk.

Then for a flash a second, he imagined another label right next to it.

Vice President Williams.

Ah! This has a nicer ring to it. Evan Williams smiled as the door shut behind him.

When Alex Pedroza's phone rang, it usually meant someone in his community needed something. Alex was a resident of a Latino-dominant West Dallas community. Every need in the community went through him. Be it setting up a health camp for vaccination rollouts, or distributing food and supplies during some crisis, or building repair work after damages due to rain or wind, someone or the other called Alex for help. And he enjoyed being the center of a support system that the community relied on. Alex worked as a landscaper for more than fifteen years. And now he owned a landscaping company. Most of his workers were from his neighborhood. He and his family lived in one of the relatively wealthier neighborhoods of this community, a city called Eagle Ford.

"Wait till I come!" he yelled from a distance to his worker.

The crew was working on a yard in Frisco today. The owners weren't home. Alex had two crews working on two different projects that day—both in different parts of Metro Dallas. He stopped to check on this crew, which was just getting started. He had to walk them through the design, explain the challenges he expected them to face, and ensure everyone had the required knowledge to finish their tasks for the day. He usually gave them a specific milestone to reach by the end of the day.

And after giving his daily instructions to his crews in the morning, he never failed to ask them "¿Trajiste tus almuerzos?" *Did you bring your lunches?* If he suspected anyone in the crew lying in the affirmative, he had the knack of spotting them. He called that crew member to his pickup truck alone and gave them a lunch bag that he had packed from home. He brought a few extra pre-packed lunch bags from home every day. He knew there would always be a couple of his workers who couldn't afford to bring lunch.

Alex Pedroza was a hardworking man, well-respected by everyone in the community. That naturally meant politicians saw his clout as a powerful one when it came to elections. Alex was fully aware of that. He played a crucial role in getting more than ninety percent of his community to vote yes in the latest referendum, and in return, he was promised that when the state legislature drew the new congressional maps, they would get their own district.

A Latino-dominant congressional district in Metro Dallas meant a lot. This had been Alex's dream for more than ten years. For those Latinos older than Alex, they never even could have dreamt of a day like that. So, Alex had been going for many of the pre-referendum rallies and meetings in the past few months. He thought he had built a good relationship with his local congressman, Gary Roberts, who had even arranged for a two-minute one on one with Governor Fisher once. Alex really was feeling good about all of these and was quite optimistic for his community.

Fisher and his party had successfully managed to coerce the Latino community throughout the state into trusting them more than their opponents by using God and church as unifying factors. Like Alex, Fisher's team had identified local community leaders across the state and promised them a political prize in return for their votes. It was a twenty-year strategy that the party had adopted long before Fisher took the office—a strategy that had started to pay off during the last six years, going by the polls. More than seventy percent of Latino voters usually voted on election day, which usually was a much higher turnout than the overall state average of sixty two percent. Fisher's party now had a guarantee of getting more than sixty-five percent of the Latino vote share in every election.

Alex had just started the engine when his phone rang.

"Qué?" Alex answered in a state of shock.

"Miguel? The one working with the crew in Richardson? Oh, my God!"

He was still recovering from the shocking news he received on the phone. He removed the phone from his right ear and moved it away, as if he was looking at the number. He didn't want his workers outside to see his face through the truck window, so he rolled it up.

"Please tell me there was no one else."

Alex Pedroza started driving. The person who had called him had just broken the bad news. There was a drive-by shooting where his other crew was working in Richardson. And one of his workers named Miguel had died. The person calling Alex did tell him that more people were shot but didn't know exactly how many. The police were on the scene, and the shooter, someone who drove by in a white car, had fled the scene.

In the five years of owning his landscaping business, Alex had never had to deal with a tragedy like this. The drive from Frisco to Richardson usually was about forty minutes. But on that day, it felt like forty hours for him. As he reached the neighborhood where his crew was supposed to be working, he decided to park his pickup truck in the next lane. He approached the new crime scene on foot.

"Señor Pedroza! We told you. I told you. They don't want us here. And you forced us to vote yes. See what those bastards did!" One of his workers was crying as soon as he saw Alex walking towards them. The man who was weeping was bleeding profusely on his legs and was lying down on the sidewalk with temporary bandages administered by paramedics on the scene, while they were attending to the more seriously injured ones first.

"This was a hate crime, señor. The sin will be on them forever!" another injured worked yelled.

A white male cop saw Alex and asked him to stop.

"Sir, you can't come here. Stay outside the yellow tape!"

"I am their employer. I want to know what happened."

"So you are Mr. Alex Pedroza? Can you just wait here? I will send the officer who oversees the case to you in a minute. He will fill you in."

The officer came up to Alex and asked him about the landscaping project details. He wanted to know Alex's relationship with the owners and if he had any suspicions on them. The owners of the house were not home at that moment, and it appeared both the husband and the wife were at work. The officer wouldn't reveal how many of his workers had died. He simply told him they had taken four to the hospital already. And the ones who were there would be taken too in a few minutes, but their injuries were apparently not life-threatening.

Alex listened to the officer's official summary of the incident, which was really a version meant for public and media. So he didn't really get any more details than what he already knew. He asked the officer if he could go to the hospital to see those admitted.

"That's up to the hospital. There will be someone from our department. Identify yourself and then they will advise. But honestly, Mr. Pedroza, I would suggest you go home first and wait for our call. We would tell you when to go to the hospital. Also, we want you to be available if we needed you to come to the station to record any statement. There will be more paperwork in the next few days because you are their employer. It's a bit of a process," the officer concluded.

Tears were welling up in Alex's eyes. He quietly walked back to his pickup truck. He didn't remember all the faces of the men who were supposed to be here today. Images of Miguel's face kept flickering before his eyes when he tried to remember the other workers. He just knew he had a crew of eight. He didn't even know if all eight had already been there when the shooting happened. He sat on the driver seat and closed his eyes. Faces of women and children from his community flashed in front of his eyes, and tears started to flow down in streams. He tried to cover his face with his hands, and they became wet soon.

"Señor! The killer . . . that killer said this was just the beginning. He said they are going to get rid of all of us pests and cleanse this country!" the worker screamed in agony.

What the worker cried after kept ringing in Alex's ears until he got home.

"You made a deal with the devil, señor. We are paying for it now. You know it, Señor Pedroza."

Senator Albert Newell was meeting with a group of legal experts in his office in DC. His staff members were told to be available twenty-four seven for the next three days. There were a couple of other senators from his party who had also joined him in his office for the meeting.

Newell had appeared alongside Dodson, Fisher, and Williams at a couple of campaign rallies for the referendum. He had also conducted his own referendum-related donor events where he had shown his soft support for the movement. Anyone who had followed Newell's position on the referendum and what came after would know that he was not the most vocal proponent of Texas leaving the Union. Even in the handful of televised interviews he had appeared on, one could sense a certain pessimism in his tone about the future of Texas. He was a cold-blooded conservative, but he came from the old school and had not been influenced by any recent rightward cultural shift within his party.

It was during the last general elections he realized how poorly he had miscalculated the seismic shift that was happening within his party and how the voters of not just his state but all over the country had now become sources of their own news cycles. Facts were waging an increasingly futile battle against convenient false narratives peddled through the echo chambers of the conservative movement. He realized that to stay relevant, he had no choice but to play the same game along with the rest of the party. After he won the last election and retained his senatorial seat, he had decided that this would be his last term and that he wasn't going to seek reelection. He hadn't made any public announcement about any of this yet, as there were bigger issues to keep his focus on.

One of the legal experts weighed in for a question Newell had posed earlier.

"There is a precedent. But we must go all the way back to 1861. *Texas v. White.* This court, though, with a seven-two split, will never use that precedent. It's a done deal as far as SCOTUS goes. This is going to congress." He banged the table and shook his head.

The question was, "When SCOTUS takes the *Texas v. Harrison County* case from the docket, what should we be prepared for?"

"So then, are you saying we are on the verge of SCOTUS overturning *Texas v. White?* Un-fucking-believable." Senator Newell was fuming.

Although he appeared to have supported Texas leaving the Union, he knew better than most senators, congressmen, and women that the process of economic separation and establishment of border control among other things would bring down at least a generation with it. There was no easy way for him to educate the pro-referendum people of his party. The damage had been done a while ago, and now it was an emotional issue.

He turned towards the senators who were there at the table.

"Now promise me again, gentleman. You are with me in my pursuit of convincing the United States Congress to not pass the approval of TEXIT. Right?"

Both the senators nodded their heads in acknowledgment.

If he waited until SCOTUS overturned *Texas v. White*, then Newell knew he would have very little time to act before Congress took up the vote. So he had already put together a swift team with his staff members. They had started reaching out to the Congress members individually, and they had been on this task for more than two weeks now. The swift team had given its latest data to

Newell just that morning.

He pulled out that datasheet and shared it with the other two senators.

"We lost more than twenty votes in two weeks. How did this happen? Right now, I don't know how much we can rely on the remaining fifteen." Newell was furious.

"Senator Newell, if I may say so, this is no achievement for Dodson. It's all Williams. That blue-eyed boy of Dodson is playing well with the cards he has been dealt. He seems to know all the right buttons to push."

"Either I am losing sense of the heart of our party and where its core sentiment is, or I am just losing my political wit."

"Senator, we still have two weeks to go. Trust your swift team to do the work. I will guide them. We will make sure we don't lose these fifteen votes," said Senator Brynes from Nebraska.

"If this swift team is so good, then why haven't they fucking done anything about it already? Two weeks is a painfully long time, senator! You know better than most!" Newell's anger had not subsided.

"I'll crack my whip. We'll get it done," responded Brynes, making direct eye contact with Newell.

CHAPTER 3

THE ROAD TO REFERENDUM

A spirations to secede and leave the Union have been a standard feature of much of America's politics, in some states more than others. In the history of the United States of America, there have been only two instances of successful secessions—when portions of the Louisiana Purchase, north of the 49th parallel, seceded to become a part of Canada, and the Treaty of Manila, which made the Commonwealth of Philippines an independent country in 1818.

When eleven Southern states attempted to secede by forming the Confederate States of America, the effort eventually collapsed after the Union sent its forces to quell the rebel states, thereby resulting in the Civil War.

But what made secession almost unconstitutional was when the Supreme Court of the US decided to take up the *Texas v. White* case. Justice Chase, who wrote the majority opinion in the case, said:

> *The Union of the States never was a purely artificial and arbitrary relation. It began among the Colonies, and grew out of common origin, mutual sympathies, kindred principles, similar interests, and geographical relations. It was confirmed and strengthened by the necessities of war and received definite form and character and sanction from the Articles of Confederation. By these, the Union was solemnly declared to "be perpetual." And when these Articles were found to be inadequate to the exigencies of the country, the Constitution was ordained "to form a more perfect Union." It is difficult to convey the idea of indissoluble unity more clearly than by these words. What can be indissoluble if a perpetual Union, made more perfect, is not?*

This didn't mean that politicians in a few states had stopped to perpetuate the fantasy of seceding from the Union. Besides, 1869 was so long ago.

About two years ago, a little-known conservative businessman from Texas shared a Facebook media post which simply said *TEXIT NOW.* Historians in the future may look back at that post and say that it was the beginning of the Texas's political landscape shifting.

The pro-TEXIT movement grew in popularity over the course of next few months. Its supporters ranged from those who shared social media posts in favor of secession, to those who walked around in *TEXIT NOW* T-shirts and hats. The general elections were just around the corner when the TEXIT movement started taking afoot at the conservative grassroots level. It didn't take long for politicians like Derek Fisher, who was running to be the next Governor of Texas, to exploit the sentiment. Soon, TEXIT became the foundation of Fisher's election platform. This was when conservative politicians like Newell, who never thought they would have had to deal with this during their lifetime, stopped ignoring the movement.

After taking office, one of the first things Governor Fisher did was to establish a TEXIT task force. The task force, among other things, identified all the challenges that lay ahead of them before even they could take this for a formal and official public referendum. The referendum, though, would be the official first step in the process; the secession itself and thereby the success of TEXIT depended on a couple of things before the referendum stage.

The task force identified that one of the first things the state of Texas needed to do was to establish that there was an intent of revolution, because in the same majority opinion, Justice Chase also wrote:

"However, the Court's decision recognized some possibility of the divisibility through revolution, or through consent of the States."

The state started a signature campaign first to prove the intent. Once they managed to get more than a million signatures in favor of TEXIT, they were able to present a case to the state legislature to formally approve a public referendum to be held within six weeks.

Both senators Dodson and Newell, DC politicians and largely perceived to be Texas outsiders, were skeptical at first. But the junior senator from the state, Dodson, was the first one to jump on the TEXIT bandwagon thanks to Congressman Williams. He had sensed that this movement was gaining traction fast, and anyone who stayed out of it had no future in the party—at least not in the state of Texas now, and definitely not in the Commonwealth of Texas in the future.

Fisher pumped the entire state machinery into this campaign. From propaganda pamphlets at all government offices to social media advertising, the budget he had set aside for TEXIT was close to ten percent of the state's quarterly overall budget. And it worked. For six weeks, it felt like there was a special carnival in the state of Texas. There were TEXIT themed county and city fairs, music and food festivals, political rallies, special church services, and more. Public schools were forced to participate in the referendum, and they were given strict instructions to take only a pro-TEXIT stance. Special officers were assigned to schools to monitor them, conducting mock future Senate proceedings, constitutional readings, et cetera. If anyone had visited Texas during that time, they would have felt that they were perceptively in an entirely different country, which literally the state would be in future if things went as planned.

The referendum, much to Fisher's unpleasant surprise, passed only with seventy-point-five percent voting in favor. He and his team, after successfully restricting voting access at many black community polling stations, were really hoping to cross the seventy-five percent mark. Although anything over sixty-seven percent was good enough to establish the cause of "revolution" in front of the judicial and legislative branches in DC, falling shorter than their target meant that Fisher had more work to do.

No one knew exactly how all of this would play out eventually. Constitutional legal experts, historians, political pundits, senior journalists, et al., were all only coming up with theories as to how this would play out. And needless to add, it kept the TV pundits busy. There was no reference from history for anyone to quote or borrow teachable moments, since this was a situation that no other state had ever been in since 1777.

What most experts agreed on as the next logical steps were as followed:

1) The US House of Congress passes a resolution ratifying the referendum results

2) The ratification goes to the US Senate where it must get at least 60 votes for final approval

3) The President of the United States formally signs the secession motion and gives Texas 12 months to formally secede from the Union after they pass Article 49 in the state assembly

4) The state assembly passes Article 49

5) The state assembly appoints a temporary President

6) Framers of the new Commonwealth of Texas draft a new constitution and have it signed by the governor and the interim President

7) In 12 months, the interim President puts together an economic, social, and defense plan for complete independence from the Union

8) The state assembly ratifies the plan

9) Interim President sends the signed independence plan to the US Congress

10) The US Congress approves the plan and sends it to the President of the USA

11) The President of the United States of America signs the plan and formally declares the new country independent from the Union

12) State assembly is dissolved, and the interim President takes office and forms a temporary cabinet

13) The interim President announces a date for the Presidential election, and it should be held within 6 months after complete independence

14) An independent election council appointed by the state assembly before its dissolution supervises the election

15) The first formally elected President and of the new country takes office and appoints a new cabinet

The referendum was scheduled for early spring. Before the referendum was officially called for, one of the many political strategies Fisher adopted was to make the legislature ram through a series of bills that he could sign. These bills were extremely populist measures among his far-right base and were meant to excite them, project him as a doer, and get them to do anything for him. He needed a certain momentum going into the referendum, and it didn't hurt to ride on the popularity wave all the way to presidency.

Total abortion ban was one of the first bills he signed. Under this bill, there were no exceptions to mother's health or the conditions under which the mother became pregnant. The new bill would criminalize both the mother and the doctor who performed the abortion, and everyone involved would face extreme punishments, with the doctor having the possibility of facing even death penalty. Even though the majority of Texans did not support a total abortion ban, Fisher, like any other conservative politician in the country, figured out that the Christian right and their emotional connection with his campaign was critical to his success. So, he decided to court them early.

Next on his agenda was public schools. The conservative war on education began some twenty years ago. There was an increasing backlash within their echo chamber on how liberal teachers were indoctrinating the children at schools with anti-white and anti-Christian agendas. Texas was the first state in the country to pass a ban on all books that talked about or referenced LGBTQ in school libraries. Florida and Alabama used Texas as a precedent and passed similar bills soon. So, Fisher decided to push the state of Texas one step ahead. That's how he ended up banning all science books with evolutionary references. He doubled down on book bans and started to defund public schools that defied the bans. The war on education was taken up with such urgency that he even signed an executive order that gave complete power to local police authority to act on citizen tips to take actions against teachers and educators who continued to teach LGBTQ content or evolution-related science in public school properties or at their homes. The police could simply show up and take teachers into custody if one of the parents called and reported that he or she was teaching something inappropriate. This rogue law was the reason why an honest and passionate teacher like Ava Walters was on the run.

The final and the most critical bill he signed into law was the one that restricted press freedom. This was an important bill for Fisher and the pro-TEXIT movement. Because they wanted to do everything, they could keep any kind of negative coverage on TEXIT or on the post-TEXIT state of affairs as far away as possible.

The Fisher TEXIT task force had discussed many strategies before the referendum. And they ranged from some really scandalous plans to manipulate the referendum results before they went for official counting to contesting the referendum results if they didn't go their way. No one knew to this date if Fisher's team was even partially successful with this plan to manipulate the results. The press had no access to any of these task force meetings or data. Nor were the journalists allowed to interview anyone working with the task force, election officials, and more. It was simply a violation of the state law to approach any of them, and journalists could be arrested for simply interviewing a prohibitive figure.

With so many controls in place, Fisher was very confident of having the referendum go their way. Yet he needed to be out in the front and be on top of nationwide news coverage daily. His referendum-related campaign events for six weeks were hectic, with his speech team ensuring there was always at least one hot new headline that could come of out of each of his speeches. With a designated team working the many social media channels, all they needed was that one clickbait headline to keep Fisher in the news continuously. The press took the bait, and they joyously covered Fisher for six weeks positively and without a single damaging piece.

Fisher was not really keen on having Dodson and Williams by his side during some of these rallies. But once his team convinced him how they could plan these events in such a way that he was always the star of the rallies, he was satisfied. Dodson and Williams were always the opening acts at these events, which they didn't mind for the time being, while Fisher was the main act. He was more comfortable having Daly and a couple of other state congressmen by his side during his marquee speeches.

There were a few important community-specific rallies that Fisher's team had identified, and they wanted to make sure only Fisher was present at those events. The Eagle Ford rally was one such rally where Fisher was able to spend time with Alex Pedroza, the local Latino community champion. Congresswoman Daly had met with Pedroza multiple times before the rally and was very familiar with all the issues he had brought up. So, in the short time he had, Fisher, the savvy politician he was becoming, spoke directly and in a very relatable way with Alex Pedroza. Alex was both impressed and moved. He felt a soft corner and admiration for Fisher right away and did not see any harm in supporting TEXIT. After all, everything that Daly and Fisher were saying seemed totally possible. The future that Fished had painted for the Latino community throughout the state of Texas and specifically for those in Eagle Ford looked very promising and appealing, which was why he decided to take it as a mission upon himself to convince his community to vote yes in the referendum. And he delivered.

The sea rarely turned blanket-blue in the Gulf of Mexico. It was always murky brown with a sickly greenish yellow color. Ambling by the seashore during the evening hours of the early spring season in Galveston had always been the most blissful thing in Vanessa's life. The beach seemed dupped in earthshine-gold with the sun's rays reflecting off the grains of sand. Clumps of seaweed had washed up on the beach. Vanessa Glass bent down and removed the ones that got tangled in her feet. There were a few palm trees that lined in serried rows, and they dipped their heads in obedience to the sea.

The anchored yachts and ships in the distance rocked like cradles. The glassy air that filled the evening had a faint smell of perfume. But it also carried with it a galaxy of familiar otherworldly smells with it. It felt like a vial was uncorked as the air touched her nostrils. Suddenly, Vanessa had a moment of realization. The smell—it was the scent of food drifting from the restaurants and roadside food carts. She could detect fried chicken, barbecue, onions, and more. The carnival of toothsome aroma tantalizing her noses with richness made her stomach sound like bottled thunder. Then she recognized her most favorite smell. That of grilled tuna. She turned in the direction of the crowd devouring these delicacies and absorbed the beautiful scenery of people enjoying their food. She heard them laugh. Her heart felt full. Soon, she turned on her heel and made her way back to reality.

Her thought cloud was already filled with grilled tuna and her grandma. Her grandma used to tell stories about her parents, Vanessa's great grandparents, and how they were products of the chattel slavery system that still existed in this part of the country even after President Lincoln had signed the Emancipation Proclamation.

"They hell didn't know. No one told them. They continued living underground in their little cages and doing donkey's work for fifteen hours a day. It was two years after Lincoln signed the Emancipation Proclamation that Major Granger came to Galveston. And then we all became free."

That's how her grandma reminisced the end of slavery in Galveston. Vanessa's great grandparents didn't know what to do when they became free. They were old and had two little children. And that's how they ended up being fish mongers on the beaches of Galveston. Everything Vanessa's grandma learned about seafood and fishes; she owed it to her parents' occupation. As a teenager, Vanessa's grandma realized she was a good cook. She started cooking a few dishes at home and sold them along with the fish caught from the sea. Those who came to buy fish from her by the seaside also bought her cooked food and soon started returning just for the cook food.

Thus was born the first entrepreneur of the Glass family. She set up a food cart, and so it went on. Grilled tuna was her most favorite thing to cook, and she had prepared a special seasoning that made all the difference. She never passed on the seasoning recipe to anyone in the family, so no one could reproduce the exact taste after her passing away.

Vanessa Glass worked as a nurse for four days a week at a hospital and as a private nurse for a wealthy old man for the remaining three. She also volunteered at a local old age home whenever she could. She still had her grandma's food cart at home, which she pulled out when she really felt nostalgic and entertained her family with random recipes, often overcoming her family's resistance.

Grilled tuna tonight, she thought to herself as we walked back home. She didn't have to report for her private nurse job the next morning until 10:00 AM.

"Let me try to try to decode my grandma's seasoning recipe again tonight," she murmured.

There was a blue Cadillac parked outside her house. She recognized from a distance that the car belonged to her patient—the wealthy man.

Hugh Haddock had been paralyzed below the waist for the past six months after he fell from his bed one night. He had a house full of servants available when he needed help, but this was a fall no one could have prevented. Now he relied on personal nurses to be with him twenty-four seven. Vanessa was one of the five.

Oh, no. Did something happen to him? Or did someone not show up? Vanessa thought to herself as she walked into her house.

The main door was not latched from inside, and she could hear her husband talking to a voice she could recognize. It was Roy, Mr. Haddock's house manager. She pushed open the door and walked in.

"Good evening, Mr. Roy!"

"Good evening, Ms. Glass. Apologies in advance for showing up at your house unannounced." Roy was trying to be polite.

"That's all right, Mr. Roy. I suspect there is an emergency. I hope it has nothing to do with Mr. Haddock's health."

"No. Not at all. He is doing just fine. And the nurse on duty right now is taking excellent care of him," said Roy.

"That's good to hear."

"I was just beginning to explain to Mr. Glass the reason for my sudden visit. It's all good. Nothing to worry about." Roy cleared his throat.

"As I was saying, Mr. Haddock is hosting a dinner for a very special guest this weekend. A high-profile one, I might add. Someone from DC. A Texan, really. Senator Newell. I am sure you know him. And Mr. Haddock has been putting together a short list of local guests he would like to grace the occasion. It's really a low-key dinner, and he doesn't want the media to get a whiff of it. But since Mr. Haddock holds you in high regard, Ms. Glass, he insisted on ensuring you would be there." Roy completed conveying that long invitation from Mr. Haddock without any stutter.

"That's so generous and kind of Mr. Haddock," Mr. Glass said with a smile and a tinge of excitement.

"Mr. Roy, thanks you so much for the invitation. It's really very kind of Mr. Haddock to invite us. I am not sure how and why we deserve this honor. I hope you will allow us an evening to consider the invitation before we give our response. We would be very honored to be there, of course. We just would like to consult with each other as a family tonight and...and I hope you understand, Mr. Roy."

"Of course, Mr. and Mrs. Glass. Of course. If you could let me know by tomorrow morning when you come for your shift, that would be enough. Now, please allow me to take your leave. And apologies again for interrupting your family time." Roy got up from his seat and started walking.

"Goodbye, Mr. Roy. And have a good evening!" Mr. and Mrs. Glass shut the door close as soon as Roy left their house.

They looked at each other, smiled, and took a deep breath.

"What was all that about?" Vanessa was shaking her head.

"I think I know what exactly this is all about."

"What?"

"You know it."

"I highly recommend you try their steak tartare. Let me order some to start with and we could share." Senator Dodson was pointing at the menu.

"Then I will order Salmon. Balance my meal a bit." Senator Newell laughed.

The senior and junior senators from Texas were dining at the BLT Restaurant in DC. The restaurant was always busy and crowded. For a Tuesday evening in January, the wait staff's workload was more than one hundred percent.

"So, Fisher tells me you are all in on TEXIT?" Newell asked Dodson.

"That shouldn't be a surprise. Should it?" Dodson was sarcastic.

"Listen, I am going to be all in, too, until the referendum. There's not much of a choice for me there. But let's say the referendum succeeds. What are the odds we will make it all the way through?" Newell was direct and open about sharing his skepticism with his colleague on TEXIT long before the referendum was conducted.

"I get it, senator. It's not been done before. Not like this. When there's no one who has jumped into the water, the only way to find out if your balls would freeze or not is jump in and find out." Dodson was clearly not amused. He wasn't willing to show sympathy towards Newell's rational argument.

"I am going to jump with you. I have made that decision. The question is what if we went into a septic shock as soon as we jumped in. Frozen balls don't matter. Do they? What's our first aid plan?" posited Newell.

"Senator, I can't tell you what all could go wrong. That's why we have the experts. We are going to ask them to tell us what all could go wrong and come up with a plan for each. We got more than a year to work this through."

"What if all of it... I mean every single thing that is there… went wrong? Who is our team of experts who can paint us the doomsday picture clearly and tell us what signs to look for? You know, I am not sure if the rookie motherfucker Fisher knows what he is doing."

"On Fisher matters, there is no fissure between us, senator." Dodson guffawed, proud of that word play.

"So, what are you planning? Don't you see the longer we wait, the easier it is going to be for Fisher to take control? It's got to be you or . . . I mean . . . you and me, senator. *We* are the ones who can save Texas."

"There are things I have been considering, senator. I have already put together an exploration committee, and the committee members are looking into my prospects in the state. I will be unofficially launching my campaign to be the first President of Texas very soon. You are welcome to endorse me and join my team in some capacity. I am sure I can use your economic insights. You are the best mind in the Senate when it comes to matter of finance and economics."

"Phew! That's interesting. I was expecting this meeting to be about that. You know. We sit and talk and make our plans on perhaps forming a ticket together." Newell was still processing the shocking revelation he had just received from Dodson and was trying to hide his disappointment and anger.

"You should have said something about your ambitions the last time we met, Senator Newell. With your skepticism, I am not sure I would have wanted you on my ticket anyway. I want someone who is fully committed to TEXIT, someone who is passionate about creating a brand-new Texas," said Dodson.

"A fair amount of skepticism is a must in administration and leadership."

"You don't try to teach me any bullshit." Dodson was upset.

The meeting had slowly turned sour. Both the senators were clearly bringing out their pent-up frustrations and anger on each other. Both their dinner plates were only half-eaten. The waiter came to check on them.

"Please pour the rest of the wine for him. I am done with my meal." Newell removed his napkin from his lap and wiped his mouth.

"And I will pick up the tab for both of us." Dodson instructed the waiter to bring the check to him.

"Allow me. Please." He looked at Newell as if he were pleading.

Senator Albert Newell didn't say anything. He got up from his seat, pulled out a twenty-dollar bill, and dropped it on the table as a tip for the waiter. He looked at Dodson as if he were about to burst out into a long rant. And then he stopped.

"Thank you for the meal then, senator. It was a good dinner. And I will see you somewhere on the campaign trail. Soon," said Newell and left.

At the neighboring table, there was a group of three eating quietly. One of them looked at Newell walking out of the door through the corner of his eye and immediately unlocked his phone. He had been listening to the senators' conversation the whole time.

He sent a text to one of the contacts in his favorites list.

Got a major scoop. FT in about an hour?

How about 90 minutes? came the response.

Lisa Barkley couldn't avoid revisiting her traumatic experiences from one of the darkest days of her life. She was on her regular shift at the Mexican restaurant waiting tables when she received a call from Caleb, her husband. She ignored it the first time, but Caleb kept calling her. Eventually, she found a quick minute between her tables and walked to the aisle leading to the pantry.

Caleb told her that their daughter fell from the swing while they were playing at the local school park and fell unconscious. He didn't even have the presence of mind to call 911 until Lisa asked him. That was her first question before she had time to process and panic. Caleb called 911, and Lisa spoke to her shift manager, who was not happy to lose a waiting staff on a busy afternoon. But a family emergency was something she couldn't be tonally and emotionally apathetic to.

When Lisa and Caleb met at the urgent care, he saw Caleb no longer had the shiver in his voice. In fact, he had completely forgotten about the incident and was on the phone with his buddies discussing their upcoming boys' weekend at the casino. Lisa was mad. They had not been divorced yet but had called it quits on their marital relationship as soon as their daughter was born. Lisa did not want to have a child this early in their marriage, but Caleb somehow convinced her that they could make this work. He promised the sun and the moon as far as how he would be a great wonderful co-parent. All that lasted for just one week. Then Caleb was back to his ways. Drinking with his friends every night and not being home when Lisa needed help with childcare.

Caleb was not all that worried about the divorce itself, but he certainly was not too keen on the alimony he would have had to pay. So he was not going to initiate the divorce proceedings from his end and instead did what he could do to work out a co-living deal with Lisa. The house that they had inherited from Lisa's parents after their passing was an upgrade for Caleb from where he grew up in East San Antonio. Lisa let him live in the house as a paying guest for a very nominal rent and under one condition: He would babysit their daughter twice a week when she was at work.

When the doctor who attended her daughter told Lisa that she was already awake and smiling, Lisa was relieved. Caleb hadn't been paying attention to her conversation with the doctor, as he was still on his phone. Lisa went inside to check on her daughter.

After four hours at the urgent care, the hospital released them. There was nothing to worry about, and Lily was just fine after recovering from possibly a minor concussion. Lisa drove home separately in her car, while Caleb quite nonchalantly decided to hang out with his friends. He gave Lily a quick hug and left. Lisa didn't say a word.

When Lisa and Lily got home, she thought that the worst was over. But what happened later that evening was the kind of trauma she would not wish upon any women. Caleb brought home a couple of his drinking buddies after 10:00 PM. Once he confirmed Lily was asleep, he asked Lisa to join them. Since they all knew each other, Lisa smiled at Caleb's friends and joined them in the living room for a few minutes. But Lisa could barely tolerate the fused stench of alcohol and tobacco filling her living room. She stood up and reminded Caleb in demanding terms how she was extremely disappointed that he forgot the no-cigarette rule inside her house.

"I am so sorry, babe. This will be the last one," Caleb fake-apologized.

And as soon as she left the room, he whispered, "Bitch."

His friends laughed.

At 1:00 AM, after his friends left, Caleb walked into Lily's room. She was fast asleep. He quietly closed the door and walked into Lisa's bedroom.

Caleb sat on the mattress. His senses were aroused as soon he saw Lisa's slender figure lying. All he could think of at that moment was only one thing.

"She looks like an angel," he whispered.

Lisa, a light sleeper in general, was already having a disturbed night thinking about Lily's fall. She was startled to hear a voice so close and so late. She could feel Caleb's warm breath with cigarette stench.

"What the fuck are you doing here, Caleb?"

He held her hand and rubbed it on his crotch.

"You know what would help you right now?" he asked.

"Sleep. Go to your room, Caleb. Get the fuck out."

"You know what the problem with you is Lisa? You talk too much. Even at 1:00 fucking AM."

Before Lisa could respond, Caleb brought his hand and covered her mouth and pulled her night pajamas down. He got on top of her.

Lisa was struggling to breathe when she felt a loud slap on her face. Her mind was fully shut at that moment, and with that, her body, too. All she remembered the next morning was Lily standing next to her bed, pointing at the blood on her sheets, and asking with all the tender care:

"Are you okay, Mommy?"

Alex Pedroza's parents didn't live long enough to share with him their family roots and history. All he learned about his family was through his neighbors, who took turns in caring for him as foster parents. He didn't even know any different as a six-year-old boy caught in a foreign land. Alex thought all young children lived in different houses every month and had different parents as they grew older. When he turned eighteen, he was left to live his life on his own just as Alex had understood how the social norms worked in the country. Alex Pedroza was a Latino American just like many second-generation immigrants he knew of. All of whom were proud to call Texas as their homeland while still finding themselves as visitors when they stepped out of their communities. The challenges for immigrants trying to integrate their communities with the local culture and balancing it with their desires to stay in touch with their own cultures were real.

 Alex was four when his parents immigrated to the USA from Honduras. And they moved to the Dallas area because they had friends who had already settled there. Alex had no vivid memory of his parents. All he remembered thanks to repeated retelling of that dreadful moment in his life was that both his mother and father went to work one day and never returned. It was as if they had disappeared. To this day, he didn't know what might have happened to them, and he just assumed the worst. All his foster parents over the years had told him the same, and they never talked about Alex's biological parents with him in detail. They didn't tell him his father was hired by a local businessman to murder someone and that his father fatally failed in his first hitman job. His mother found out what had happened, then went to seek compensation for her husband's death from the man who had hired her husband, but she never returned home.

When Alex was eighteen, he fell in love with Maria, who was of the same age. They agreed they would get married when they turned twenty-one or when they had saved enough money to buy a car. It was through Maria that Alex learned what happened to his parents. He was very indifferent when he found out that his father and mother were murdered. He had lost the desire to cling onto his past. He was looking forward to the future he wanted to build with Maria. So he did just that.

They built a family with two children, and life was not too bad as a landscaper. Maria, a second-generation immigrant from Guatemala, started working as a freelance Spanish teacher for elementary and middle school children in and around her neighborhood. She could work a few hours a week just to be able to get out of the house. More than the little money she earned, it was the opportunity to meet and interact with people that gave her the most satisfaction for those few years. Alex was very proud of Maria's work, and he was also very protective of her.

Maria was only thirty-three when her doctor diagnosed a chronic heart condition in her and recommended a surgery, one which they needed to take care of immediately. With no health insurance, life was always a gamble for people like Alex and Maria. Their local hospital, supported by the church, provided basic medical services for the members without insurance. Most of the community members relied on this hospital, but this place wasn't meant for advanced treatments and surgeries like what Maria needed. So Alex left the fate of Maria in the hands of his family's and friends' prayers, and the goodwill he had hoped he had earned. Maria passed away before she turned thirty-four.

Alex became a rudderless ship for the next few months. His only anchor was his children, and they kept him stay afloat. That was a big transformative period in his life. He decided to quit his daily labor job to become an entrepreneur. He started his own landscaping business. He had no prior experience in being an entrepreneur, but he was good with people. With his landscaping experience and the relationships with customers he had built directly while he worked for other landscaping companies, he was confident about turning many of them into his customers within a few months. So he did just that.

Alex started to become angry at the political system; despite the Latino community's contribution to the Dallas economy and the Texas economy in general, city and state politicians were treating the community members simply as a vote bank they could make deposits into a few weeks before the elections and withdraw their deposits in the form of votes, then forget about these communities for four years. He was frustrated that the young adults of his community did not have counseling or guidance, and that they all kept living their lives caught in a vicious cycle. Most young men and women were wired to taking up only jobs that were in a selected list—jobs they had seen their parents and grandparents do. Alex used to feel helpless to see the younger generation around him lacking imagination. They did not know that they had the freedom to do other things and they could shape their futures differently. Alex made this one of his missions—to counsel the youth.

Alex was also unhappy with the healthcare system like most Americans. About seventy percent of the Latino community members didn't have any form of health insurance, and they all heavily depended on the local hospital that treated them either free or at a very low cost, depending on their income range. The hospital offered very basic medical services because it was funded entirely through individual donor contributions and occasionally by a few wealthy donors from the Dallas area. They were writing checks either for their own PR's sake or for their own tax purposes. Or both.

Alex vowed to take good care of his employees in his landscaping business by paying them well, i.e., by paying fare wages. Over a period of time, as his children grew older, he became invested in many community activities—like youth career counseling, disaster relief and distribution, off-school learning opportunities for young and old, English speaking and writing classes for old, et cetera. He personally started educating his community members about the importance of buying health insurance, taught them how to buy health insurance through the affordable care public market, and gave them tips on how they could save some money and put that aside for health insurance or health emergencies. Gradually, Alex became the go-to person for everything in the Eagle Ford community. His clout had increased beyond what he knew of because everything he did until then was from his heart and was out of empathy with no ulterior motives.

When Sima Daly was working with the Fisher campaign before the last gubernatorial elections, her strategists told her about Eagle Ford, the number of votes there, their primary issues, and of course, about Alex Pedroza.

It was only natural that Daly invited Pedroza for a personal meeting. Alex had no idea what to expect when he went for the meeting. He didn't even know how to make a big deal out of having an opportunity to meet with a state representative.

At the outset, the meeting was a successful one. Sima Daly, the savvy politician she was, gauged Alex in no time. She crafted and tailored her pitch in such a convincing manner to him that Alex felt saying no would have been the biggest mistake of his life. They didn't talk about the referendum, as it was not a thing yet. Daly convinced Alex that the other party, with their socialist policies and through all their progressive worldviews, would make Alex's vision for his community extremely hard to be transferred to the next generations, and that their regulations would make some of his activities challenging to implement. She convinced him that if he wanted to continue providing valuable services like he already was; either directly or indirectly, he really needed to back her party. She did not even wait for Alex to acknowledge her pitch before writing a $250,000 check right in front of him. One of her aides tore it open right there and handed it to him.

"For the hospital," Sima Daly said.

"Muchas gracias, señora!" Alex was pleasantly surprised with such a generous gesture as he waved goodbye to her before leaving her office.

It was another dreary January day at work. Gavin Forbes wasn't complaining. He was working as a linesman at Oncar, one of the few transmission companies in Texas. Gavin was considered an expert by his colleagues, and he was always protected by the crew working under him on any job.

Winter was perhaps the hardest season to be out on the field as a linesman. Even in Southern Texas. The electric grid situation in Texas made national news these days. Year after year, during peak summers and peak winters, ERCOT—Electric Reliability Council of Texas—was used to running war rooms to manage the inevitable crises that would hit the state due to the imbalance in demand and supply. In winters it was always disruption to the supply side of things and in summers it was always disruption to the demand side of things.

"Will we ever get a break from this shit, man?" one of Gavin's crew members vented.

"No. Not in the near future. Not until we hook to the national grid, man," another crew member said.

"Fuck, no!" Gavin screamed angrily.

The crew members were not shocked at Gavin's livid reaction. They had known Gavin and his politics. But it was 1:00 AM. This crew of five was working on a transformer in a residential area that got burned due to a fire caused by falling of a tree. The winter storms in San Antonio in that week had been a bit too harsh, with temperatures falling below freezing point throughout the nights. The last thing any of them wanted at that time of the night was to argue over a political matter which they had no control over. It was important they stick together at that moment to get the job done and go home.

"Fuck, no. Don't be feeding off that fake news media junk, man." Gavin was still angry.

"What do you mean, Gavin?"

Historians could argue that Texas's secessionist ambitions were already successful. Because the USA has three grids in total—the Eastern Interconnection, the Western Interconnection, and Texas Interconnection. The Texas grid, barring a couple of minor exceptions, has always stayed independent.

It was called ERCOT, although there were two other smaller grids within the state—El Paso was on one of them, while the Upper Panhandle and a part of East Texas were on another one, owing largely to their geographical proximities to other bigger grids.

The separation of the Texas grid from the rest of the country began early last century, even as early as when Edison turned on the country's first power plant in Manhattan, aiding the war effort. Multiple utilities within Texas eventually linked with each other to form the Texas Interconnected System, and so far, they had managed to stay out of being governed by federal regulations, which had always been their primary goal.

In the aftermath of a major blackout in 1965, ERCOT was formed in 1970. It pushed ERCOT into assuming additional responsibilities, and as a result many electric deregulations happened in Texas a decade or so ago. To this day, ERCOT remained beyond FERC, or the Federal Energy Regulatory Commission.

"We will talk over a beer one of these days, man. This is politics you won't understand, kid." Gavin was visibly annoyed.

"Let's finish the job and go home, boys. I need to catch a break. Call me

Saturday. I will tell you exactly why we have the best system in place." Gavin, much to the relief of the rest of the crew, brought that unpleasant discission to a closure.

Gavin Forbes was born in a family of electricians. His father, Gavin Forbes, Sr., was the smartest man he ever knew. He could identify an electric problem often by just listening to the symptoms. He was an employee of Oncar, too. Growing up in an environment like that had made Gavin who he was today. At six-two, Gavin was well-built, single, and looking to settle down with his longtime girlfriend. He never hid his political opinions or views, and always wore it proudly on his sleeve. Whenever he was shooting breeze with his friends or at a bar, Gavin couldn't keep quiet when it came to politics.

He hated the party that had not been in power in Texas for decades now.

"Blue wusses. That's what they are." Gavin would laugh loudly after coming up with nicknames like this. Like his father, he believed Texas couldn't attain its full potential, yet because Texans had been stifled by the feds all these years, the only way Texas could attain its full potential was by acting independent first and then becoming truly independent eventually.

Gavin, like many of his like-minded friends, had been upset with many of the past governors of the state, representing the party he feverishly supported. Because none of them acted with courage. None of them took an objectively measurable step when it came to seceding from the Union.

That was, until the day Gavin saw Derek Fisher during a campaign event in San Antonio. Gavin couldn't possibly explain what exactly he saw in Fisher. But he would go on and on from the next morning about how confident he was with Fisher for finishing the job of secession quickly. Gavin paid $500 to have dinner with Fisher the second time he came to San Antonio to campaign. He even got a photo opp.

"Promise me one thing, sir. TEXIT first before you do anything else," he said with a smile to Fisher when he was standing next to him.

"TEXIT first!" Fisher shook hands with Gavin.

"And your name?"

"Gavin Forbes. Fighting for independent Texas from the day I was born, sir!"

There was an echo of laugher on that stage.

Jason Greer started his media career as a reporter for *The Washington Post*. A Houston native, Jason's interests towards political reporting came about when he was in high school. The press club in his high school worked on an underground publication, without an official approval from the school administrators. The weekly magazine had a cheesy title (*Hey, Houston!*) and it covered all things Houston. From restaurant reviews to concert schedules, from mayoral election politics to infrastructure issues, from local celebrity gossips to interviews with these figures, the magazine tried to cover a range of topics. A bit too ambitious for a high school monthly. Jason was the only political columnist in that magazine, and he happened to cover one mayoral election from end to end. He was fascinated by the breadth and depth of electoral politics. Growing up in a liberal family—relatively liberal for Texas standards, that is—Jason always found it amusing how faith played a critical part in electoral politics.

The underground publication lasted exactly for eleven months, or twelve issues, before it got busted by the school administration. The main reason for getting busted was Jason's controversial column in the twelfth issue where he was very critical of the Houston-based megachurches and how they were turning into shelters for scandal ridden politicians of the conservative party governing the state. One of the students' parents was a member of the megachurch, and they outed the magazine to the school principal.

It was Jason's English teacher who defended Jason and made sure he got way with just one week of suspension. Mrs. Magdalene saw something in Jason, and she became his informal career counselor. To this date, the now retired former English teacher would send an email to Jason immediately after reading a new column of his.

Her latest email to Jason read:

Dear Jason,

I happened to read your latest column on the Post, *and I couldn't help but point how awful and inconsistent your application of capitalization rules is.*

I would be very grateful if you simply didn't mention my name if anyone asked you who your English teacher was.

As embarrassed as I am about teaching you English for four years in high school, I can't be lying if I don't mention that I am equally proud of all the reporting work you are doing out there.

Political reporting can be dangerous. As they say, there is always another Watergate story to be broken. You just have to have the patience and determination to find your Deep Throat.

Be safe out there!

Yours sincerely,

Mrs. Magdalene.

As Jason progressed in his political reporting career in DC, it was Mrs. Magdalene who convinced him that he should move to Texas for a couple of years. She, like many Texans, knew that a Fisher win was inevitable. But she sensed that with Fisher would come TEXIT. Unlike his predecessors, Mrs. Magdalene noticed that Derek Fisher had an unmistakable tone deafness when he talked about human sufferings, a tone that lacked complete empathy. She sent an email to Jason asking him to seriously consider shifting his base to Texas before the gubernatorial elections and stay through till he was sure TEXIT didn't happen. If it did happen, then he would never regret his decision to move back to Texas, for he would become the first national political reporter from *The Washington Post* to have had access to information from the epicenter of the biggest political earthquake to rock the country.

Jason Greer listened to Mrs. Magdalene's advice. He got a one-month temporary assignment and moved to Austin. Once he moved back to Austin and got his feet fully wet, he realized that Texas politics was different. The coverage he would be able get from Austin through a national outlet like *The Washington Post* would not do justice to the amount of reporting he wanted to do. He wanted to report on everything that was happening. The reporter in him was excited, while the liberal Texan in him was nervous. He wanted to have access to a publication that would give him complete independence to whatever story he wanted to cover and when to cover them.

The Austin Star came close to meeting his requirements. They gave him the freedom to choose stories to cover and report on, but he didn't get complete editorial control to the stories he wanted to publish. He was assigned to a supervising editor, Myra Bristow, with whom he established a very tight working relationship within no time. He found out that Myra was as keen on reporting a side of Texas politics that most publications did not pay close attention to, and was as nervous as he was for the future of the state of Texas.

The first story he covered for *The Austin Star* was about the rising star of the ruling party, Richard Harvey, who, by textbook definition, was the antithesis of everything the party stood for and yet was able to weave his way through the grassroots of the party. Jason did research on Harvey's school years, interviewed neighbors from his elementary school days, talked to teachers from his school and college, and even contacted his Wall Street colleagues to learn about his actual day to day work. Jason's column on Richard Harvey came out as a three-part series, and it painted Harvey as an astute centrist whose heart for the day was where his mind told him it should be when he woke up every morning. It was an objective coverage on the trajectory of Harvey's political career. Jason extensively talked about how Harvey chose to place his bet on the conservative party for his political future despite him personally deriding some of the party's positions on issues such as education and women's rights. He fell short of calling Harvey a hypocrite who knew where the wind was blowing.

Harvey making hay and the sun is shining.

That was the title of Jason's column.

Richard Harvey's name became widely popular within the ruling party members, and suddenly Harvey realized that he didn't have to restrict himself to local Austin politics for too long. His release to state politics was accelerated by Jason's column, and for that he was always grateful to Jason.

Richard Harvey decided to run for the state senate.

Sima Daly's first paid internship during her junior year was at GTO. The HR manager who hired her didn't know who her father was, and Sima got her internship through her academic credentials alone. She was assigned to a biweekly rotating shift. Sima worked in the accounting department for two weeks, the PR department for two weeks, and finally at the legal department for two weeks. Even though Sima did not have any prior experience in the oil industry, politics and oil in Texas have always been inseparable. Being a daughter of a politically influential father meant that Sima had been exposed to oil industry jargons without her paying close attention to any of them.

During her internship at GTO, she impressed her supervisors with her astuteness when they would try to explain a specific concept before asking to work on specific tasks. They trusted her enough to give a fair amount of independence to her because they knew they would be largely pleased with her work. She was majoring in American history and minoring in accounting at college. But she didn't enjoy her two weeks in the accounting department one bit. To her credit though, she did try to learn everything she could while she performed tasks that were assigned to her. The most enjoyable two weeks rotation for her was when she got to work in the PR department.

When she was there, there was a major oil spill in the Gulf, and it was not from one of GTO's oil rigs. Yet all the oil companies usually came together during crises like these. The public relations departments of these companies were working overtime to create campaigns to downplay the effects of climate change and the environmental impact of such oil spills. Even though they are used to battling climate change activism through PR campaigns throughout the year, the oil spills were a different PR monster to deal with. It was during her short stint with the PR department there that Sima got to know Steve Riggs. She had drafted an email response to something a national newspaper had asked GTO for, specifically Steve Riggs. It was about oil spills and how one of GTO's own oil spills from twelve years ago still had reeling effects on the marine life in a part of the sea where the accident took place.

Steve Riggs was quite impressed with Sima's draft. It was short, to the point, and sounded very authoritative—like from someone who had been in the industry for decades. He immediately wanted to find out who had drafted this response and said he wanted to meet her. Amanda arranged for a meeting in Steve's office that afternoon. Sima knew who Steve Riggs was, but it was only during that meeting Steve found out who Sima was.

"Ah! You are Devon Daly's daughter. No surprise," he had remarked.

"Thank you, Mr. Riggs. I am a big admirer of your executive leadership style," Sima said politely and with confidence.

"So, what's next for you?"

"I think I will be running for public office soon. Maybe five years from now. When I am twenty-six or twenty-seven. Till then GTO can benefit from my services if you want to hire me."

That's how Sima Daly ended up working for GTO in the PR department after graduation. Within a year of her joining, she got promoted to be the head the department, and became in charge of monitoring and approving all of Steve's official emails to media. She even traveled with him when he had to meet journalists for interviews or when he was attending conferences and seminars that were not oil industry specific. Sima seemed to have a knack for reading the pulse of the audience in the room or the readers. Steve trusted her instincts and usually got a five-minute brief from her before he addressed these gatherings or before he spoke in any of those breakout sessions.

As much as GTO's overall favorability ratings and hitherto the stock price increased during Sima's time, she had not wavered from her long-term career objective. And Steve continued to encourage her and advised her about politics whenever he could. He had been working with national political leaders for a couple of decades now and knew a thing or two about how DC operated.

When it was time for Sima to leave GTO, Steve personally worked with her and got himself coached on the nuances of drafting email responses in the most effective manner. In return, he gave her several tips about electoral politics and how he would approach state politics very differently from national politics.

"GTO may be a Texas company. But the whole world is our customer. I can't be acting the same way in front of a global audience. I must pretend I like sushi and drink wine with a smile. And it could be the opposite for you." Steve was trying to differentiate.

"End of the day, remember this, Sima. When the next government is formed in the state of Texas, when Derek Fisher becomes the next governor—God forbid if he doesn't—he is going to change the landscape very fast. I know that. So, you better get on Team Derek before someone else jumps ahead of you in the line." Steve was coaching Sima.

"Thank you for that tip, Mr. Riggs."

"And I better get used to calling you Congresswoman Ms. Daly." Riggs laughed.

Sima Daly had been working for this moment for the past couple of years. Even before she filed her nomination, her victory was a guaranteed one in TX-43. It was not only a testament to how influential Devon Daly had been, but also to how hard Sima Daly had worked to build credibility of her own and for her brand among the conservative grassroots.

"Mr. Riggs, I am sure we will be doing some amazing work together for the state of Texas and perhaps even for the new nation of Texas. Soon," Sima assured him.

"You bet we will!"

Russell Weston and Emily Chase went to college together. But their paths never crossed until there was a sexual harassment incident that implicated a sports team coach in their college. Like what happened in a few other universities, here, too, the authorities tried to shove the issue under the rug. It was when Russell Weston overheard a conversation between a couple of staff members in the locker room things started to take a turn.

He launched a solo protest for "truth and justice," which soon became a campus-wide phenomenon. Eventually the coach was dismissed, and proper legal course was taken. Emily Chase, who also played an active role in the student protest of the university administration, was one of the many senior student advocacy council members who saw Russell as a very principled individual. But Emily and Russell had somehow lost touch after graduation.

Emily Chase, a New York native, had moved to Texas for work after graduation. And it was a happenstance that she and Russell ran into each other at a coffee shop in Austin.

"Russell?" Emily beamed a wide smile full of surprise. She walked towards the table where Russell was sitting.

"Emily?" Russell responded in equal amazement. He got up from his chair.

"Well. Well. Well. Let me guess. You are here for the oil spill and climate change rally?" Emily was trying to guess.

"Haha. I actually work here. Work for a nonprofit in Austin. But you are right. Will be going to Houston for the rally tomorrow."

"Haven't changed one bit. Have you?"

"Tell me. What have you been up to?"

After Emily explained her monotonous software development job and how she was ready for a change, she listened to Russell. She was impressed by Russell's commitment to activism and noticed how Russell's passion for social justice had been undiminished. In fact, it felt like Russell had a much more purposeful life now and had somehow figured out what his mission was.

As they split paths at the coffee shop, a spark of joy rippled through Emily's body, and she decided right in that moment that she would join Russell for the rally.

"Hey . . . can I come to Houston tomorrow?"

Russell was startled for a second. "Of course. You're serious, right?"

That's how Russell's and Emily's collaborative activism in Texas commenced. Both non-natives of Texas, they started to fight the system for causes they believed in and for the people of Texas. They soon realized that there was never a dearth for causes they wanted to fight for in the state, and the hours they could honestly spend their energy in were just not enough.

So, during the course of next two to three years, after lending their voices to multiple causes, ranging from climate change to police discrimination, they decided to launch a very focused advocacy group— the Texas Women's Rights Advocacy, or TWRA. The advocacy group had been preparing for the inevitable attack on women from all corners of the legislative and justice systems. They knew it was only a matter of time once Fisher took the oath as the next Governor of Texas.

In American politics, and perhaps in geopolitics in general, whether someone is from the old school traditional politics or from the new age social media infused politics, when they hold onto a very strong core belief and are suddenly presented with some evidence that shows the fallacy of their belief, their ego gets bruised. They tend to become very uncomfortable. They are forced to stand up for their beliefs because they have developed cognitive dissonance, and they start rationalizing their words and actions, and start denying things that are remotely against their belief framework. Until they humiliate themselves.

But there is one seemingly big difference between the old school politicians and the new age ones. The traditional politicians were used to having only one or two sources of information they considered reliable. So, when they were caught in a situation of having to defend the weak foundation of their core beliefs that have been exposed, they tend to come around to a compromising position. In contrast, the new age politicians have an endless supply of sources of information in their own bubbles, and they can tailor their sources to provide the information that would play to reinforcing their beliefs and thereby making their cognitive dissonance immensely stronger. In short, once they get caught in an echo chamber, there is no escaping it. The humiliation no longer matters in the latter's case because it's not just the politicians who are caught in their echo chambers, but also their followers and those who would vote for them who are caught in the same echo chambers.

When Richard Harvey decided to run for office, the first person he reached out to was someone he had worked with during his stint on Wall Street, who was also currently running for office in Texas.

Sima Daly, when she was running the PR department at GTO, managed to nurture an excellent working relationship with Richard Harvey, who, among other things, was running a hedge fund and had built enough clout in his firm to leverage favors when needed. GTO never had a rough day in the stock market during the five years Sima was with GTO. Even on days when other stocks had to paddle through choppy waters, GTO somehow never disappointed its investors. Not even for a day. Richard Harvey may have played a small role in how GTO fared, and Sima never forgot all that Harvey did for her.

"That's a surprise, Richard. Why don't we meet for dinner? Tuesday night? I am going to be in Austin," Sima asked over the phone.

"I would love to. Will message you a couple of options. Sort of low-key places. No one would recognize us."

"That works. See you soon, Richard."

Sima was three years younger than Richard. But by average Texan political standards, both were way too young to be considered serious politicians. When they met for dinner, Sima Daly was as impressed as she was when Richard would rattle off financial data and analysis to justify what he did to save GTO on a bad stock market day.

"Wow. Senate run, huh?" said Sima, wiping her hands with the napkin.

"I know this sounds crazy. But the congressional race is a rough one here. For someone with my background, that is. If you know what I mean. TX-14 offers me just enough challenge to keep this election exciting and at the same time gives me hope. Because I have run numbers…and…" Richard went on.

"Hold on. Did you say numbers? I trust you, Richard. I am sure you have looked at the data and know what you need to win this. What can I do? I mean, from the outside it may look like 43 is a done deal for me. That may be true. But it's not over till it's over right? So, I will have to keep my focus on 42. Besides, I don't know anything about TX-14. Not been our district for the past four elections. I'm happy to do whatever I can. Tell me."

"Exactly. That's why I need your help, Sima. Put in a word with Fisher for me. Please. All I need is for him to rouse the grassroots a bit here. There are many of them who think 14 is a lost cause. They still can't believe I beat their favorite in the primaries."

"Rudolph Mattiazo?"

"Right. I just want Fisher to do one rally with me. That should do. You think you can help?

"Of course. As a matter of fact, I am meeting him tomorrow. Will check."

"I know I can count on you, Sima. Stop by in one of my rallies if you can. A Daly on stage in TX-14 may not hurt. In fact, it will be an honor."

"I will. I will." Sima checked time on her phone and continued. "If you'd excuse me, I'd have to leave now. 'Twas lovely seeing you, Richard. Thanks for the dinner." Sima gave a quick hug to Richard and left.

Both Sima and Richard were what one would mistakenly label as new age social media politicians who feed off their echo chambers—and it's not anyone's fault if they did so because these were young politicians. But both, for entirely different reasons, had managed to imbibe a certain quality of politics from the old school—that when you were challenged, you were vigilant and didn't just get your ego boosted through your echo chambers alone. They made sure one felt the humiliation from those outside the chambers. They listened to everyone. They were rational and looked at all the possibilities and arrived at a compromise without their egos getting bruised. If they could, that's the route to take.

Any book on Texas political history would have to have a dedicated chapter for Governor Harold Willkie. He served two full terms, and his popularity ratings remained above sixty percent throughout those two terms. Most Texans, conservatives and liberals alike, treated him with respect because he believed in the overall goodness of Texans. There was no official video or audio record of Governor Willkie insulting anyone in public.

His policies were conservative, but he respected the near majority that his opposition party had in the state legislature, so he was always very careful with his executive outreach. If he could bring both sides together to the table to negotiate on a particular issue, he gave that a shot first. At sixty-eight, during the middle of his second term, he learned that he had to deal with cancer at home. His wife Paula was diagnosed with a rare form of ovarian cancer. And he just decided he wouldn't run for public office anymore.

When Willkie announced he wouldn't be seeking reelection, there were many names who were considered favorites within the party, but how a relatively unknown grocery chain owner, Derek Fisher, became a favorite to win the primaries, should be a chapter on its own in that history book. Derek Fisher had learned the art of doing conservative politics in the twenty-first century by observing the best in the business. From Hungary to Turkey, from New York to Texas, he had been keeping his hungry political stomach open to consume food that would satiate him. He was very successful in creating a unique mix of a political style that drew from all the above different styles.

Fisher announced his arrival to the political scene in style. He showed up at ten different grocery stores of his chain in ten different cities and offered to pay up the grocery bills for everyone who was at the store at that moment. The customers, who were mostly women during that time of the day, were in a pleasant state shock when the cashiers announced that the "future Governor Fisher" was taking care of their groceries on that day.

Needless to add, this was the kind of positive campaign message that connected Fisher with every Texan instantaneously.

His campaign slogan lacked innovation, but it was so simple that it had a long-standing resonating power: "Git-er-done."

Derek Fisher did not have to do much after that sort of a powerful launch. He avoided the usual "gotchas" in interviews and managed to say less in general. He relied a lot on actions, and every time he did something, his team ensured that the videos were being circulated on social media tirelessly until they either became viral or the local TV channels picked them up for further coverage. Within two months, he became the favorite to win the party's nomination in the primaries.

It was the sort of dream campaign anyone would like to run. Derek Fisher did it all by himself. He didn't have data analysts working for him. Every single campaign-related action he did was conceived by him. Every single speech he gave until the primaries was carefully written by him. Every single interview he gave until then, he vetted the media outlets he wanted to speak to, and worked directly with the journalists and interviewers. He worked really hard to avoid even the smallest of gaffes politicians in this era are used to making.

A self-taught politician like Derek Fisher came occasionally in American politics, and when they did come, they made it big. Really big.

Derek Fisher was ready to become the next Governor of Texas.

CHAPTER 4

CURRENT DAY

The windows were fully raised, and there was air conditioning in the car. The Pecos River was quiet like it usually was. And it was not because it was well past 3:00 AM. Ava Walters was resisting her eyes from shutting down. She was clutching onto her backpack that was on her lap. She was not paying attention to the beautiful parks alongside the road as the car zoomed past them, or to the moonlight that was reflecting off the flowing river. There was a full moon in the sky.

"I'm sorry. I didn't have time to introduce myself. My name is Joanna. Joanna Ridge. Rosaline shared everything about you. I am so proud of what you did, and I am so sorry that you are being put through this," the driver said.

"That's all right, Joanna. Thank you for doing this. Not really sure if what I did was courageous or foolishness. Didn't have to put Bradley and Eveline through this, you know." She paused when she realized Joanna didn't know who they were. "My husband and my daughter." Ava sounded tired but composed.

"For your own safety, I am going to share very minimal information with you. I hope you have your phone turned off. If not, please do that immediately. Once we reach the house, I will go through some safety protocol. Till we figure this out, I'm gonna make you stay off the grid completely. Can't risk it." Joanna had thought this through.

"That's fine. I get it." Ava looked at Joanna and then showed her phone. "It's turned off by the way."

There was not much traffic at that time of the morning. Lights turned from green to red and from red to green, and no matter in what order they did, theirs was the only car for almost seven miles. It looked like the car was leaving the heart of Carlsbad.

"Why don't you get some shut-eye?" Joanna asked Ava to get some rest.

"We've got at least another hour to go."

The red Chevy Impala they were on was heading towards a small town

North of Carlsbad. As they drove through the silence of a clean summer night, the jagged New Mexico landscape unfolded like a storybook. The red rocks and dusty earth that Ava saw through the windows made her imagine the snow-capped mountains in the distance and earthen Pueblo villages dotting the rolling hills. She was no stranger to New Mexico but hadn't really explored the state. This land, as she had read in books, was alive with history and mystery, and it was no wonder so many writers had been drawn to its power.

There's something about this rugged landscape that stirs one's imagination, she thought to herself.

"Should take Eveline on a weeklong road trip. We should drive through the lengths and breadths of this state. It's as if it's calling out to those who are looking for a little magic in their lives."

New Mexico, a place where time seemed to move more slowly than anywhere else. A place where the rhythms of life were dictated by the ebbs and flows of the seasons. In Ava's life, the season of turbulence may have just begun.

The car pulled in front of a small house in the middle of nowhere. There was no paved road to get to the house. In fact, they had not been driving on paved roads at least for the past twenty minutes. Joanna drove the car to the back of the house and parked the car inside what appeared to be a makeshift garage. An open-roof garage that just had six-feet walls around it on three sides. Unless one took the aerial route, from a distance, no one could see there was a car parked there.

Joanna patted on Ava's shoulders.

"This is it. Jump out of the car quickly and follow me. I will get you set up inside. I cannot stay long here. I must leave soon for my morning shift."

Ava followed Joanna, making as little noise as possible.

"So, I assume we are no longer in Carlsbad?"

"No. It's better you don't know where we are exactly. At least for the time being."

No one knew for sure how this old house ended up there, in the middle of nowhere. Joanna thought it was a vacation home that someone had abandoned, but a few others she had talked to said it was cursed and no one should stay there for long. The house had just two rooms. The windows were boarded up, the small backyard—if one could call that—was overgrown, and there was an eerie feeling that came with everything with a house like that. Ava wasn't curious about any of that. She hoped that she would only have to stay there for a night or two.

Joanna unfolded a cot and dusted a couple of sheets. She threw two pillows on the cot. She reached for a sleeping bag from the top shelf of the lone closet in that room.

"Don't know how dusty and moldy they are. Please make do with these for now. There is a single burner grill. Coal fueled. But nothing else really. No electricity. Flowing water is a few hundred feet away from the house. When the sunlight breaks, just go fill these two buckets. Should get you through the day. My only advice is this: Do not go out more than once a day except to fill water. Got it?"

"Think so. Thank you."

"And be honest and please give me all pieces of electronic equipment you have on you. Need to take them with me and run a few checks. Don't want anyone to be tracking you to this place. Includes your laptop computer, phone, anything. This is critical." Joanna was firm.

"My computer, too? That is my life," Ava announced in a pleading voice.

"Don't worry. No harm will be done to your data. Will bring them back when I come back later tonight." Joanna collected all the equipment from Ava and was about to leave.

"Oh. Almost forgot. About food. I have a couple of cereal bars in my handbag. I'll leave them here."

"Thank you." She and Ava lifted the grocery bag.

"I still got this grocery bag. It's in your car. A human being can survive on raw veggies, fruits, and bread for a few days, I am sure." Ava was trying to make light of the situation.

Joanna went outside and picked up the grocery bag.

"Here. Lock the door from inside. I'll see you when I see you. Take care now, Ava!", Joanna left through the back door.

Senator Newell was an Iraq War veteran. He was widely considered as a fair and an honest man by many of his constituents. As a sixty-two-year-old conservative politician, Newell, over the years, had made an effort to paint a picture of himself as someone willing to listen to different points of view. His military experience had given him a deep respect for the rule of law and a strong commitment to defending the Constitution. As a senator, like many old school conservative politicians of his age, he had been a strong advocate for fiscal responsibility and limited government. He was a devout Christian and a strong supporter of gun rights. These two usually went together in Texas. He and his wife had two children and four grandchildren.

Newell had a two-prong approach to derailing TEXIT. One was at the federal —to make sure the US Congress didn't ratify TEXIT. And the second approach was at the state level—to try to sabotage or delay the passing of Article 49. They both needed different strategies, and that's why he had two different swift teams working on them simultaneously. His Austin-based team had to work in a clandestine mode and fly totally under the radar, for any mistake would not only have the remainder of his Senate career ruined, but he was afraid that he would perhaps face the possibility of becoming a Texas exile with his family coming under immense danger.

His inside allies in Austin were Alan Marks and Vivienne Creasey. Both were serving in the state congress. Vivienne was not from Newell's party, but they went a long way back. All the way back to Iraq. For Article 49 to pass, the TEXIT movement needed 101 votes in Congress and twenty-one votes in the Senate. With the governing party holding more than 110 seats in the House, getting ten "nay" votes from the ruling party felt close to impossible. So instead the swift team set their focus on the Senate. They just needed to flip four votes.

Vivienne was the minority leader in the Senate. Alan Marks was chairman of the Ways and Means Committee. Among other things, this committee controlled all bills and resolutions proposing to raise state revenue, all bills or resolutions proposing to levy state taxes or other fees, all proposals to modify, amend, or change any existing state tax or revenue statute, et cetera.

One of the presentations essential to passing Article 49 in the House was going to be the detailed report of what the Ways and Means Committee would propose for the next five years and what their overall outlook for the future independent Texas would be. The committee had already started having initial discussions on this even though the US Congress hadn't yet ratified TEXIT. This was by the far the most complicated and unprecedented task that the committee had ever to deal with. They were in the process of hiring a team of economists and accountant to get them through with these proposals, forecast, and analyses.

For the committee to paint gloom and doom for the next five years, they needed to have enough projected scenarios. Alan Marks, an economist in his former career, had to work on the assumption of the worst and ask questions that would propel the team to come up with projected worst-case scenarios. In many ways, Newell couldn't have found a better ally. Or so he thought. For if the Texas house got to review a pessimistic outlook from the Ways and Means Committee, then the chances of Article 49 failing in the House are somewhat high. And the chances of the House delaying the vote by another year or so are even higher.

Newell and Marks were meeting at a hotel lobby in Houston, Texas. It was a public spot, but they had assumed that this meeting was not going to raise any eyebrows, given Marks and Newell had worked together in the past to pass a strong veteran protection bill in the state. They were sitting very closely to each other, and no one would have been able to eavesdrop into their conversation unless the couches they were sitting on were bugged.

"Marks, give me some good news!"

"Senator, all I can say is that we are on the right track. Gonna take some time to start looking at actual numbers and scenarios and such. But trust me, this looks better than what I thought two months back." Marks was sharing his assessment.

"So, you are telling me you can deliver. That's impressive. I have a more serious question. Are you really into this or are you more like me?"

"More like you? What does that mean, senator?"

"I mean. I got on the TEXIT bandwagon cause you know . . . there was nothing else some of us old schoolers could have done. Now that the referendum has passed, I am getting the jitters. That's why, of late, I am spending way too many sleepless nights more than I should. For my age, at least." Newell laughed.

"I really was a TEXIT believer, sir. I reckon I never thought I'd get to see this in my lifetime. Tell you the truth, 'twas only after the referendum and all I started feeling the nerves. My gosh! What have we gotten ourselves into? This is going to be a disaster. I'm worried for my kids. Do I want them to grow up in this uncertain land?" Marks sounded anxious and concerned.

"Exactly. That's my concern, too." Newell looked around after hearing some footsteps and then saw a man approaching them. He continued.

"Congressman, as I always say, I appreciate what you're doing. I mean it from the bottom of my heart. We will connect within a week."

"My pleasure, senator. Let's keep this between us. I will loop . . ." Marks paused to check if anyone was near. "I will loop Vivienne in as soon as I can. She has a tremendous perception on issues that I never can have. She will have a few pointers."

"You bet," said Newell, getting out of his seat.

"Next time we will meet for dinner. It will be on me. I want to take you to my favorite steakhouse in Austin."

"Can't wait!"

Alex Pedroza was sitting in his living room. There was a photo of Maria, his wife, right next to him on the side table. He looked at the photo and started whispering.

"Did I make a mistake, Maria? Miguel was only as old as our boy, Diego. What will I tell his parents? How can I even look at them in their eyes?" Alex was writhing in mental pain, and tears just flowed down his cheeks.

Till that day, Alex had never thought about any other implications of TEXIT. There were people in his community who would ask him to tread cautiously and not throw in his support behind Fisher and everything he did blindly. There were a few who felt comfortable enough to ask him if he thought TEXIT would really be good for the Latino community.

He simply asked back, "What is our alternative? Not supporting it? Then we would have earned a near enemy forever, whether this passes or fails."

Alex spent several weeks caught in a quandary. He had to decide and let Fisher know—a difficult choice that would not make him popular with his community members who had been behind him all these years, but he felt it was the best one for his community. He rationalized his decision by thinking that the community members would understand eventually—that is, when they got their own congressional district. And even if they didn't, his heart told him that he had made the right choice. He knew once he made the decision, however unpopular it may be, the majority of the community would follow his lead and deliver it for him. That's what they did. He got to deliver ninety percent "yes" from his community for Fisher in the referendum.

All that rationalized thinking changed today. For the first time, he started questioning his decision. Why did the killers target his workers? Did the

TEXIT referendum results accelerate racial hatred? What if all those who warned him against betting on TEXIT were right? His mind kept wandering between consoling Miguel's family and that other worker at the site who screamed, "You made a deal with the devil, señor!"

His phone rang.

"Mr. Pedroza. I am the detective assigned to your case. We need you to stop by our office. And sign some paperwork. It should be quick. When can you come, sir?"

"Oh . . . err . . . good morning, detective. Your office, I mean the police station next to the civic center, right?"

"That's right."

"Will be there in twenty minutes, detective."

When Alex went to the police station, he was handed a bunch of forms and was asked to sign wherever it said *Employer Signature.*

For the next few minutes he sat there waiting for someone to give him an update on the case and on the health condition of his other workers who were injured. There was no one who even showed any inclination of talking to him. So he got up from his seat and walked towards the reception area.

"Excuse me. Who should I talk to about the Richardson case? There was a shooting this morning and . . ."

"Which one? The drive-by shooting or the one at the gas station?" the officer manning the reception desk asked.

"There were two this morning? This . . . this is the drive-by one."

The detective who spoke to him over the phone came out of his office to meet with Alex. The detective shared a few details from the hospital, and none of them was specific or helpful. His update was as trite and repetitive as what he already had heard from the police officer guarding the crime site. Alex expressed his displeasure and helplessness quite visibly. He told the detective that it was quite unacceptable that even after five hours, he, the person who was responsible for the well-being of those injured, had no idea what he was dealing with. The detective tried to smoothen the nature of the situation and sugarcoat the official police update again, something he had been trained to do all these years.

"We are doing everything in our power to ensure the injured receive the best care. Their condition is being observed by the emergency doctors. When there is a significant update from the hospital, I will personally call you to update you. For now, just sit tight and pray."

A thoroughly displeased Alex Pedroza nodded his head in disbelief and left the police precinct quickly.

Alex couldn't shake the feeling that something was wrong. He wished he could quite put his finger on it, but there was a sense of foreboding that hung over him. In that moment, everything felt hopeless, like there was no point in his fight and struggle for the community. Part of him knew he should keep fighting, but another part of Alex just wanted to give up and let the darkness of this moment consume him. He was caught between guilt and commitment. The conflict raged within him, and he didn't know what to do.

He needed to talk to someone. He called his daughter.

"Juana, I can only hope that someday I'll find a way out of this darkness and get back into the light."

"Papa, don't worry! You are fighting the good fight. Everybody knows that. This battle is what your life is all about. This is what defines you, Papa. Don't give up. Even if it feels like you are fighting in the darkness right now".

Those words of comfort from his eighteen-year-old daughter made him feel better. He knew this fight, what he was doing for the Latino community, was what his life was all about. He couldn't let anyone else get the better of his commitment.

For now, he would have to deal with the loss of Miguel. He would have to take responsibility for what happened and face the consequences. And at that moment, he decided that he was not going to let the police bureaucracy delay what he felt was his most important duty as an employer. Alex Pedroza drove to the hospital where his injured workers were admitted.

The Austin Star occupied just two floors in an unassuming building. In the digital age, traditional print media outlets like *The Austin Star* no doubt were struggling to stay afloat. Advertising revenues had declined, and many publications had been forced to cut costs or close their doors entirely. The situation was particularly even more dire for local newspapers, which had seen their readership drop precipitously in recent years. While there were still some holdouts who preferred the physicality of print media, it seemed increasingly likely that the days of newsprint were numbered.

It was the leading daily newspaper in Austin, but like most newspapers *The Austin Star* had also embraced the eventual death of their print form and had been in the process of growing its presence digitally in multiple formats. On the second floor was the editors' conference room. Jason Greer was sitting in that large room, alone, with his computer opened. He was waiting for Myra Bristow to show up.

Myra had been thinking about Jason's text since she received it. And she wanted to hold onto the story that focused on Russell Weston and Emily Chase. She was trying to reason it out with Jason that they should perhaps focus only on the rally and the sudden breakout of violence in their coverage of that day's proceedings at the rally. And not wander into the unknown. Her logic was that if they didn't know enough about the story, then it could come across speculative. But Jason was not ready to buy her logic. His rationale was that Russell and Emily were not well-known names outside the activists' circle and that even if they gave a speculative spin to the story today, they would have lit the flare. Flare that hopefully was bright and warm enough for the cockroaches to fall out of the cracks. They—Jason and Myra—could always do a follow-up.

With so much anti-Fisher coverage in recent times, *The Austin Star* was already carrying the "Fake News" label. How much more harm could another story linking the police to the staged arrest of two activists bring? Myra was usually quick to make decisions under such situations, as she, by nature, seemed to have the instinct when stories were more straightforward and of black-and-white in nature. There was something about the arrests earlier today that didn't sit well with Myra. There were lots of gray in this story, and she felt that they should focus only on what they thought were just black or white. She thought untangling this lead needed time, and it may not be a simple case of someone from the pro-Fisher circle trying to threaten two annoying activists who had been on the news much too frequently of late. She tried to tell Jason that his theory of Fisher himself being directly involved with this did not make much sense. There was nothing that they did recently as activists against the Fisher government that could have triggered such a panic reaction. As far as Myra could tell, there was nothing that they did recently that would annoy Fisher more than what they had done over the last two years. So Myra's theory was that there was more to the story than met the eye.

"The last thing we want, Jason, is to alert those who are behind this. Any focus on Russell and Emily's arrest could halt them from what they were going to do next. Or worse. Either way, I reckon you wouldn't be able to write the conclusion if you went with your speculative slant today."

"I thought about that Myra. What if their next target is something worse? Or someone else? What if it's me? Or you?"

"Jason. Stop right there!" Myra was trying to laugh through her fake anger.

She continued, "I don't know who your source is. I don't need to know. But if they are credible, I am sure you'd get to know the next target, too. So stop imagining. Stop overanalyzing. We need to report what we know."

"Excuse me. I think I need a break, Myra. Maybe I am too consumed by this theory. How about we reconnect in about an hour? I promise I will finalize the draft after that meeting."

An hour later when Jason and Myra met, he agreed with her logic. He seemed to have thought through the consequences of publishing the story like he had originally pitched. In his career, Jason had come across a few stories that just didn't seem quite right or the details just didn't add up at first. But he was able to use his sources' information and his own investigation to develop a certain kind of journalistic instinct before publishing these stories with an investigative slant. He realized this was not one of those stories. Even though the incident itself was insignificant in the larger context of what was happening in Texas at that time, to be able to arrive at an investigative slant with what little he knew, Jason understood the high stakes involved. He was once again glad and relieved that he had Myra as her supervisor and a bouncing board. Someone who could guide him out of making a career breaking mistake.

"Thanks Myra." Jason smiled.

"For saving your ass?"

"For that, too." Jason laughed.

"You have two hours to finish the draft then. See you later."

After Myra left the room, Jason opened his computer and moved the story draft he had already typed up to another folder. He took and a deep breath and started typing.

Chaos in Austin Rally!

The split screen on his computer had his X (Twitter) feed open on the right half.

Something caught Jason's eyes.

Politico was reporting that the Texas Women's Rights Advocacy, the nonprofit organization founded by Russell Weston and Emily Chase, was under investigation for violation of political and lobbying compliance and falsification of financial records.

"What the actual fuck!" Jason reacted.

Just outside Governor Fisher's office in the Capitol, Senator Harvey and Congresswomen Daly were waiting in the lobby and waiting for him to show up.

"So, got any scoop?" Harvey was trying to make some small talk.

8:30 AM was not too early for Daly for small talks, but it was Monday. Caffeine was taking extra few minutes to kick in and awaken her spirits.

"What did you ask? I have a severe case of the Mondays," said Daly.

"Fisher showing up will fix that for ya," said Harvey, trying to lighten her mood.

Sima Daly continued to stare blankly into her phone, ignoring Harvey's remark.

Governor Fisher entered his office at 8:33 AM. He was usually very punctual, and today was an exception.

He checked his private desk phone for voicemail alerts, as his executive assistant usually forwarded only important voicemails to this message box. There was nothing. Then he checked his daily schedule that the executive assistant had printed for him. She usually kept that printed schedule right in the middle of his desk so he couldn't miss it. In addition, the daily planner was also sent to him in a text message every morning.

He picked up his phone and asked the assistant to send Daly and Harvey in. He stared outside the window and took in the beauty of the serene Austin skies for a couple of seconds. Then he walked towards the coffee machine behind the large couch in lounge like area. Fisher usually drank coffee less for the caffeine but more for the combined taste of milk and sugar. He also liked the smell of fresh coffee brewing.

Outside, the sun had already started blazing down on the State Capitol, its heat waves shimmering in the distance. The legislative building was bustling with activity, as lobbyists and politicians alike congregated in its air conditioned halls. Monday mornings were almost always busy until the legislators went on their summer recess.

A dozen demonstrators were chanting and carrying signs outside, about 100 feet from the gate. The police were keeping a close eye on them. Amid all this activity, a group of tourists walked by, eager to take in the sights and sounds of Austin during the summer. They stopped to take photos in front of the Capitol before continuing their walking tour. In short, it was politics as usual in Austin during the summer morning hours.

"'Morning governor!" Daly and Harvey walked in.

"Good morning! Pretty warm day. How are y'all doing? Be honest," said Fisher.

"Not as anxious as you are, I reckon," replied Daly.

"Lay it out for me. Any new scoop from your sources? Why did Dodson call for this meeting?" Fisher's voice certainly showed his anxiety.

"Sorry to say that there is nothing significant to add, governor. Nothing more than what we already know," answered Daly.

"Or not know." Harvey looked at Daly with a smile and turned towards Fisher. "If I may, governor, do you think he has made up his mind and perhaps he just wants to let you know? An aggressive first move?" posited Harvey.

"That would be my guess, too. But why now? That's what I want to know. We have plenty of time for this talk. He should be keeping his ass glued in DC and deliver the votes in Congress, the votes he has promised. That's what he should be doing. Why is he here breathing down my neck?"

"Unless . . ." said Daly.

"Spit it out, Sima!" ordered Fisher.

"Unless. There is a problem with that. Maybe he can't deliver those votes and he needs your help?"

"Hmm. That's an interesting thought. At least this meeting wasn't completely useless. You've given me something to think about and prepare for."

"You are welcome." Daly was happy she could provide some valuable input.

For the next few minutes the three of them kept going back and forth about how much they were unable to stand the contemptuous nature of Dodson and how patronizing he always was when he talked to any of the state level conservative politicians from Texas.

When it was time for Fisher to take an urgent call from his cabinet member, he decided to bring this meeting to an end. He told Daly and Harvey that his assistant would reach out to their offices to set up the next meeting depending on how his Dodson show went.

It was 10:00 AM.

The executive assistant had been given strict instructions that she should let Dodson and his team into Fisher's office as soon as they arrived. Since Fisher didn't know how many people he was to expect for the meeting, he had assumed the worst, and let his assistant know that there could be five or six people.

"Hey! Good morning, governor!" Dodson, a hefty man in his late fifties, with a navy blue blazer and khaki pants, pushed open the door and walked in.

"Top of the morning to see you, senator! What a pleasure to see you in my office. If I recall, this may be the first time you are stopping by our office. Right?" said Fisher.

"Well. I am not keeping count, exactly."

They both laughed, gave each other a quick hug, and shook hands.

"May I offer you Austin's best coffee?" Fisher started walking towards the coffee machine.

"Ah! Nespresso. I bet it's the Austin water that makes all the difference. I will have a small cup." Dodson smiled.

They both grabbed their cups of coffee and sat down in the middle. The sofa where the governor usually hosted his guests. From cabinet ministers to DC politicians to lobbyists, this was the playing field in Fisher's office.

"Let me get to the point, governor. I am sure you must be wondering if I am going to drop my hat in the ring to be the first President of Texas. But that's a long away. I am still thinking about it. This meeting is about Newell."

"Senator Newell?" Fisher was mildly relieved that this discussion was not going to be what he thought it would be.

"Yes. The senior senator from Texas. He—pardon my French—that giant piece of senile turd, he has been working behind the scenes to sabotage TEXIT. At least that's what I've been made to believe."

"What? You better not fucking kidding me. How do you know?" Fisher was clearly not expecting this.

"I, too, have sources, governor. But that's not the point. I wanted to meet you face to face today so I could ask you what's your take on Newell?"

"What do you mean, senator?"

"Well. If it's between me and Newell, who would you choose?"

"That's not how it works. I have high regards for both of you. Newell has been serving in the Senate for a long time. He has done a lot of good things for the people of Texas. And so have you. In your short time in DC."

"Let's cut the bullshit. If Newell and I throw our hats in the ring, who would you back to be the first President of Texas?"

"It's too hypothetical. I can't answer that question now." Fisher was feeling the heat.

"Can I at least count on your vote? Not an endorsement. At least not now." Dodson was trying to prod Fisher even more.

"Sure. You may. But only hypothetically speaking," clarified Fisher.

"That's enough for now, governor. Although, to tell you the truth, I am not convinced. But let me tell you something. None of this would matter if Newell were able to pull off his heist."

"How do you think he is going to pull that off?"

"Please surround yourself with people who understand Article 49, governor. There are so many ways Article 49 could fail in the legislature. Newell just needs to find the right person to get his ideas in. And that would be the end."

"I do have a great team, senator. Don't be so condescending."

"Well. Then it looks like you have it under control. Will see you on the other side when all this matters."

"Nice of you stop by, senator. Have a good day!" Fisher waved goodbye to Dodson.

"Good day to you!"

According to the Submerged Lands Act, individual states had rights to the natural resources of submerged lands from the coastline to no more than three nautical miles. That was in the Atlantic, Pacific, the Arctic Oceans, and the Gulf of Mexico. The only exceptions to this rule were Texas and the west coast of Florida, where state jurisdiction extended from the coastline to no more than three marine leagues, or sixteen-point-two kilometers into the Gulf of Mexico.

The SLA also reaffirmed the federal claim to the lands of the Outer Continental Shelf, or OCS, which consists of those submerged lands seaward of state jurisdiction. The SLA paved the way for the Outer Continental Shelf Lands Act, or OCSLA, later in 1953. The OCSLA and subsequent amendments, in later years, outlined the federal responsibility over the submerged lands of the OCS. Additionally, it authorized the Secretary of the Interior to lease those lands for mineral development.

These make the whole the ownership of offshore and onshore drilling quite complicated should Texas eventually secede from the Union. The US Bureau of Land Management, or BLM, oversaw all onshore oil fields, while leasing and drilling on federal offshore seabed was controlled by the Bureau of Ocean Energy Management (BOEM), and the Bureau of Safety and Environmental Enforcement (BSEE), formerly named the Minerals Management Service (MMS).

There were potentially three different ways the Union and the new government of Texas could come to an agreement.

1) Both the Union and Texas could agree upon some terms and conditions under which BLM, BOEM/BSEE would lease these fields out to Texas for ninety-nine years (most practical lease term). Texas could decide how to lease these out to individual companies.

2) Both the Union and Texas could agree upon some terms and conditions under which individual Texas-based oil companies or drilling companies would go for open bidding through the standard and existing process, and they would lease directly from BLM, BOEM/BSEE.

3) Both the Union and Texas could agree upon some terms and conditions under which BLM, BOEM/BSEE would lease out only certain areas and fields to Texas for ninety-nine years (most practical lease term) while the rest would remain with the Union and they would decide how to lease those fields out directly to the oil companies.

The enormity of analyzing permutations and combinations of all the terms, conditions, and pricing would be a cumbersome and time-consuming undertaking. As soon as the referendum passed, Derek Fisher's chief economic advisor had mentioned about this being the most complicated step during the final stages before Article 49 got tabled for voting and then again during the final stages of the US Congress approving the independence plan.

As soon as the referendum passed, on his chief economic advisor's prompt, Governor Fisher had appointed Abhinav Agarwal, CEO of RapFuel, as his oil czar. Abhinav Agarwal was no muck with numbers. He was an economics professor before taking up a consulting career in the oil industry. His economics background, combined with his extraordinary people skills and analytical mind, pushed him up the ladder slowly and steadily in the oil industry, all the way to the top at RapFuel.

One of the first things Abhinav did was to call for an all-executive meeting involving Texas-based oil companies. Every single CEO attended the meeting. To begin with, Abhinav wanted to know if all of them were really onboard with TEXIT. If they responded yes, then he wanted to learn more about each one of the executive's individual proposals to make the oil industry make the best of both the worlds. Abhinav got a varied list of proposals. He was thrilled that he found out how many executives were onboard with TEXIT. But he was also disappointed that so many of these executives couldn't even do basic forecasting of their own businesses.

By the end of the two-day meeting, Abhinav had a sack full of useless proposals and a few good ones. Abhinav meticulously went through the good proposals and studied them closely. The numbers man he was, Abhinav was aghast that many of the proposals had made some calculation errors. Eventually, by borrowing a couple of ideas that he thought were brilliant in the above proposals, he started putting together a final proposal for Governor Fisher.

CHAPTER 5

A FEW DAYS BEFORE REFERENDUM

Keith Glass had managed to get someone else to switch his shift at the plant with him. He was not sure what to expect of this evening. He had met Mr. Haddock only once before, but he really did not get to spend much time with him. All he remembered about Haddock was that he was wheelchair-bound, but for a man in his eighties, he was very sharp and seemed to have an amazing sense of memory. One thing stood out for Keith from that brief meeting. Mr. Haddock was very kind to Vanessa, and that was all Keith cared about.

Vanessa walked out of her bedroom looking for her purse and caught Keith sitting on the couch watching TV.

"Please don't tell me you are going to come dressed like that." She was clearly not amused by Keith's evening wear.

"I ain't gonna dress up just cause we've been invited to a rich white man's party. This is what I wear when I go out with my boys. What's wrong with this?"

"This isn't just another white people party, Keith. We are going to meet the senator."

Vanessa had picked her most favorite dress from her wardrobe. A green and blue combination, which she thought brought out her best features elegantly. Keith loved this dress on Vanessa, too. She always reserved this dress only for the best occasion, which came by once every two or three years.

She had never visited Mr. Haddock's house during non-working hours or without her uniform. She had been privy to a couple of small private parties that Mr. Haddock had hosted when she was on duty. Both the parties were restricted to the resting lounge, the guest room, and the grand dining room, and the parties were quiet for the most part except when they all gathered in the resting lounge post-dinner. There was some music and loud laughter, which Vanessa presumed was because the guests were playing some games.

Mr. Haddock had an eclectic music taste, and he had a huge vinyl collection. During the daytime, he would have the music playing almost nonstop, even when he took short naps. Vanessa had learned a whole lot about a wide array of classical musicians and opera voices she had never heard of before. He was particular about how the vinyl records were arranged in his shelf, and Vanessa had learned it the hard way.

"Are you ready, honey?" Vanessa yelled.

"Almost!"

They drove in Keith's car. A metallic blue Ford Escape. Keith had changed into one of his two formal wears. A sky-blue shirt, khakis, and a dark brown sports coat that gave him a dignified look. Or so he thought.

"Keep your eyes on the road and hands on the wheels, Keith. It's nothing you haven't seen or touched before," said Vanessa, playfully chiding Keith the moment he saw shades of romance clouding his eyes.

When they reached Haddock's house, Vanessa wondered if they were late because the road was busy. There were two dozen cars parked on both sides of the road and they had to drive around to the next road to find a spot to park. As they walked into Haddock's house, there was a greeter who welcomed them and asked for their names. He immediately picked up his phone and called someone.

"Vanessa Glass and Keith Glass," said the greeter, waiting for a response.

"Yes. Just two. Okay. They are on their way."

He handed them a small card that had the agenda for the evening and menu on the other side.

Haddock's house didn't tower over the other houses on the block. But the external appearance of the house could have been misleading. As soon as Keith entered the house, it was clear to him that no expense had been spared in its construction. The front door was made of solid mahogany, and the windows were adorned with intricate stained-glass designs. But the most impressive room by far was the formal living room. The walls were covered in rich silk wallpaper, and the floor was carpeted with an expensive rug. A grand piano stood in one corner, and in the center of the room was a beautiful chandelier. The furniture was all upholstered in fine fabrics, and there were delicate figurines on every surface. Vanessa had never been to this room until then. It was clear that this room was meant for entertaining guests, and it certainly seemed to impress them.

Keith took a deep breath in, breathed out, and muttered, "Fancy!"

There were about fifty odd people in the room standing with their drink glasses and hobnobbing with their standing neighbors. There were a couple of waitstaff walking around with trays of hors d'oeuvres and drinks. Vanessa and Keith looked around to see if there were any familiar faces. They were not able to spot any.

"Champagne or wine, ma'am?" a waiter asked.

"Err … I … ummm … champagne, please," said Vanessa.

"Do you have anything else?" asked Keith.

"Sure. What do you want sir?"

After a few minutes, and after a few more guests had slipped into that room, Keith was sipping his glass of bourbon filled with ice, while Vanessa was roving her eyes around the room to see if anyone else was gazing at them.

"There must be a reason why Mr. Haddock wanted us here." Vanessa was trying to think hard.

"Ladies and gentlemen, the senior Senator of Texas, Mr. Albert Newell!" someone announced his arrival to the center of the room. The guests formed a circle around him. There must had been about 100 people in that room, waitstaff excluded.

"What an honor to be in this part of the country. I love Galveston. I do. And I wish I traveled here more often. It's an absolute honor for me to be hosted by the kindest man I have ever known—my father's good friend, and Galveston's pride, Mr. Haddock. Thank you, Mr. Haddock, for having me. By the way, this is not a political event. So, no speech. And no solicitation for donation." Newell paused and smiled, while the guests laughed.

"Enjoy your evening. I hope to stop by and talk to each of you individually."

Vanessa saw Mr. Haddock in his chair at the corner of the living room with the wheelchair parked next to it. Newell was sitting across him with a small table separating them. From a distance Vanessa could tell these men had known each other for a long time. She felt someone tapping on her shoulders.

"Ms. Glass, I am glad you and Mr. Glass could come," Roy greeted her.

"Oh . . . yeah. We are glad, too. Thank you again for inviting us."

"Mr. Haddock wanted me to let you know that he and Senator Newell would like to talk to you in private whenever you are ready. Now . . . preferably," suggested Roy.

"Now . . . now should be fine. Keith, are you ready to go meet the senator?" Vanessa tapped on his shoulder while he was trying to pick up a shrimp cocktail glass from the tray the waiter was holding.

"What, now? Sure." He reluctantly left the glass back on the tray.

Roy led both to the corner of the room. Everyone in the room could see what was happening in that corner, but no one could hear. There were exactly four chairs placed around that table. So Newell and Haddock could meet only up to two guests at a time.

"Good evening, Mr. Haddock! Thank you for having us here." Vanessa greeted Haddock with a sense of warm familiarity. She extended her cheeks and bent down for Haddock to let him kiss her on her cheek as a token of welcoming her. And she lifted her right hand to shake his.

"Indeed, a pleasure to have you, Vanessa. You look dazzling in that dress. Senator Newell, this is Vanessa Glass, and the gentleman next to her is Keith Glass. You wanted to meet them. Here they are. In flesh and blood."

"It's an absolute honor to meet you, senator!" Vanessa shook Newell's hands.

It was early morning when Burl awoke to the sound of cicadas humming in the trees. The sun was already hot, and the day promised to be another scorcher.

He pulled on his overalls and headed out to the peanut field. The peanuts were just beginning to flower, and the plants were waist-high. He spent the first few minutes walking up and down the rows, quickly inspecting the irrigation system that he had installed and ensuring that it was working properly.

On his way to the truck after checking the irrigation systems, he saw the creek that ran on the other side of the road. He was reminded of his childhood days when he, Dudley, and a bunch of other friends would come and play here. He felt sad that children from his town wouldn't be able to enjoy the creek as much this year due to the drought. He looked up at the sky to see if there were any dark clouds. He had already checked his weather app as soon as he woke up and knew there was no rain forecasted. And yet.

He drove to the warehouse, where he usually spent most of his mornings in a small office room located at the back of the warehouse. His workers would come in by 9:00 AM. There were a few unopened mails on his table. Burl took the one on top that was from USDA. He was mad for a second for no reason. Then he collected his emotions and opened that mail. It was an invitation from USDA to attend an award ceremony where he was being recognized as one of the awardees in the Young Farmers category. It was a global event organized by USDA.

He was ready to tear the invitation off when something caught his eye. On the morning of the award ceremony there was a free seminar being hosted by USDA for all farmers. The topic was "How to get equipped for twenty-first century farming and stay competent. Modern techniques, methods, tools, and more." He really wanted to attend this event. He knew his father would disown him if he ever saw him holding that invitation for more time than was needed to tear it and throw it into a trash can.

He looked at the date. The event was scheduled exactly on the day of the referendum. And he had to travel to Chicago if he chose to go. At first, this felt like a sign. He thought he was sinning by thinking about it too much. Enough signs to discourage him from going to the ceremony were already there. And yet the passionate farmer in him kept whispering in his ears that this was the learning opportunity he had been waiting for. To meet other farmers from other parts of the country, to exchange ideas, to meet a few global pioneers in modern farming, to learn from them, to ask questions, et cetera.

"I am gonna lose it, Dud. I am gonna be fucking wasting my vote in the referendum." Burl called his best friend and was speaking with Dudley on the phone.

Dudley was like a bouncing board for Burl. He was not a farmer, but growing up in Stansley, one had to know enough about farming even if they were not directly in the industry.

"Burlster, you learn all that modern shit from those feds and implement them here. Right here in Stansley. When Texas breaks free, you will be the king. You can teach all Texas farmers about modern farming and all that shit dude." Dudley was encouraging Burl to go.

"What about my vote?"

"Fuck it. If we are gonna lose the referendum by one vote, then we didn't earn it anyway."

Burl Fogg was not convinced by Dudley's response about the vote. But he did see value in Dudley's point on how he could leverage all this learning in a post-TEXIT independent Texas. After contemplating over this for twenty-four hours, Burl Fogg had concluded that this was an event he couldn't afford to miss.

If one were to walk into a Sima Daly's office right now, they would immediately notice that the mood in her office was optimistic. Right from the day she got elected, there was a feeling of hope and possibility in the air in the office. Everything seemed possible. Even the most difficult problems seemed like they could be overcome. Sima Daly's staff seemed to have imbibed that quality and always came across optimistic, too. They believed in their boss and their ability to make a difference. They were confident that they could make a strong and positive impact on the political landscape of Texas. There was a sense of purpose and excitement in the air. It felt like anything was possible.

Sima was sitting at her desk, catching up on the latest news on her iPad. Her secretary knocked and opened the door. She wanted to let Sima know that Aaron was there.

Aaron Naylor had always been interested in politics. So when he saw an internship opening in Congresswoman Daly's office, he jumped at the chance. As an intern, Aaron was responsible for a variety of tasks, from answering phone calls to helping with research for an interview sound-bite. But he quickly realized that the most important part of his job was simply being there for the constituents who needed help and for the congresswoman, whom he had developed a deep admiration and liking for within a few days of joining her office.

Daly pushed her iPad away on her table and looked up at Aaron.

"I don't think we have had a one-on-one before this meeting. I have been hearing good things about you. Glad you could be part of our team. Aaron, right?"

"Likewise, congresswoman. I mean . . . ma'am. I have been learning a lot and I quite like what you do and where your priorities are." Aaron was trying to impress his boss.

"Listen, I know Meghan would have briefed you. This is one of those tasks we can't put it on a paper. You know what I am saying? No emails, no voice-mails. So I hope you know what you are getting into." Sima was very hesitant.

"Absolutely, ma'am. I know exactly what I am going to do. I know my responsibilities. Don't worry about me, ma'am. Will report back after I finish the task in four to five days."

"Good. That's really good. Just want to make sure that we are not forcing you to do something which you are not into whole heartedly." Sima wanted to confirm one last time that Aaron was willing to take upon the task.

"Once again, no worries about me, ma'am. Besides, I do like Senator Richard Harvey. I sure do. He has got a … ummm … a certain presence … about him … umm … that can't be matched easily," offered Aaron with a smile.

Sima dismissed Aaron from her room and immediately started drafting an email.

Jason Greer and Myra Bristow were sitting in Myra's office when Jason's phone buzzed. There was a text message from his source in DC.

Got a major scoop. FT in about an hour?

Jason responded, *How about 90 minutes?*

He finished his meeting with Myra and left for home. It had already been a very long day. He was wondering where he would be in the next forty minutes if he started driving home right then. His driving instinct told him he could make it home in thirty minutes.

He dropped his bag and went to the refrigerator to pick a bottle of beer for himself. Even though they were not his most favorite beer, he usually had a few bottles of Red Stripe in his refrigerator because they had twist tops. He opened a bottle and sat on his couch, scrolling through X (Twitter) and waiting for the call from DC.

His phone rang.

"Hey, Lee! Whassup?"

"I am doing all right, brother. How is Austin treating you? How are you keeping cool in all this political heat?"

Jason showed him the bottle of Red Stripe through the camera.

Leer and Jason used to work together at *The Washington Post*. While Lee continued to work for *The Post*, Jason had moved to Texas, prompted largely because of an advice given by his former English teacher, Mrs. Magdalene. Lee continued to stay in touch with Jason, and they both continued to share political gossips every now and then.

"Are you sure? Dodson and Newell are both in it? Wow. Dodson was a given. But Newell too?"

"That's why I am looping you in. You should find out more from Houston."

Jason thanked Lee for the scoop.

The next morning, when Jason had the daily editorial meeting with his team and Myra, he pitched this lead and asked Myra if he could work on this as his next story.

"I have a very reliable source, and I know both senators want to run."

Myra convinced Jason that this story was too premature and perhaps needed more vetting. She was also not comfortable with giving this story a lift at that point of time given it could become unworthy if the referendum failed.

"Jason, I have no problem you want to dig into this. Find more details. Keep the flame alive. But we are not pushing this now."

An avid music and dog lover, Evan Williams was elected to represent the people of TX-02 in the last election. He was born in Louisiana and was raised mostly in Texas. His family moved to Houston when he was three. Evan was the oldest of three siblings. He went to the Colorado Christian College and graduated with a degree in political science. After college, he worked as a staff member in Senator Ryan Dodson's reelection campaign. He then went on to work for the National Republican Congressional Committee. Running for public office was something he started to think about seriously while he was in college where he ran and won a student council election. When he decided to run for congress, Dodson was the first most prominent conservative politician to endorse him. He had officially become a mentee of Dodson since the time he started working for him. Until now, there had not been a single issue in the US Congress that Williams voted independently and out of his own conscience alone. He had always consulted with Dodson before voting. Such was Dodson's influence in his political career.

When Dodson decided to join Fisher during the referendum and pro-TEXIT campaign rallies, it was because Williams had advised him to do so. Evan's strong grassroots connections had indicated that the pro-TEXIT wave this time around had really been significant and that there was a perception in the state of Texas that Dodson was trying to dodge his stance on this. When Williams met Dodson on the flight to DC the following Monday morning, he had shared his personal advice and recommendation to Dodson.

"Senator, if I may, I think you should go all in. If the referendum doesn't pass, I guess there's nothing to lose. We all go back to doing what we are doing now. But if it does pass, then we, too, will become the faces of the movement. It is not going to be just Fisher."

"Hell, son. That makes a lot of sense. What you just said."

As soon as their plane landed in DC, Dodson called his Senate staff to schedule a Fox News interview in one of the primetime shows for that evening. He also went on all major conservative media news outlets the next day and started delivered passionate stump speeches on TEXIT and why he had to take his time to decide where exactly he stood on this issue.

"It's not whether I am pro- or anti-TEXIT. I have always been very clear when it comes to Texas's independence. It was always a question of timing. Are we ready now? Is Texas ready now for this? That needed some understanding of the issues on the ground, and I took my time. Here I am. And the answer is yes. A resounding *yes*. We are ready to get it done."

That media blitz seemed to have helped mitigate the danger of Texans viewing Dodson as going soft on TEXIT. Not only that, but it had also put pressure on Senator Newell to come out and take a similar stance, which he ended up doing the following week.

Dodson, Williams, and Newell were supposed to appear alongside Fisher today at a rally. Both Dodson and Newell did not think highly of Fisher. Williams had never openly shared with anyone what he thought of Fisher's ascent to governorship. But since he was Team Dodson, the perception was naturally that he wasn't a fan of Fisher either. On the other side, neither Dodson nor Newell had forgotten their conversation at the restaurant in DC a few weeks ago. And the bitterness between them had only thickened since then. But tonight, they all knew what the stakes were. They had to project a united front. Alongside Fisher.

The campaign event was kicked off with a local school choir singing "Texas, Our Texas". It was followed by another band performing a rock version of "Miles and Miles of Texas." And so on. Then it was time for rallying speeches. Evan Williams welcomed the supporters who had gathered. Every time he mentioned Fisher's name the entire arena reverberated with cheers. The same could not be said about how the crowd reacted when Dodson and Newell's names were mentioned. Evan noticed the difference. So did Dodson and Newell. They all knew Fisher was the star. He had been instrumental in getting the momentum for the referendum thus far.

When Dodson spoke, he slyly remarked with a sarcastic tone that the senior senator from Texas, Albert Newell, had such an illustrious career, how he had been a great mentor for young senators like him and for state politicians like Derek Fisher. Dodson went on to add that Newell's special efforts to encourage next generation politicians were an example for how senior politicians should make away for younger ones when the time came. Newell did not appreciate Dodson taking a dig at his age to make his potential presidential run a nonstarter. On the other hand, Newell did not come prepared to talk about Dodson. So he decided not to take any potshots back at Dodson. He kept his speech short and focused on what great things an independent Texas could achieve. He also talked about the challenges that lay ahead once the referendum passed in their favor. He specifically talked about how achieving economic independence was not going to be easy and how securing the border now would become entirely their responsibility. The crowd wasn't paying attention to much of that. They were there to cheer for Fisher—and for TEXIT.

Finally, when Fisher spoke—rather, tried to speak—his voice was drowned by the sheer noise coming from the stands. He barely got out a couple of sentences when someone started fireworks outside the arena. There was even more noise. He gave his usual stump speech.

And ended his speech with his trademark chant: "TEXIT NOW!"

When Russell Wilson learned of how RapFuel had managed to cover up the effects of the oil spill from a few years ago, he was naturally enraged and wanted to take this fight up. This was before Fisher had taken office. Russell got engaged in this fight and got to work with a group of environmental activists for a short time before moving on to his other activism projects. But he just did not and could not let go off RapFuel.

When he had the opportunity to come back to Houston to join another protest rally along with Emily Chase, he got in touch with the environmental activist group to see where they were with the oil spill fight. Russell and Emily learned that the case was now with a US district court, but it did not look that promising for the advocacy group. The legal team representing the environmental advocacy group, which was fighting on behalf of the coastal area residents and the fishermen, was using the BP oil spill judgment as the basis and reference. They wanted to prove in the court that RapFuel's decisions to continue to operate certain rigs was entirely driven by profits and as a result they consciously chose to disregard known heavy risks. They wanted the compensation to the tune of seven-point-five billion in total. RapFuel was contending that this was an unfortunate accident, and they did everything as per their safety guidelines to keep the rig operationally safe. And that there was no intentional negligence on their part.

Russell and Emily got more invested in the case during their time there in Houston. They understood that to fight a large corporation like RapFuel, their traditional rallies and protests were not going to be enough, as it was now a matter of winning the legal battle for which they needed more evidence. They spent the next few months doing thorough homework in understanding company's daily operations, finances, executive decisions, and changes in the business graph of the company over the years, especially from one year before the oil spill to one year after. They were able to get their hands on some sensitive data about the company through their relentless pursuit.

With the help of engineers and auditors in the environmental advocacy group, Russell and Emily were able to put together a solid evidence document that the group could now produce in court. That was exactly what they did. When the case reached its final hearings, it was clear that RapFuel had lost its advantage.

The US district court judge assigned RapFuel the majority of the blame for the accident. "Gross negligence on RapFuel's part" was the judge's verdict. And he even cited the BP oil spill case as a precedent for paying close attention to the evidence produced by the prosecution and he could not help notice the striking similarities between both the cases. The judge concluded that the company owed a cumulative penalty to the tune of nine-point-two billion in total to the affected parties. The environmental advocacy group was delighted with the verdict, and they were thankful for the efforts put in by Russell and Emily, especially in the last few months to bring them to this favorable closure.

Abhinav Agarwal, the CEO of RapFuel, said that RapFuel completely disagreed with the judgment, as the case did not prove gross negligence, because the bar to prove that was very high as per law. He also added that RapFuel would nevertheless honor the verdict and pay the penalty as adjudicated over the next three years.

The day on which the judge passed the verdict was the day Agarwal learned of the names of the two activists who brought him and RapFuel there. During the final proceedings, one of the attorneys in his legal team pointed to Abhinav, where Russell and Emily were seated inside the courtroom. There they were, sitting in the last row, completely overwhelmed by emotions as soon as the judge read his verdict. They got up and hugged each other while other members of the advocacy group inside the courtroom were also equally elated.

Meanwhile, from a distance, Abhinav was staring at Russell and Emily. He was wondering how two no-name activists could cause so much harm to his reputation and his company's. After all, this case was going completely in RapFuel's favor just a few months ago. In Abhinav's mind, it was clearly etched that these two were the main reason for the prosecution getting an upper hand at the right time. With every passing moment of that stare inside the courtroom, the vengeance that was harboring deep inside Abhinav Agarwal only intensified more and more.

Of all the places to find a quiet gay bar in Austin, one would never expect to find it to be in the back of a dusty old bookstore. But there it was, a small sign in the window with a rainbow flag next to it. Aaron pushed open the door and stepped inside.

The bar was dimly lit, with a few small tables scattered around. There was a stage in one corner, and a piano in another. The walls were lined with bookshelves, and there was a small dance floor in the center of the room. The bar matched all the description Aaron was looking for, and he knew he was at the right place.

He ordered a gin and tonic and sat down at one of the barstools facing the bartender. Soon he was joined by a couple of other patrons. They chatted quietly, enjoying the peace and quiet of the place. As the evening went on, more people came in, and the atmosphere grew more festive. But even then, it never got too loud or rowdy. It was just the right amount of queer for someone like Richard Harvey.

Harvey walked in when the place was almost full and when all the tables were occupied. There was one table at the far end that was empty, away from the crowd, one that no one could easily spot if they walked in through the main door. The table was left empty by the management on Thursday and Friday evenings. They knew Harvey could come any of those evenings and at any time. Harvey took a seat facing away from the entrance.

About fifteen to twenty feet away from that seat was Aaron, sitting on a barstool with his right elbow leaning on the bar counter. Through the corner of his eyes, he spotted Harvey across the room. He had visualized this moment multiple times and had played through a few scenarios. The usual first trick of making a move with stranger at a bar was to try to make eye contact. In this case, since Harvey was sitting away from the bar, that was not possible. Aaron took a take a deep breath and started to walk towards him.

"I like your shirt—linen?" asked Aaron quietly, as he approached the table. His eyes met Harvey's.

"Yes. Easy giveaway, huh?" Harvey smiled. He sounded like he was warm to having conversations with a stranger at a bar.

"Hey, I'm Aaron. Didn't we go to high school together?" The tall, dark-haired Aaron extended his hand with a friendly toothy smile.

"No, I don't think so. Does that pickup line actually work?" Harvey replied while shaking his head. Harvey was probably two inches shorter than Aaron, with blond hair and piercing blue eyes. "I just moved here from out of state."

What a liar! Aaron thought to himself. "Ah, that explains it," he chuckled. "So what brings you to this neck of the woods?"

"I'm actually in town on business," Harvey replied. "I'm staying for a week or two, I don't really know, and then I'll be headed back home."

"That's splendid. I'm happy to have made my first friend in Austin. I'm from Corpus Christi," Aaron said. "Hope you don't mind me calling you my friend."

"No problem at all. Likewise, I am glad to make a new friend, too."

The two new friends ordered more drinks, and as alcohol continued to warm their throats and stomachs, Harvey was loosening up quite a bit. The music kept changing, and the overall noise in the bar kept increasing. Suddenly,

Harvey leaned forward and kissed Aaron on his lips. Aaron was not expecting this. But he was hoping for this moment.

"I'm sorry. I don't know what I was thinking," said Harvey.

"Well. I do hope you are thinking what I am thinking," Aaron said with a naughty smile. "I quite liked it."

The warm evening progressed into a cooler night with the two of them holding hands at the far table and no one paying attention to them. At some point, Harvey looked at his phone and realized it was late.

"Listen, I got to go. Have a meeting in the morning. But …"

"But what?"

"Can we meet here again tomorrow night?

They both kissed each other again, and this time it was a much longer kiss. Harvey got up and picked up his coat and hat.

"Hey, stranger! You never told me your name," said Aaron.

"Call me Richard."

"And cover you with kisses?" Aaron chuckled in an obvious reference to the Blondie song.

As soon as Richard Harvey walked out of the bar, Aaron got up from his seat with a victorious smile. His night had gone exactly as planned and he hoped the next night would also go just like he had planned. Then he may just be able to go back home much earlier than what he had anticipated before meeting Harvey.

It was Saturday morning. Sima Daly was sitting on the porch in her backyard, watching the lawn sprinklers spray jet streams of cold water onto the grass, and sipping her first cup of coffee. That was when she received a text message from her secretary.

"Plumber called. Successfully plugged the leak. Said he'd send invoice and pics later. Want me to take care of the invoice?"

"Great. Yes!" Sima Daly was smiling.

She leaned back in her lawn chair with a satisfied smirk on her face. She had reluctantly and shamefully worked long and hard to get to this point, and it had all paid off. From the secretary's message, she was sure that the scheme had been successful, even though she had yet to see any photographic proof. She believed she was now one step closer to her goal. Sima Daly would not let anything—or anyone—stop her from achieving what she had set out to do.

During her days at GTO when she was working with Richard Harvey on a regular basis, she had sent her contacts in New York to do a background check on Harvey. Everything came out on the positive, but there was one thing she was not expecting. Richard Harvey was gay, and he had not come out of the closet yet. Not that this news shocked Sima personally. She took time to process the revelation and moved on. She had no idea that years later, what she had learned about Richard Harvey, that day would come in handy for advancing her own political career.

She was fully aware that Richard Harvey treated her with utmost respect and as his only ally inside the party. At times he even looked up to her and sought her advice. So, to do this—to set Aaron up for a carefully planned "random" encounter at a bar, to patiently follow the target, to seduce, and to eventually make him yield and indulge? This was not something Sima wished to do. But she *had* to.

Aaron was an openly gay man, and he had come out during his high school senior year. Sima did not know Aaron was gay when she hired him, but within a few weeks after he started interning, everyone in her office knew Aaron was gay. This was her plan. That she would send Aaron Naylor, her intern, with his full consent, to Austin. If Aaron were to become successful in his attempts to woo Harvey, then Aaron should somehow find a way to capture photographic or videographic evidence of what happened in the hotel room. Once she had access to the photographic evidence of the encounter, she would have complete leverage over Richard Harvey.

Richard Harvey was always a loose cannon in Derek Fisher's books. Harvey was righteous and moderate. His demeanor, his intellect, his politics, and his collective personality could have earned him a ticket in the opposition party, too. And people would have still voted for him. But by making a choice to be in the conservative party, he knew the personal sacrifices he had to make. For instance, hiding his sexuality.

When Fisher's internal polls started showing weakening support for TEXIT among moderate members of his party, he knew Richard Harvey was the man they needed to go after to restore faith in Fisher's commitment to an independent Texas. Fisher remembered how Sima had specifically requested him to appear in a campaign rally alongside Richard before his Senate election. So he called Sima and asked her if she was still in the good books of Harvey, and if she was, then what could she do to cement long-term commitment from Harvey for TEXIT. He wanted Sima to ensure that Harvey would stand along with Fisher and pro-TEXIT members of his team during selected referendum campaign rallies.

As the sun started beating down on the morning lawn, the grass began to shimmer in the heat. The sprinkler continued to hurl thousands of droplets of water into the air. Loops of rainbow-colored light appeared in the spray as the sun shone through the water. At about seventy-five feet away from the sprinkler, Sima Daly was sitting on a patio chair. She had just finished her coffee and kept staring at the sprinkler. Sima was in a state of conflict. She was relieved that the most challenging part of her plan had just been executed without any harm to anyone. But she was also questioning her own integrity for exploiting the personal weakness of someone who considered her as a political guide. The smile she had earlier vanished and now she had moved onto the next step. Her phone beeped again.

A new text message from her secretary read:

Repair pictures received from the plumber. Verified. Cleared invoice.

Hundreds of miles away, in a metallic gray Ford Mustang, was Aaron. He was driving back home. The joy on his face was visible even to the drivers of the cars passing by. He had not still come out disbelief and happy shock. It was a huge payday for him. Fifty times bigger than his monthly salary as an intern. His car windows were rolled down, and he sang along with the music playing in his car, quite loudly. "Call me, call me on the line! Call me, call me, any, anytime!"

CHAPTER 6

CURRENT DAY

One of the most well-known hospitals in San Antonio was the Methodist Hospital. The Methodist Hospital was a private, not-for-profit hospital that had been serving the community for over 100 years. The hospital offered a wide range of services, from emergency care to cancer treatment. In addition, the hospital had a Level 1 trauma center and was a teaching hospital for the University of Texas Health Science Center. The Methodist Hospital was also home to the renowned Texas Transplant Institute, which provided life-saving organ transplants for patients from all over the world.

Lisa Barkley sat in a hard plastic chair, her hands clutching her purse tightly in her lap. She was wearing a bright floral dress and matching shoes, and her hair was styled in a neat bob. She looked around the lobby, taking in the drab wallpaper, and worn carpet. The only other person in the room was an older man, who was reading a magazine. Lisa began tapping her foot impatiently, waiting for the doctor to call her. After what felt like an eternity, the door opened, and the attending nurse appeared with her notepad. She hurried over to Lisa, apologizing for the delay. Lisa stood up and followed the nurse into the examination room.

A few minutes after Lisa went inside, Gavin Forbes walked into the lounge with his girlfriend. They walked to the counter and checked themselves in. Then they both found two empty seats across the old man reading a newspaper. Beth, his longtime girlfriend and soon-to-be wife, was six months pregnant, and it was her fortnightly checkup with the gynecologist. There were a few magazines on the coffee table in the center of the room, the latest being from three months ago. Gavin grabbed a couple of magazines, gave one to Beth, and sat down.

Beth held Gavin's hands tightly when she saw a woman walk in. She looked fully pregnant. Both women exchanged smiles. That's when Gavin noticed a familiar face walk out of the doctor's office. Lisa stopped by the counter to check herself out. Gavin told Beth that he knew the woman standing at the counter and she was one of her customers. This was the first time he was seeing her after that day he went to her home to fix the air conditioner. He did not know she was pregnant. Gavin got up from his seat and took a few steps towards the main door, hoping to say hello to Lisa. She finished checking out and was ready to leave.

"Hey, Ms. Barkley. Thought I have seen you somewhere," said Gavin.

"Hey … is this … I am …"

"Yes. I am Gavin. I don't have my baseball hat on," Gavin chuckled.

"That's right. What brings you here? I mean. Sorry. That didn't sound right." Lisa realized the awkwardness of her question given they were standing inside an ob-gyn office.

"That's all right, Ms. Barkley. It's Beth. My fiancée. She's six months in." Gavin was excited to share the news.

"Congratulations, Gavin! That's wonderful." Lisa smiled at him.

"What about you? I know it's not appropriate to ask."

"Well. Why else do women with swollen tummies visit their gynecologists, right? Me, too," Lisa responded in a tone of helplessness, and Gavin couldn't help but notice a tinge of sadness in her eyes. He was not a mind reader, but anyone could have seen that Lisa was not particularly happy when sharing the news of being pregnant.

"Oh, wow! Congratulations. Lily will make a great big sister." Gavin was doing his best to hide his curiosity. Lisa nodded her head in acknowledgment.

"Thanks, Gavin. And good luck to you and Beth. By the way, the air conditioner is working well." She smiled again. "See you around," said Lisa, indicating she was ready to leave.

Gavin controlled his urge to ask her if everything was all right. He didn't really know her well to ask a personal question like that. After saying goodbye to her, he walked back to Beth and told her how he felt. Beth told Gavin that she also noticed from Lisa's body language that all was not well. And the two of them continued to talk a bit more about Lisa before the nurse came out to call for Beth.

On their way home, in the car, Gavin told Beth what he knew about Lisa's life, she being a single mom, and the rumor how her ex-husband, Caleb, was a bit of a jerk, and more. Gavin could not get the sadness he saw in Lisa's eyes out of his mind. He asked if Beth would like to get to know Lisa better.

"Maybe as a new mom or to-be mom, you could ask her for some tips?" suggested Gavin.

"I will find a way, Gavin. You know what? This is why I love you so much. You really care for others. So proud of you, honey. Our baby will be proud to have a father like you." Beth kissed him on his cheek.

"I'm driving. Don't distract me." Gavin let out a fake scream for help.

The remote village of Atoka was located in the southeastern part of New Mexico. About thirty-five miles to the north of Carlsbad. The village was only accessible by a long and winding dirt road, and it was surrounded by nothing but dusty hills. The air was clean and fresh, and the scenery was mostly brown with patches of green. The population of Atoka was about 1,200, and people who lived there were mostly farmers and ranchers. Life in the village was simple and slow-paced. There was one grocery store, a couple of restaurants, and a bar. Cell phone service was patchy depending on where you stood, and broadband internet was a luxury.

The house where Joanna locked Ava Walters in was five miles to the west of the heart of Atoka. A dirt road would take you for about three miles, and then if one was inclined to drive all the way to that house, they'd better carry a compass with them and have a good knowledge of the bumpy terrain.

Joanna was not a professional cross-border trafficker. Nor was she a police dodger. She lived in Atoka and worked in Carlsbad at a grocery store. She was also a natural when it came to matters of technology. Joanna was a self-taught computer geek. Rosaline, Ava's friend from Midland Texas, needed some urgent tech help with her computer when she was staying in Carlsbad once. She had posted a message in an online forum (this was before the age of social media) and was approached by a user who claimed she could do it. Rosaline met Joanna at the grocery store parking lot and was impressed with how quickly Joanna diagnosed the problem. Within fifteen minutes, she was able to hand Rosaline's computer back in fully working condition. And Joanna had still fifteen minutes left in her lunchbreak. Rosaline thanked her profusely and paid her twice the amount Joanna asked for. Both remained in touch as the digital era evolved. Joanna had visited Midland a couple of times in the last sixteen years while Rosaline had visited Carlsbad a couple of times herself.

So, when Rosaline asked Joanna for help, there were no questions asked. It was only after she picked up Ava from the gas station that Rosaline shared bits of information about the danger Ava was in and why she was running away. Rosaline knew better not to call or text Joanna. So she communicated with Joanna only through those old forum message boxes, which were not easily traceable.

Ava managed to sleep for a few hours. She was thoroughly exhausted after that incredible adrenaline-filled fugitive run to nowhere. Never in her childhood did she imagine that a day would come when state police would be looking to arrest her and that she would be on the run. This was not what a teacher should be doing. When she woke up, it was past noon. She got out of the cot and then saw how dirty the sheet she slept on was. It looked like a large piece of rag that had just been used to clean the floor. The sleeping bag, on the other hand, looked marginally cleaner.

She was beginning to feel thirsty, so she picked up the two buckets that Joanna asked her to use and peeped out of the window through the backyard. That was the direction Joanna had pointed to when she talked about flowing water. She tried to recollect if Joanna was more specific. Was she talking about flowing water, as in a river? Or was there a tap? She decided to check it out for herself. She opened the back door and walked through the backyard. She was very careful with her first few steps. Ava looked around 360 degrees. There was some wildlife she could spot—birds, squirrels, and what she assumed were mites and moths.

Once she realized that she was absolutely the only human being in that vast expanse of land, a land that was in the middle of nowhere and one she had no clue about, she felt a sense of fear, sadness, and excitement run through her, all at once. There was something both exhilarating and terrifying about being lost in a remote place like this. On one hand, she was free from the constraints of the society and from the burden of everything that chased her until last night. She could explore to her heart's content. On the other hand, she was completely at the mercy of the natural elements and Joanna, with no guarantee that she would make it back home to Bradley and her daughter, Eveline. But for now, there was something uniquely thrilling about being cut off from the world, even if it's just for a little while.

Her own footsteps reverberated in her ears. Every sound was amplified, every scent was more pungent, and every movement was full of purpose. The handles of the aluminum buckets she was carrying were rattling as they kept rubbing against the body. She was on a mission to find the flowing water. After reaching what appeared to be a dead-end of sorts, beyond which one couldn't walk normally, she guessed that it couldn't have been a river that Joanna was talking about. She turned back and tried to locate the house. She was able to remember her path, although she could not see the house. She was sure at that point that she must have walked more than one thousand feet. She found some shade under a lone tree on that dead-end hill. Her thirst had peaked. She dropped the buckets on the ground and looked around. There it was. A single tap ran straight out of the ground, right next to a rock. She had to walk back a few feet towards the house to get to that tap.

Ava ran towards it, and as she got closer, she could see that it was wet and was leaking drops of water. She opened the tap, put her mouth to the spout, and drank deeply, quenching her thirst at first. The water tasted fresh. She was happy to have found flowing water, but she knew she needed to get back the house quickly after filling those buckets. She regretted not bringing the dirty sheet with her, else she could have given it a quick rinse. Ava filled the two buckets with fresh water and walked back to the house.

When she reached the house, she looked at the grocery bag and was trying to plan her survival for the next few days. She remembered she had four apples, three bananas, a loaf of sliced bread, a can of milk, a stick of butter, a box of strawberries, a dozen eggs, mustard, and a dozen yogurt cups. The science teacher in her swung into action. She was looking for a dark corner in the house. She made some perforations in the grocery bag and took the bag to that dark corner. She figured eggs, apples, mustard, and bread could come out of the bags. As for the remaining items inside the bag, she knew milk would be the one that would perish first. The organized woman she was, she planned her meal for the rest of the day and for the next day as well. Milk and banana now. Milk, banana, yogurt for the next meal. And so on.

The day gave way to dusk and soon it became dark. Ava was getting a little restless. The only connection that she had with the real world was her wristwatch. Without her phone and computer, she was completely disoriented. It was almost midnight, and Ava was beginning to lose hope if Joanna would come back tonight or not. And she fell asleep.

At half past one, Ava heard some noise, and when she opened her eyes, she could see lights reflecting through the back door and window cracks. She guessed it must be Joanna's car. The footsteps got closer to the door, and she heard someone unlock the front door. As the door opened, Joanna turned on the camp light she brought with her.

"Hey, Ava. Did you get some sleep?" Joanna left the bag she brought with her on the floor.

"Yes. I did. Thank you. How was your day, Joanna?" asked Ava.

"I'm guessing it went better than yours. At least I was not stuck inside four walls like you." Joanna smiled.

She handed the camp light to Ava and told her it was hers. She had also brought a couple of bottles of soda and a quarter pounder from McDonald's.

"Not sure if you are hungry."

"I will save it for tomorrow. Thank you." Ava nodded.

"Your electronics . . . you will get them tomorrow. When I come back. I don't know how long I am going to need to keep you holed up here. I may need to find a power source for you if this situation is going to last more than a couple of days." Joanna was really committed to making sure Ava was comfortable. Comfortable under the circumstances, anyway.

"I know I'm not supposed to ask a lot of questions till you tell me to. But can you just let me know if Bradley and Eveline are okay?" said Ava, finally sensing an opportunity to find out what was going on Midland.

"About that . . ." Joanna quietly began to share the latest updates she had from Midland.

Senator Dodson was livid after his meeting with Fisher. He never liked him, but the meeting earlier today went not the way he had envisioned it would. Fisher's ambition to become the first President of Texas was not an open secret. At this point, if after the US Congress ratified TEXIT and Article 49 indeed got passed, the kind of momentum Fisher was riding on would become even more formidable. Dodson knew that.

He called his secretary to check if Williams was still in town and asked him to come to his office if he was. After about an hour or so, Eval Williams was in Dodson's office. He could see Dodson's stiff face and immediately concluded that the meeting did not go well.

"That son of a bitch is no longer hiding that he has the upper hand." Dodson was fuming.

"Senator, was he surprised when you told him that you are in contention, too?"

"No. I didn't get to do that. I decided to play differently sensing his tone. I figured it'd be better for us if I can convince him to be our ally instead of Newell's."

"And . . .?" Williams was curious.

"He read through. He fucking read through my mind. Do they teach politics at grocery stores? Where did he learn all this? Our only trump card is our DC game." Dodson had calmed down a bit.

"Yes, sir. I think it's about time we play it a bit dirty, too. Fifteen more votes. Fifteen more days. My gut tells me there's still enough time to make a deal with Fisher. For that, we need a small team in Austin, senator."

"Who do you have in mind?"

"Grace Ashworth and Edward Coll."

"Grace Ashworth? Get going on that, son. I don't really need to know who they are. I trust you." Dodson checked his watch. "Oh, shit. I have a flight to catch in a couple of hours. Are you on the same one?"

"I was. I was going to be on that flight until this moment. But now I guess I have some work to do in Austin today. So I will fly into DC tomorrow," said Williams with a smile.

Mondays at big city airports were chaos. The George Bush Airport in Houston was a place of constant motion—with suitcases gliding by on conveyer belts, people hurrying to their gates, children running to keep up with tired parents, and more. The air outside was particularly more humid today, and the air inside the airport was thick with the smell of coffee and fast food. There were thunderstorms in the vicinity, and the PA system continued to crackle announcements throughout the terminal—flight cancellations, gate changes, delayed flights, et cetera. In the background was the constant drone of hundreds of conversations and the hum of idling engines. At the center of it all were the security checkpoints, where travelers presented their IDs and boarding passes before putting themselves through what had now been normalized but a somewhat ridiculous ritual of removing their shoes, belts, watches, et cetera, to get to their gates through scanners.

In short, a daunting scene for first-time travelers, but for frequent flyers like Senator Newell, it was just another Monday and was part of the journey. Senator Newell was already inside and waiting near his gate. Being a senior senator from the state, serving in the Senate for more than fifteen years now, his face had appeared quite often on televisions, so his face had a more familiarity quotient compared to many state congressmen and senators. He had done his best to minimize attention in the airport and was wearing a large pair of sunglasses and a baseball hat. He had his iPad open and was checking his emails.

An email from Senator Brynes gave him hope and a quick churn in his stomach at the same time. He lifted his head and looked around. He contemplated about calling Brynes and talking to him immediately but curtailed his own urge because of where he was and the possibility of someone around him overhearing their conversation. He couldn't wait to get to DC to find out more.

The first thing that anyone noticed upon entering Elizabeth Greenburg's office was a huge painting of an oil rig. An abstract painting done by a contemporary artist from Texas. It stood tall and was dominating the rich mahogany paneling on the walls and the plush leather sofa in the corner. The desk was massive and imposing, made from a single slab of polished granite. And behind it sat an equally imposing figure: a well-dressed man in his early sixties with piercing blue eyes and a no-nonsense expression. This was Elizabeth Greenburg's father, a well-known lobbyist himself, who was now retired.

As one took a seat across from her, she usually got straight down to business. She would start by telling one about the latest developments in the oil industry, both good and bad. She usually didn't shy away from discussing the environmental impact of oil production and distribution, but she usually spun it in such a way that made it seem like not such a big deal. After all, as she usually explained, there were much worse things that we could be doing to the planet. She would always end her initial monologue with how we needed oil to power our economy and our way of life, and why oil was not going anywhere anytime soon.

She would then ask one what one's views were on oil production and its impact on the environment. She listened intently as one shared one's thoughts, and she then provided her own counterarguments in a way that didn't come across like she was disagreeing. She was clearly very knowledgeable on the subject, and she knew how to push all the right buttons to make one question one's own views. By the end of the conversation, any normal person would not be very sure where they stood on the issue anymore or why they felt strongly about taking a stand against the oil industry in the first place. Elizabeth Greenburg was friendly and very persuasive, and commanded respect from the audience for her knowledge and expertise.

The sign of a good lobbyist, as her father kept reminding her, was to know how to get what he or she *wanted*.

Elizabeth Greenburg took over as the CEO of GB, Inc., a powerful lobbying firm in DC, about two years ago. Among other smaller companies, Elizabeth and GB, Inc. also represented four of the oil giants, namely Exxon Mobil, Marathon Petroleum, Valero Energy, and GTO. Elizabeth was responsible for managing all the client-relationship-related activities at these four major oil industry clients, and she had already built strong trust with the respective CEOs within a few months after she took over.

Even though fossil fuel big spenders like GB, Inc. worked round the clock, the changing DC political climate had an impact on how they spent their money in any given year and dictated how their priorities shifted. For now, Elizabeth was focused on lobbying for limiting the disclosure of climate change impacts. This, according to Elizabeth, was snuck into a major bipartisan infrastructure bill by the progressive wing and it had no place there in the bill. She was relying on ten congressmen to flip their votes and make a difference in the end. These were congressmen she had closely worked with and had promised desirable contributions to their reelection funds.

She saw her phone ring, and her caller ID displayed a Houston number. She could tell it was from GTO based on the middle three digits. It was Amanda, Steve Riggs's secretary. Amanda had wanted to check with Elizabeth if she was available for an in-person meeting with Steve Riggs in her office sometime next week. Once they agreed on a mutually convenient time slot, she hung up the phone.

Elizabeth Greenburg knew how to read a client's mood or intent even when they didn't tell her why they wanted to meet. GTO was one of the biggest spenders last year at GB, Inc. With GB's total lobbying spending for the previous year being twelve million dollars, GTO alone was responsible for thirty percent of it. That was the highest GTO had ever spent on lobbying in DC. It was all because of the recent change in leadership at the company and how aggressive the new leadership had been in trying to prioritize their issues, and in getting their voices heard in DC through lobbyists.

Elizabeth knew that Steve Riggs was personally flying to DC to meet with her for only one reason. She thought somehow his priorities at GTO had changed and she guessed that he wanted to use her and GB's voice on the hill to disrupt the congressional ratification of TEXIT. She knew that the oil industry would be one of the worst hit industries for Texas in a post-TEXIT world. She was also sure that she and GB would be called sooner or later to push the layered agenda of the oil industry in DC.

It was 8:00 AM, Wednesday morning. Elizabeth was already in the conference room, where she was going to meet Steve Riggs. The room was large enough to comfortably seat over a hundred people. But today, there was going to be only a handful. The rich table at the center of the room was polished to a high shine, and the walls were adorned with artwork from local artists. The windows ran from floor to ceiling, providing a stunning view of the capital city. The room was well-lit, but not so bright that it was uncomfortable to look at. The chairs were cozy, and there was plenty of legroom for everyone.

"Good morning, Lizzy!" Steve Riggs walked in with his arms wide open.

"Oh, my God! Good to see you, Steve. How have you been?" Elizabeth stretched her arms for a hug, too.

They embraced, and Steve gave a couple of formal pecks on her cheek.

"All good. All good. How is your father doing?"

"Well. He is doing quite all right. Sharp as ever and cheerful. Given everything I should say, he is doing very well. Thank you for asking."

"Should we get started? Or are you expecting anyone else?" asked Elizabeth.

"No. This is it," responded Elizabeth with a smile.

So the meeting went on. Elizabeth started to feel a bit embarrassed, because her instinct failed her this time. Steve was not there to ask for help to disrupt the congressional ratification. In fact, he had embraced the idea of TEXIT. Most of his conversation with Elizabeth was about how to start building the future for GTO and for Texas from scratch, and how to engage with the potential new government.

"Why don't you shift to Austin for a few months? I want you to build a brand-new GB, Inc. from scratch and serve only Texan companies."

"That sounds ridiculous, Steve. Why would I? Leaving all these? No fucking way."

Steve Riggs smiled and said, "Please allow me to convince you."

"Go on!"

"It will be fun," he said. "I promise."

Elizabeth was hesitant, but Steve's pitch to her was convincing. He promised that she would feel empowered, and should something go wrong, he would be there to help her. The good leader he was, he understood negotiation was more than just haggling over one issue. The most important thing he understood was Elizabeth's own goals and objectives. Once he knew what she wanted to achieve, he threw out a couple of strategies, literally pulled from thin air. He repeatedly told her that her focus could continue to remain in DC, but for the next few months alone, being in Austin could energize her—she would feel connected to the roots again. He tried to convince her a short break like this would let her see things differently and when she came back to DC, she could do much more for GB, Inc.

"It's going to be the best challenge you have ever had, Lizzy. That, I guarantee."

It was a very atypical day at the Midland precinct—phones ringing off the hook, detectives hurrying to and fro, and the incessant sound of keyboards clacking from the admin pool. Coffee pots percolated in every corner, and the air was thick with the smell of seared chicken from Pete's diner down the street. At the center of it all was Captain Ramirez, his booming voice carrying over the din as he barked out orders to someone on the phone. Papers littered his desk, and his tie was askew. It was clear that he was in for another long evening, making it the second consecutive day.

"What the fuck should I do with that kid? Take her home with me?" Ramirez was yelling at someone.

When one of the officers brought a file with him and waited in front of his desk, Ramirez waved at him to go. But the officer insisted on staying there. Ramirez muted his phone by cupping the speaker with his hand, and asked the officer "What?" in an annoying tone.

"Sir, there was an Ava sighting at the H-E-B parking lot."

Captain Ramirez spoke on the phone now. "I'm going to have to call you back." He hung up the phone.

"What have you done since you got the information?" He was looking at the officer.

The officer who had shared the news did not have any further updates.

"I'm sorry. I don't have any more information." He was worried how the captain may react.

Captain Ramirez emerged from his cubicle and walked to the middle of the main room. The captain's face was red with anger after listening to the officer's response. He started shouting at everyone in the office. His veins bulged and his fists were clenched tightly. He slammed his hands on a table he was standing next to, making the glasses shake. The officers looked at him, their expressions a mix of fear and confusion.

"I'm not sure how I should make this clearer. If you are going to bring me some information, make sure you do that after you do a thorough follow-up. Only complete information please. Now, someone call Officer Ken, who is handling Ava's case, and find out what's going on!" screamed Ramirez as he stormed back to his cubicle.

That's when the phone rang.

"Sir, we have an update."

It was officer Ken who had called. He was able to go to the grocery store and corroborate Ava's presence a few minutes before 5:00 PM at the checkout counter. He was also able to get CCTV footage to identify Ava, who was wearing a pair of blue jeans and a green top. Since there was no CCTV camera outside the door she had used to leave the store, Ken wasn't able to get any video proof of where she left. Ken brought Bradley, Ava's husband, with him and he was able to identify Ava's car, which was left locked in the parking lot. There was no sign of any damage to the car. By then, Ramirez had moved near the phone.

"So we think someone picked her up from the parking lot. And it was not Bradley. Bradley said he didn't know who might have picked her up. I got a search warrant to go over his phone and was able to confirm Bradley did not receive any message or call from Ava about her whereabouts. She had simply asked him to stay calm and take care of Eveline. And specifically asked him not to come to the grocery store. She didn't want to put Bradley and her daughter in danger. That was the only and the last message from Ava."

"Smart woman," said Ramirez. "What next, Ken?"

"Well. Sir, we are going through her close friends list and will try to get search warrants to go over their properties."

"Call me when you find something," said Ramirez.

For officers with an investigative nature, Ava's case offered everything thrilling about a police investigation. The feeling that one could get if they were able to crack the case was what a typical police officer yearned for. But Ava's case could neither be simplified as a missing person's case nor as a criminal-on-the run case. This case was a political ticking bomb. The longer this case remained unsolved, Captain Ramirez knew the more Midland Police would be drawn to media limelight. He was already imagining appearing before a pool of national media outlets and reading a prepared statement, followed by taking a few questions. He had seen a few of those on TV and had always hoped he would never have to be in that position.

It had been a long, hard day for Ramirez. He finally decided to take a logical break with what he was working on and leave the precinct. As he pulled into his driveway, he felt more exhausted than he had in a long time. All he wanted to do was spend some time with his wife and the dog and forget about the challenges of the day. However, he knew Camila was particularly interested in Ava's case. Camila was not a fan of Governor Fisher's attack on science education. And she had often mentioned this to her husband that she believed the state of Texas was entering a dangerous period. When she heard of Ava's case the previous evening, her immediate reaction was, "I hope you never find her."

As he walked into the house, he could see Camila sitting on the couch, waiting for him. She had poured a cold glass of Modelo for him, and she looked concerned. He sat down next to her and began to recount the day's events. He told her about the latest updates. As they talked, he could feel his stress begin to dissipate. He was not even concerned if Ava was listening to him. He unloaded the burdens he had been carrying all day.

"Honey, please promise me if you ever find her, you won't harm her in any which way. Please."

"I promise," Ramirez said and gave her a kiss.

About 320 miles southeast of Midland, the mood at the Austin police precinct was completely different. It was a quiet night. Most of the officers had already finished their paperwork and were now milling about, waiting for their shift to end. Some were chatting idly, while others were playing cards or reading magazines. Outside, the city was still and peaceful, the only sound the occasional car passing by on the street. It was a welcome respite from the usual hustle and bustle of the precinct during daytime. The tranquility was broken when a sudden scream pierced the air.

It was Travis County sheriff. The officers who were playing cards quickly packed them and hid them away. Everyone was wondering why the sheriff decided to show up this late. The sheriff's loud voice had reached everyone inside before he physically pushed opened the door and appeared in front of everyone.

"Where are those spineless activists?"

One of the officers pointed at the lockup cell. The sheriff walked over quietly. Since it was dark, he couldn't see clearly inside the lockup cell. He assumed that they were sleeping.

"Release them. I will sign the paperwork. No questions asked. No explanations need to be given," he instructed the officer.

The officer quickly unlocked the cell door and called them out. Russell and Emily were already disturbed by all the commotion, and they could hear the sheriff give instructions to the officer. They quietly got up and gathered their belongings.

"You may leave now! You are free!" the sheriff yelled at them.

Russell and Emily were perplexed. When they were arrested at the protest site the day before, they were not told why they were being arrested. Notwithstanding the fact that they did not incur any physical injuries, they had no idea why they were being brought to police custody. It was only late in the evening when the sheriff stopped by, and they were informed that they were arrested for instigating violence at a rally. When they asked for an attorney to speak to, they were simply told that they would be let go the next morning and there was no need to involve an attorney. The officers had confiscated all their belongings and sent them inside the ten-by-ten lockup cell. But the officers in the precinct were courteous to them and even fed them Chinese takeout for dinner and doughnuts in the morning.

When the sheriff said they could leave, both Russell and Emily wanted to know what had transpired in the last twenty-four hours that they were being released unconditionally. They also wanted a copy of their arrest record.

"I said you are free. There is no record!" the sheriff was still yelling.

Russell and Emily looked at each other. Then Emily looked at her watch. It was past 9:30 PM. Without speaking another word, they quietly walked out of the police precinct.

Outside, about a few hundred feet away, standing under a tree in the corner of 1st and Main Street was Jason Greer with his camera.

The parking lot was a madhouse. Cars were circling around, trying to find a spot. Restless drivers were honking and yelling, forgetting that they were in a hospital. It was like a scene from a movie. The hospital parking lot was packed with cars, and the air was thick with exhaust. The sun was beating down and the pavement was hot. All Alex saw was how chaotic and confusing the place was. He kept circling around till he found a spot far away from the main building.

He took a deep breath and opened his wallet. There was Maria's photo in it. He whispered something to the photo, kissed it, and put it back in his pocket. Alex was there to see how his workers were doing and nothing more. He was fully aware that the police detective at the station specifically asked him not to go to the hospital, but here he was.

Entering the Roberts hospital through the main door was a breeze. Alex stopped by the building map and tried to guess where his workers would be. After much deliberation and hesitation, he decided to ask the woman at the information desk. He was directed to the trauma center. The lady wasn't certain if the patients he was looking for were necessarily there, but that would have been the most logical place to search for them. He entered the trauma center, located in the adjacent building but connected to the main building through a corridor.

The waiting lobby at the trauma center was surprisingly busy. People of all ages and races were anxiously seated there in the many chairs available, waiting for news of their loved ones or simply waiting to be seen. The air was thick with the scent of antiseptic and fear. The atmosphere was one of tense anticipation, as though at any moment someone might burst into tears or laughter. The tick of the clock echoed in the silent waiting room, punctuating the anxious breathing of those who waited. Occasionally, a doctor or nurse would hurry through, their white coats flapping like flags in a storm. Alex didn't know what kind of people he expected to see there. There was a woman knitting, a man who looked like someone who would read the newspaper from front to back, a couple who whispered to each other, an old lady leaning on her granddaughter's shoulder with her eyes closed and with dried-up tears, a woman who was holding onto her beads and saying prayers, and so on. But what caught Alex's eye was a young girl who was sitting all alone. She looked Hispanic to Alex. This girl, no more than ten years old, was sitting in the corner of one side, clutching a battered teddy bear. She looked utterly out of place surrounded by adults, and her big eyes were full of fear. No one said anything to her; and those who walked by, they simply went about their business as if she wasn't there. She didn't seem to mind, though; she was content to sit in the corner with her teddy bear and wait with hope. There was a seat available right next to her. Alex's mind raced to making many assumptions.

"Did the police already inform the families of those who are being treated? If they did, then he would have found out somehow. And maybe if they did, then they should have also informed him. So maybe this girl is not related to any of my guys. Who is she? Why is she alone? Jesus, bless this girl, please. Amen."

When Alex approached the seat next to the girl, she did not react at all. She kept staring at the TV playing an old football game.

"Cómo se llama?" he said, pointing at the teddy bear.

At first, she did not realize he was talking to her. It took Alex another try before she responded.

"Teddy!" she replied, smiling as an afterthought.

"Bonito nombre," he said, complimenting her on the name.

"Gracias," she said politely and continued to watch TV.

"¿Dónde están tus padres?" he asked, checking to see if she had any adult supervision there.

The girl pointed in the direction of the sign that read *Intensive Care Unit*. Alex was not sure if she really meant that or if she was pointing in the general direction of the corridor that led to other rooms. Since the girl wasn't very comfortable engaging him, he decided to wait for a few minutes before persisting with his questions. It also gave him a few minutes to observe the trauma center. Alex did not want to go ask the officers who were perhaps guarding the room where his workers were being treated. He knew they wouldn't let him in and that would be the end of it. So he was looking for ways to check on them somehow.

After a few minutes, he saw a couple of uniformed cops walk from the corridor and towards the lobby area. They approached the girl sitting close to

Alex. He wasn't reacting.

"Hey, come with me," one of the cops said.

The girl quietly got up from her seat, still clutching onto her teddy bear. She walked past Alex and turned to make an eye contact with him. Alex waved at her, and she didn't respond. She kept walking with the officers and turned into the corridor towards the general direction of ICU.

Alex got up from his seat and decided to follow them. He kept a safe distance, so the cops didn't notice him in that busy corridor. The cops walked past the door on the right that said *ICU*. Alex got even more curious. The linoleum floors on the corridor were polished but worn and scuffed, the walls were a dingy white, and a couple of fluorescent lights flickered overhead. Every time a door opened, Alex heard the beeping sounds the machines and he saw doctors and nurses in scrubs, lost in their own world. Alex saw a stream of patients being wheeled in on stretchers near another door. He saw waiting families pacing back and forth near another door. He felt some tension in all their faces. He thought at any moment someone's life could forever be changed.

The cops were about 200 feet ahead of him. There were not many rooms in this side of the corridor, and the overall traffic had come down. Alex knew that the cops could hear his footsteps and could turn back to see him, notwithstanding the flickering lights. He became a little conscious and paused for a few seconds, seeking refuge behind a small partition wall. He saw the cops stop ahead, and the girl was let in through the door on the right side by someone else. The cops stayed outside. Alex waited. After a few minutes, the girl was led out but someone else, and that woman gave her a hug before handing her over to the cops. The cops turned back and started walking towards Alex. He wasn't sure what to do. So he decided to walk back to the lobby at a much faster pace. He wanted to get through the next possible door and let the cops go past him. When he saw the sign *Trauma Orthopedics*, he pushed open the door and walked in at a brisk pace. After a few seconds, he stopped to listen to the footsteps outside.

Once he was sure the cops and girl had walked past the door, he used his shoulder to gently push open the door again as silently as possible and stepped onto the corridor again. He turned to his right to ensure the cops and the girl were well ahead the other way. Alex started walking to his left on the corridor. He remembered exactly where the cops waited and let the girl in through the door on the right side. He increased his walking pace. Finally, he reached the exact stop where he saw the girl walk in.

The sign on the door read: *MORTUARY.*

Burl Fogg was expecting a bad year. So were the farmers in his vicinity. The heat—blistering, to put it mildly, had been the biggest enemy for the farmers for the past two years. One-hundred-degree days beginning from as early as May were wilting the cotton crops in the neighbor's farms and Burl had heard that somewhere else in the farms that grew melons, they had been turned into pressure cookers. Most farmers in this part of Texas practiced "dryland farming"—meaning they were entirely dependent on rainfall. Burl was the first one in Stansley to implement "scattered irrigation" for his farm, and he invested quite a bit for that. So his peanut crops could just do okay when compared to his counterparts in Stansley.

Burl knew how he might not just survive this year but actually make some profit, too. However, the same could not be said about the Goodmans' farm for example. The Goodmans were about $125,000 in debt already and were expecting to go up by $175,000 by the end of this season. Bill collectors were hounding on them regularly for the tractor they bought using a loan lats year. The family of four made just enough money to cover their mortgage cost for the past eight months. The father and the mother no longer wanted to plan a future for their children in the farm. For now, getting through with their lives on a weekly basis was their focus. The story was the same for many farmers across the country, and not just in Texas.

Burl Fogg had been following the struggles of Eastmans and other farmers in Stansley like him. These struggling farmers were beginning to rely more and more on Burl Fogg's wisdom and his smartness to guide them out of their misery eventually. The entire town of Stansley was very proud of what their local boy had managed to achieve in a short time. Burl Fogg was both conscious and self-aware of the growing responsibility he was beginning to have—responsibility that he didn't choose to have but one that naturally came his way. He was embracing it wholeheartedly.

As a matter of fact, a couple of weeks ago, Burl Fogg wrote a long email to the Commissioner of the Texas Department of Agriculture as a follow-up to their meeting.

The email read as followed:

Respected Commissioner,

Thank you again for inviting me to the annual summit and for giving me your personal time to meet with me.

Like I had mentioned, I am no expert in farming. I am learning.

What I do know very well is the plight of my fellow farmers in Stansley and in Lubbock County. From what I have been reading, the stories are very similar across this big land called America.

It hurts me every time when I see or hear an average American's version of a family farm. Or an average Texan's version for that matter. These family farms, as they imagine, are set in picturesque locations, with vast expanse of lush green fields. Sort of like how they are on Hallmark cards. But the truth is that such farms are declining in number quite rapidly. And that average American and Texan are not being informed of this rapid decline. Whatever be the reasons for the decline—trade wars, politicization of farm bills, overall global economy, and our dependence on the same, increasing droughts in recent years, et cetera—it's the responsibility of departments like yours to be proactive and not always be caught in a reactive mode. If the Texas Department of Agriculture wants to be in a mode where they want to be writing checks to farmers after the fact, then I am afraid, you would be drowned doing just that forever, and things will only get worse.

As per the public records available for bankruptcies in Texas, we have seen Chapter 12 farm bankruptcies go up by thirteen percent just in the last year alone. This is an alarming number.

As I indicated during our meeting, I have been a firm supporter of TEXIT. Now we are on the cusp of our independence becoming a reality. As exciting as this is for a Texan who has been dreaming of this all my life, let me also be very practical and state that your department and the Texas government leadership had not even talked about what this means for the farming sector. There are several questions to be addressed before the farmers of Texas understand the changes coming their way. And we have less than a year to work through the details. That is, if we all somehow survive the effects of this year's drought and make it through to the next year.

I do remember my promise to you that I would prepare a document on "Sustainable Farming." As you may have been made aware, I won a global award recently at an USDA event. More than the award, the event gave me an opportunity to learn a lot about how farmers around the world are coping up with climate-related changes. I was able to appreciate the technological advancements made in general in the field of agriculture. I was also briefly exposed to learning about how governments get involved with the farming sector in different countries quite differently. For me to put together a meaningful document on Sustainable Farming for a future independent Texas, I need more information and hence more time. Some of the information I need will be dependent on the plans and policies to be announced by the Texas government. I hope you appreciate the reasoning for the delay.

Should you have a need to discuss any of these matters further, I am more than available to be of assistance.

Regards,

Burl Fogg

There had not been a response from the commissioner or from his office to date.

It was another hot and humid day in Galveston. The kind of day that made one want to take a cold shower and sit in front of a fan. Or better yet, jump in the ocean if one had one nearby. Every time Vanessa and Keith decided to go to the beach on days like these, Vanessa always remembered her grandmother's story of how much she, as a young girl and then as a woman, yearned for a swim on hot days like these. She never could go to public beaches because of segregation, and when public beaches were finally desegregated, she was too old and physically not in a position to go for a swim.

Vanessa and Keith carried beach chairs and umbrellas with them. They always had them in the car. After taking a quick dip in the ocean to cool them off, they walked back to the beach and sat on their chairs. They watched the ocean quietly as the waves crashed against the shore. They must have looked like a mirage to the people walking by—two black figures, sitting so close to the water, but never touching it.

Vanessa saw Keith had closed his eyes.

"Are you sleeping, honey?"

"I was. Not anymore."

"I need to get on the phone and talk to Senator Newell this week. We have already taken enough time. If we say no, then he probably would want to talk to someone else about it," said Vanessa.

"Are we really saying no?" Keith stared at Vanessa.

"No. I mean, I want to say yes. But it will change our lives forever. Don't know for the better or worse, honey." Vanessa sounded a bit concerned.

"Either way, we will have some time to get used to it." Keith smiled.

There were few things more exhilarating than sitting down at a poker table and going head-to-head with other players. The stakes were high, and the sense of anticipation was electric. But at the same time, poker was entirely a game of strategy and psychology, requiring a sharp mind and nerves of steel. Most professional players would tell another that success in poker comes down to three things: knowing one's opponents, playing the odds, and keeping a cool head under pressure.

In any given hand, one needed to be able to size up their opponents and figure out what they were likely to do. Were they tight or loose? Were they aggressive or passive? Did they tend to bluff or play it safe? The better one knew one's opponents, the better one's chances of winning. But even the best players couldn't control the cards, so it was also important to understand probability and know when to take a risk. Sometimes one must go against the odds in order to come out ahead in the long run. And finally, no matter how good one's strategy was, there was always moments of doubt and stress. Again, a professional poker player like Edward Coll would tell another why it was essential to be able to keep one's emotions in check and make decisions quickly and without hesitation.

Born into a wealthy family, Grace Ashworth was accustomed to a life of luxury. However, after a chance encounter with a streetwise model, she found herself captivated by the fashion world and decided to pursue a career in modeling. She quickly rose to the top of the industry, graced the runway for many years, but eventually became disillusioned with the superficiality of the modeling world. Grace then decided to launch her own clothing line. Her designs were an instant hit among her followers thanks to her social media influencer power. After five years of running a profitable boutique, she decided to sell it off for an undisclosed amount to someone from the industry. Then, Grace started flipping houses at the age of thirty-seven. She bought her first house for $120,000 and sold it for $250,000 six months later. Since then, she had flipped over thirty houses until then and with all her wealth from her previous careers included, she was worth over thirty-five million dollars. Grace Ashworth, now a busy socialite, was a permanent fixture in all high-profile parties in Austin, and over the years, she had managed to know the who-is-who of the Austin power circle.

Grace Ashworth and Edward Coll had met each other only a couple of times in the past. But they knew of each other very well. After all, if somebody was one of the members of the power circle in Austin, it was not easy to miss knowing most others. Besides, they both had such unique backgrounds that it was hard to forget names after the first introduction.

Tonight, they both had been asked to join Congressman Evan Williams for a dinner meeting. They didn't know they were going to meet each other.

Evan Williams was the first to arrive at the restaurant. The host directed him to a private room with two tables and eight chairs. He ordered a bottle of Egon Müller Riesling and asked the waiter to pour a little in his glass. He swirled the glass and smelled the wine. He had always enjoyed Riesling on stressful days like this. About ten minutes into his meditation with Riesling, he heard the door open and he saw the waiter bringing in Edward and Grace together.

"Good evening, congressman. Pleasure meeting you," said Grace Ashworth with a beaming smile.

"Pleasure is mine," said Evan as he got up from his seat to shake Grace's hands.

"And good evening to you too, Edward!" Williams extended his hand to Edward.

After they sat down, their wine glasses were filled right away.

"I will get to the point right away as to why I invited you both. An unusual combination of guests at my dinner table. And I mean as it as a compliment for both of you." Williams laughed.

"Nothing unusual, congressman. A socialite like me can attach herself to any group," said Grace.

"That's right!" Edward guffawed and continued. "I had not seen Ms. Grace in at least three years, I think. Can you believe that? She's right. She can fit into any group."

"Well, I need a favor. From both of you. And it involves Derek Fisher." Williams opened his arms and stretched them forward, pointing at each of them.

CHAPTER 7

FOUR DAYS BEFORE REFERENDUM

Her hand trembled as she ripped open the packaging and pulled out the stick. Lisa eyed the stick in her hand with trepidation. She felt like she was going to vomit. She walked into the bathroom carrying the stick and hoping for the best. After a few minutes, she got off the toilet seat. Her hands were shaking as she set the stick down on the bathroom counter and stepped away. She willed herself to take a deep breath and calm down before she picked it up again. She saw two pink lines on the stick. Her heart sank when she realized the test was positive. She turned the box around to read the instructions again to confirm what two pink lines meant. She leaned against the counter for support as the reality of her situation sunk in.

She was pregnant. Lisa felt like she was going to faint. She took a few deep breaths and splashed some water on her face before she left the bathroom.

Lisa had been feeling off for a few days. She was exhausted all the time, despite getting plenty of sleep, and her stomach had been acting up. She wasn't sure what was wrong, but she had a sneaking suspicion. Tentatively, she reached for the box on the shelf. She had bought it the day after Caleb forced himself on her and hadn't dared to use it until she really felt it was time. She had to call Caleb.

Lisa moved to the living room and sat on the couch. Then she slowly fell on the couch. Lily, who was playing on the floor with her toys, sensed something was wrong and ran towards Lisa to check on her. Lisa gave Lily a big hug and told her that there was nothing to worry about and that Mommy was having a bad headache. Lily went back to playing with her toys.

After a few minutes, she called Lily.

"Hey, Lily, do you want to go play with Zack? Mommy has to step outside to the pharmacy and get some medicines. I will be back in an hour."

Zack was a five-year-old boy who lived a few doors down the street. Zack went to the same playschool as Lily. His mom didn't mind watching Lily over for an hour or two whenever Lisa had urgent errands to run. And Lisa did the same when Zack needed adult supervision. But that situation arose less frequently in Zack's case, as Zack's mom was not a single mom.

"Sure, Mom. Come back soon please. I want to finish building this." Lily got up quickly and was ready to go. This was one thing Lisa was proud of. Lily would stop doing anything, even her most favorite activity in the world, the moment she heard Lisa give her instructions or asked her to run a chore.

Lisa dropped Lily off at Zack's house and drove to the meat packaging plant where Caleb worked. It was a small plant and had only five to six people working in any given shift. Lisa had been there several times when Caleb and she were together, and a few times since they were separated. Caleb would sometimes ask Lisa to come and pick Lily up from the plant because he was running late in the morning. The supervisor of the plant knew Lisa fairly well.

Lisa's car pulled to the side of the plant where Caleb usually parked his old white Saturn. Today, Lisa did not find his car. So she decided to go into the plant and check for herself. The moment she stepped to the side door through which employees usually entered, a man from inside pushed open the door and walked outside. He had come out to smoke. As soon as he saw Lisa, he held the door open for her. She thanked her and went in. The supervisor on duty recognized her immediately.

"Hey, Lisa! How are you?"

"Good, I guess. Please tell me you haven't fired Caleb." She was curious.

"I wish I had. He's a jerk. An arrogant son of a gun. You know that. But he is the best I've got here. So, no. Not yet, Lisa," the supervisor said, making other employees who were working there shake their heads.

"Then where the fuck is he?" Lisa was shaking.

"He must be running late. Come on. Why don't you sit in that little office there? I'll get some water for you. We don't want you to be all agitated when he gets here. With all these sharp objects lying around here, I don't want to deal with any human meat." The supervisor was trying to calm Lisa down.

Lisa followed his directions and went into the office room. She sat down.

Her headache had worsened, and she realized she hadn't eaten anything since the morning. She asked the supervisor if she could have some coffee. The stale warm coffee in the coffee pot sitting on the warmer would have normally made Lisa throw up. But when the supervisor poured it in a Styrofoam cup and handed it over to her, she somehow enjoyed the coffee. She thanked the supervisor and started looking on the walls around her in that small office. Calendars with schedules, a notice board with a bunch of sticky notes and printed notes, a few posters of the local sports teams, et cetera.

Caleb walked in.

"There goes twenty minutes off your paycheck," the supervisor commented.

"Dare me," Caleb said as he went to his corner table inside the plant to leave his lunch bag and other things. He removed the overalls hanging on a hook and wore it on top of his jeans and T-shirt. He was ready to chop some liver. That was when he noticed Lisa through the glass window, sitting inside the supervisor's office. Lisa had not seen him until then as she was busy reading the shift schedules on the wall.

"Has she taken over your job?" he yelled at the supervisor while pointing at Lisa.

"Come on, now. Be nice to her. She seems to be in some panic," the supervisor, about ten years older than Caleb, advised him.

Caleb dropped his tools on the table and briskly walked into the office room.

"Hey! What's up? What are you doing here? Where is Lily?"

"Lily's fine. She is at Zack's." Lisa got up from her seat, walked towards the door, and closed it. "I'm pregnant."

"What?" said Caleb.

"I said I'm pregnant, Caleb. With a child I did not want. With a child forced on me by *you*." She was angry.

"What the fuck are you talking about?" asked Caleb.

"I don't have time for this, Caleb. You know what you did. Now cut the crap and tell me what should I do. I can't bring another child into this world, Caleb. I am struggling to raise Lily already. I am an awful mom to one child. I don't want to be an awful mom to two."

"Calm down, Lisa. Calm down. Let's talk it through. When did you find out?"

"An hour ago."

"Maybe you should do another test."

"How does that matter? Will you raise this child?" Lisa got up from her seat again.

Caleb felt a mix of emotions—and none of them related to happiness. Only fear, anger, confusion. But he didn't know what to say. He covered his face with both palms and started pacing in back and forth. Meanwhile, through the window, the supervisor and Caleb's colleagues were watching the animated discussion. They could tell from Caleb's body language that he felt angry and nervous. Lisa's body language, on the other hand, told them she was feeling helpless.

"How do I know it's my child?" Caleb asked the worst question he could have under the circumstances.

"What did you ask?" Lisa was livid.

"How do I know it's my child? It's not like I know who all you sleep with. What if…"

Before Caleb could finish his sentence, Lisa threw the coffee pot with the warm stale coffee at him. The pot didn't really hurt him, and the lukewarm coffee didn't burn him, but it definitely stained his T-shirt.

"You bitch!" Caleb ran towards Lisa, grabbed her hair, and pulled her towards him.

The supervisor sensed that he needed to step in, and he ran towards the door and pushed it open. They had not locked it from inside.

"Hey, hey, cut it, you two! Whatever it is, you both should calm down. Now. I would say take this fight to your home. Goddammit. I know you both damn too well. You are better than this, kids. Listen, take the day off, Caleb. Go home. Breathe. Talk it through. And Lisa, you go home first. I will talk to Caleb and send him home."

Lisa decided not to persist with making the scene worse than what it already was. Her objective of letting Caleb know that she was pregnant had been met. She picked up her handbag and keys and left. Before she stepped outside the office room, and as she walked past Caleb, she turned towards him to make eye contact.

"You know you did it. Be a man. Own it."

Science education had been Ava's passion since she was a little girl. When she became a teacher, she was very clear about one thing—that she would inspire the next generation of scientists. After graduating from high school, she attended the University of Texas, where she earned her degree in education. While she was in college, she met her future husband, Bradley Walters. They married after graduation, and had their only daughter, Eveline, after two years. Ava was a dedicated teacher who loved her job. She was recently honored with the Presidential Medal for her work in helping her middle school students to achieve excellence in science. Ava was a role model for her students, a well-recognized teacher in the school district, and an inspiration to everyone who knew her.

Even before Derek Fisher took office, Governor Willkie had introduced a few amendments to public school funding. Funding—specifically for science—was cut by twenty percent under Wilkie, and that money was set aside to arm schoolteachers. After Fisher took office, as Ava feared, things got progressively worse in a very short time. She had been finding it increasingly difficult to teach science in the prevailing conservative political climate in the state. The state government was no longer hiding its hostility towards public education in general, but their vitriol towards science education was something even Ava did not expect. As a result, Ava, like hundreds of other science teachers across the state, had been adjusting to teaching with fewer resources and less support. Despite these challenges, Ava continued to stay committed to her students and determined to give them the best science education possible. There was a reason why the children in her school admired and respected her.

The latest policy change that banned any books that talked about evolution meant science teachers like Ava were no longer able to perform their duties as educators and justify their purpose to their conscience.

It was a quiet Friday evening at home for Ava and Bradley. They had just finished dinner and were now relaxing in the living room. The TV was on, and Eveline was watching an animated movie, half-asleep. She should be going to bed in another thirty minutes. Bradley was reading a book while Ava was correcting some school test papers. Every so often, they would exchange a few words or share a smile. It was a comfortable silence between them, one that was filled with love and understanding. They were content just being in each other's company.

There was a commercial break on TV, and there was a political ad sponsored by a pro-TEXIT PAC, reminding all Texans to vote yes and help make Texas the greatest country in the world.

Ava and Bradley looked at each other. There was a long silence again but this time with both staring into each other's eyes. A thousand words were exchanged in those few seconds of silence and the eye exchange. They both had talked about this many times ever since Fisher was elected. Ava was the kind of woman who did not want to give up without fighting, while Bradley was the kind of man who would look for a safe exit if that was an option. That meant Bradley was hoping he could somehow convince Ava about leaving Texas within the next two years, after the referendum passed. He had short-listed Colorado as his most preferred place to move to and had even taken Ava and Eveline for a skiing trip to Breckenridge during the last winter break. Ava knew Bradley was being very supportive of her perseverance. But she also understood where Bradley's heart lay, and that he wanted the best for hers and Eveline's future.

Ava couldn't think past the future of her schoolchildren. She knew that not every child in her school had the choice or option of moving to another state where there was no attack on public education, and where the wonderful world of science could continue to be taught in such a way that it raised curiosity in young minds. Her conscience kept pointing at how guilty she would be if she just gave up on her schoolchildren in order to secure a safer future for her own child.

Eveline had fallen asleep. Ava had just finished correcting her papers. She got up and looked at Bradley.

"Thank you for supporting me always. You are my rock, Bradley. You know that. I love you," she said and leaned forward to kiss Bradley. Bradley gave her a gentle hug and pouted his lips.

"Good night, baby!" she whispered in Bradley's ears.

Bradley looked at his wife with a sense of appreciation and love. He noticed the way her hair curled perfectly around her face, how her eyes shone brightly, and how her lips always managed to look soft and inviting. He also appreciated the way Ava was always so kind and patient, even when dealing with the most difficult situations. In that moment, he was filled with gratitude for everything she was and everything Ava did. He knew that she was his best friend, his rock, and the love of his life. And he was determined to never take her for granted.

"Love you and good night." He closed his eyes and kissed her deeply.

Ava carried Eveline on her shoulders to put her to sleep in her bed. After she lay her in bed, she carefully arranged her favorite soft toys around Eveline, turned on the night lamp in her room, and quietly walked away to their bedroom.

Bradley continued to look at Ava with a smile and determination. He vowed to be the best partner she has ever had in her lifetime.

It was late in the evening by the time the analyst finally finished her report on the latest oil spill. She had been working on it for days, and she was exhausted. As she gathered her things to leave, Abhinav Agarwal, the CEO of the company, walked in. He looked angry, and he demanded to know why the report was not finished yet. She was clearly shocked to see the CEO of her company walk to her cubicle. Doing her best not to lose composure, she tried to explain to him that it had been a complex situation, but he was not interested in excuses. He demanded her that if the report was not finished by the next morning, she would be fired. She was really annoyed by his tone and told herself she should resign if this continued for one more time. Abhinav had been on her case for the past few days—since the verdict, to be precise. He had been angry at his staff almost all the time and had been seen intolerant of even minor misgivings. Abhinav was convinced that there had been a leak from inside and there was no way the environmental advocacy group or the activists would have been able to produce the evidence they did. He took it upon himself to find out who these people were. But this was the first time he walked right to her desk.

Meanwhile, Russell and Emily had gone back to their base in Austin. With the kind of reputation they had built from the RapFuel case, many oil-company-related complaints and pending cases had started coming to them for their attention. Some of them were individual complainants while some were advocacy groups or small corporations affected by the oil companies. But all of them were hoping Russell and Emily would be able to help them find a breakthrough in their respective cases as well, just like they did with the RapFuel case.

Today was not a typical day in the office for Russell and Emily. Their team was working on a new campaign to raise awareness about the latest women's rights issue and the state's complete abortion ban. They were busy brainstorming ideas for social media posts and drafting press releases. Russell was on the phone with a reporter, trying to get coverage for their upcoming rally in Austin. Emily was working on a grant proposal and meeting with potential donors. In between all of this, both Russell and Emily were monitoring the latest news on X (Twitter) and other social media feeds, RapFuel case follow-ups, and responding to emails.

With the amount of data piling up from those who had reached out to them about individual oil companies, Russell and Emily had to employ a set of data analysts, one petroleum engineer, one civil engineer, two auditors, and an accountant specifically for a team that would concentrate only on oil-company-related complaints, including the additional data that Russell and Emily managed to obtain from RapFuel during the case period. It was lot of work, and something that was a deviation from the main objective of TWRA, but Russell and Emily wanted to bring these complaints to a logical conclusion before turning them to over to someone else—either to the press or a more focused advocacy group that had been working only on oil-company-related issues.

Every evening they would meet with the team for a debrief on what kind of breakthroughs they had made by scouring over the data. It was quite a tedious job for all of them. One of the first reviews the team did was about the environmental group Earth First! and the data they had turned in. This group had released over 100 gigabytes of data they had acquired from RapFuel for Russel's and Emily's team. The data, which included everything from contract information to many confidential financial documents, had been obtained through a sophisticated phishing attack, targeting specific RapFuel employees. Once they had the data, Earth First! began combing through it. What they found was a series of accounting discrepancies totaling over ten billion dollars. While it was unclear to the Earth First! group whether these discrepancies were intentional or not, they had decided to turn the data over to Russell and Emily for further review. Russell and Emily's team used this data along with the more comprehensive financial documents they already had collected for the case and started drawing a few preliminary conclusions.

Every evening when Russell and Emily met with this team was a revelation to all of them and it kept them excited. They knew they were onto something big. Within a week of reviewing all data they had the team had about RapFuel, there was something very clear. RapFuel was using off-balance sheet Special Purpose Vehicles (SPV) to hide its toxic assets and debts from its creditors and investors. This was illegal. And on top of that, the team also concluded that the company had been using illicit entities to create capital projects to divert money. The revelation that shocked Russell and Emily the most was the one that showed a direct connection between RapFuel and Governor Derek Fisher. From an accounting standpoint, the entries were kept clean, but it was anyone's guess what kind of legitimate business deal Derek Fisher, either in capacity as a grocery chain owner or in his capacity as an individual, could have with RapFuel. This was a red flag in Russell and Emily's world.

Russell and Emily spent the next week drafting the conclusions with inserted copies of proof from the data and documents they had received. They now had a well-documented proof on RapFuel's accounting fraud and a potential political scandal connecting Abhinav Agarwal and Derek Fisher. After much deliberation, they decided that it was best to leak the story to the press. A legal battle was an option, but, in this case, there was no plaintiff who would come forward. They could directly have an agency like SEC get involved. But with TEXIT on the horizon, what kind of hold SEC would really like to have on Texas-based companies was not something Russell and Emily were willing to speculate. So they decided to defame the company immediately, which they hoped would benefit Texas the independent country in the long run, and hoped that law would take its due course.

The Austin Star was their first choice. So that night they gave the task to one of the members in the team to package their conclusions document, save it in a storage device, encrypt it, put it in an envelope, seal it, and keep it ready for the next morning. When Russell and Emily left home that night, little did they suspect that there would be any foul play before the document reached *The Austin Star*.

The two men sat in the hotel room nursing their drinks and venting their frustration. The congressman from Texas, Evan Williams, was fuming about the governor's latest decision, the attack on women's rights, and the total ban on abortion, while the junior senator from Texas, Ryan Dodson, did not really care much about that issue. Both hated the governor's guts, but they were fully aware that there was nothing they could do as DC politicians. They were stuck working with him for TEXIT, at least for a few more days. It was enough to drive any man insane. Still, they had to keep up friendly appearances at these rallies. It was not based on the governor's ask, but they were doing it to prop their own reputations. They could not let the public see them not on the same page with the governor on the issue of TEXIT. They had to act like they were one team fighting for independent Texas.

It was a steamy hot day in Dallas and the two men had just finished their last rally appearance of the day. They were sitting in Dodson's room, trying to come up with a plan to override the governor's popularity, whom they all hated. They heard a knock on the door. It was Newell.

"Look at us here. What in the name of God's earth has brought three of us together in the same damn hotel room!" said Newell with a sense of fake amusement. His tone still had a bitter tinge to it—residual bitterness from their meeting in DC.

"For starters, this is not DC. We are supposed to be in the same team here, senator. Let's go easy, shall we?" laughed Dodson.

Newell poured himself a drink, bourbon—neat—and walked back to the couch.

"To our future!" Newell raised his class.

The other two joined and raised their glasses, too. "To our future!"

Senator Newell was in a quandary. Should he share the information about his plans to throw his hat in the ring for presidency post-TEXIT? Or was it too early? After all, if word got out, he could get into a lot of trouble for bringing the cart before the horse. On the other hand, he remembered his junior colleague had made it clear during their bitter meeting at a restaurant in DC a few days ago that he was going to do something similar. After much deliberation, Newell decided to not take the risk and share his thought at that moment. It was the right thing to do, and he decided that he would just play along until the referendum was passed.

Dodson sensed the uncomfortable mood that seemed to have seeped into the room suddenly. He refilled his glass and asked the others if they wanted a refill.

And then he looked around the room and raised his glass to say a toast.

"To the first President of Texas, whoever he may be, may God bless him and his family!"

"Amen!"

"When people look back and read their history books, I want them to tell their kids that I was the only one who could have held the office as the President of Texas in the year when the state got its independence. I don't know if I want to be the most famous Texan, but I would like to be the only one to be remembered for having enough of a national platform to represent the entire country of Texas and trusted by majority of the people. I will serve as the president for all citizens."

"Wait right there. You mean for *all* citizens? You don't mean that, do you?"

"I mean it, of course. That's what I mean."

"Not just for Christian white men?"

"Well. If you put it that way . . ." Derek Fisher laughed.

His wife, Gloria, was lying in bed and reading a book as she saw her husband pace back and forth in front of their bed in pajamas and practice his presidential announcement. The couple had seen many ups and downs in their lives. They had lost their younger son to cancer at a young age and now their older son was in college, away in Italy, studying at the Catholic University. The family had always been devout Christians, but after their younger son passed away, Derek started taking special interest in talking about his faith more often and more publicly. When he decided to enter politics, his devout Christian personality suddenly became one of his biggest political assets, as his opponents in the fray found it extremely difficult to fight him against his faith. Eventually, after he took office, his faith started dictating policies, which then started affecting millions of people. Even some of his cabinet members were beginning to feel worried about the governor being pulled by strings from the extreme right. They tried to intervene but failed. Derek Fisher was easily swayed by the 3vangelical Christian lobby in the state and it was an open secret.

"So, what kind of president will you be?" Gloria was trying to entertain her husband.

"You just wait and see." Fisher laughed. "I will be the best president ever. I will be the best *Christian* president ever."

"Do you think the people of Texas are ready for you?" asked Gloria.

"They chose me as their governor, didn't they? I think they are happy with their decision. Just go around the state, darling. Ask Texans what they think of me. They love me, honey. Isn't that the greatest feeling? To be loved by so many? If they are happy with me as their governor, I will be the same kind of president they voted me to be. Someone who works hard for preserving the fundamental right to exist as a white Christian in Texas more than anything else. I tell ya, the people of Texas won't ever regret choosing me over that douchebag Dodson or whoever. Watch me steamroll them!" He sounded as optimistic as ever. Gloria had been eyeing him all the while with lustful eyes and finally decided to make a move as soon he finished his speech. She dragged him onto the bed by holding her arms around his neck and started kissing him. He responded with equal ardor, kissing her passionately and wrapping his legs around her. Soon they were making love and moved together as one, their bodies slick with sweat and lust.

The Austin Capitol Building was an imposing sight. Rising from the heart of downtown Austin, the white granite building soared to a height of 302 feet, offering sweeping views of the cityscape below. Built in 1888, the Capitol was the third-oldest state capitol in continuous use in the United States. The interior of the building was just as impressive as its exterior, with a grand staircase leading up to the rotunda and several beautiful murals depicting scenes from Texas history. The building was designed by Elijah E. Myers and completed in 1888. The design was a mix of Romanesque Revival and Renaissance Revival architecture. The front facade featured a central clock tower with four dials that could be seen from afar. Above the clock were the words *STATE OF TEXAS*.

The Legislative Reference Library was also located in the Capitol Building. This library was one of the oldest and the most comprehensive libraries in Texas, and it served as a valuable resource for lawmakers and staff members. It was a place of hushed concentration. Amid the low buzz of murmured conversation and the scratching of pencil on paper, it was usually the staffers of the lawmakers who were spending most of their time here. The shelves were lined with law books, financial reports, and government records, dating back centuries. The thing that made this library unique when compared to public libraries in general was that there was a sense of weighty importance in the air, as if the very walls were absorbing the knowledge contained within them. The atmosphere was one of calm diligence, a sharp contrast to the hustle and bustle of the rest of the Capitol Building.

The library was a refuge for those who seek answers, a respite from the outside world. In this place, one could find peace in the pursuit of understanding. It was also a place for secret congressional deals that were made over handshakes and occasionally a place for the blackmailers to threaten their victims.

State Congresswoman Sima Daly had been waiting at the far end of the library at a table, all alone. She had texted Richard Harvey in the morning and had asked him to meet her inside the library at noon. He had agreed and did not ask why. At 11:55 AM, he texted Daly to let her know that he was running a few minutes late. Sima did not have any books in front of her. There were a couple of newspapers, and she was browsing through the newspapers, but her mind was not on any of the news. She had never done this before. The younger version of herself appeared in front of her to tell her how ashamed she was for growing up to be a blackmailer who was exploiting a friendship for personal pollical gains. She gasped for a second as the visual faded out. She picked up the phone to see if Harvey had texted her. He had. The last message said, *On my way!*

Richard Harvey walked into the library with a broad smile, completely unaware of what was going to unfold in front of him. As soon as he spotted Sima, he started walking towards her. She had not noticed him and was busy looking at something on her phone.

"Hey, congresswoman! Feels weird to address you like that. Let me just call you Sima." He tried to stretch his arms as if he wanted to give her a hug.

Sima was startled by that but recovered quickly. She got up and reciprocated the stretching arms gesture. They both hugged each other for a brief second.

"Give it to me. What's the breaking news from the TEXIT world?" he asked her.

"Going well, I think. Richard, listen. I will keep it short. We want you on our team. Derek wants you on Team TEXIT very badly. Not just support it. But be a champion for the cause. Show up at rallies. Speak. We are in the home stretch. Just a few more days for the referendum and your voice will make a lot of difference." Sima was trying to list what all they wanted from him.

"We've already had this conversation. I am a moderate . . . a moderate conservative. Whatever that means these days. You know me, Sima. I can't. This is not what I want. I believe we are bringing the future lives of thousands and millions of Texans down by this. The damages I see this is going to cause are unfathomable. I am really hoping this movement fails at some stage."

"What can we do to convince you?" Sima raised her voice, no longer in a favor requesting mode.

"Nothing at all. Just leave me alone. You do your thing. I will continue to campaign against this wherever I can. And hope the referendum fails."

"What if it doesn't?" Sima asked Harvey.

"Then I will shift my focus to DC for the congressional ratification and then to Austin to meddle with Article 49. I am going to keep fighting this, Sima."

"The governor thinks very highly of you. He says you've got a great future. Only if you get on the same page on TEXIT. He can ruin your career if he chooses to," Sima reminded him in a mildly threatening tone.

"Threatening me? Bring it on!" Harvey challenged her with a fake laugh.

"I haven't even started threatening you," Sima informed him with a wry smile. She opened her handbag and picked another phone from inside. She unlocked it and opened an app. Then she flipped the phone for Richard Harvey to see.

On the screen was a video playing. There they were.

Aaron Naylor and Richard Harvey were completely naked on a hotel bed. Harvey's face and his audible moaning showed he was enjoying the oral pleasure given to him by Aaron while he held Aaron's head firmly against his pelvis. The video was two minutes long.

Richard Harvey was staring at the screen for two whole minutes. His mind had become numb, and he was beginning to sweat. There were no signs of the embarrassment of being outed as a gay. But there were signs of anger and disappointment.

"You? Out of all people, you, Sima? I never imagined you could do this to me."

"I didn't have a choice, and I needed a leverage, Richard. I'm sorry. This is politics. This is how things work. You know it. I have to do what I have to do. I know none of my reasoning matters to you right now. Feel free to be angry with me," Sima offered in an unapologetic yet self-consciously friendly tone.

It was never easy to deal with betrayal, especially when it came from someone one thought one could trust. The pain and hurt can run deep, and it can be hard to forgive and move on. But betrayal was also a part of life, and it was something that everyone had to deal with at one time or another. Richard Harvey's mind was trying to process the act of betrayal by Sima. First, he was willing to give Sima a pass, thinking she may have made a poor choice and there was no need to judge her as a bad person. It was a difficult experience for him. A part of him was relieved that he was finally out of the closet in some ambiguous way, and he was thankful to Sima for that. He wanted to stand in the middle of the library and scream, "I am gay!" But the other part of him was angry. That someone he trusted would carefully plan a scheme to create a circumstance to exploit his weakness and then use that against him. He got up and walked away without saying a word.

Sima was staring at him as he walked away from her. She whispered, "I'm sorry, Richard." And put her phone back in the bag. She grabbed her other phone, which was on the table, and her handbag, and left the library.

The librarian near the door recognized her and said, "Have a beautiful day, Congresswoman Daly!"

Sima responded, "I have a feeling it's going to get more beautiful."

When Russell and Emily got to the office the next morning, they went looking for the package that was to be sent to *The Austin Star*. They had asked the team member to leave the package in a specific storage shelf in the office which was to be locked. They did not suspect anything, as the shelf was locked and there was a sealed package inside exactly where they had asked the team member to leave it. The package had a Post-it note affixed with the sign *To The Austin Star*. They took it to the mail room and asked the attendant there to send it urgently to *The Austin Star* with the envelope addressed to Jason Greer. The plan was to email Jason the encryption code so he could decrypt the device once he received it.

Jason Greer, by then, had built a bit of a reputation for himself as an honest journalist who was not influenced by the political theme of the day. His past work at the *Post* combined with what he had been doing at *The Austin Star* seemed to have made him some sort of the go-to person at his media outlet if anyone wanted any state level scandals to be broken in an impartial manner. "Jason wouldn't just publish a story" was the word on the street and everyone trusted his investigative reporting when he was onto something.

Russell and Emily didn't know what had happened the previous night after their team member left the sealed envelope inside the shelf and locked it. A man had been lurking in the shadows, outside the building that housed their office, waiting for his opportunity. The target was a small office building, and he knew that inside was the confidential document he had been hired to steal. He waited until all the lights were off and the building was silent before making his move.

He climbed up to a window on the second floor and used the special tools he had brought with him to break in. Once inside, he made his way to the room where the document was kept. He had a copy of the key to the shelf. He quietly opened the shelf and found the document quickly. He had brought another similar looking envelope with a storage device inside. The storage device looked exactly like the one inside the original envelope and it weighed about the same. The only difference was that the envelope he swapped with had a blank storage device with absolutely no data in it. The job was successful, and the hired thief got away cleanly with the document he had been asked to steal.

When Jason Greer walked to his desk, he saw an envelope that was addressed to him. It read it was from *Russell and Emily, TWRA*. He was not familiar with Russell and Emily, so he did a quick online search for both the names: Russell Weston and Emily Chase. He got two dozen hits for each of them. He started reading about them and was soon thoroughly impressed by the work they had been doing. He was particularly drawn to their remarkable success in the RapFuel case. Once he knew who they were, he felt comfortable enough to open the envelope. Within seconds, he connected the device to his computer only to find out that it had been encrypted. He was tempted to call them and ask for the code, but his instinct told him to check his email. There it was. An email with the encryption code. He hastily typed the code to unlock and decrypt the device data. A few seconds later, he stared at the screen in amusement. It was an empty storage device with zero files.

Is this some kind of a joke? he thought to himself. But he quickly realized that this may have been a foul play. He almost picked up his phone again to call Russell and Emily, and let them know of the ruse, but only in a sarcastic way. Then he concluded that there was no possibility of this being a play on him. It became increasingly clear to his investigative brain that this was one on them. That was why he decided not to shock them immediately over a phone call.

After a couple of hours of sitting on this and brooding over the plans, he decided he needed to talk to Russell and Emily in person to sort this out. He got out of his office building and started walking towards their office, which was only three blocks away. During his walk, he was wondering what kind of information they wanted to share with him. Again, his logical thought process took him to RapFuel and Abhinav Agarwal. He was sure that they were sending him something explosive that possibly fell outside any legal purvey for now. He reached a modest two-story building with no big sign outside. This was an advocacy group functioning entirely off donor money, and that showed in the appearance. As he got closer to the main door, he saw a small sign that said, *TWRA*, for Texas Women's Rights Advocacy. He neither waited nor hesitated, but knocked on the main door.

"Good morning! How can we help you?" a volunteer greeted him, opening the door with a smile.

"I would like to meet Russell Weston and Emily Chase, please. They will recognize me if you mention my name. It's Jason. Jason Greer," he introduced himself, handing over his business card to the volunteer.

This would be the first time he would be meeting with Russell and Emily. And none of them had any idea how this meeting would trigger a series of events, eventually bearing heavy on the TEXIT future of Texas. The butterfly effect was about to be set in motion.

After a couple of minutes, Jason Greer was let inside the office building by the volunteer. Jason smiled at him and stepped in. He felt a bit excited to meet Russell and Emily—the kind of excitement a reporter like him usually got only when they were going to meet high profile individuals, holding high public offices, or industry leaders, or someone he had been asked to interview—someone who happened to be in the middle of a huge story he was working on.

The inside of Russell's and Emily's office was abuzz with activity, exactly like what he had expected. Volunteers were preparing mailings, answering phones, drafting new social media campaigns, responding to social media posts, and sorting donations in the computers. The shelves were lined with books on the history of women's rights in the USA, around the world, and in Texas, as well as other books and publications on feminism, and the walls were covered with posters highlighting famous women and men who advocated for equality throughout history. The atmosphere was one of excitement and determination. But the place was also way too disorganized for Jason's liking.

"Hey, Jason! It's great to meet you finally," called Russell Weston, walked out of his office room.

"Likewise. You have no idea how excited I am to finally meet you," Jason admitted with a wide smile.

"Coffee? Coke? Water?" Russell was walking to the kitchen area to get himself a cup of coffee. Emily was standing there in the kitchen refilling her water bottle.

"Emily, this is Jason Greer," Russell introduced them.

"Oh, wow. Didn't expect to see you here. At least not so soon. Pardon our mess. This is how we operate." Emily shook Jason's hands and smiled embarrassingly.

"That's all right. I understand." Jason helped himself to a bottle of water from the refrigerator. "I have so much to talk to you about. But let me cut to the chase. Did you send me some material marked confidential today?"

"Yes, we did. We thought you are here to talk exactly about that." said Russell.

"I'm sorry. But it was a blank document. The storage device in the envelope was empty. Zero files. There was nothing in it. First, I thought you were trying to pull one on me. But something didn't sit right. I figured the victims here may actually be you. You wanted to send me something. But someone got hold of them." Jason was talking like an investigator.

"Oh, God! How? We were here last night and we sealed the envelope," said Emily in a surprised tone.

"No, Emily. We didn't stay until the envelope was sealed. We gave that task to Mike. Remember?" Russell reminder her.

As he was responding to Emily, Russell walked to the shelf where the printed documents with data they had received from different sources were kept and tried to see if anything else stood out. The disorganized appearance of the office notwithstanding, the shelf was one place and perhaps the only place in the office that was very well-organized. And Russell and Emily spent extra time sorting through their document shelves and keeping them organized. As far as Russell could tell, nothing looked out of place. He randomly picked a few files to see if any of them raised suspicion. Everything looked just like he expected.

"Wow. Someone must have broken in. I don't know if we should get police involved, as that will pretty much ruin everything and bring this to an end. All the time we have spent for the last three months will mean nothing." Russell took a deep breath. "But . . ."

"What?" Jason looked puzzled.

"Did the encryption code we sent you work?" asked Emily.

"Yes. It did. I mean, the empty device was encrypted, and I was able to decrypt it using the code you sent," Jason responded.

"Wow. That's incredible. Our team created this specific document to be shared with you, and we should have a copy of that in our drive. To create this explosive and speculative document, we needed all those gazillions of printed pages that thankfully we were able to get hold of through many sources." Emily started walking towards her office to look for the document on her computer.

Russell and Jason followed her. Anyone looking at Emily's computer for the first time would immediately be impressed with how organized her computer was. Every file was neatly labeled and stored in its own designated folder. The desktop was clean, with only a few key shortcuts visible. Emily quickly got to the folder she wanted to access, which was secured with two layers of authentication. Russell was impressed, making a note to himself about which folders he should add these additional layers of security to. Emily was able to find the document, which was also password protected. When she opened it after typing the password, she was shocked. Emily stared at the computer for a few seconds.

The document was blank. This was the file they thought they sent to Jason.

"What the fuck is going on?" Emily was clearly flustered.

Emily sat down on her chair with her chin resting on her palm. Russell was pacing back and forth in his room. He was thinking of all the possible actions they could take and the options available in front of them. They could continue to act normal and pretend like nothing had happened. Or they could try to meet with every single volunteer one-on-one, starting with Mike, the person who was supposed to have left the envelope sealed in the shelf the previous night, and hope they may be able to narrow down the suspects. Or they could take this whole case to the Austin police, whom they did not trust very much given the sensitive nature of this document and the people involved. Russell kept thinking about all the options again and again. Then a new thought struck him.

"We must find out who the mole is. Whoever did this could even break into your computer, Emily. That's serious shit. Not some old school break-in to the office and steal papers kind of heist."

"Oh, fuck! They probably have access to my cloud account, too." Emily suddenly realized that it was possible if they were able to crack the password for the document. She logged into iCloud to check if her folders and files were there, and heaved a sigh of relieved. "They look okay." She went on to changing all her passwords while listening to Russell.

"Where was I? Yeah. We have to find out who the mole is. But what is really our priority now? Sharing this explosive information with the press or tracking down this asshole who hacked into your account? Thing big picture, Russell. Think big." Russell appeared to be talking to himself, but he was really venting out and sharing the challenges that lay ahead.

"Why don't we reconstruct everything from scratch? And we can create a new document within a week. And Jason could watch us as we go through this," offered Emily.

"Exactly my thoughts, too," concurred Russell.

With that, the trio agreed to comb through the gazillion documents on their own and identify the data they needed to expose the people involved.

Russell went out of Emily's room and looked around. The office was relatively thinner that day. He spoke in a very loud voice and asked all the volunteers who were working there to take the rest of the day off and come back tomorrow. He also said that he and Emily had come across some interesting information, and they needed to work on it—storyboard possibilities—before they could decide if this lead was worth everyone's time investment. There was a moment of shock and silence in the office since this was the first time something like this had ever happened; Russell and Emily clearly wanted everyone to leave the building because they wanted to discuss something in private. After about two minutes, all of them packed their bags and left. There were quiet murmurs as they stepped out. Russell heard them, but he at that point he didn't care.

He yelled again, "Don't come before 2:00 PM tomorrow! We need some time!"

Jason looked at his watch. It was 1:30 PM.

"We have exactly twenty-four hours. There is no accountant among us, no auditor, but heck, why bother with any of them? We know what we are doing. Right?" said Emily.

Jason smiled, and Russell let out a wry laughter.

Russell walked to the document shelf and started bringing out the boxes they needed for this work. Emily helped him carry them one by one, placing them on the floor. Jason walked to the main door and locked it from inside. The three of them sat on the floor and swiftly started going through the endless documents.

CHAPTER 8

CURRENT DAY

With over forty million passengers annually, Washington Dulles airport is one of the busiest airports in the world. Senator Newell breezed through the crowd inside the airport and stepped outside looking for his cab. He was hoping it would be his regular driver. Someone who was familiar with his routine, so he didn't have to talk a whole lot. As the taxi pulled up to the curb, Newell was relieved to see the familiar face behind the steering wheel. He quickly got in, but before he could settle in and give time for the driver to pull away, he saw a throng of reporters and paparazzi surrounding the taxi right by the curbside. He had been dreading this moment ever since his plane had landed.

Senator Brynes had shared something with him before he took off, had warned Newell that there could be reporters waiting outside the airport. Taking a deep breath, he steeled himself for the onslaught and stepped out of the cab. Immediately, he was swarmed by the press. Cameras flashed in his face and questions were shouted at him from all sides. He did his best to keep calm and answer the queries as best as he could in the most ambiguous ways possible. After taking about half a dozen questions, he waved goodbye to the press. He made his way back to the safety of the taxi to escape the maddening crowd. As the taxi pulled away, he let out a sigh of relief. It was going to be a long week.

When he reached his office in the Capitol, the first thing he did was to send a message to Brynes. Senator Brynes had been waiting for the arrival of Newell. The two decided to meet in Brynes's office. It was midmorning and there was enough time for another cup of coffee. So the senators grabbed themselves hot cups and settled down in Brynes's office.

Hailing from Nebraska, Senator Brynes was a conservative politician who had been in office for over twenty years. During his time in the Senate, he had managed to build a reputation of being reasonable to reconciliation and bipartisanship, a rare quality among the DC ilk these days. He had opposed bills that would increase funding for education and healthcare, and he had voted to slash funding for food assistance programs. But to his credit, Senator Brynes had consistently voted to raise the minimum wage or to provide paid sick leave for workers. Despite his mixed track record, Senator Brynes continued to get elected by a wide margin every six years. And that was largely because of his connect with his constituents, big businesses, and wealthy donors—not to mention, a couple of bills that the Senate had passed during his time benefitted the infrastructure initiatives in Nebraska immensely and would continue to do so for years to come.

"Brynes, I know things change rapidly in DC. But so much in seventy-two hours? How did he manage to do this?"

"Your boy, Williams. He is a dealmaker, senator. He wasn't even here, and the ball he set rolling before he left DC, I think has hit the right pockets."

"Son of a gun. Anything we can do?"

"Too late, I think. He still hasn't got all fifteen votes yet. But he is very close from what I hear."

"Shit." Newell showed his frustration.

What Congressman Williams had been working on to secure the fifteen votes they needed for Congress to ratify TEXIT was as followed:

He and Dodson had put together a proposal that if they got the votes, ten percent of the public offshore drilling leases in Texas would be given to the companies from states these congressmen represented. If the states did not have companies that were capable of drilling, then the proposal also took care of compensating such states through circumventive shell company structures. Ten percent was a huge deal. There were still many uncertainties, and these leases would not come into effect for at least another three to four years, but the sheer volume of the promise such a deal offered was something these congressmen and women could easily say no to.

"We will keep trying. This is just a proposal. And it depends on so many factors. So, getting all fifteen votes may not be that easy." Brynes was still trying to keep his optimism alive.

"And what about the leak? How did that happen?"

"BLT is a fucking eavesdropping party. Was it Dodson's choice? Did he pick that restaurant that night? I wouldn't let it past him that he planted a bug there. Or it just happened. You know. This is DC. Can't escape them."

"I don't remember. Yes. He may have suggested BLT. There was press at the airport. Thanks to your tip I was prepared. Think I managed to dodge a bullet for today. As long as Dodson doesn't crap out of his mouth, we can let this story die quietly," said Newell.

Lee Sung, the reporter who had overheard the conversation between Senators Dodson and Newell at the restaurant, had shared this tip with Jason Greer immediately. And he was expecting an explosive headline the next day. But when Jason Greer and Myra Bristow decided not to act on the scoop, Lee Sung was disappointed. From Jason and Myra's perspectives, this was a story that needed more legs to stand on, so they had decided to do more investigative follow-up, even though, at first, Jason thought they should publish the story right away. Young, restless, and a reporter craving for attention, Lee Sung wanted this story to take over the news cycle at least for a day or two. So he decided to leak that scoop to someone else from his DC media circle of friends.

The New York Post did not think too long before picking up this story, and they paid him handsomely for the scoop, then decided to do a half-page column based on the Dodson-Newell feud. They reached out to both the senators offices for follow-up, which was an unwritten protocol among the DC press. Tabloids like *The New York Post* did not really have to wait for a clean follow-up or responses from the parties affected or any kind of closure before publishing their stories, because their very model was pure sensationalism. They reached out to the senators' offices only to check off a formality clause. Since there was no one in Newell's office over the weekend, the reporter who was doing the follow-up reached out to the offices of a couple of other senators' offices, senators who were considered allies of Senator Newell. Senator Brynes was one of them.

As soon as Brynes got a whiff of the story to be published by *The New York Post*, he had alerted Newell through an email the previous night. Newell, a politician from the old school, was someone who was not connected to his devices all the time. So he got to see Brynes's email only this morning when he was at the airport. By then *The New York Post* had already published the story. This was the reason Senator Brynes had also alerted Newell before he took off on his flight from Houston that he should expect reporters as soon as he arrived. Newell did not give away anything to the press at the airport, and he stuck to the same response: "It is ridiculous to talk about a Texas presidency when there are so many more hurdles to cross before the state becomes independent. Right now, Senator Dodson and I are committed to working together to get the best deal for *all* Texans. There is no truth to the story except maybe a small part. I did have steak tartare at BLT. And I highly recommend it."

"By the way, the word on the street is that the president has called for a meeting with Dodson this week. Don't know what the meeting is for." Brynes casually dropped another bombshell of a news for Newell.

That was the last straw in Newell's morning of many mishaps. He was completely livid, annoyed, and beginning to feeling dejected.

Meanwhile, Senator Brynes walked over to the other room, grabbed a copy of today's *New York Post* from his secretary's table, and dropped it on the table in front of Newell.

Senator Newell opened *The New York Post* and flipped through the pages to see where this story was.

Right there, on page five, he read the half-page column with the headline:

HIGH STEAKS FOR TEXAS PRESIDENCY

Dodson v Newell Duel at BLT

Reading that sign on the door startled Alex a bit. He took a step back, closed his eyes, reached for his locket, and opened it. He whispered, "Todo es para tu gloria!" *Everything is for your glory!* He hesitated to look into the mortuary, as he was mentally not prepared for this moment. But since he was already there, he decided to check it out. He looked through the small glass pane on the door. There was no one near the door. The only sight of any live human inside was about ten meters away from the door. And the person in the scrubs with a head gear had their back towards the door. Alex knew they couldn't see him. But he had one hitch. He needed a badge to open the door.

He was lost so much in the thought of how to get in while staring inside that he completely ignored a hospital staff in uniform walk up to the door.

"Excuse me, how may I help you?" he asked.

Alex was startled again. He was trying to regain his composure to come up with the best response.

"Sorry. I didn't see you. Umm . . . err . . . that little girl who was just here with the cops. Soy su tio. Sorry. I am her uncle. She left her favorite toy inside. I came to pick it up."

"Oh. That shooting victim? What tragedy! Poor girl. She has now lost the only surviving parent. Wait. Let me open the door for you.", said the man as he opened the door. He stepped in first and signaled to Alex that he could follow him.

Hoping to avoid any sudden movements, Alex stepped timidly into the room and quietly closed the door behind him. The first thing that hit him was the overwhelming smell of bleach. His eyes watered and he had to fight the urge to cover his nose with his shirt. The tile floors were spotless, as were the white walls. Every surface gleamed, including the large metal table in the center of the room. There were drains in the tabletop, and hoses were hanging on hooks along the wall. He could only imagine what those were used for. The room was cold, and a chill ran down his spine. He tried not to think about why that might be as he took a few steps closer to the table. And then Alex saw it. Lying on the table was a body covered in a white sheet. He could not see the face, but he guessed this was the man the girl came to see and perhaps identify. And in that moment, he realized that this was how life ended. It was a sobering thought, but one, he told himself, that everyone must face someday.

The hospital staff pointed at the lifeless body. "That's the girl's father, Miguel. I am sorry for your loss. How are you related to him?"

"I'm his cousin," said Alex without thinking twice.

As the man left Alex alone there, he stared at the covered body of Miguel, his employee who lost his life because he came to work on an Alex contract. If it was not for Alex's project, Miguel would have probably stayed home or worked on some other project. He would not have gone to Richardson, and he would have gone home alive. That little girl would have had a father to care for her not just for the night, but forever. All these guilty thoughts kept hounding Alex as he pretended to search for the teddy bear on the floor.

When that staff came back to where he was standing, he quickly recovered and said, "Sorry. I can't find it here. Maybe she dropped it somewhere else. Do you know how many other shooting victims were there along with Miguel? I heard there were three other coworkers of Miguel they brought to hospital. How are they doing?"

"Listen, I know it must be hard to process this. They all are dead. We still haven't brought their bodies out here. We will do that one by one."

Alex apologized to the staff member for wasting his time and thanked him for letting him in. He said he would continue to look for the teddy bear in the corridor. After a few seconds, he was back there. But this time around, he was walking back to the lobby very slowly. His mind had been numbed after he heard what he just did. He had lost four of his workers. These were all members of his community, either from Eagle Ford or other nearby Latino settlements in Metro Dallas.

Alex thought how strange life was. It had a way of sneaking up on someone when they least expected it. One minute you were living your life, going about your business, seeing your daughter off to school, packing your lunch for work, and the next, you were faced with your own mortality. Just because death was an inevitable part of life, it didn't make it any easier to accept. Not when death was thrust upon someone against their will by somebody else. Miguel didn't deserve to die like this. Nor did the other three.

Wonder how many children are going to be without their fathers tonight, Alex thought to himself. He continued to wander aimlessly for the next hour or so in the corridor, consumed by his own depressing and guilty thoughts. What was the point of it all? Why bother going on? Alex felt like he had let his people down. And maybe it was God's way of telling him he had failed to fulfill his purpose in life.

Alex reached for his locket again. He stopped and moved to the side of the corridor and leaned against the wall. As he opened the locket and said, "Perdona mis pecados, Padre!" *Pardon my sins, Father!* he heard a voice. It was faint at first, but it gradually grew louder and more insistent.

"You have to keep going," the voice said. "You can't give up now." And in that moment, Alex felt strange, as if he had found a new purpose. He tried to shake his head and make sure he was not dreaming. The voice was only getting clearer and clearer. The depressing thoughts slowly cleared way for more positive ones. He realized that even on the darkest days, there was always something worth fighting for. So he picked himself up and started walking briskly back to his car. He was determined more than ever to fight for his community. He was determined for the first time in his life with so much conviction to fight for a specific cause. A bigger cause that was always overshadowed by so many shortsighted smaller ones over the years that had eventually brought him here at the cost of four lives.

"I am going to make you answer for all this, Derek Fisher!", he muttered quite energetically, pumping his fist.

For the rest of the world, Jason had never met Russell and Emily. Only the three of them and the volunteer who let Jason inside their office knew that Jason had come to meet Russell and Emily in their office a few days before the referendum. The trio spent close to twenty-three hours sieving through giga bytes of accounting data, contracting data, and hundreds of pages of documents, emails, reports, and more. Based mostly on Russell and Emily's memory from their meeting with their team the previous night and the notes they took, they were able to create a conclusion document, which more or less matched word for word with the original document they tried sending to Jason earlier.

Jason took the document back to his office and met with his supervisor, Myra. From his perspective, this was an explosive page one story, and he was ready to write. But it was Myra who stopped him from doing that. Her reasoning was that the conclusions were highly speculative. With so much at stake with TEXIT, what with the congressional ratification pending and the politics behind it all, Myra thought this story would surely be considered a hit piece by most people, especially a hit piece on the pro-TEXIT movement overall. Although the story itself had nothing to do with TEXIT, because of the people it targeted, Myra was worried. Myra also knew that if they were to pursue the investigation to the point of collecting more firsthand quotes or soundbites, she needed to let Jason spend more time on the field, and that meant less time for the low-hanging fruits of the day like TEXIT-related news coverage. After all, news business was becoming a rough one these days, and even *The Austin Star* needed those low-hanging fruits to pay their bills.

Jason, after much deliberation, agreed quite disappointingly to delaying the story. Myra did not ask for his sources. She never did unless he himself volunteered some information. The story got put back in the back burner for lack of time on Jason's part. And he had forgotten about it temporarily. But Myra had not. She knew that this was the kind of story that could do to him and her what the Watergate scandal did to Carl Bernstein and Bob Woodward. Myra wanted to be part of the story. And she just needed to find the right moment.

Meantime, Russell and Emily got busy with their campaigns and rallies that were more in-line with TWRA's main objective.

The wings of the butterfly that fluttered a few weeks ago had set in motion a tiny marble, which had rolled in front of Jason Greer today.

He was sitting with Myra and talking about how his source must have decided to take his story about the Dodson-Newell tiff at the restaurant to *The New York Post* because *The Austin Star* didn't do anything with his lead.

"Jason, *The New York Post* is a tabloid. They could afford to publish whatever they want. One can't really hold them accountable for anything they publish. We are not a tabloid. We have guidelines."

"I know," said Jason. Myra could feel the disappointment in his voice.

As Jason was scrolling thorough *The New York Post* pages in his computer, a photograph on page six struck him. There was a photograph of State Senator Richard Harvey with Governor Fisher, standing with champagne glasses, at what appeared to be a reception of some sorts. Behind them was Abhinav Agarwal, whose face would have skipped many readers' interests, as he was about ten feet away from the main subject of the photo. But Jason spotted him. He scrolled back up to see what the column was about. There was no written piece to go with the photograph. But the photo had a caption: *Texas Politicians, slick with their donors.*

Jason's mind raced to that night at TWRA office. He thought about the data they had collated and the document they had drafted. And how this vast network of corrupt individuals continued to become more and more wealthy and powerful. He wondered why he did not read about or talk about corruption much during his younger days. He wondered if it was because corruption was not this deep-rooted in America back then and if things had progressively changed for the worse. Or with more access to politicians and businessmen in the modern era, people were getting to see corruption more. Either way, he concluded that there was more corruption now than before. He was thinking about the changes that had happened in America to make it a fertile ground for political corruption. But why did political corruption happen?

There were several different theories about the causes of political corruption. One theory posited that corruption was a natural outgrowth of the exercise of power. This view suggested that because those in power have access to resources and privileges that were not available to others, they were more likely to abuse their position for personal gain. Another theory attributed corruption to the structure of government institutions. This view held that certain features of government institutions, such as an excessively centralized bureaucracy or an unaccountable judiciary, created incentives for officials to engage in corrupt practices. Still another theory emphasized the role of cultural factors in explaining why some societies were more corrupt than others. This perspective argued that certain values and norms, such as a belief in individualism or a lack of concern for public welfare, encouraged corrupt behavior. While each of these theories had some merit, it was likely that all played a role in explaining why political corruption occurred in America.

Jason's mind kept bringing back memories of the data they had collected and the voices of Russell and Emily saying there was so many accounting screw-ups that any expert could put together a case against RapFuel. Jason looked at Myra and nodded his head once again as if to let her know that he understood why *The New York Post* could do what they did and why *The Austin Star* could not.

The office was almost empty. Even Myra, who usually ate her lunch at her desk, had a lunch meeting, and left the office. Jason had brought a sandwich from home, and he was nibbling through the corners while staring at the photograph. It was as if there was a calling. He stuffed his sandwich back in the brown bag, wiped his hands with a napkin, took a sip of water, and got up from his seat. He decided he was going to take the rest of the day off, as he wanted to clear his head. He sent a short email to Myra from his phone saying he was not feeling all that well and that he would like to go home.

And then as an afterthought, he added a line before clicking send.

PS: Feel free to call me in case there's something.

Jason stepped outside his office and looked down at the pavement. He noticed the cracks in the concrete, the patches of moss, and the gum that had been trodden into the ground. He looked up at the buildings, some tall and some short, and saw the windows reflecting the sunlight, the people walking past, and the cars driving by. He heard scratching sounds, tires on the road, and horns honking. He also heard people talking. There was something about these sounds. Sounds he had heard before. But they suddenly started to annoy him. He brought both his index fingers and tried covering both his ears. He took a deep breath. With his aural senses temporarily blocked, his mind focused on the olfactory senses. He could smell the pungent exhaust fumes and the aromatic smell of cooking wafting through the windows of the restaurants nearby.

He felt the warm sun on his skin and a breeze blowing through his hair. And for a moment, he just stood there and took it all in, with his ears closed. The breath of fresh air and this solitary moment made Jason forget everything for a few seconds. When he regained his senses, he removed his fingers from his ears. He could still hear people talking. It was still intent. But no longer annoying. He remembered he had a task to complete in the afternoon. He pulled out his phone from his jeans pocket and dialed Emily Chase's number.

"Hey, it's Jason. Jason Greer. Any chance we could meet soon?"

Russell Weston had chosen not to share his number with anyone outside his small-knit activist friends after the authorities started investigating TWRA. Both he and Emily had to surrender his phone to the authorities, who were investigating, and now he had a different number. Emily was using a friend's secondary phone as her primary one for the time being.

Within ninety minutes, Jason was at the Potters Creek Park, about forty miles from Austin. Russell and Emily's car pulled in. They hugged each other and shook hands before finding a quiet spot away from the parking lot. The shade under the tree and its canopy provided a nice shelter. Jason noticed Russell had started growing a beard. He looked different. And Emily was dressed more casually than she normally did. Jason had not shared with them about how closely he followed them since the time they were arrested at the rally.

In fact, Jason found out about the new whereabouts of Russell and Emily only after they were released by the Austin PD. He was waiting when they got out of the precinct, and Jason followed them for more than an hour before seeing them go into a friend's house—the same friend who had come to pick them up from the station. Jason employed his friendly investigative journalistic tactics for the next few days before getting hold of Emily's new number.

"Sorry, you guys are having to go through this. I followed your arrest story. In fact, I was not too far away from you when they pulled you into the sheriff's car. And I was there when you got out. That's how I got hold of your number," said Jason with a sheepish smile.

"I figured you got in touch with the very people we have shared this number with. Good work, Jason. You don't look too bad yourself," said Russell.

"If it's permissible legally. Only if it is, what's going on with TWRA? You guys doing okay?" Jason carefully trudged the subject.

"We are done. At least for now. And how we operated. There is no official TWRA anymore. We have all the legal shit to take care of, man. We're back to being two individual activists who will continue to fight for the causes we believe in. But we have lost access to all our funds." Russell sounded dejected.

"Bastards!" Emily cried, seething with anger.

"I am so sorry." Jason didn't know what else to say.

"They got nothing, man. They know that. It was all planted evidence. It will come out in the courtroom. We won't let those motherfuckers get away with this. I know who they are. We just need proof." Russell sounded very determined to go after those who were responsible for all the unfortunate incidents in their lives recently.

"About that. The reason why I reached out to you is because something clicked today and I wanted to pick up that work we did from where we left off." Jason was a bit hesitant.

"That's when we lost trust in you, Jason. You are all the same. Aren't you? Why did you decide to drop the story? We had something. You agreed we had something big. We put it together, man." Emily wanted to know why Jason and *The Austin Star* never published the story based on the explosive document they produced.

"I apologize. I know. I know. It's too late for all that. But at least I owe you an explanation," said Jason, then went onto explain how Myra prevented him from publishing the story back then because of the timing before the referendum, and why she wanted him to pursue the story by investigating further so he could bring more tangible evidence.

"Myra is so into this story, guys. I know it's hard to convince you right now. But she wants to be part of this. And she wants to get it right. By the way, she doesn't know I am meeting you today. But check this out." Jason opened his phone and opened *The New York Post*. He scrolled to the page where he saw the photograph.

"Recognize these people? This photo was the reason I am talking to you today. Something told me I need to pick up the story again. This was some oil industry gala. From two or three days ago." Jason was very animated.

"What's new here, Jason? I mean. We already knew this right?" Russell.

"Fair enough. But something else about Harvey that I didn't know until recently has made me curious to dig more into his case. So can you guys help me? I promise, I won't let you down this time around." Jason was trying to convince Russell and Emily.

"We have nothing in our possession anymore, Jason. All those documents, our computers, phones, we don't have access to them. Unless you are asking if we want to start from scratch. If that's what we want to do, I was able to retrieve a few documents from my cloud account and I have printed them. Because if I had tried downloading them then it would have been just a matter of time before they tracked that download activity and asked me to hand those over as well," said Emily.

"Not to add, but that would have been an additional crime you would be charged with," Jason informed them.

After a few minutes of blank stares and quiet exchanges of smiles, nods, and heavy breaths, Russell and Emily told Jason that they needed a day or two to think about this. They wanted to figure out how they could offload some of the work they were currently involved with and chalk out a financial support plan for their own survival for the next few months. Jason thought that was a fair ask and told them not to rush into making any decision. And if they were in with his plan to start this new investigation, he would get Myra's buy-in even before they set off. This was to avoid any disappointments later because of Myra's editorial decisions. They hugged one another and slowly made their way back to their cars.

Jason got into his car and picked his phone up to check notifications. There was a missed call from Myra.

Elsewhere in the park, a butterfly fluttered through the air, its wings a kaleidoscope of colors. It floated atop a breeze, drifting lazily from flower to flower.

It was pitch-black outside. The only light came from the moon, which was barely visible through the trees. And what little that scattered through the cracks of the window and the door was all the light inside the house. Ava could barely see Joanna and yet she sensed what she was about to say. It was as if Ava could sense danger for Bradley and Eveline even before Joanna could complete her sentence.

"About that, Joanna?" Ava was curious.

Joanna paused and took a deep breath. She started to explain the recent turn of events in Midland. The cops had taken Bradley for questioning and did not let him go home for the night

This meant Eveline had to be taken care of by the CPS for the night. All Joanna was aware of at that point was that Eveline was in a safe home environment. Rosaline could not visit her yet, as she did not want to raise any suspicion. If Bradley did not cooperate for another day or two, according to Texas state laws, CPS would start looking for a long-term foster home for Eveline. Needless to say, Ava was beginning to tear up, and Joanna could hear audible gasps as she was narrating what she had read in an email Rosaline had sent her earlier that evening.

"No other family in Midland for you?" Joanna asked Ava in a very concerned tone.

"Bradley's parents are in Colorado. My parents? I don't know where they are. Bradley's parents are too sick to travel to Texas," Ava replied.

Ava's mind was full of dark thoughts, and her heart felt heavy with sadness. She thought of Eveline and wondered what she would be doing right now. If she even understood what was going on. The mother in her missed her daughter so much that it felt like a physical ache. She wondered if she was happy, sad, anxious, fearful, or disoriented, if she was eating properly, if she was being bullied at school, and so on. For a moment she imagined herself holding Eveline in her arms tightly, and her mind did not want to let go of that moment.

"Maybe this is the turning point. What kind of mother am I if I am going to let this happen and do nothing about it?" she asked with despair.

"I can't tell you. But you are trying to make a point. You are standing up against an authoritarian rule. You are trying to do your best for hundreds of school children. Maybe this pain you are going through right now. Maybe this is all worth bearing for a few days, you think? I don't know. Think of it as a temporary pain you'd have to put up with, Ava," offered Joanna, who was not the best when it came to providing words of comfort to someone in need.

As the dark thoughts continued to cloud her mind, the mother in Ava kept telling her that she was not doing enough, and she was failing her daughter. Joanna's words about the pain being worth bearing echoed in her ears. The science teacher in her felt a punch in her stomach. She remembered talking to Bradley about the worst thing that could happen to them if the police came for her. They had agreed that the worst thing would be for Ava to spend a few months in prison. The teacher in her drew a parallel between that and where she was now.

Ava got up and walked to the back window and opened it. She gazed out at the vast, dark sky. The clear dark sky was dazzling here and there with bright stars. The dark thoughts in her mind were also dazzling now with bright thoughts.

"I understand, Joanna. This was a choice I made. I need fight till the end."

"The fight is going to get only harder now, Ava. I think it's just a matter of time before they connect you to Rosaline. And by natural order of progression and elimination, they would get to me soon. So I think I may have four to five days, at my pessimistic best, to come up with a relocation plan for you." Joanna was sharing what she thought was the most likely scenario and how they could prepare for it.

"Or ..." Ava trailed off.

"Or what?" asked Joanna.

"What if we put them on the defensive? I do not know why I didn't think of this sooner. Can you leak this situation to someone reliable in the press? Perhaps national media outlets? Or *The Austin Star* even?" Ava asked Joanna with a thought that occurred to her while standing by the window.

"*The Austin Star,* the last bastion of free press in the state of Texas," said Joanna.

Joanna liked the idea. She even acknowledged that Ava, despite being sleep deprived and being stuck in a dark and remote house in the middle of nowhere, had her mind working quite acutely. She took a sip from the bottle of soda she had brought for herself.

"The quickest way to get the story out would be through a tabloid. But it ain't doing any good for any of us. *The Austin Star* is the best bet, I reckon," decided Joanna.

"Will you do this tomorrow?" Ava asked Joanna.

"Of course. First thing in the morning. But I am going to be practical and continue to plan for the worst-case scenario. What if *The Austin Star* doesn't want to take this story up? Or they take one more week before they get it out? I definitely got to come up with a relocation plan. Stay strong, kiddo. I will see you tomorrow." Joanna got up and started walking towards Aba.

She gave a quick tight hug to Ava and gave the same instructions she gave her the previous night. And with that she left the house through the back door and got into her car. The car drove away, its engine a low rumble that gradually receded into the distance. For a moment, all was silent. And then, slowly but surely, the sounds of nature began to assert themselves once again. The rustle of leaves in the wind, the chirping of crickets in the grass—all these sounds reassert themselves, filling the void left by the car.

On the cot, Ava took a bite off that burger Joanna had brought her. It felt like a soothing balm for her wound, a cool breeze on a warm night, a real treat for her starving soul. And then she remembered the last time she and Eveline had gone out to McDonald's and how much fun they had playing a word game. Ava also remembered how Eveline refused to eat burgers that day because she did not want to eat dead animals anymore. When Bradley and Ava thought that this was just a one-day resolution, Eveline continued to surprise them by staying away from eating anything that she knew for sure were made of animal meat.

It had been exactly a week since Edward Coll and Grace Ashworth met with Congressman Evan Williams. The congressman gave them very crisp instructions and had a very specific ask. There was a reason why he had picked

Edward and Grace for this task.

"Well. I need a favor. From both of you. And it involves Derek Fisher." Williams opened his arms and stretched them forward with an arm pointed at each of them.

"As long as it doesn't land me in prison, I am open to listening to your request, congressman," said Edward, looking at Grace.

"Tune us into what you are looking for, congressman," Grace said with a smile. She added, "As long as I continue to remain the queen of Austin socialite club, sure."

Before leaving the restaurant that night, the congressman asked them for a very simple favor. He wanted dirt on Fisher. Edward was picked by Williams because he knew Fisher was a poker player. Not many even in his close circles knew about his habit. If he was in Austin, he made sure he joined his small group of friends every Wednesday for "poker night." There was not much information available about these poker nights, like what stakes did they play for, who all get together along with Fisher, or any wild stories from their encounters. So Williams wanted to use Edward's help in possibly digging some wild scoops from Fisher's weekly poker rendezvous. Grace was picked simply because she was the socialite diva of the Austin circle, and as a woman of supreme talent and taste, who had an inclination to get judgmental of others' personal life choices, she seemed to be particularly attracted to juicy and delicate personal information about those in her in circle. Williams was hoping Grace would be able to identify someone in her social circle who knew someone who in turn knew someone who in turn could find out any Fisher weaknesses of scandalous nature.

For tonight's second meeting, Williams had invited them to a country club. It was a Tuesday evening, and that usually meant there were not many patrons at the club bar. Williams had already notified the club receptionist about the guests he was expecting, so Edward and Grace did not have a problem getting in.

Both Edward and Grace had been to this club many times even though they themselves were not members. So they were not distracted by the opulence of the club—from marble floors to intricate chandeliers, from enormous paintings by masters on the walls to custom-made furniture, none of these posed any distraction to them as they walked to the bar. The staff was attentive as always and they greeted them with glasses of champagne as soon as they entered the bar. There was someone waiting at the welcome desk to take them to the table where Williams was seated, which was far away from the main door, presumably because he wanted this evening to be the least conspicuous public appearance he had ever made.

It was the kind of bar where one could find well-dressed men and women sipping on cocktails and laughing politely at each other's jokes. The kind of place where everyone knew each other's name, but nobody really knew anything about one another. It was the perfect place to go for a stiff drink and some light conversation. There was something about the atmosphere that made it seem like anything and everything was possible.

"Good evening, Mr. Coll and Ms. Ashworth!" Williams greeted them as soon as he saw them walking towards the table.

"Please. Call me Grace."

"How gracious!" Williams retorted quickly.

The three of them sat at the table, with Edward and Grace on one side of the table facing Williams. The waiter handed them the menu and said he would come back in five minutes to get their order.

"Why don't we get our drinks taken care of first before we start discussing our subject?" suggested Williams.

When the waiter came back after five minutes, they ordered what they wanted: cosmopolitan for Grace, gin and tonic for Edward, and an old fashioned for Williams. The waiter was about to ask them if they were going to order some food, but he sensed the mood of the table and of all the individuals seated and decided to move away. Evan Williams did not want to wait too long, not until the waiter brought their drinks, so he started talking. He cut down to the chase.

"Give me the rundown, Edward. Your email was cryptic."

"So Goose meets with about fifteen friends every Wednesday for his poker night

Technically this is a boys-only club. And they keep changing the venue every week, so they don't meet at the same location for two consecutive weeks unless if they decided to meet in December or January, because of holidays. Last week for example, poker night took place at one of the friends' houses."

Edward went on to narrate what he had personally inquired and found out about Derek Fisher's poker habits. With every new piece of information Edward had shared, Williams's jaw kept dropping lower and lower. Next to Edward was Grace, who was also getting to know more about this facet of Goose. Her facial expression did not indicate if she was really shocked by any of this.

After their first meeting a few days ago, the trio had started communicating periodically through email. One of the first things Williams suggested to Edward and Grace was to stop referring to their subject by their real name. "No real name," he had said in that email. He also suggested that they come up with a nickname immediately. And it was Edward who had picked "Goose" for Fisher. Since then, the trio had been referring to Fisher only as Goose. What Williams found out from Edward was stunning and not what he had expected in the least to find out from this operation.

According to Edward, Goose and his group of poker friends belonged to a registered poker club. The club had been operating completely underground as a private one, with the public not having any knowledge of the existence of the same. And as far as Edward could dig into, he could not find Goose's name being associated with the club registration in any form. The poker club had been registered as a game room, which meant gambling regulations of Texas oversaw it. But since the gambling laws in Texas were so complex, it was hard to determine if the specific poker club that Fisher had been part of had done anything that broke the law or not. In addition, Texas law gave counties and cities the authority to create their own ordinances to regulate game rooms that fell under their jurisdictions.

Edward had no idea if this poker club was registered in Austin or in some other location or if the club had a physical address at all. But if the numbers he had heard were true, then the club had been generating profits to the tune of close to two million dollars during the course of the last five years consistently, and it was only after the recent raids in the Harris County involving other game rooms that this club had started reporting slightly lower profits. The Harris County raids opened up a can of worms in terms of how many cities and counties in Texas started interpreting the overall framework for gambling. When private poker clubs reported profits, they were typically from the subscription fee they generated, from alcohol and food sales, et cetera. But this particular club, with a total membership of only twenty or fewer, had been reporting high profits without any of the above. What made this case even more curious for Williams was when he found out that the club had somehow managed to pay zero federal taxes and very minimal state taxes thus far.

What Edward shared next certainly made this whole operation "Dirt on Goose" totally worth the time and effort. This poker club had been directly linked to a PAC, the chairman of which resided in the suburbs of Dallas. And that PAC had been paying off a few county commissioners, sheriffs, city mayors, and even a few city council members in the form of campaign donations. Even though Edward admitted that he had not seen any proof for the PAC link and the donations as yet, he was optimistic that his sources were reliable, and he would totally trust them to provide the required evidence before their next meeting.

"Wow. That's something, Mr. Coll. Impressive," said Williams, still in shock.

"Edward. You may call me Edward, congressman."

Both Evan and Grace gulped down what was left in their glasses, and Williams signaled to the waiter for a repeat. Taking the cue, both Edward and Grace did the same.

"Unfortunately, I don't have much time. So if there is any kind of evidence you can bring that may link the Goose to any of this what you just mentioned, let's say, within a week or so, I would really appreciate it," said Williams.

"Just a week? Now your demands are increasingly putting pressure on us, congressman. What are we getting in return?" Edward smiled and asked the question that had been lingering in his mind since he met Evan Williams the first time a few days ago.

"Yes. I would like to know that, too. If you don't mind . . ." Grace joined Edward in a playful but serious tone.

"Well. Let's just say I will have an open door for you in the first President of Texas's office. I don't forget people who do me crucial favors like this, ever. This one, if you are right, will not only bring down the Goose but will ensure we—I hope you know who I am talking about—we have a clear path to presidency." Williams was pretty honest about the quid pro quo, as he laid it out openly.

"And what if you don't ever go near the presidency? Even after all that we do for you?" Grace asked.

"Good question. Give me a number. Or tell me what you want. I will see what I can do. Like I said, I don't forget people who do me crucial favors ever." Williams smiled.

"Fair enough!" Edward said.

"So, Grace, if I may, do you have anything for me?" Williams turned towards her.

"As a matter of fact, I do. I very much do. This doesn't involve the Goose. But the Gander." Grace let out a mischievous smile.

"Ooooh. I bet your story is going to be more interesting than Edward's," said Williams.

Grace then went on to share what she was able to find out about the

Goose. It did not take long for Grace to learn that things were once not all that well between the Goose and the Gander, and they were about to go their separate ways. This was in the first year after their move to Austin in their official capacity. Apparently, the Gander, who was completely lost in the high that her newfound power lifestyle gave her after they moved to Austin, was looking for ways to keep herself occupied. With the Goose being away from her most of the time, she got more and more desperate and, in the process, ended up getting a little raunchy with a Secret Service agent in her own house. And this continued for three months before someone let the secret out to the Goose himself.

The Goose and the Gander had a major blowout, which was witnessed by most of the domestic staff, and they decided to separate. But then two of the Goose's advisors, who were also very close family friends from their pre-Austin days, stepped in and made them reconsider their decision for the sake of the future of their own fortune and for the that of their future in an independent Texas. Grace mentioned that this was an open secret among all his close associates and the domestic staff. But what also surprised all of them who were privy to the blowout was how quickly they learned to put this behind them and managed to put on a picture-perfect portrayal of a power couple in love in the public eye.

"Trust Grace to come up with the juiciest story of the evening." Edward winked at Grace.

"That's true. Grace, this Is an amazing scoop. I mean, I don't mean any harm to their relationship. Bless their loving souls and all that. My God, how did I not know about this? This is incredible." Williams still could not believe his luck. He didn't think this operation would give him two explosive dirt bombs on the Goose in such a short time. He continued, "Same ask as Edward. Any proof you can bring me within a week will be greatly appreciated. My next move, my success—our success—depends on the proof I can lay my hands on."

"Understood, congressman," Grace responded politely.

"Excuse me, Edward and Grace. Now, if you don't mind, I have to get on a call right now. I will email you about our next meeting. This has been a very productive evening. Until we meet again." Williams got up from his chair, shook hands with his guests, and left.

When the waiter came back to check with Edward and Grace if they wanted anything else, they looked at each other and said no. The waiter told them that the congressman had already taken care of the check and it was his pleasure serving them tonight.

"He's an interesting man, isn't he?" Edward asked Grace.

"That's the only kind you see in politics. If you're not interesting, you're not cut out for politics, are you?" observed Grace.

"You are right!"

As the light started to fade inside the bar, the few customers still there ordered their last drinks. The music had been turned off. The only sound inside the bar was the soft clinking of glasses and the occasional scattered bursts of laughter. But soon even that would come to an end for the night. When Grace and Edward said goodbye to each other and got into their respective cars, the parking lot was almost empty. The fluorescent lights above the asphalt laid parking lot buzzed, casting a harsh glow over the empty lot. A solitary moth fluttered around the light, its wings casting delicate shadows on the ground.

The overnight rain had left the streets of Washington, DC gleaming in the morning light. Puddles had formed in the dips and depressions of the asphalt, and the gutters were overflowing with fast-moving streams of water. Cars drove through the puddles with a splash, sending up arcs of sparkling droplets. The air was fresh and clean, filled with the smell of wet pavement and damp leaves. Even the city seemed to be holding its breath, waiting for the sun to come out and dry up the evidence of the storm. Outside the Capitol Building was the usual security corridor of policemen and women guarding the place, while a few tourists braved the weather and the road conditions and reached the area early in the morning for photographs that could tell their story of the city from different perspectives.

Inside the Capitol was Senator Newell, huddled in his office with a couple of his senior staff members. One of them was drafting an email to be sent to the fifteen congressmen who were going to decide the future of Texas. Newell had to work clandestinely on this proposal, as none of them should find out that he was working against the ratification of TEXIT. And Senator Brynes had agreed to be the front for his proposal. The other staff member was preparing a proposal document. This proposal was not going to be shared with anyone in written form, but Newell wanted to put his proposal on paper so the fifteen congressmen and women would know the seriousness of the same.

It was Senator Brynes's idea to create a counterproposal for Williams's proposal. What Brynes was offering through the proposal to the fifteen congressmen and women who were undecided until then was in the scale of the notorious Teapot Dome scandal—an opportunity to bid at lower rates for a handful of oil of projects for the next twenty years. Of course, the whole proposal was for Texas oil projects only and Newell was relying on his connections in the oil industry to deliver the goods for him when he had to use this card to play and when the time came. Senator Brynes would present this proposal as if it were his, and he was doing it on behalf of a few oil companies who were not keen on an independent Texas, as they did not want to bet on an optimistic future for an independent Texas based on the nonexistent trade policies and trade agreements.

Senator Newell reviewed the draft proposal, and he asked the staff member to make a couple of minor corrections. Once he got the revised proposal, he quickly gave his approval. He asked the staff member to print just a single copy, seal it in a confidential envelope, and drop it off at Brynes's office. Meanwhile, the other staff member asked Newell if the draft email she had composed was good enough to be sent to Senator Brynes's office communication secretary.

This was the email that Senator Brynes would send to the fifteen congressmen and women inviting them for a very important one-on-one meeting to discuss confidential matters related to TEXIT ratification. Newell approved that draft email.

The moment he said that the draft email was good to go, he noticed that he had a notification on his phone about a new email.

It was from Vanessa Glass.

When Senator Newell opened his email app on his phone, clicked on the new email, and read it, he felt a sense of anguish and frustration rushing through his body. Quite unaware of his surroundings for a moment, he shook his head. The two staff members who were still sitting with him in his room did not miss noticing his body language.

"Hope everything is all right, senator.", one of them said.

"Umm. Yes. I think, so." The senator lifted his head from the phone and responded, "It turns out there is going to be some delay in getting the good news I am expecting."

The short email from Vanessa simply read:

How much time do I have?

Senator Newell quickly typed a response. Equally short.

Assuming Congress ratifies, you have until the day after ratification.

CHAPTER 9

THE REFERENDUM

The Derek Fisher Administration had declared the voting day a state holiday. He wanted Texans to take the referendum seriously. And they sure did if the early voting percentage was to go by. Texans take their elections seriously in general. More seriously than many other states. The polls were open from 7:00 AM to 7:00 PM, giving everyone plenty of time to cast their vote. By 10:30 AM, there was one count that reported the overall voting percentage in the state was already close to twenty-five percent. It was a warm day in Texas, and to state that the sun beating down on this summer day was as redundant as saying Fisher was hoping the yes votes would beat the no votes. The air was thick with humidity, and the smell of barbecue wafted through the air. 10:30 AM was not too early for barbecue in Texas. There were makeshift vendors with their grills on the curbs selling barbecues with sides in their makeshift food carts near many polling stations. But despite the heat, people were lined up at polling stations across the state, eager to exercise their right to vote on this critical matter of independence for Texas. This truly was a big day that would determine the future of Texas, and many were proud to make their voices heard. Some had been waiting for hours, but they didn't mind. They knew that their vote could make a difference.

Like with all elections, election workers were an essential part of the democratic process. The referendum day was no different. Amid the bustle of this most important day in Texas were the election workers, who played a vital role in ensuring that the process ran smoothly. Many of them were volunteers, giving up their time to ensure that then democratic process thrived. The day before the referendum, they could be seen setting up poll booths. On the day of the referendum, they could be seen checking voter registrations, and handing out "I Voted" stickers after each person registered their vote. It was usually a long day for them, but their efforts were essential in ensuring that everyone had a chance to have their say. Some of the workers in remote polling stations would have to stay late to transport the polling boxes to the nearest authorized counting centers.

Derek Fisher and his wife Gloria were in line early in the morning at their assigned polling station, and they were the first ones to vote in their polling station in Austin. At about noon, Fisher had called his chief of staff to give him the latest voting numbers. He was very encouraged to learn that the voting percentage had crossed thirty-three percent by noon. In the last general elections, in which Fisher ran and won, the voting percentage by noon was only twenty-one percent. He thought this was an encouraging sign for the pro-TEXIT side of the referendum.

Elsewhere in Austin, Senator Richard Harvey just got off the phone with Congresswoman Sima Daly. Sima had called to check on Harvey's assessment on how his campaign for TEXIT would play out. Harvey was very optimistic that he could swing at least fifty-five to sixty percent of his supporters in his constituency to the yes camp all within a few days since he got onboard. Two weeks since the day Daly quite skillfully blackmailed Harvey into becoming a TEXIT loyalist and a committed public face on Fisher's platform campaigning for TEXIT, the fifty-five to sixty percent assessment that Richard Harvey gave matched with Sima's internal team's projection.

When Sima had met Fisher prior to her meeting with Harvey and made the deal, it was clear to her that Fisher was really needing some help to get past the threshold of sixty-seven percent. All his internal polling showed that the pro-TEXIT side would very narrowly go past the sixty-seven percent but they all had a +/- two percent margin of error, which was always the error range that made all politicians nervous. Fisher needed help wherever he could. And one of the areas he was hoping he could get help was from the moderate conservative camp—that is, those who identified more with Richard Harvey's platform as well as Senator Albert Newell's. His need from these camps was more than his need from his own or Ryan Dodson's camps for that matter.

So when Sima assured Fisher that she could deliver a small chunk of that gap he was worried about, he was elated. Sima didn't ask for anything in return, and she was hoping that it was understood. She had not set her eyes on making long-term ambitions yet. She wanted to keep her options open. Her reasoning was, what if it was Dodson who became the first president? She needed Dodson to know that she was the person to go to at the Austin Capitol should he need a deal to be closed, or should he need to huddle for a few votes. Having observed how her father dealt with politicians and the kind of advice he usually gave them; she knew that it was always prudent to not pick a horse she wanted to bet on too early in the race. "Wait till you run out of options and your gut would tell you," he often advised. That was what she was holding dear to her heart.

It would be nice to be on the Fisher ticket, but what does that really get me in the long run? she asked herself. Her rationale was if she waited out either as an outsider but as a strong ally of whoever became the next president, she could play her cards carefully when her chance came a few years from now. Her gut told her that no matter who became first President of Texas, the first few years were going to be turbulent. S, when she assured Fisher that she would deliver a good chunk of Harvey voters for him, she did not want to really make a deal with Fisher. She knew what she may ask him could be much bigger if she waited it out.

It was 6:00 PM.

The polls would be closing in an hour. There were lines of people snaking out the door of many a school gymnasium or cafeteria, all eager to have their voices heard. There was a sense of excitement in the air, a feeling that anything was possible. For the next few hours, all eyes would be glued to the television screens, waiting for the results to come in. It was an exciting time, full of hope and possibility for many Texans. No matter what the outcome was going to be, the sentiment of majority of Texans was pro-TEXIT. The only challenge for the pro-TEXITers was if enough Texans came out to vote. As many experts had been saying, the results of the referendum could come down to a few counties, so every vote would make a difference.

It was 7:00 PM. The polls were closed. As per the Texas election laws, if people were already in line at 7:00 PM, they would still be allowed to enter the polling station to cast their ballots. Many polling stations had people waiting in line. So by the time all voters cast their ballots, it was 7:45 PM. The official time of the last voter in Texas to cast his ballot was 7:57 PM, and it was at a polling station in Houston. The election counting process was always a long and complicated one, with many different steps involved. The referendum vote counting would follow the same process. The first step was to collect all the ballots from the polling stations. Once all the ballots had been collected, they were brought to the election office or an official counting center in the county, where they were sorted by precinct. Once the ballots were sorted, they were counted by a machine. After the machine counting is complete, a team of human observers checked the results to make sure that they were accurate. Finally, the results were finalized at the county level, certified by the local election board, and then sent to the Secretary of State. The Secretary of State's office officially announced the results to the public. The entire process could take a few days to complete. Unlike other elections, since this was a choice between yes and no, and there were no political party observers needed at the counting premises, some of the bureaucratic delays associated with these steps could be reduced. The best-case scenario for the referendum results to be announced officially would be thirty-six hours from poll closing time. But unofficially, through exit polls and other means, TV networks and other media outlets could be calling the results of the referendum much earlier than that.

Fisher was having a quiet dinner with Gloria that evening. The butlers were asked to serve their meal and leave the dining hall. The Fishers had an iPad on the table, and their son from Italy was on a video call. He was curious to know how the referendum went and wanted to check how his father was doing. Since there was no absentee ballot or mail-in voting option for this referendum, he could not really make his voice heard in the referendum. If the pro-TEXIT lost the referendum with a very thin margin, then Fisher would probably regret his fight to eliminate mail-in ballots and absentee ballots. This was something he fought for during his election and was one of his campaign promises. He and the state legislature were able to work through a series of election reform bills during his first year in the office. One of them was eliminating absentee ballots and mail-in ballots all together.

It was 2:15 AM in Italy, but Chris Fisher was not asleep. He said he was nervous for his father. Fisher assured him he was doing well and feeling very optimistic. He was going to wait for AP's official call before celebrating. Gloria was eating her meal silently. She would occasionally interrupt the conversation between the son and father by asking her son about his health, his food, his tests, et cetera. When Derek and Gloria finished their meal, they waved goodbye to Chris and moved to their family room. Governor Derek Fisher sat on a couch with his iPad and phone next to him.

Gloria sat on the love seat right next to the couch with a book and stretched herself comfortably within a few minutes. The TV was on. Derek Fisher was flipping through the channels and stopped when Fox News came on. He opened his iPad and opened the CNN website. On his phone, he opened his X (Twitter) newsfeed. With access to three different sources of information, Fisher called out for his butler to fix him a drink. When the panel on Fox News said that they expected to release their first official projections at 9:30 PM Central Time, the butler brought Fisher's staple drink for this time of the night. Bourbon on rocks. Served with exactly three ice cubes.

Fisher's phone rang. It was his chief of staff, who wanted to know if he should keep any of his cabinet members on call should there be a need. He Fisher discussed a couple of options, and they both agreed that it would be prudent on their part to have all his cabinet members on call in case there was a need to meet later that night. Gloria's breathing increased to a heavier but more rhythmic pattern. Fisher turned around and looked at her eyes being closed, realizing she had already gone to a state of deep sleep.

The governor had issued strict instructions to his chief of staff not to call him with any early results that he may have obtained from multiple sources. Fisher wanted to go through the emotions of following the results live like every single Texan. At 9:40 PM, the chyron on Fox News changed. And the camera cut to the panel again, with the lead anchor speaking.

"Today was an historic day in Texas. In a record voter turnout in the state of Texas, seventy-seven of voters came out to vote for the TEXIT referendum today. That's twelve percent more than the voter turnout in our last general election. This is amazing. A cause of celebration. And what have they all said? Well. Our sources at AP say that AP is not ready to call the results yet. This is not unusual. This has happened in the past, too, when the results were too close to call, or when they were too close and there was fear of the projected losing party resorting to violent means to exhibit their unpleasantness. Because of the potential consequence it may have if the early projection of the results turns out to be incorrect, AP just announced that they would make the call only after their data analysts feel absolutely sure. So, stay tuned."

Derek Fisher had already moved on to his second drink for the night. It was 11:00 PM. Gloria had not moved an inch, and her breathing had settled into a much more restful pattern. Fisher closed his phone and was reading an article on CNN that was unrelated to the referendum. The load of a million thoughts and the dread of being at an historical moment bore heavy on Fisher, and he let out a long yawn.

Somewhere else in Western Texas, Burl Fogg was opening a bottle of beer. His third one for the night. He was sitting on his couch in his living room, his mom on a single seater chair, and his dog on the carpet, lying very close to his feet. He took the remote and was looking to take a break from following election results. He found a channel playing the movie *Independence Day* and stopped. This was one of his favorite movies of all time. He smiled when he saw Will Smith and Jeff Goldblum light their cigars.

"Do you think they have any clue what's about to happen to them?"

"Haha. Not a chance in hell. Good night!"

Burl decided to stay with the movie. No matter how many times he may have watched i6, he still got sucked into it whenever he saw it playing somewhere. As he settled down, his phone rang. He picked up to see it was his buddy Dudley.

"Dude, looks like they are going to call it finally. Get ready!" Dudley shared an update he had just received.

Burl halfheartedly decided to forego his fifty-first viewing the film and flipped through his remote to Fox News.

It was 11:20 PM.

"The wait is finally over. AP is ready to project. Based on AP's projected results and projected results from two other sources, we at Fox News are ready to call it. The referendum passes by a margin of seventy to thirty percent. The final percentages may vary. But yes, Texas is on its way to gaining its independence for the first time since joining the Union on December 29th, 1845. There are many more steps to cross before Texas becomes its own nation. But what happened today is truly historic. I can't control my emotions," the anchor said as he started to visibly shake in happiness in front of the camera. The camera cut to a live feed in front of the Austin Capitol. There was already a large crowd that had gathered there, and they started celebrating loudly with applause and cheers. Fireworks were lit at a distance.

Inside the governor's mansion, Derek Fisher saw the projection on TV and got up from the couch, pumping his fist to celebrate. A couple of butlers who were following the results from the kitchen let out a scream in celebration. The noise made Gloria wake up. It did not take long for everything to register in her. She looked at Derek and broke a smile. He went near her and gave her a tight hug, and they pecked one another on the lips quickly.

"You did it, honey!" Gloria congratulated her.

"*We* did it. We have a promising future to look forward to, Gloria," said Derek Fisher, sounding quite excited.

He called the chief of staff and told him that there wouldn't be a need to meet the cabinet tonight, and he could release them from the on-call list for the night.

"Congratulations, governor! We did it!" announced the chief of staff, trying to shake Fisher's hands.

"Congratulations! And thank you for everything," said Fisher.

Somewhere else in Austin, Dodson and Williams were following the results on TV in a hotel room. As soon as Fox News made the official projection, they both poured themselves another shot of Tequila, said a toast to the future of Texas, took a swig, and shook each other's hands.

They called Governor Fisher to wish him well immediately. Although he had not planned this party out yet, Fisher invited them both to a dinner celebration the day after tomorrow. They agreed. The thin walls of the hotel room continued to absorb fumes from the alcohol.

Soon, Governor Derek Fisher also invited Senator Newell for the dinner he was throwing the day after tomorrow. In fact, Newell was the first one to call Fisher as soon as he heard of the AP results through another source. By the time he got to speak to Fisher after multiple missed calls, Fisher himself had found out about the results. So it was not surprising for Newell to catch him in high spirits. It was Sima and Richard Harvey who spoke to Fisher after Newell. They had decided to dial in together through a conference bridge, and called Fisher to congratulate him.

"You delivered as promised, Harvey! I owe you one," Fisher thanked Harvey.

"I told ya. The boy has got the goods." Sima smiled through the phone.

"He certainly has, Sima. He certainly has," agreed Fisher.

"Congratulations, governor!" said Harvey in a slightly nervous yet relieved tone.

"Oh! Look who is here. Thank you, Senator Harvey. You did us a huge favor. I will find ways to thank you sooner than you think," said Fisher

"You're welcome, governor, and soon-to-be-President of Texas!" Harvey smiled this time around.

A pregnant woman's mood was often hard to decipher. She may be elated one minute and crying the next. Her emotions might be all over the place, and she may have difficulty concentrating or sleeping. However, there was one constant mood that pregnant women seemed to experience: happiness. Despite the challenges of pregnancy, most women report feeling happy during this time. They enjoy the process of creating new life and feel a sense of connection to their baby. This sense of happiness often continued after the baby was born, making pregnancy an incredibly special time for both mother and child.

Lisa Barkley did not belong to that group of women who experienced happiness during pregnancy. Since the day she found out she was pregnant, she had been going through only the worst. Being a single mother of a young girl was only making things very difficult for her. She managed to get into her eighth week of pregnancy without letting anyone finding about her health condition—not even Lily. She worked at a local attorney's office as a receptionist for thirty hours a week, and she did not have to interact with too many coworkers in the office. But she knew she could not go on for long without others finding out about it.

She thought of spending the rest of her pregnancy at her mom's place, which was about two hours from San Antonio. But she didn't want her mom to find out all the problems she had been having with Caleb. So she had decided that the best course would be for her to continue to work, manage Lily with the little help she got from Caleb twice a week, and utilize her neighbor's help for the rest of the time whenever she needed, as long as she could. She was not mentally ready to have the second child as of yet. But she was fully aware that the only thing she could not stop was time. And with every passing day, the embryo in her womb was slowly growing into a human being.

Lisa worked through her nausea and vomiting during the first trimester of Lily's pregnancy, and with the second child, it seemed it was a little different. She did not have perpetual nausea, but she had vomiting. She seemed to have an upset stomach more often and the abdominal cramps that were far and few during Lily's pregnancy were now more frequent. But what made all these miserable for Lisa was the dizziness and the extreme fatigue that accompanied them. She did not experience this kind of dizziness or fatigue while carrying Lily. The dizziness was the one she found it difficult to manage. She had talked to her ob-gyn about her these symptoms and had been taking over-the-counter medications and supplements prescribed by her. None of which seemed to help, as it got progressively worse. And today, for the first time, Lisa was beginning to get worried if hospitalization may be necessary. She called her doctor's office and managed to get an appointment for the same day, citing emergency.

Caleb had not been in touch with Lisa since she showed up at his workplace unannounced. He kept lamenting with his friends that Lisa embarrassed him in front of his coworkers and supervisor. Lisa had not bothered to drop Lily off with him the past three weeks since that encounter. She did not want to give Caleb any power to make any decisions for her with this pregnancy. She wanted Caleb to know that he inseminated her without her consent and that had resulted in her becoming pregnant. And that she was prepared to take any legal action needed against Caleb for violating her privacy and for raping her. The more distant Caleb stayed away from her, the stronger her case against him became. Or so she thought.

Caleb, on the other hand, did miss seeing Lily. He felt a void in his weekly routine. Tuesdays and Thursdays were not the same for the past three weeks because she was not with him. He missed taking her out to her favorite pizza diner and getting her a root beer float. He missed the two hours he got to spend every Thursday evening at an arcade with her, when he transformed into a child, dropping coins in the slots of those arcade game machines, collecting those winning tickets, and counting them at the end of the night to see if they could buy another soft toy or a packet of candy. He missed reading her a book and giving her a good night hug. Caleb managed the first week without seeing Lily at all because he was so angry with Lisa. But things became a bit harder in the second week, so he would try to take a sneak peek at Lily from a distance when Lisa would come to drop her off at school in the morning. It was in the third week that he really started to feel her absence. Lily gave him some structure to the week. He realized he had lost that structure now that she was not coming to see him.

Lisa arrived for her appointment a few minutes early. Lily was at school. She filled out the necessary paperwork and took a seat in the waiting room. She remembered running into Gavin Forbes and his wife during her last visit. After a short wait, the nurse called her in. She took her to the examination room. Lisa changed into a gown and got up on the exam table. The nurse asked her some questions, filled a form with her notes for the ob-gyn to read, and took her vitals. The ob-gyn came in five minutes after the nurse left the exam room. She started asking Lisa the basic questions, and asked her what specifically brought her there that day. The nurse's notes already made it clear to the doctor that the fatigue was becoming a bit too much for her to handle. Based on Lisa's specific answers to the questions she asked, the doctor concluded she needed to do more tests. So the ob-gyn called the nurse again to bring her a few more equipment.

The doctor ran a couple of more tests on Lisa. Ultrasonography and beta-hCG measurement. She also asked Lisa to give them a urine sample for additional confirmation through a urine pregnancy test. The ob-gyn was almost certain that an ectopic pregnancy may have occurred in her case based on the symptoms she had been sharing. But these tests pretty much confirmed that to the doctor. The doctor finished all the tests and asked Lisa to change back to her regular clothes. Lisa was told to meet the doctor in another private room, to which the nurse would take her once she was ready. Lisa was nervous when she entered the private office of her ob-gyn.

"Come on in, Lisa!" the doctor said.

"Thank you."

"Is your husband with you today?" the doctor asked her.

"No. He won't be coming here. Ever."

"Anyone else? Friend or family accompanied you?"

"No, doctor. I drove alone." Lisa was not sure why her doctor was asking all these questions, and her mind had already started imaging something terrible.

"I usually do not share this if the patient is alone. But I do know your situation. So . . ." The doctor paused.

"Are you going to share some bad news, doctor?" Lisa's eyes were welling up.

"I guess so, Lisa. I am afraid an ectopic pregnancy has occurred in your case." The doctor did not want to prolong this any further.

"What does that mean?" Lisa had no idea what an ectopic pregnancy was.

The doctor went onto explain how an ectopic pregnancy occurred. She told Lisa it occurred when a fertilized egg becomes implanted outside of the uterus. And that it was a serious medical condition. In most cases, the doctor said the egg was implanted in the fallopian tubes, but sometimes it could also occur in the ovaries, cervix, or abdominal cavity. If left untreated or if right treatment was not made available or the pregnant woman did not respond to any treatment, an ectopic pregnancy could be life-threatening.

"So what does this all mean, doctor? Is the baby going to be okay?" asked

Lisa, trying to compose herself.

"Ectopic pregnancy is a dangerous thing to begin with. In your case, even if the child somehow makes it through the first month of your third trimester, you will not make it." The ob-gyn was once again keeping it simple and did not try to sugarcoat the dire situation.

"I could die?" clarified Lisa.

"Yes. If you and the baby somehow make it till the third trimester, then the risk to your life increases much more, and I may not have too many choices to treat you that late."

"What do you recommend I do, doctor?" Lisa wanted to know what she should be doing.

"Listen. I practice medicine in the state of Texas. I cannot recommend anything that is considered illegal in the state." The doctor paused.

Lisa Barkley understood what the doctor was implying. Even though she did not remember the specific medical term for ectopic pregnancies, she had heard of them and how women have had to make very painful decisions of aborting their pregnancies in rare cases like these, in order to save themselves and to potentially keep their bodies healthy for future pregnancies.

"Is that the only option?" asked Lisa.

"I did not tell you anything. And you did not get any recommendation from me. Got it?" The doctor looked her in the eye. "If I were to recommend the medically right course of action, I risk losing my license."

"I understand, doctor."

"And after today's referendum, we do not know how things will shape. And how deep this legislative control over women's bodies will grow. There may be more restrictions coming along. I don't know. The bottom line is I do not have the strength or boldness to stand up for what I feel is right against the state. The medical practitioner's conscience in me will never forgive me. But I have two kids and a family to go to in the evening whom I don't want to lose," the doctor confessed in a very compassionate and apologetic tone.

"I am not suggesting or putting words in your mouth, doctor. I just wanted to make sure I understood what you said." Lisa wiped her tears.

"You did, Lisa. You sure did."

Before Lisa left the office, the doctor gave her a prescription. She asked Lisa to take those medicines for the next two weeks or so, before she decided the next steps. She wished Lisa the best. Lisa moved two steps forward to grab the prescription sheets from the doctor's hands and realized there were two sheets. On the top sheet were the medicine names, dosage, recommended interval, et cetera. There was another sheet below the prescription. That sheet also had handwritten notes from the doctor but that did not look like a prescription. Lisa read it carefully.

Contact Russell Weston and Emily Chase at TWRA. This is their email ID. Note this information down on your phone and give this sheet of paper back to me right now.

Lisa looked at the doctor, who nodded with a tight lip. It was as if she were asking Lisa to hurry up and copy the details onto her phone quickly. Lisa did just that. And she gave that sheet of paper back to the doctor and left.

The ob-gyn tore that sheet of paper she got back from Lisa into tiny bits with her hands and shoved the torn pieces into the right pocket of the white hospital coat she was wearing.

Richard Harvey had had life experiences ranging from love, breakup, loss, sadness, achievement, betrayal, et cetera. There was a special kind of pain that came with betrayal though. It was a sharp stab to the heart that leaves one reeling, struggling to understand how someone they trusted could hurt them so deeply. It was a deep-seated anger that burned hotter than any other, fueled by a sense of anger and hatred. And it's a feeling of profound sadness because betrayal always carried with it the sting of loss. When someone close betrayed one's trust, it felt like a part of one's very soul had been ripped away.

They feel numb and lost, like they'll never be able to trust anyone again. And some betrayal more than others makes it hard to breathe.

He had been around in the finance industry for a while and had his share of professional betrayals. They were very hurtful as soon as the act happened, but he could get over those situations. Because, even amid pain, there was hope for him. These situations helped him see the world more clearly and to build better professional relationships that were based on trust and respect. Pain caused by personal betrayals, on the other hand, were not easy to forget. Harvey was no exception. Every time someone he trusted or knew well personally did some backstabbing, he found it extremely difficult to reconcile or to forgive that person. But what Sima had done to him belonged to a different betrayal bucket as far as Harvey was concerned

He was seething in rage one moment and plotting vengeance the other. He was sad one moment for losing a mentor whom he could trust and frustrated with himself the other for letting his guard down. There was nothing Sima could do now that would make Harvey rebuild the kind of relationship he had with her before the blackmailing incident.

Meanwhile, Sima was fully aware of what Harvey may have been going through. She knew she caught him completely off-guard by setting him up for that weak moment and capturing it on video. She personally did not care much for Harvey's sexual orientation, but she also knew how much her voters cared for Harvey's sexual preferences. The conservative movement around the country had made significant strides backwards in recent years on many social issues. Women's rights, homosexuality, anti-trans movements were three major social issues on which the conservative movement had set its eyes on.

For many conservatives, the very idea of gay marriage was still an affront to traditional values. And thanks largely to a certain kind of politicians who have chosen to wage a cultural war using issues such as these, and take advantage of the spewing hatred, the conservatives around the country had gone back to ramping up the old belief that marriage should be only between a man and a woman, and that homosexual relationships and transsexual proclivities were an abomination in the eyes of God. Texas conservatives were ranked among the top two or three in the country when it came to becoming increasingly vocal in their opposition to gay rights, including the right to marry. There had been instances in recent past where this anger had turned violent with conservatives attacking LGBTQ individuals, especially trans people, and vandalizing their property. There were even half a dozen shootings at gay gatherings in Texas, especially at gay bars, in the last six months or so. The second amendment protectionism combined with homophobic and transphobic anger were slowly pushing the lives of the LGBTQAI community over the edge in Texas.

Sima had been living and breathing the conservative way of life from the day she was born, and she could not miss a beat when it came to the conservative cultural mood in Texas, for she knew that it was unlikely that the conservative movement would ever fully accept homosexuality. So, using Richard Harvey's sexual orientation—which, when leaked to public, could cause a huge conservative uproar and thereby make him resign his public office immediately—as her blackmail card, to make him support TEXIT more vocally. As much as a part of her was feeling guilty for what she had become, the more ambitious part of her was proud of her own work for being able to pull this off.

The evening after Sima met Harvey at the library and threatened him with the video, he was seen at the same bar again. He was at his usual seat and trying to replay that night's events. How he met Aaron Naylor, and how easy it was for him to fall for Aaron. Harvey was doing some self-introspection as the bartender kept coming back for refills. Something told him that even though Aaron was there to perform his task and deliver the goods for Sima, he was really attracted to Harvey. And Richard was not someone who would easily take a conversation he had with a stranger at a bar to his bedroom the same night. He, too, felt something for Aaron. When they parted the next morning, they had promised each other that they would meet again the next month. Which was why it kept bothering him that he could not see through Aaron's play. Not for a second.

Today was the day of referendum. Most of the conservative politicians of the state were either anxious or excited. But not Harvey. He was in a particularly somber mood and avoided all social obligations. He went out to vote first thing in the morning and made sure there were photographers who were able to capture the moment he walked out of his polling station. And after that, he cocooned himself in his bedroom, bracing for the results. Harvey was not sure which was better for his political future—the referendum passing or not. He had not shared the deal he had had with Sima with anyone in his circle of political advisors. After all, Sima was supposed to be his primary advisor. So this deliberation about his future within the party was something he had to do on his own.

He so wished he had his mom by his side. Not that he relied on his mom for her political wisdom or her insightful strategies, but he relied on her to lend her shoulders to lean onto. She was the only in the whole world Harvey could consider as his confidante, someone who empathized with his feelings no matter what he went through. Long before he discovered his own sexuality, his mom knew. And when he decided to come out to his mom, who raised him as a single parent after the divorce, he really did not have to say anything. It was as if his mom understood he was ready to talk about it. They just spoke through their eyes, and Harvey had happy tears rolling along his cheeks the moment his mom said, "I knew. And I will always love you." Richard Harvey was nineteen then. He had grown a bit distant from his mom in the past few years and that was because he was lost in his world of ambitions and greed.

Harvey turned his phone off as soon as he came home after voting. And he did not turn it on until the polls closed. The first call he received as soon as that happened and after he turned his phone on was from Sima. She wanted to prepare him for the call with Derek Fisher later that night. She had a script prepared for both the scenarios. She told Harvey he did not have to say much if the referendum passed, as Fisher was likely to be in a congratulatory mood and not much would register. On the other hand, should the referendum fail, she said, Harvey may have to do some analytical talk to boost Fisher's morale and should be ready to answer some questions, which Fisher was likely to ask. When she hung up, Harvey's calm mind was once again reminded of the betrayal. He yelled "Bitch!" and threw his phone on the bed.

Meanwhile, somewhere else, in Corpus Christi to be precise, Sima was getting on with her day. It was a big day for the state of Texas, so she had called all her staff members to come to her office in the evening after 5:00 PM, and after they all had voted. She wanted to have a poll closing happy hour and then have a result watch party with her staff. It was a sort of tradition her father had created in his office, even if he never ran for public office. Election evenings were celebratory times in the Daly office.

"Meghan, is everyone in the office? How much more time should we give before we open the bar?" Sima Daly asked her assistant.

"Yes. Except Aaron Naylor," replied Meghan.

"That's pretty good attendance then. Let's get rock and rolling. I will join you guys in a minute," Sima said, raising her arms and swaying her body from her sitting position.

"I will let the bartender know. About Aaron, ma'am. This is probably not the best time to let you know of this. Aaron has not been coming to the office for more than three days, and there has been no communication from him at all. His contract for his internship with us doesn't end for another month. So, knowing him, if he was leaving for another job, I am sure he would have said something. Tried calling him and emailing him. No word. I thought you should know." Meghan sounded very concerned about Aaron.

"This is serious, Meghan. I'm concerned. Thank you for sharing this. But you could have said something about this sooner. Have you sent trackers for him? Make sure all Ts are crossed and Is are dotted. I will follow up with you on this tomorrow again." Sima got up from her seat to join her staff for the poll closing happy hour.

Sima tried to shake the feeling of unease that had taken root in her mind. It was silly, she told herself, to be worried about Aaron. He was a grown man, after all, and interning with her for a while. Surely, he was entitled to take a couple of days off without letting her know, she thought. Or maybe he had personal issues he could not share with anyone. But try as she might, she could not get the image of Aaron's empty desk out of her head. She told herself not to be ridiculous—of course Aaron existed. But the longer she thought about it, the more her anxiety grew. She started to imagine all the terrible possibilities that Aaron could present her. What if he went to the police or to a reporter and provided proof of what he did for Sima Daly? What if he went to Richard Harvey himself and let him know that he was sorry for putting him through this? And what if Richard Harvey asked him to do a favor and they both decided to bring Sima down? What if Aaron Naylor committed suicide after being unable to bear the burden of his guilt of what he did to Richard Harvey? What if someone murdered Richard Harvey? And what if they stole the proof he had, which could implicate Sima? The many questions, the many possibilities, and the many terrible consequences.

What if Aaron Naylor is dead? Sima thought to herself just before she entered the lounge area in her office where a temporary bar had been set up.

"Happy referendum, y'all!", she cheered as soon as she saw her staff members waiting for her to join. There was upbeat music playing. They all had their drinks in their hands, and she got herself a margarita.

As she was sipping her drink, the thought *What if Aaron Naylor is dead? Is this really bad for me?* kept ringing in her head.

The celebratory party was in full swing at the governor's mansion. Balloons, streamers, and confetti decorated the room in a chaotic but festive way. Music blared from the speakers, and people danced and laughed, enjoying the momentous occasion. It was a night to remember for everyone involved. The pro-TEXIT victorious camp had everything to celebrate, and they were celebrating in style. The percentage in favor of yes was not as overwhelming, and the final official tally signed by the Secretary of State was seventy-point-five percent, slightly better than the earliest AP projections on the election night. Drinks were flowing, and the mood was jubilant. It was clear that the attendees were relieved and elated that their campaign had paid off. They were ready to move forward with the future, optimistic about what lay ahead. The next two years would be filled with challenges, but they were ready to face them head-on. There was the congressional ratification, there was the Article 49, there was the actual secession plan, and finally the Union presidential sign-off. None of that was in anyone's mind. The only thing that was in everyone's euphoric mind that night that this was the beginning of a new era for Texas.

The invitees were all politicians, businessmen, and women. Those who stood alongside Governor Fisher publicly in his campaign for TEXIT, those who extended their support from a distance, the heavy donors, and those who did none of the above but were going to play a crucial role in the shaping of Texas's future. This was not a night to take political revenge. This was a night of unity. This was a night to show solidarity to the rest of the country. This was a night to tell the world that Texas stood on a single united platform, and that they knew exactly what they were doing. At first, Derek Fisher had planned on giving a formal speech to the gathering, but he scrapped the idea. As one of his cabinet members advised, it was important that everyone felt that they were really part of this TEXIT movement and that they all individually owned the secession. It should not be about Fisher owning the TEXIT win. At least for that night.

Gloria Fisher was being wonderfully gracious with the guests as she navigated through the crowd smoothly, stopping by to say hello and exchanging quick pleasantries with each and every one who had gathered. She was not only the first lady of the state, but also the hostess of the party that evening. Derek Fisher was doing the same in the other half of the room. And their paths crossed somewhere in the middle. They exchanged a warm smile. Derek leaned forward and gave Gloria a peck on her cheek, and a few in the crowd went, "Awww!"

Steve Riggs and Abhinav Agarwal were in attendance, too. They flew together from Houston in Abhinav's private jet and had landed in Austin earlier that afternoon. Both were dressed almost alike. Plaid sky-blue sports jackets, white shirts, navy blue trousers, and black shoes, with each one of these accessories screaming loudly that they were expensive designer brands. They were holding mojito glasses with neatly trimmed mint sprigs capping the glass tops.

When Fisher approached them, he stopped and smiled. He took a deep breath and stretched his arms to hug. It was Abhinav who came forward to reciprocate the hug first. The two men embraced each other tightly, with Fisher patting on Abhinav's back quite violently before moving onto Riggs. He just could not stop laughing.

"What a night!" he said with a beaming smile.

"Indeed, governor. What a night. Congratulations! You delivered this," said Abhinav Agarwal.

"We did. We all did. This belongs to you all," Fisher thanked them, while continuing to smile.

"This evening is all about celebration, governor. You deserve it. And thank you for including us in this jubilee," said Riggs.

"Are you fucking kidding me? My oil czar and the kingpin of GTO are not going to be at this TEXIT celebration party? That would be sacrilege," said Fisher.

"Don't let us hold your celebrations. Please. Carry on, governor! We are still on for tomorrow's meeting? Much to discuss," said Abhinav, reminding the governor about their scheduled meeting for the next day. When Abhinav reached out to the governor's office yesterday and said they had to meet urgently, the governor was able to accommodate them for an hour-long meeting first thing in the morning the next day.

As the drink continued to flow, the mood continued to evolve. The laughter grew louder, and the voices became jumbled. There was food and nonstop music. There was nothing quite like a political party to get the blood flowing and the feet moving. The music was upbeat and celebratory, the food was plentiful and delicious, and the dance floor gradually started to get packed with people of all ages and backgrounds. The DJ cleverly kept mixing "Texas, Our Texas" and "Miles and Miles of Texas" between whatever song he was playing to get the crowd going. There was not a single person in that room who did not dance that night. When the last guest left the venue, it was 1:00 AM. Derek and Gloria Fisher had retired for the night at midnight as Derek remembered that he had to be in his office by 9:00 AM for his meeting with Steve Riggs and Abhinav Agarwal.

The next day came.

It was one of those rare Austin mornings where the humidity had not yet started to build, and the air was still cool and fresh. A light rain was falling, tapping gently against the windows, and filling the air with a gentle ministerial music. The streets were mostly deserted, except for an occasional car or bike that would speed past, its tires hissing on the wet pavement. The trees and bushes were heavy with droplets of water, and the leaves shone brightly in the morning light. It was a beautiful day. Derek Fisher stood outside on his balcony and took in the view of the beautiful morning as it was blossoming.

At exactly 8:55 AM, Riggs and Abhinav walked into Fisher's office and were asked to wait right outside in the lounge area. Riggs looked fine while Abhinav was nursing a hangover, which was visible on his face. The assistant let them into the governor's suite at 9:00 AM.

"Good morning, gentlemen! Pleasure to see you again," Fisher greeted them with a cup of coffee in his hand.

Abhinav pointed at the coffee machine and asked Fisher, "May I?" then waited for his approving nod before helping himself with a cup of coffee. He walked back to the couch.

"So, Congressman Williams had been pestering me with requests. And I don't know if you are in the loop or not," announced Abhinav.

"Requests for what?" wondered Fisher.

"Public offshore leases. He wants a percentage set aside in case he needs to throw this as an incentive to congressmen or women whose votes become crucial for the ratification." Riggs shrugged his shoulders.

"That son of a gun. Heck, no. He didn't talk to me about this. I bet Dodson is behind this, too." Fisher was taken aback by this news.

As Fisher noted during their conversation, he was open to negotiations with Dodson and Williams to seal the ratification. And he was already prepared for some trade incentive deals when the time came. But this was a line too far. Public offshore leases were a bit too risky, and if he became the first President of Texas, this would forever be a scar on his record. He wanted to know what Abhinav and Steve really thought of the plausibility of such a deal. They both felt extremely uncomfortable to offer something like that.

"Why can't he pitch the same kind of deal like you all do—I mean it with all due respect governor—the usual stuff, you know? We keep writing campaign contribution checks through PACs. It's a tried and tested method," Abhinav asked.

"This whole TEXIT is not a tried and tested method though." Steve was trying to play devil's advocate.

"Gentlemen, keep him guessing. That's all I would say. Do not commit to anything until we get to talk. I need to meet with Dodson soon to sort out a few other things. I bet I would be able to gauge this situation better after." Fisher was ready to wind this meeting down and get ready for his next phone meeting with Franklin Cooper, the President of the United States of America.

Before Riggs and Agarwal left the room, Riggs, almost as an afterthought, paused, turned towards Fisher, and said, "The other thing you wanted me to look at? It's all under control, governor. Thought you might want to know."

CHAPTER 10

CURRENT DAY

I t was still bright outside this summer evening, but the inside of his house was covered in darkness, and the only sound in the room was the ticking of the clock on the wall. Alex Pedroza sat in his chair, staring at the blank television screen in front of him. His mind was reeling from the events of the day. Until two days ago, he had a routine. He would visit his sites, greet his workers, occasionally share meals with some of them, meet his community members in his office, visit them in hospitals, schools, or wherever, and then come home to an empty house very late in the evening. He liked that routine. And now, he was sitting alone in his living room on a Tuesday. A senseless act of violence had taken four of his workers' lives, and he was struggling to make sense of it all. He felt numb, as if he could not feel anything at all. But at the same time, his heart was heavy with grief and guilt. He mourned for his lost workers and wondered how their families would cope with this tragedy. Sitting in the darkness, he tried to find some measure of peace. But it was hard to find amid all the pain and confusion.

Earlier that day, he visited all the bereaved families. There were three houses he had to visit. He could not gather enough courage to meet Miguel's daughter, who was with a neighbor. When he visited the families, he really found it hard to meet the family members in their eyes. Nor could he find the right words to console them. He sat with them, hugged them, and cried with them. When he left, he said sorry to every single person he met there. And his sense of guilt only deepened with every passing minute.

His crew from his other site had called him in the morning and asked him if he was going to come over to do quality check before they started off their next task. He simply had asked them to leave him alone and let the houseowners know of the turn of events. He had asked the houseowners to excuse him for a couple of days. He was not in any state of mind to resume work. Juana, his daughter, had been checking on him a couple of times a day. He was haunted by grief initially. But over the past twenty-four hours, his grief had manifested into betrayal and anger. He felt betrayed by Sima Daly and Derek Fisher, neither of whom he knew was directly responsible for the shooting incident. But the violent rhetoric they had been spewing out during their TEXIT campaign rallies was always going to have direct consequences. Alex became increasingly convinced that Sima, Derek, and the entire group of politicians who piled up anger against immigrants in order to win votes were responsible for what happened.

Derek was known for his brash and unapologetic rhetoric. He never hesitated to speak his mind, even if it meant offending others. It was not that he relished in stirring up controversy and making headlines for his inflammatory comments. But when he did make headlines because of a controversial speech or an offensive remark, the polling usually showed an uptick in his ratings. So his advisors did not discourage him from doing that often. His views on gay rights and women's rights had always remained the same. Conservative to the core—and not much different from the bedrock of Texas conservatism. But when it came to his views on public education, especially science education, and his views on race, they used to be different when he was an entrepreneur. During the course of his gubernatorial campaign, he had been changing his rhetoric gradually and steadily. He had learned to push the white supremacy theories mostly by observing the sentiments of his loyal vocal voters at the grassroots level, and partly through what his advisors had been feeding him.

During the pro-TEXIT campaign rallies, he spoke vehemently against immigration from across the border, subtly implying his party was acceptable to the more respectable white-collar immigrants but not the blue-collar ones. Sensing the success of growing white nationalistic far-right sentiments in Eastern Europe, Fisher, too, started to become a strong advocate of white supremacy, and he regularly made disparaging remarks about minorities. And the more divisive his rhetoric was, the stronger his personal favorability grew. Many Texans were drawn to his charismatic personality for being able to offend others, speak their language, and say things other politicians were afraid of saying all these years. They appreciated that he was not afraid to voice his opinions, no matter how unpopular they may be. In short, with every passing week, Derek Fisher and his band of pro-TEXIT politicians understood what the Texas conservative voters really wanted to hear, and they kept delivering it through speeches day in and day out.

The consequences of all their words and actions were to be felt today by anyone who cared to pay attention. Even before the referendum passed, there had been several incidents of hate crimes committed against minorities in the state of Texas. If the crime did not involve any fatality, the law enforcement officials had been largely successful in ensuring the news did not break out in national media. Whenever there was a serious crime involving fatalities, the officials made sure that the news did not last multiple news cycles.

Alex decided that he would confront Sima Daly first, in person, and talk about the damage she and the pro-TEXIT wing of her party, including the governor himself, had done to minorities like him and to the Latino community in Dallas, and then ask for reparations. Even if she or Fisher did not apologize publicly, the least he wanted them to do was to compensate the victims, and then assure a more accommodating deal for his community—a deal he could hold them accountable to.

"Papa, maybe this is a bit too much for one person like you to take on. You should get more community leaders involved. From other cities in Texas. The only way powerful politicians can be held accountable is through solidarity. Solidarity in larger numbers," Juana told him over the phone.

Alex was proud of the incredibly smart, mature, and very understanding young woman Juana had turned into. She lived about thirty miles away from him and was working as an IT consultant for a telecom company. She was making a good living and was enjoying every minute of her independent life. As a father, Alex understood that. He never leaned on her for anything. He wanted her daughter to live her life to the fullest with no commitments. He wondered how on earth she managed to acquire a sense of political wisdom that someone like him who had been working with people was not able to. Until the moment Juana talked about turning this into a big political movement against Fisher, Sima, and the likes, Alex Pedroza was dealing with it as an episode in his personal revenge drama.

Alex woke up the next morning to the most wonderful light cascading in through his bedroom window. It was as if the sun itself was smiling down upon him, and he suddenly felt a surge of energy coursing through his veins. He leapt out of bed, eager to start the day. For the first time in days, he had a sense of purpose. He knew what he wanted to do with his day, and he was determined to make it happen. He was going to put together a plan, and execute every step of it, one by one. The first order of the day was to do research on the number of hate crimes against minorities that had taken place in the state of Texas since Fisher took office. He had spoken to Juana the previous night and she had shared with him a few tips on how to search for news archives online, what search results to rely on, how to filter through fake news articles, et cetera. Alex was more eager than ever to look beyond his community. His mind had opened for a larger cause. He was going to seek and share the pain many people in the state of Texas could be experiencing much like him because of their race. Juana was going to meet him for lunch the next day, and she had given him some homework. Alex was working on it already.

Russell Weston and Emily Chase had lost access to their TWRA bank account. That account was not only the funding source for all their activities that they were doing through the advocacy group, but that was the only one they had access to that was paying their own bills. Now they were reliant on their friends in the short run. They knew they would be able to get their donors back if they resumed their advocacy activities more formally. But for now, their focus was to get down to the bottom of RapFuel and the potentially serious conclusion they could draw from the documents that could implicate a few big names in the state of Texas. And for that, they needed to plan their expenses and arrange a stream of funds.

The friend whose house they were staying in was Emily's friend from high school and she was more than willing to let them stay there for as long as they wanted, with no expectations in return. In the meantime, Russell had also reached out to his friends from other advocacy groups operating out of Texas. The situation was not pretty but was manageable. They did not know how long this mission would take, and they were relying on Jason Greer to make something meaningful out of the mission, and bring this to a closure. They certainly did have access to immediate cash that would be enough for at least a month, before which Russell was confident he would be able to mobilize more funds should they need them.

Russell was sitting on the floor and looking thorough a box of files and folders. He picked one folder and opened it. It had a list of all the women they had helped or were actively helping through TWRA. Women who were having difficult pregnancies and didn't know where to go or how to go about making decisions that would save their lives.

"Two hundred eleven!" Russell exclaimed. "That's how many women who reached out to us at TWRA in out short existence."

"Wonder how many more are out there with no counseling, guidance, or help. And how many are already dead," said Emily. "That reminds me, can we pull out those women whom we are in the middle of helping out but have not brought them to a closure yet?"

"Absolutely," said Russell.

Within ten minutes, he was able to pull out twelve files. These were twelve women who had been in touch with TWRA up till that point and needed further follow-up.

"Twelve? Not too bad," said Emily as she looked through the files and opened the first one.

"Lisa Barkley. That San Antonio single mother. I wonder where she is with her decisions."

She made a note to herself that they should call her and check on her.

Russell and Emily went through the other eleven folders and made appropriate notes. Emily organized these files alphabetically in a separate folder and moved the folder aside. Russell packed that folder inside an empty box with a label *TO CARRY*. A box they were going to carry with them as they embarked on this investigative trip with Jason Greer and wherever it took them.

Around the same time, in *The Austin Star* office, Jason Greer was going through a bunch of documents that were draft articles he had written but were never published because of some last minute editorial calls or because he never concluded his investigation to complete those stories. He had copies of all of them on his personal computer, but the printed ones had notes, annotations from Myra, and more. He wanted to find a couple of old draft articles he had started writing about RapFuel, and the lobbying power of the oil industry. As he was flipping through these documents, another incomplete column caught his eye. It was a profile on Abhinav Agarwal. This was around the time when Abhinav Agarwal was announced as the next CEO by the board, and he was about to take over from his predecessor.

Jason remembered how he was very confident of finding something scandalous when he followed a lead from his source, but he could not in the end. He took that document out and glanced through the annotations. Instinctively he took it out and put it aside. After he picked the other two documents, he took all three documents to the print room and made two copies each. He put the original documents back in the folder and locked them in his draw. He placed both the copies in a file and left them on his table, covered by a book. He checked his watch, remembered that he had called for a meeting with Myra, and she was always on time. So he ran to the conference room.

The air was gentle with no tension inside the conference room, and Myra was sitting with her iPad in front of her. This was a room where lives could be changed with a single word, where decisions were made that would have a ripple effect for years to come. This was a room where history was being made. At least that's what reporters like Jason Greer and editors like Myra Bristow, journalists of integrity still believed. When Jason walked in, Myra greeted him. She acknowledged that she was early for the meeting, and he need not have apologized. Since it was just the two of them, she asked him to get started.

For the next ten minutes, Jason Greer painstakingly narrated the sequence of events since the time when someone tried to play with Russell and Emily by sending a blank storage device to him, his subsequent meeting with them, their scouring over hundreds documents related to RapFuel, trying to recreate the conclusive document Russell and Emily's star team created, hid following them after they were released from the police custody, meeting them in the park, and their current plan.

"Wait a minute! So you knew Russell and Emily all along? Even before their arrests? And I did not catch you letting that one out when we were talking about their arrest and how upset you were when I asked you not to publish that story. I'm impressed, Jason. I am." Myra was clapping her hands.

"Yes. I have known them for a while." Jason blushed.

"Tell me again. Your current plan is to jump on a road trip with two activists who have just been charged with accounting fraud? What could go wrong?" Myra was not very happy with Jason's plan.

"You know, Myra. They are not guilty. This whole thing is a setup. Please give me two weeks. That's all I ask for. We will narrow this down. Not only will you get a great story, but also an opportunity to make history. Right here. In this room. Like you always say." Jason was trying to convince Myra that this was a very crucial mission for him and *The Austin Star*.

After that emotional plea, Jason leaned back in his chair, gazing at Myra's eyes for reaction.

After a moment, he continued calmly, "This story is important," he said quietly. "It needs to be told. And you know that." Myra's skeptical look had not changed.

"This story has the power to change a lot of things, Myra. Trust me," said Jason again, in a pleading tone.

"But there is no story. Not yet. You want me to send you on a two-week field trip with two accounting criminals to write this story." Her voice had changed a bit.

Jason could see the doubt start to dissipate from his editor's face, and he knew he had convinced her.

"See you in two weeks!" said Myra, walking out.

"They are not criminals! They have been framed!" Jason yelled out.

The hotel lobby was a hive of activity. Guests were coming and going, luggage was being carried to and fro, and the concierge was busy answering questions and giving directions. In the midst of all this activity, one man stood out. He was impeccably dressed, with a cane in one hand and a top hat in the other. He walked with a regal bearing, and his eyes surveyed the scene with an air of calm authority. It was clear that he was not just another guest; he was the owner of the hotel. And as he made his way through the lobby, everyone stopped what they were doing to bow or curtsy in respect. It was a small gesture, but it spoke volumes about the man's stature within the hotel. This was not the biggest hotel in Washington, DC, but Senator Newell picked this venue exactly for that reason. That it offered an intimate setting where people were not going to judge someone. When the owner walked past Senator Newell, he acknowledged his presence with a quick nod and kept walking.

Newell was waiting for Alan Marks. He knew Alan was flying in from Austin and his flight was delayed. Despite the hustle and bustle, the atmosphere in the lobby was still very calm and relaxed. This was due in part to the plush furniture and warm colors that have been used throughout the space.

Senator Newell had a file with him, and he was reviewing the email Alan Marks had sent him earlier today. Being old school still, he had his staff print that email and put it in his file. Alan Marks entered the hotel exactly at 6:15 PM. Newell caught him, and he waited for the concierge to bring Alan to his waiting couch.

"Good evening, senator! Sorry to keep you waiting," Alan Marks apologized.

"I knew you were caught in a flight delay, congressman. You want a drink before we get into business?"

Alan looked for concierge assistance again, and as soon as he caught a staff's eye, he asked for water.

For the next sixty minutes. Alan Marks, the Chairman of Texas's Ways and Means Committee, shared with Senator Newell how bleak his realistic forecast looked for an independent Texas, at least for the next three years. He did not even have to play any favorites while putting together his initial draft of this forecast. These were numbers as he saw them and as his team saw them. In the short term, which according to the Ways and Means Committee was a twelve-to-eighteen-month period, his team of economists were predicting that TEXIT would cause market uncertainty and a decrease in investment. This was because businesses were unsure about what the future held for the Texas-USA relationship.

According to the committee, the long term was five to ten years, though some economists believed that TEXIT could actually be positive for the Texas economy because they argued that leaving the Union would give Texas more control over its trade policy and would allow it to pursue more free trade agreements with other countries. But then, these economists who had an optimistic take on Texas's long-term economic stability had no numbers to back their optimism up with and no historic reference to rely on. So the only numbers they had that they could use to project the economic future of Texas put them at a decline in GDP in the long-term range, from the current three-point-five percent to less than two-point-two percent in five years.

According to his team of not-so-optimistic economists, who were relying on numbers only, there were longer term implications of TEXIT. The new graduate class entering the workforce in the next year or two would face a tremendous economic crisis as they got started in their careers. The chances of wages rising were extremely low, and in fact, the current indicators pointed to a wage suppression. So there was a very good chance that they could lose this workforce to other states in the Union, thereby causing a long-term effect on Texas's own skilled labor supply. This would lead to a further fiscal crisis in Texas.

"So you are saying that you really didn't have to do anything to paint this not so rosy picture?" Senator Newell was smiling.

"No, senator. The only thing that stands between my realistic summary—in no uncertain terms that would spell out the economic disaster for Texas, post-TEXIT, and flipping the four Senate votes—is, I think, the optimistic outlook as well, which I am bound to include in my report to the congress." Alan was explaining how he thought there was still a possibility that Article 49 would pass without a problem. "How do we fix that? Is Vivienne in the loop with any of this?" Newell asked, while waving at the waiting staff to bring him another bourbon—neat.

"Yes, of course. If I may suggest, perhaps it is time to work on Plan B and Vivienne's strategy," Alan added.

"She told me she had to stay in Austin for a vote this evening. It's a shame she couldn't be here tonight. Are you in town tomorrow, Alan?" Newell asked him.

"No, sir. I'm catching the first flight out. I'm meeting with an old friend in town for dinner tonight. Will try to catch a wink or two before I leave tomorrow," Alan told him.

"That's all right, Alan. Why we couldn't have done this over the phone, you may ask, but I am still old school. I like to look into the other person's eyes when I am discussing something important." Newell got up and took a big swig from his glass and emptied it. He added, "Thank you for coming all the way. The next meeting will be with Vivienne."

Senator Newell walked back slowly to the door and waited for the doorman to open. His cab was waiting right by the curb, and the driver was holding the door open for him to get in.

Inside the lobby, Alan Marks was typing a short email to Vivienne Creasey.

With the kind of profession Gavin Forbes was in, Sundays did not mean anything special. He worked on shifts and rotations. But he loved Sundays when he was off because he and his wife Beth would be able to do things together. Beth had a more traditional Monday through Friday, nine to five kind of a job, so she usually looked forward to her weekends. More so after she got pregnant.

On this particular Sunday, both Gavin and Beth were looking forward to just relax in the house and take things easy. Gavin woke up early morning and decided to make breakfast for his pregnant wife. He prepared her favorite meal of scrambled eggs, bacon, and toast. Beth was still lying in her bed, but she was fully awake. She could smell bacon and eggs being made. She had somehow got through most of her first trimester without much morning sickness. And she was craving for bacon every single meal. She was overjoyed at Gavin's thoughtful gesture and could not wait to taste what was being cooked. So she got out of the bed and rushed to the kitchen. Gavin kissed her and served breakfast in two separate plates, with Beth's plate having twice as much bacon as his. They enjoyed their meal together. Afterwards, Gavin sat down with Beth on the couch in their living room and they discussed their plans for the day. Their plans included a walk in the neighborhood park, grocery shopping, lunch at their favorite Chinese restaurant, and visiting Lisa Barkley before coming home for a nap. Gavin was content with the thought that they were going to have a perfect Sunday.

The park was extremely busy, so Gavin and Beth decided to cut short their walk. Since Lisa was his client, Gavin had her number. He texted her to see if she would be available between 1:30 and 3:00 PM. He told her that Beth wanted to meet her to talk about her pregnancy experiences and get some tips from her. It felt like she was trying to avoid meeting them at first, but upon insisting how important it was for Beth to talk to her, Lisa reluctantly agreed to meet them.

It was a typical Sunday afternoon at their favorite Chinese restaurant. As they perused the menu, they joked back-and-forth about their various options. They both knew that they would eventually end up ordering their usuals: Beth would get the sweet-and-sour chicken and Gavin would get the General Tso's shrimp—but it was still fun to pretend to be adventurous. After they placed their orders, the conversation turned to Lisa. Gavin was wondering why she was reluctant at first when he told her Beth wanted to get some tips from her. Beth asked him not to read much into her reluctance. She told him he did not even see her, and it was a mere speculation on his part that she was reluctant based on the tone of her text messages. But they both agreed that Lisa did not look all that happy and healthy when they met her briefly at the ob-gyn office.

The food arrived in about fifteen minutes, and unsurprisingly, they devoured what was served in front of them without taking much of a break. Beth was going through a sweet-and-sour chicken phase in her pregnancy and Gavin did not have worry if he would end up eating her leftovers, too. They wiped their plates clean.

They arrived at Lisa's house at 1:40 PM. Lily was riding her tricycle outside, and she recognized Gavin as soon as she saw him. She just stopped her tricycle, jumped out, and ran inside the house to warn her mom.

"Mom, it's Mr. Electricity! He is here with a girl!" Lily was screaming from the main door, and Gavin and Beth could both hear her scream.

Lisa came to the front door, pushed it open, smiled at them, and let them in. The three of them exchanged pleasantries and Lisa guided Gavin and Beth to the kitchen area where there was a dining table. While Lisa sat on one side of the table, Gavin and Beth sitting on the other.

"Hey, thanks for having us. I know . . ." Beth started.

"It's okay. I'm happy to answer any questions," said Lisa, still looking visibly tired. She poured herself a glass of water and started drinking.

"I wanted to ask you about your first pregnancy. Which trimester was the toughest? I, for some reason, am having a not-so-painful first trimester. Wondering . . ." Before Beth could finish her question, Lisa got up and said, "Excuse me, I'll be right back," and rushed to the restroom.

Both Gavin and Beth looked at each other, slightly puzzled and concerned. They could hear Lisa throwing up. The sound of vomiting was followed by loud coughs, clearing of throat, gargling, and a door being opened.

"I'm sorry guys. I'm just not feeling well." Lisa was apologetic as she came back to her seat.

"It's all right, We can come back some other time," said Gavin, noticing that there were tears forming in Lisa's eyes.

When Lisa's eyes made contact with Gavin's and she realized an empathetic look on his face, she started breaking down and couldn't control herself. She sobbed hysterically for the next two minutes, and Beth got close to Lisa to give her a tight hug. She saw Lisa was running a temperature.

"Do you want to go to the doctor's? Your body feels warm," observed Beth.

"That's normal when this happens. I have meds," Lisa replied.

Lisa did not know Beth at all. And her relationship with Gavin was only as a client who continued to have electric problems in her house and who had been using Gavin's services to ger things fixed at reasonable prices. And yet, at this moment, Lisa was extremely relieved to have an empathetic adult in her house who would not judge her. She was relieved because she had found an outlet through which she could vent her emotions, and a shoulder, quite literally, to lean onto.

"I have not shared this with anyone. So please keep this to yourself. I don't know why. But I trust you guys." Lisa wiped her tears and went onto explain the complications in her pregnancy as revealed by her ob-gyn during her last emergency visit. Neither Gavin and Beth had heard of ectopic pregnancies and Lisa had to draw with her fingers in the air, to try to make them visualize the seriousness of ectopic pregnancy. She told them why the doctor could not recommend any procedures for her. Lisa, notwithstanding Gavin's staunch political leanings, did not mince her words when sharing how she felt about the draconian laws of the Fisher Administration that were being made very clearly to control women. She could see Gavin squirm in his seat and inching to tell Lisa something. Beth sensed the mood, too, and she held his hand tightly and did not let him get out of his chair. They both let Lisa continue to vent. And she did.

After a few minutes, Lisa was no longer crying, but there was still pain and helplessness in her voice. Finally, she summarized her condition by saying she had two choices. Either she continued to live, be a good mom for Lily, and raise her to be a good woman. Or she died delivering this new baby, who may or may not survive after she came into this cruel world.

"The problem is Fisher and his administration have decided that I cannot have any right when it comes to deciding which of the above two choices is better for me. They decide it for me." Lisa wiped her tears, which were slowly drying up on her cheeks.

"I am so sorry." Beth gave her another hug.

"This is not a political ideology. This is not me trying to be a bad Christian. This is my life. I want to live and see Lily grow up to be a beautiful woman."

"What are you going to do?" Beth asked.

"I'll be a fucking criminal in Texas if I did anything to my womb. No matter how sick I am. My doctor wouldn't help me. They would much rather I die than do anything else. So I have contacted TWRA. And they came to see me a few days ago. They gave me this." Lisa showed an envelope.

It all came together in a flash right in front of Gavin's eyes now. He remembered how a few days ago, he made a trip to Lisa's house to fix her air conditioner but turned back because he saw through the window whom Lisa was having a pensive conversation with two people—a man and woman, after which Lisa sat down cupping her face with both her palms. She was sitting on the exact same seat where she was sitting right now.

"TWRA? The women's activist group that's gotten into some financial cheating scandal?" Gavin asked.

"Long story. But yeah. Them," Lisa responded.

Gavin and Beth spent the next few minutes getting more information about TWRA from Lisa. Upon her insistence, they opened the envelope and quickly flipped through the pages that were inside. They consoled her again with words of encouragement and motivation. And then they left.

On their drive back home, Beth noticed Gavin's mood has changed. He looked like a completely different person. He did not want to talk to Beth. He had his eyes on the road and kept driving.

Gavin was in a dilemma, and he was torn between two competing impulses: the desire to help someone in dire need and save her life, and the equally strong desire to uphold and stand up for his political principles. On the one hand, he knew that by helping Lisa, he would be going against one of the core conservative tenants. But on the other hand, he also knew that if he did not help, Lisa may just die. Gavin, the man who was known to help people around him if he could, was trapped in a difficult situation, and it was not clear to him what the right thing to do was. With every passing minute on the road that night, an agony of helplessness thrusted upon Gavin like he had never felt before. He gently pushed Beth's hands away when she tried to lend a touch of support.

The day after his meeting with Alan Marks, Senator Newell was feeling optimistic about his own political future. Between the counterproposal he had been working on through Senator Brynes and the Alan-Vivienne play he has set in motion to jeopardize Article 49, he, for the first time since Fisher announced the TEXIT referendum in the state, was feeling like he was in control of the narrative. Newell finally started to feel like he had an upper hand over the junior senator from his state. He knew Dodson and Williams were very good in such power plays, but this was an opportunity for him, the senior senator from Texas, to show he could engage in a bit of a political game himself. That made him feel good.

As soon as he reached his Senate office in the Capitol, he asked one of his staff members to send out a message to Dodson's office or call his office to find out if he was available for a short meeting. Dodson's office responded immediately, and they agreed to meet over lunch in Newell's office.

Newell had his staff get lunch for both of them, and when Dodson arrived in his office, the lunch was already on his table.

"What a crazy week this has been, huh, senator? How have you been doing? How have you been handling all the media attention?" Dodson walked in with a big smile and a loud voice. He was referring to *The New York Post* story.

"Mmm. This smells good. I am starving," Dodson said and sat down.

"The media attention was on you, too, Ryan. Somehow, I was made out to be the bad guy in the story. It smells like it was planted." Newell was trying to be as direct as he could.

"Are you accusing me of something?" Dodson took a bite from his chicken sandwich.

"Don't react if you aren't guilty," Newell responded and grabbed his lunch bowl.

Newell opened his Cobb salad bowl and took a bite. He could hear Dodson chew his food loudly. And it annoyed him. He forced himself to ignore the loud chewing noise and continued to eat.

"Senator, I am not sure why would you invite me to your office and accuse me of something ridiculous—I mean, this sounds entirely speculative," Dodson said.

"Speculative or not, you know the truth, Ryan. Anyway, I did not invite you to talk about that at all. You brought it up, didn't you? Listen, I'm ready to move on. Here, take a look." Newell changed the topic of conversation to his main agenda for the meeting.

"What is this?" Dodson asked, opening the document.

Senator Newell had put together a proposal for reconciliation between the two senators of Texas. Even though he did not name Williams or Fisher anywhere in the document, it was obvious to Dodson which reference belonged to whom. The gist of the proposal was that Newell was fully aware of the deals that Williams was trying to make to get enough votes for ratification. Notwithstanding the fact that some of these deals could bring legal trouble for Williams and for Dodson, Newell mentioned in the proposal that he was willing to ignore them if Dodson agreed to a few conditions after Texas became independent.

The first condition was to support his presidential bid.

Dodson did not read any further. He was fuming with anger. He felt insulted and got up from his seat. He pushed his half-eaten sandwich to the other side of the table.

"I've seen worse insults. You should work harder, senator," said Dodson.

"I take it then that you don't like the proposal?" asked Newell.

"Fuck, no. Pardon my French. We have already had this conversation at the restaurant. Nothing has changed since. If anything, my position has only become stronger. You think I would work so hard all these months only to give my dreams up just because you pushed a single page proposal at my face?"

"In that case, I will set my Plan B in motion." Senator Newell was angry at the absolute arrogance of Dodson.

"We'll see. Good luck, senator!"

"To you, too, Ryan!"

It was early morning, and the sun was just starting to peek over the horizon.

The air was still and cool, and the only sound was the gentle rustling of the leaves in the breeze. In the distance, a rooster crowed, announcing the start of another day. Birds started singing, insects started buzzing, and small animals could be heard scurrying about in the underbrush. The world was coming to life again after a long night's sleep. And in the midst of all this natural activity was a lone figure: Burl Fogg, working in his field. He moved methodically, tending to his crops with care.

His phone rang, and since he had both his hands occupied, he ignored the call. Within two minutes it started ringing again. The caller kept calling him relentlessly every two minutes. Finally, Burl had to give up his farming task, remove his gloves, and pick up his phone. It was an unknown number. Burl waited for the caller to call again. In a few minutes, there it was. He picked up the phone.

"Mr. Fogg?" said the caller, a female voice.

"Speaking."

"Calling from the Commissioner of Texas Department of Agriculture's office. The commissioner would like to set up an in-person meeting with you at the earliest of your convenience. When do you think you can come over to Austin?" the commissioner's executive assistant asked.

That was how a meeting was set up between Burl Fogg and the commissioner for the following Wednesday. Burl Fogg did not know what the agenda was, but he knew the commissioner would be talking to him about the letter he had sent him. In fact, this was the first time he had heard directly from the commissioner or from his office since he mailed that letter. But to Burl Fogg, it felt like the letter was sent in a different era. He had learned much more since then. Much more about the current state of affairs in the state of Texas and how that would impact the farming industry as a whole. If he had to write that letter today, he knew he would have added more information and been more direct in asking for an urgent meeting with the commissioner and the Fisher Administration.

Stansley to Austin on road is about 380 miles and it took upwards of six hours to drive. Burl Fogg had asked Dudley if he would accompany him and be his travel companion for the road trip. Dudley agreed readily. So, there they were, on their Ford F-150 setting out of Stansley at 12:30 PM on the following Tuesday. Burl's meeting with the commissioner was going to be at 10:00 AM the next morning. So they would have enough time to check into a hotel for the night, rest, and be fresh for the meeting.

The F-150 shifted into fifth gear and the odometer ticked over to eighty miles per hour. But even with the accelerator pressed down, the truck could not maintain speed on the short uphill stretch of the state highway. Burl Fogg, not a stressed driver normally, cursed under his breath and pulled his foot off the gas, letting the truck coast down the hill. As he drove, his mind wandered to the events of the past few months. Dudley, sitting next to him in the passenger seat, was fast asleep. Burl could even hear him snore. The wind whipped through Burl's hair as he continued to cruise down the open road stretched out before them. There was a country music radio station playing Hank Williams, Jr., who belted out a hit song with his usual vigor. Burl started singing along without realizing and hearing that Dudley woke up.

"Where are we?" wondered Dudley, wiping his drool from the mouth.

"A few more miles to Coleman. Maybe another two and a half to three hours to Austin," Burl said, still singing along with Hank, Jr.

"Can you pull over at the next gas station? Need to take a leak, dude. All that soda, I tell ya." Dudley smiled.

"Now, only if you'll promise me that you won't fall asleep till we find that gas station. The whole point of you going with me is to be my driving companion, dude," mentioned Burl.

"All right. All right. I apologize. Was a late night last night. I'm awake now. Don't get too salty now," countered Dudley in a defensive tone.

As they approached Coleman, they found a Texaco not too far from the highway, and they pulled in. Burl decided to fill the tank since they had stopped. This 2021 F-150 was relatively less of a gas guzzler. With a twenty-six-gallon capacity, and his tank still being only half-empty, Burl was sure he could get to Austin with whatever fuel he had, but he just felt incomplete not filling the tank up after having stopped at a gas station. Dudley went in looking for a restroom. Burl paid at the pump, filled the gas, moved the truck to the parking space on the side, and went into the gas station to relieve himself.

Dudley decided to pick up another bottle of Dr. Pepper and a bag of chips. He was waiting to pay at the cashier's desk when he overheard the conversation between a young woman and the cashier. The woman was standing there with a girl. They both looked reasonably well-dressed. At least that was the impression they made on Dudley, because he was clearly surprised when he heard the woman asking the cashier if he could buy them one of those cold sandwiches as they did not have any money on them.

"My daughter is six. She has not eaten anything in twenty-four hours. Please. Just one sandwich," the woman was heard pleading.

There was a tug in Dudley's heart, and he suddenly felt guilty standing behind them with food in his hands. He stepped forward and told the cashier that he would be paying for the sandwich and asked him to add one more sandwich to the bill along with Dr. Pepper and the bag of chips he was holding. The woman turned back and looked at him with gratitude in her eyes. She moved aside and walked towards the door with her daughter. Dudley paid and stepped outside to look for the woman. She was standing a few feet away from the door. He handed over the sandwiches along with the drink and chips to her.

"Here. If she hasn't eaten anything for twenty-four hours, you haven't eaten anything for longer. Am I right?" Dudley asked her, almost rhetorically.

"Thank you, sir. I don't know if I will be able to pay you back." She was beginning to choke.

"And I don't expect you to. So . . ." Dudley was going to ask a question about her background and what she was doing there but checked himself in the last second, and decided not to ask.

"I know what you were going to ask. What am I doing here? With my daughter? With no money…in the middle of nowhere? It's a sad story. I don't believe you'd want to hear," she said.

"Well, if you put it that way. I do want to hear. Please. Try it on me." Dudley was all ears.

So the woman spent the next five minutes explaining what brought her to the streets and how she ended up there at that gas station. Dudley was thoroughly gutted hearing that story. Her account was one of loss and heartache. She had been through so much in such a short time, and as far as Dudley could tell, he could not see much of that in her weary eyes. He thought maybe she had not had time to process it all since all of what she had narrated seemed to have happened in such a short period of time, and at that moment, all she was doing was to survive and help her daughter do the same. Dudley was a simple Texan man with a very kind heart. The world he grew up in Stansley was all he had been exposed to. The people, the traditions, the food, the conservative ideas—he was brought up with were the only worldview he has ever had. Unlike many of his friends and family in Stansley, Dudley never hated people because they did not hold the same conservative ideologies as he did. He had always treated people as people and trusted them all equally.

As the woman spoke, Dudley listened intently, his heart going out to her with every passing word. He had never heard anything like the woman's story before. He may had been naïve, but he was not stupid. He could understand the root cause of what this woman had been through. He could connect the dots and decipher why this may have happened to her. And he was very upset.

"I am sorry," Dudley said.

"Please. Why are you being sorry? Mashallah!" she said, with her hands pointing towards the heaven.

By then, Burl had spotted Dudley and started walking towards him.

"Sorry to interrupt. Are we ready to go?" he asked.

Dudley had not recovered from the story he had just heard. He was still lost and fumbling for words. He wanted to do something to help the woman and her daughter. But he did not know how. He whispered in Burl's ears and smiled at the woman. Burl was puzzled, but he acknowledged and moved a few yards behind her to the grass area.

Dudley looked at the woman again and asked her to wait there while he talked to Burl quickly. "Will be back in a few seconds."

When Burl and Dudley stepped aside, Dudley tried to give a condensed version of the woman's story. He told Burl that the woman was from Houston. Her parents had migrated from Iran a year before she was born here. Her husband, who was also born into a Muslim immigrant family from Iran, was working as a bank teller in Fort Worth, which was where they were living. She received a call about a week ago. It was the police informing her that her husband had been shot dead. She was not given much information, and when she went to the hospital to identify her dead husband, she saw three other Muslim women waiting in the hospital to do the same. It did not take long for her to conclude that her husband was a victim of hate crime. Her anger took over her grief and she wanted answers from the police.

She kept following up with the Fort Worth police till one day two police officers asked her to come to the station to sign some papers. When she went, she took her daughter with her, too. She signed a couple of documents related to her version of the complaint. The police officers treated her very nicely and invited her and her daughter to share a pizza. That was the last thing she remembered, and the next thing she could recollect was she being on the side of a highway, safely tucked under a bush with a sleeping bag. Her daughter was by her side, fast asleep. The woman was disoriented, and it took her a while to gather some energy to walk all the way to the nearest safe spot she could find, which happened to be this Texaco gas station.

Burl was processing everything Dudley said and was unable to comprehend how any of this could be real. He kept staring at Dudley. Both men stood silent for a minute.

Then Dudley asked, "The least we could do is give her a ride to Austin. Find a safe shelter for them. Don't you think?"

"I . . . err . . . You read my mind, Dudster. That's the least we could do," said Burl. So that is what they did.

When they went back to the place where the woman and her daughter were standing, she had finished eating the sandwich and was taking a sip of Dr. Pepper.

"Do you want us to take you to Austin? We are headed that way," Burl asked. "Maybe we could find a safe shelter for you in the short run? While you try to figure out how to fight for your survival and for your husband. You know."

The woman and daughter thanked Burl and Dudley profusely and agreed to go with them to Austin.

Burl left the radio on. But for the rest of the drive, both he and Dudley did not exchange many words while the woman and the daughter sat in the back seat and slept. Dudley had his phone opened and was Googling for shelter-related information in Austin. He was not sure where to drop them off. If a homeless shelter would be the easiest place to start with or if there were any nonprofit charity groups, he could call for help. After much deliberation, he suggested to Burl that a homeless shelter would be the easiest place to drop them off for the night since Burl had an important day ahead of him the next day. And then if they had the time, they could help them further after Burl's meeting with the commissioner. Burl agreed, although neither of them was completely satisfied with what they planned to do. They knew it was the best solution under the circumstances. There would not be much paperwork to complete, nor processes to be taken care of at that time of the night if they were to drop them off at the homeless shelter. Dudley made a call to one of the shelters and made sure they could take them in.

When they reached the shelter, Burl opened his wallet and gave fifty dollars to the woman. He told her to stay safe and promised her that they would come and check on her the next day after their meeting. The little girl waved them goodbye with a beautiful smile that warmed the cockles of both their hearts. For a woman whose life had been mysteriously upended for no explicable reason and had been left stranded in the middle of nowhere with a young daughter to care for, the woman seemed to be in good spirits.

When they left Stansley earlier that afternoon, Burl and Dudley sure were hoping for an uneventful drive to Austin, a nice meal, and a good night's rest. Little did they expect their day to take a complete emotional detour. Suddenly, his farming challenges seemed so trivial to Burl. The meeting that he was so looking forward to the next day looked meaningless in the larger scheme of things when compared to the hardships this woman was facing. His mind kept going back to the little girl who would grow up fatherless. They decided to have a simple meal and call it a night. Dudley had trouble sleeping that night. The little girl's warm goodbye wave and her beautiful smile kept him awake. He wished he could do more for them right at that moment.

The next morning, Burl Fogg reached the Department of Agriculture office at 9:45 AM. Since Burl was already there, and since the commissioner did not have any other earlier appointment, he decided to meet Burl at 9:50 AM.

"Good morning, Burl! So good to see you again," the commissioner greeted him.

"Good morning, sir. Likewise." Burl shook the commissioner's hands and sat down.

The commissioner said he had read the letter Burl had sent as soon as he received it. He said he was so caught up in the post-referendum frenzy and the hundreds of reports he had to prepare for the many congressional committees who were working on Article 49 resolution, he did not have time to get back to Burl. Which really was why he had thought a face-to-face exchange would be more effective and could avoid mail-related delays.

Burl agreed. "Under the circumstances, yes, this is much better. Although I am a better communicator when I am writing," Burl said with a nervous laughter.

For the next hour the commissioner was listening to a passionate Burl unfurl his extensive thoughts on sustainable farming, why Texas was so ill-prepared, the TEXIT impact on farming, his disappointment with the Fisher Administration for taking the farm sector for granted and not investing any time or expertise in addressing all issues in the farming sector, and more.

Burl started off his conversation by asking, "If you recall during our last meeting, I told you how my dad hated the feds," and added that he was like that, too, when he met the commissioner last time around. Right now, Burl said, he had more disappointments and apprehensions about the whole direction in which Texas was going. And TEXIT may have only made matters more complicated for him in his mind—about the promising future Texas may not have as his dad had hoped and as he was made to believe.

"I appreciate you being candid here, Burl," the commissioner said.

"The question is, what can you do about it?" asked Burl.

"How about I set up a meeting with you and Governor Fisher? I think you would become the first farmer the governor would officially meet post-referendum," the commissioner asked Burl.

Burl began to sweat. He was not sure if this was real or if he was living in a dream. He kept staring at the commissioner. For all the courageous farmer advocacy causes he was taking up in his mind on behalf of many farmers in Texas, the very thought of meeting the Governor of Texas sent a streak of excitement through his spine.

"Burl? Hello . . . Burl, do you want to meet the governor?" The commissioner was trying to make sure Burl was still conscious.

"Yes. I'm sorry. Yes. Of course," Burl responded startlingly. He was still recovering.

Within a few minutes the commissioner called his executive assistant and asked her to get on the governor's calendar as soon as possible. He heard back from the assistant soon.

"Friday? At noon?" He covered the microphone on the phone and looked at Burl. "Friday works for you?"

Burl was unprepared for the suddenness of such an important meeting being possible. He tried to recover from the shock and surprise.

"Day after tomorrow? Yes. Why not? Umm. Let me check. Should be possible, I think. I will extend my stay in Austin. Friday should work," said Burl. When he walked back from the commissioner's office to his car, there was an extra spring in his step.

Dudley was waiting in the hotel. When he learned that they were going to spend another two days in Austin, he was relieved. The first thought that occurred to him was what he could do to help that woman and her daughter in the next two days.

Officer Ken pulled his car in front of a house in a middle-class neighborhood. The house was unremarkable in every way. The house looked like almost every other one in the subdivision. Ken looked at the two-story house from outside and guessed it must be a four-bedroom home. The lawn was neatly trimmed, and the flower beds were well-tended. There was a basketball hoop in the driveway, and a trampoline in the backyard. The windows were clean, and the gutters were free of leaves. In short, it was a perfectly ordinary house. The twilight added a tinge of beauty to the colors emanating from the flower beds. Officer Ken paused for a minute to admire that before knocking on the door.

"Excuse me, ma'am, My name is Officer Ken. I'm from the Midland Police. Are you Ms. Rosaline Doughart?" he asked the woman who opened the door.

"Yes, sir. I am." She guessed what this unannounced call was about, and she had been waiting for this moment for a while. At least from now on, she did not have to live in nervous anticipation and fear. She had considered leaving town, but since that would arise suspicion much sooner, she decided to stay home. She knew this could buy some time for Ava. Rosaline was holding onto the door, slightly open, hoping to answer Ken's questions without letting him in. But it looked like Ken had plans of his own.

"May I come in? I just need to talk to you. It won't take very long. But it is not going to be a quick two-minute thing. Also, this involves some sensitive information. You sure don't want your neighbors to listen in. Do you?" he asked.

She let him in.

Ken had not dealt with this kind of a missing person case before. So he did not have a search warrant, as there was no evidence yet in his possession that could be used to linking Rosaline with Ava's whereabouts. He was really hoping to break her through some persistent questioning, which he was good at.

"I don't like to waste my time or your time, ma'am. So tell me, where were you on the evening of Ava missing? Around 5:00 PM? You must have read in the news that we think the last place she was in Midland was at a grocery store," said Ken.

"I was on the road. I was driving home."

"You answered it like you were expecting this question to be asked, Ms. Rosaline." Ken smiled.

"I've been following Ava's case just like her other friends and family. I want her to be safe and well. And I've been replaying that evening in my mind. That's all," she responded.

For the next fifteen minutes or so, Officer Ken kept going back and forth with the same set of questions, worded slightly differently, in different tonal modulations, trying to see if Rosaline would break at some point. She did not.

So Ken went to another set of questions he had prepared. They all were related to her friendship with Ava and how well she knew Ava's family—Bradley and Eveline. Rosaline had not quite thought about this set of questions. She realized that these questions started touching a raw emotional cord in her because answering them made her think about Ava's family, her bonding with her husband and daughter. Rosaline did her best to answer these questions as cold as she could, giving the impression to Ken that she was a good friend but not that close of a friend whom Ava would call trustingly when she was in dire need. Officer Ken, after trying this new set of questions for about fifteen minutes, switched back to the first set again. And he noticed Rosaline was beginning to get annoyed with his repetitive inquisitive nature.

"Officer, you said this wouldn't take long. We have spent thirty minutes already. And all you have done is to ask the same ten questions ten times. Can we stop this now? Can you please leave? I need to get some work done," she said.

"I apologize, ma'am. I know it must be hard. But why wouldn't you want to help us find your friend? Isn't it better for her safety?" he asked.

"Are you fucking with me? You are the ones she's run away from. Why would I let you catch her?" Rosaline's resilience cracked open mildly.

"Fair point. So is it safe to assume that Ava and you had been planning her escape from Midland for a few days? How long? A week? Ten days? I mean, an operation like this needs good planning. And I know you guys are not criminals," said Officer Ken.

"We were not planning. It was an emergency," Rosaline broke and blurted out.

About 180 miles to the northwest of Midland, Texas, in the outskirts of Atoka, New Mexico, a red Chevy Impala pulled in the back of a lonely house. The sky was ablaze with colors, a deep orange mixed with reds and pinks as the sun rose in the east. The light slowly started spreading across the landscape, illuminating the desert and mountains in all their glory. The air was still and calm, and the world outside the house felt at peace. Dawn Sky in New Mexico—a time of day when anything seemed possible.

Joanna opened the front door that was locked from outside. Ava, who was fast asleep on a sleeping bag, was disturbed. She got up and ran to a corner to be safe. She did not have time to check through the door cracks if it was Joanna's car that pulled in.

"Rise and shine! Got some hot breakfast for you. Well, it was hot when I picked it up." She handed over a box with scrambled eggs and toast.

"Thank you," said Ava as she took a deep breath of relief.

"The good news is Jason Greer has the story. I made it every bit dramatic as what you've been going through," said Joanna.

"Jason? *The Austin Star?*" Ava asked.

"He is our man. Now we must sit tight for a day or so to see if there is a reaction from his side. Else, Plan B. Relocation," she said.

Then, with the morning rays peeping through the door cracks as the backdrop, the two women ate their breakfast. Both were in their shabby looking crumpled clothes, although for entirely different reasons. They took their time enjoying their meal. There was a comfortable silence between them, broken only occasionally by the sound of their chewing food or taking a sip from their coffee cups. They were both clearly focused on their food, savoring each bite. But there was also a sense of companionship in the way they shared the space. It was clear that these two women had started developing a strangely close bond, even though they did not need to say much to communicate.

Ava thought about Rosaline and wondered how her fate would have turned out had she not showed up at the grocery store on time. She looked at Joanna and smiled. A smile that conveyed one thousand thanks.

CHAPTER 11

A FEW DAYS AFTER REFERENDUM

aron Naylor had been driving for hours, and the endless stretch of highway had begun to take its toll. His mind kept wandering back to the events of the past few weeks, and he could not help but feel a profound sense of guilt. He had always been a bit of a loner, but since his meeting with Richard Harvey and handing over of the videos to Sima Daly, he felt completely lost. He had not even realized how heavy this act would weigh on him afterwards. Every exit he passed seemed to offer some sort of promise, but he never had the courage to take one. He just kept driving, searching for something that he could not quite define. Maybe one day he would find what he was looking for. Or maybe he would just keep driving until the end of the road.

When Aaron decided to leave Corpus Christi with just a suitcase and his computer bag, all he wanted to do was to get away—get away from his daily routine of meeting people who kept reminding him of everything he did. He had thought about meeting Richard Harvey in person and confessing to him about all that had transpired and all that he had done. Even if his encounter with Harvey was transactional, Aaron truly felt a strange connection with him. He could not stop thinking about him. He had also thought about meeting a reliable reporter and sharing his side of the story without naming Harvey. He had even thought about just driving out of Texas to a faraway location for good to a place where Sima could not track him easily. But mostly, he was trying to get away from his own conscience and was terrified of the consequences. When the gas meter in his car showed it had only fifty more miles to go, he decided to look for a motel. And only after that warning, he decided to bring his aimless drive to a halt and found the nearest motel. Aaron realized he had been driving for more than five hours. He had crossed the border and was about thirty miles from Lake Charles, Louisiana.

The exterior of the motel was uninviting. It was a one-story building with a flat roof and brown siding. There was a row of windows, but they were all covered with curtains. The only entrance was a glass door at the front of the building. There was a sign above the door, but it was so faded that it was difficult to read. The parking lot was empty, and there were no cars visible on the street. It looked like the kind of place where one would go to get a cheap room for the night or by the hour, but not somewhere one would want to stay for very long. In other words, the place was what Aaron was looking for that night. He went inside and found no one at the reception desk. He kept buzzing the bell for a dozen times before an old man, half-asleep, showed up. Aaron did not have a problem checking in. The old man asked Aaron to fill in his name, address, phone number, and car registration details. Aaron thought that for a small motel that did not invite a lot of guests, this was an overkill. He filled in all his details and got the room key.

When he stepped into his room, the smoke-stained walls of the dingy motel room closed in around Aaron like a prison. He could hear traffic outside, but it felt a million miles away. The only light came from a neon sign that cast an eerie glow over the bed. He sat down on the edge of the mattress and wondered how he ended up there. He went to Corpus Christi chasing a dream. Corpus Christi was a big city compared to the small town he grew up in. And all he had found now was disappointment. He thought he could make it in politics on his own despite being a gay, but he was wrong. Now, like many gays in Texas who get ridiculed, bullied, and even ostracized by their own families, friends, and communities, he understood he, too, was just another lost soul, alone and afraid. Worse, he had exploited another gay man's vulnerable moment and used it to advance his career. Something he was not proud of.

But even in this dark place, a part of Aaron kept telling him that he would not give up hope. He lifted his head up and saw the neon light. There was a moment of clarity.

I must come clean with Richard Harvey. That's the only to relieve myself of this burden, he thought to himself. Anything else he tried to do would only complicate things further. If Senator Harvey was able to forgive him, then that was enough for Aaron. All the tension he was carrying over the past few days would be gone in that moment. He rested the back of his head on the hard pillow. His eyes closed and he fell asleep within seconds.

The hallways of the Texas State Capitol were often busy, with lobbyists and other visitors crowding the halls. However, the office of Texas State Senator Richard Harvey was always a hive of activity. Despite the constant coming and going, the staff always seemed to be on top of things. It was clear that they were well-organized and efficient. The senator himself was always polite and had a ready smile for everyone he met. Having worked on Wall Street, he still carried a little of the corporate persona in him. Abhinav Agarwal had called the senator's office the previous day to get a thirty-minute time slot on the senator's calendar. The senator had an extremely busy day, but he asked his staff to bump one of the donor meetings to the following week so he could accommodate Abhinav.

Abhinav was already in Austin to join the referendum celebrations with Governor Fisher. He and Steve Riggs were able to meet with the governor the following morning after that late night party. So Abhinav thought he would take advantage of his time in Austin and meet with Harvey. Both would have ideally preferred to meet for dinner, as they could discuss things more freely and in a more relaxed manner, but Abhinav was flying back to Houston that afternoon, so they really did not have too many options.

"Welcome to my humble office, Abhinav!" said Senator Harvey.

"Pleasure is mine, senator," said Abhinav. Both men shook hands and exchanged a quick hug

When Richard Harvey was working on Wall Street, he had more than one channel of communication to the oil industry. One was through Sima Daly, who was then interning in the PR department at GTO, but the other one was through Abhinav Agarwal, the CEO of RapFuel. But the Abhinav channel was not a direct one, as it would have been very easy for SEC and other regulators to track the connection that could have proved much costly for RapFuel. There were multiple layers involved—all of them disguised properly without raising any legal suspicion. No one really knew if it was a mere coincidence or if there was something else—but during Harvey's time there, Abhinav off-loaded more than two billion dollars worth of stocks. Not RapFuel stocks, but those of other companies.

Abhinav Agarwal and Richard Harvey's friendship went a long way back. Even before Harvey started working on Wall Street. They had continued to stay in touch all the way through Harvey's Wall Street years and then after he entered politics. Agarwal was the first one to write a check for Harvey's election campaign. He did it as soon as Harvey launched his campaign. In return, Harvey had helped create two critical draft bills that would have allowed oil companies to write off more in their tax returns on the expense side if they were able to show committed investments in alternative energy sources. As the author of the bill, Harvey also worked with Congress to get this bill passed. RapFuel had been the biggest beneficiary of this bill. Not many knew back then that Abhinav had learned of the contents of the bills even before they were passed and had sufficient time to get a head start on RapFuel's alternative energy investments.

"Too bad we are not meeting at our regular rendezvous spot. I would have said much more," Harvey said to Abhinav.

"Hear you, senator. Given the place we are at, I, too, will keep it short and cryptic. I wanted to ask you just one thing. Remember the two activists? The two who were behind exposing my confidential company data in that trial?" Abhinav asked.

"Sure, I do," Harvey responded.

Abhinav Agarwal, the CEO of RapFuel, was just laying out his plans to get to the two activists who handed a defeat in the courtroom for him and his company. Since the judgment day, Abhinav had been keeping his eyes on Russell and Emily. From a distance, he had been keeping track of their work through many observers. What Abhinav wanted to do was to arrest these two activists in an upcoming rally in Austin by using a tactic he believed they could improvise with the help of the law enforcement authorities. He just wanted to give a jolt to their systems and let them experience the comfort of a prison life for a night. Because the rally was going to happen in Austin, he wanted to inform the local senator from TX-14 so he could make sure that the police turned a blind eye to his dream on that day. In addition, he really wanted the police to be part of this, orchestrating the arrest.

Richard Harvey was shocked to listen to Abhinav's plan. Even in his wildest dreams, he would have never imagined a day would come when he would become part of a group, hatching a plan to intentionally arrest two activists who were fighting for a valid cause and standing up for the oppressed.

"This sounds a bit stretched out to me. If you are asking for permission, then my response would be, 'Who am I to give you permission?'" said Harvey. "But you are not asking for permission. You want me to be part of this whole thing by engaging the police directly with this. Wow," he finished, still in a state of surprise.

"Why don't you do something white-collarish? Like framing them for some accounting fraud or something?" Harvey asked.

"Brilliant, senator. Thank you for that idea." Abhinav was truly impressed by this suggestion. And he continued, "We will do both. Let's take care of them at the rally first. Then I will make sure their heads get so deeply buried in this accounting scandal that they would never be able to do this advocacy business anymore."

"Listen. I will talk to the police to try to keep the heat down during the rally. And whoever oversees arresting them, I will brief them the day before. You know, I'm still not happy doing this. But this is for old times' sake!" Harvey raised his coffee cup while Abhinav raised his glass of water to reciprocate.

Abhinav Agarwal and Steve Riggs flew together from Houston for the referendum success party. They flew on Abhinav's private plane. The day after the party, while Abhinav was meeting with Richard Harvey, Derek Fisher had another meeting with Steve Riggs. Interestingly, both the oil executives from Houston knew nothing about this private and secret meeting the other one was having.

Governor Fisher had reached out to Steve Riggs for an early morning meeting at his residence—the governor's mansion. The Texas governor's mansion has been the official residence of the Governor of Texas since 1856. With eighteen rooms on the ground floor and a full basement, the mansion had earned its right to be added to the National Register of Historic Places and has also been recognized as a Recorded Texas Historic Landmark. The mansion was open for public tours during weekdays unless and until there were emergency repairs or alerts. Being a weekday today, Fisher thought it was best to meet Riggs before they opened the mansion for public tour. There were many private spots inside the mansion where he could meet Riggs, but when the mansion was opened for the public tour, he was only increasing the chances of exposing the Riggs visit.

Riggs arrived through the western entrance promptly at 7:00 AM. Per instructions given to him, he had his driver park his car a block away, and he simply walked to the entrance. Once in, he was whisked away to a patio facing a lawn. A small table with coffee and tea pots along with a few pastries were set up. There were just two chairs. Steve Riggs looked at the well-manicured lawn. The grass was a deep green, and the flowers were in full bloom. The few trees he saw were tall and stately, and the bushes were trimmed perfectly. It looked like a perfect spot for a cozy date. Or a business meeting.

The governor walked behind Riggs and asked, "Enjoying the flowers?"

Startled, Riggs responded, "Indeed, governor. Nothing like a quiet morning and some flowers to admire at."

"And a cup of coffee would complete that morning. Wouldn't it?" said Fisher as he poured himself a cup.

The two men, in their buttoned-down shirts and neatly pressed slacks—which many would deem quite formal for an early morning meeting—sat down sipping their coffees.

Governor Fisher wanted to talk to Steve Riggs about the state of the oil companies after Texas became independent. He had been working with his oil czar, Abhinav Agarwal, to put together a plan for gaining complete control of the oil companies that were based out of Texas and registered in the state but were leasing federal offshore public lands for their drilling. Based on the initial draft of the plan that Abhinav had put together, Fisher felt that he had enough ammunition on his side to negotiate with the Union, starting with the president himself. The plan was not circulated with other Texas oil company executives. So, essentially, Steve Riggs had not seen the plan. Fisher—the extremely savvy businessman, who could twist and bend rules when needed if he could and add an extra zero in his income—realized what an enormous opportunity he was sitting on.

Before he had a chance to meet with the POTUS and the Secretary of Energy among others to negotiate the oil company exits from the Union, Fisher wanted to know how much leverage he had individually on these oil companies to benefit his personal exchequer. GTO was a big fish, and since Steve Riggs was already in Austin, Fisher figured he would throw the bait at him first and see what he was able to catch. Fisher wanted to make deals with these Texas oil companies, wherein he or someone recommended by him would benefit directly in exchange for him negotiating a successful exit from federal leasing. In addition, he would also promise a fair deal on the new leasing opportunity that Texas, the new independent country would float.

"Now that we are done with the referendum, the difficult journey starts towards trade negotiations," said the governor.

"The fun part. Right?" Riggs was warming up and waiting to see what the governor was going to throw at him.

"Abhinav as the oil czar has been doing a wonderful job. We will have to start meeting with the DC folks soon." Fisher was getting ready to serve his ace.

"Abhinav is a very knowledgeable man who could look at numbers and understand them the way I couldn't. And he has all our backing." Riggs was letting Fisher know that the oil company executives were behind Abhinav.

"I wouldn't have chosen him to be in this role if otherwise." Fisher smiled. "Let me not beat around the bush. I have reviewed Abhinav's first draft for the negotiation. And I like it. But here's the thing." Fisher started to pitch what he was looking for, then paused.

As a young Texan, Steve Riggs had a vision for the oil industry. He saw it as a powerful and convenient source of energy that could change the world. After getting his start in the industry, he quickly rose through the ranks to become the chief executive at one of the largest oil companies in the world. But his success did not come without challenges. In difficult economic times, he was forced to make tough decisions that often put him at odds with environmentalists and government regulators. Nevertheless, he remained committed to his vision for the oil industry and continued to fight for its place in the global economy. Today, Steve Riggs was one of the most respected leaders in the oil industry in the USA, and during his times he had had his fair share of negotiations with leaders holding powerful public offices—although none like this one with the Governor of Texas himself during a time like this when the state was seceding from the Union.

Steve Riggs was waiting for the governor to finish his pitch.

Fisher continued in a whispering tone, "I need five percent in GTO."

Steve Riggs was prepared for an explosive ask from Fisher, but even in his wild imagination he would not have thought of the Governor of Texas asking for a certain percentage of stocks in his company in return for a favor he would do.

"Pardon me. Did you just ask what I think you did? I mean . . ." Riggs put his coffee cup on the table.

"I am a businessman, and I damn well understand that in business you don't get what you deserve, you get what you negotiate. We've some time Mr. Riggs. No pressure. Think about it." Fisher got up.

When Riggs saw Fisher walk back into the mansion, he followed him.

"Have a great day, governor!" said Riggs, and the first person he thought of calling at that moment was Elizabeth Greenburg.

Riggs knew that they both had something that the other person wanted. The question was what he, Steve Riggs, the CEO of GTO, was willing to give up in order to get what he wanted. And what would he gain if he gave that up?

Mrs. Saunders strolled into the motel lobby at her usual time of six in the morning. It usually took her about an hour to prepare things for her daily chores. Today was a typical day, as she went about her duties, cleaning up the breakfast mess left by guests and straightening up the rooms. She carried a room chart with her that told her which day each guest was checking out, so she knew how to approach each room she was going to straighten up and clean. She had worked as a housekeeper at this motel for over twenty years, and it was like second home to her. As she went about her work, she chatted with the other staff members, smiled, and greeted at the motel guests if she ran into them in the corridors. It was just another day at the motel for Mrs. Saunders. Until she decided to open room 106 using her master. The guest was supposed to have checked out by 11:00 AM, but there was no response to her knocking on the door.

She saw no one on the bed, so she started pulling the sheets out. As she moved around the bed to clean, something caught her eye. There was a man lying in the bathtub, and he appeared to be unresponsive. Mrs. Saunders was shocked. In all her twenty years, she had never seen anything like this. She immediately ran out and called for help. The ambulance arrived within fifteen minutes, and the man was rushed to the hospital. Mrs. Saunders could not focus on her work for the next hour or so until the motel receptionist received an update from the hospital.

"Hello, the man the paramedics brought in from your motel earlier this morning—I am sorry to say, he is dead. He was your motel guest right?" the caller asked.

"Yes."

"What is … was … his name?"

"Ummm … Aaron Naylor. From Corpus Christi, Texas."

After Vanessa and Keith Glass met Senator Newell at Mr. Haddock's residence, their life had not been the same. The time the senator spent with Vanessa and Keith at Haddock's was very brief.

After Mr. Haddock introduced Vanessa and Keith to the senator, Vanessa said, "It's an absolute honor to meet you, senator!" and shook Newell's hands.

"The pleasure is mine," said the senator. He had a certain charm that would attract anyone around him to start paying attention to what he was going to say next. And with every word he spoke in a measured tone, he commanded respect more and more from the gathered crowd.

"There is a lot I want to discuss with you, Mrs. Glass. Perhaps tonight is not the right time for it. Let us enjoy the wonderful party Mr. Haddock is throwing in my honor. And I will have one of my staff members pick you both up from your house tomorrow at around noon. Let us meet for lunch. I will tell you more. Will that work?" said Senator Newell.

Vanessa and Keith looked at each other. And it was Keith who responded first. "Yes." Vanessa stared at him and then quickly realizing that the senator was watching her, shifting her glance to the senator and said, "Yes, of course."

Needless to say, Vanessa and Keith continued to throw multiple speculative theories as to why a senator would want to meet them. They did not even vote for him in any of the general elections. Could this be about the referendum, or was it about the next presidential elections? There were many questions and theories that they kept lobbing at each other. Neither of them could sleep well that night.

One of the last thoughts Vanessa had before she fell asleep was, *What kind of food will I get to choose from when I go out for lunch tomorrow?*

Keith was still awake. After many deliberations and tossing multiple theories, he was convinced that the meeting the next day was going to be about a job offer for Vanessa.

Maybe Mr. Newell has an old family member who needs a nurse. Maybe Mr. Haddock recommended Vanessa to him, and maybe he wants us to relocate because of that. Keith thought to himself as he struggled to fall asleep.

At around 11:50 AM the next day, a black Cadillac pulled in front of their house. Vanessa and Keith were already dressed up for their lunch date with the senator, waiting in their living room, and occasionally peeking through the blinds to check if the car had arrived. The driver did not step out of the car until it was 11:58 AM, and that was when the couple got up from the couch too. They locked the door and stepped outside. Vanessa was in awe of the beautiful car, and she reacted with her mouth agape: "Wow!" It was the blackest car she had ever seen. The paint seemed to suck in all the light, leaving only a deep, impenetrable darkness. The windows were tinted so dark that it was impossible to see inside, and the chrome trim added a menacing touch. Even the tires were black, providing a stark contrast to the bright white of the road. It was an imposing sight, and one that she would never forget. The very sight of the car gave an impression of very important people traveling inside. The driver was holding the rear passenger door open, and Vanessa got in first. Keith followed her. They thanked the driver as he closed all doors before setting off.

When the car arrived at Moody Gardens Hotel, Vanessa and Keith were puzzled. The driver held the door open, and they both got out of the car. Another well-dressed gentleman received and greeted them.

"Good afternoon, Mr. and Mrs. Glass. This way, please."

The couple followed him without asking any questions. They reached a modern restaurant inside the hotel called Shearn's Seafood and Prime Steaks. The greeter asked them to follow him to a corner where it appeared they had a table reserved for them. They could see Senator Newell was already seated there. And he had two folders with him spread out on the table.

Newell saw Vanessa and Keith walk towards the table. He got up to greet them. He gently shook their hands and stretched his right arm to point at the seats. After they were seated, he ushered at the man who brought them to the restaurant to leave.

"This might seem like a lot to take in, what I am about to share. So why don't we enjoy our lunches first and then I will get to them?" Newell pointed at the folders he had with him.

Vanessa had been looking forward to this lunch all morning. As she scanned the menu, her eyes lit up when she saw one of her favorite dishes: lobster. She quickly placed her order and sat back to wait for others to order. Keith decided to get a shrimp pasta. They both looked at Newell for his order. And he got himself a lobster bisque and a salad. The food arrived after a very short wait. The three of them dived into their lunch right away. After what seemed like a very brief period, during which hardly any words were exchanged, Vanessa and Keith had finished their lunch and cleaned up their plates well, while Newell, seeing his guests clean up their plates, decided to stop eating. His fully empty soup bowl and half-empty salad plate indicated that he liked the bisque better. Vanessa was very much satisfied with her lunch. She leaned back in her chair with a contented smile on her face.

Once the waiter cleared all the plates from the table, the senator signaled for some coffee, which Vanessa and Keith stayed away from. He opened the first folder. It had old newspaper clippings and a couple of documents that looked like they were sale deeds of some kind from olden times. What the senator said next shocked Vanessa.

"My second great grandparents were slave owners. And this sale deed is proof that they purchased what I now know are your second great grandparents," Newell said, looking at Vanessa in her eyes.

"What? How? When?" Vanessa was startled, as she was clearly not prepared for this conversation. This was not even close to any of the theories she and Keith were discussing the previous night.

"Here are some newspaper clippings from the time when the Emancipation Proclamation was signed. And here are a few about the chattel slavery system when they existed. There's more here. These are not newspaper clippings, but some sort of list. A repository. The names of the people owned by different white families in the region."

"I don't know any of them. I know only my grandmother and my parents," Vanessa said in a low voice.

She was in a complete state of shock and was still gasping. She did not want to look at the images and the newspaper clippings. Her grandmother's face flashed in front of her eyes. She remembered some of the stories her grandmother had shared with her about her parents. But she did not recall anyone talking about her great grandparents and second great grandparents. Keith, on the other hand, was a little more composed and was open to receiving the folder from Newell. He flipped through the pages. The folder had been meticulously put together and laminated. And the contents were sorted in a chronological order.

Senator Newell continued to pick the second folder he had brought with himself and gave it to Keith. And asked him to go to the fifteenth page in the folder.

"According to my researchers, that photo you see there, one of the little girls in the front row. She is Vanessa's grandmother."

Vanessa immediately grabbed that folder from Keith's hands and started staring into that picture. She brought it very close to her eyes, as it was a very old image and there was no way to zoom it further.

"This is already a digitally enhanced photo. So I am not sure if you can see anything clearer than this," said Newell. "The third one from the left is your grandma, I am told."

They spent the next twenty-five minutes talking about the contents of the folder. It was mostly Newell talking and Keith occasionally interrupting with questions to understand what each newspaper clipping meant. Vanessa was still processing it all. Neither of them had any negative reaction towards Senator Newell after finding out he was descendent of a slaveholder. Vanessa tried to imagine her faceless second great grandparents who were forced to work for someone forever as slaves against their will. She thought about the inhuman conditions under which they lived, the cruelty they endured, and the strength it must have taken to survive. She thought about how possibly their sufferings had been passed down through the generations, affecting her own life in countless ways. The blood-and-sweat-soaked pages of the dark history lay bare open in front of her.

"Am I ashamed? Perhaps a little. But these were my second grandparents, and they did what they did. They owned slaves like many white folks did back then. I cannot change that fact. I do feel some responsibility now though to set some of the things right, things that are under my control and things that make sense to me. I have spent the past five years with a help of a research team to put this information together. And we have been trying to track all surviving members of the four families my ancestors owned. That brings me to why we are here today. Why I wanted to talk to you," Newell said in a hushed voice. "It's a proposal of sorts. A proposal in reparations if you will. I do not want you to respond right now. Just listen to what I have to say. It will seem like a lot to take in. And it sure is a lot to take in. So go home. Take your time. I will not put any pressure on you to respond. You will find out by when you must respond yourselves. You will know. I am sure of that. But please give this proposal a serious thought. That's all."

Vanessa and Keith kept looking at Senator Newell as they were waiting for him to share his proposal. Senator Newell took a deep breath and started talking again.

Not in a million years could Vanessa have imagined that someone would ask a question like this to her.

Sima had a cold glass of chardonnay in front of her. There was music coming out of her portable Bluetooth speaker that was placed right to her phone on the patio table. She had not taken a sip from her glass and was staring into the blankness. The afternoon rains had made the grass in her backyard gleam. There were black-throated sparrows—many of them visiting her feeder and relishing the seeds.

I did not want to become this. What would Dad think about what I have become? Sima thought to herself. Having lost both her parents in quick succession, Sima never had given herself the time to properly grieve. Every time she got sucked into a grief mode, she found excuses to break out of it. Today was no exception. A workaholic by nature, she had always found her work and her ambitions give her the outlet to stay busy. An excuse of a diversion.

A few weeks ago, when she decided to use Aaron for this assignment, the first thing she did was to have one of her security details people install a tracker app on Aaron's computer and phone. The security person worked with the IT personnel in Sima's office, who in the process of making all devices "Congress-compliant," asked all employees in Sima's office to bring their devices for regular verification. Everyone complied unsuspectingly. That included Aaron, too. The tracker app simply plotted the geolocation of the device and relayed it to a server periodically. The data on the server could be accessed from anywhere.

On the evening of the referendum when Sima had her poll-closing happy hour in her office, her mind was fixated on one thing only: how to stop Aaron. And where was he? So, as soon as the happy hour was over, she ran back to her desk and logged into her special admin account on the server, which was tracking the details of Aaron's devices. She noticed that the devices were moving. And they were moving along the biggest highways of the southeastern coastline of Texas. She kept tracking the devices until they stopped. She waited for another hour or so before confirming that Aaron was spending the night somewhere in that area, in which case she had the perfect opportunity to do what she wanted to do, unless Aaron had found out about the tracking app and he decided to discard the devices somewhere there. Either way, it was time to act. So she called her go-to person on her security details and instructed him what to do.

If the motel in which Aaron Naylor had security cameras outside, they would have been able to spot a pickup truck pull into their parking lot at 3:29 AM. The camera would have picked up a man in a baseball cap and jeans get out of that pickup truck, walk to the front door, and then pick up his cell phone to call someone. The camera would have also picked up another man walking from inside the motel, opening the front door, letting the baseball cap man inside.

If the motel's security camera on the corridor was not covered by a towel, it would have recorded the two men walking to room 106, the room in which Aaron was staying. It also would have captured the man in baseball cap walk out of Aaron's room, alone, at 3:48 AM.

If the motel had security cameras outside, they would have captured the same man in the baseball cap walk back to his truck and leave the parking lot exactly at 3:51 AM.

Sima received a call at 3:52 AM. She was home, lying on her bed and trying to go to sleep.

"It's done," said the voice on the other side. Sima took a deep breath and hung up the phone.

As she reminisced through these events, she was staring into the blankness. There was a chill in her bones. Then her phone rang, snapping her out of her hazy thoughts. It was Meghan.

"Ma'am. Sorry to share this news. They found Aaron dead at a motel near Lake Charles." Meghan sounded like she was sniffling and holding her tears.

"Lake Charles, Louisiana?" Sima asked. Not only did Sima know the answer to that question, but she also knew much more about Aaron's death than she let out. "I am not sure how to process this, Meghan. I need a minute," said Sima, gasping for breath.

"I understand. I feel sick, too, ma'am. I cannot begin to imagine," responded Meghan as she heard Sima disconnect the call.

CHAPTER 12

CURRENT DAY

"We were not planning. It was an emergency," Rosaline broke and blurted out.

That was the breakthrough Officer Ken was hoping for. He knew he had Rosaline. And Rosaline knew she was on the verge of being searched legally. When Officer Ken left her house that evening, he simply said, "I will see you soon. Just a reminder. Any attempt to leave town like your friend did, you know what the consequences will be. Don't want to make matters much worse than they are for Ava, do you?"

He had to wait until the next morning to go to the court. The judge was reluctant to listen to Officer Ken's attempt to establish a probable cause. He did not have evidence to prove how Rosaline Doughart was involved in an illegal activity. However, he tried hard to explain to the judge that Rosaline was in possession of an evidence, which was her phone, that was used to abet a crime, one committed by Ava. Even if Rosaline may or may not have been involved in committing a crime herself, Officer Ken argued that her phone record would help the Midland Police trace the whereabouts of Ava. The judge took some time before he decided to issue a warrant. And the warrant issued was not a blanket one, but it only allowed the Midland Police to search Rosaline's phone call and text records. The warrant also allowed the police to contact the carrier to obtain the corresponding records had Rosaline deleted the specific records on her device. *That's enough for the time being*, Ken thought.

Within an hour after getting the warrant, he reached Rosaline's house again. Long before Officer Ken showed up at her house, Rosaline, of course, had deleted all her text messages that she had ever exchanged with Ava. In fact, there was none after the incident. The only record that could prove Rosaline knew Ava was in trouble was when Ava called her from the grocery store parking lot.

"This was expected. A smart woman like you would have deleted everything on your phone," Ken said. "Not to worry. The warrant allows us to contact your carrier. And I already did. We should have the data in forty-eight hours."

The agony of waiting for another forty-eight hours was just too much to bear for Ken. So he had already come prepared with a plan to search Rosaline's email records from her computer. He pretended like it was part of his task and asked her to bring her computer to be investigated by his IT department. Rosaline did not go through the warrant in detail, so she brought her computer without suspecting any foul play by Ken. She knew it was only a matter of time before someone in the Midland Police Department found out more about her communication with Joanna. She had been in touch with Joanna almost daily since the time Ava was picked up by her. Barring the first email she had sent to Joanna asking for immediate help, since then, based on Joanna's suggestion, they had been using the same online forum where they met for the first time. That forum allowed private messages, and that had been the mode of communication between the two.

The IT expert whom Midland Police employed for such matters was already outside the house. He was waiting for a call from Ken before he went inside. As soon as Ken got hold of the computer, he called him. The twenty-something guy, not a stereotypical computer nerd, walked in with his computers and other gear, and took a seat at Rosaline's dining table. He opened Rosaline's computer and with her help, logged into all email accounts. After searching for a few minutes, he gave a thumbs-down to Officer Ken. He enjoyed these kinds of challenges. That evening would have turned out to be another boring evening for him if it was simply a matter of searching through someone's emails. Now he had a chance to do something more.

He set up his computer right next to Rosaline's on the dining table and logged into a few different applications. After finding out which IP addresses pertained to Rosaline's home, he was able to download an history of all the websites Rosaline had visited in the past one week. He had a tool where he could feed this browsing history and it would generate a report with warnings—warnings of sites that were worth looking into further. That's how he narrowed his search down to three websites that Rosaline had been frequently visiting in the past week. One was the online forum that she used for communication with Joanna. And then other two websites were language learning websites that were flagged by the tool because they were being hosted in Russia.

Officer Ken thanked the IT expert and asked him to send the invoice for his time before letting him go. Ken now had all the details of Rosaline's communication with Joanna.

He looked at her with an evil smile and said, "Now, if this is not incriminating evidence, I don't know what it is." He did not let her respond. He called Captain Ramirez right away and informed him of the progress he had made. It was Ramirez's call now to make the next move. Ken had shared with Ramirez that Joanna was from Carlsbad, New Mexico. Ken knew that now they were dealing with an interstate crime, and given the nature of the crime for which they were going after Ava, it would be highly unlikely that it became a federal crime. Officer Ken understood Captain Ramirez needed his time to come up with a plan. Before the IT expert left, Ken had asked him to do some more digging on Joanna's background like her address, phone number, employment information, and more. The IT expert said he would get back to Ken as soon as he had more information.

Captain Ramirez was out on a patrol duty when he received this call from Ken. Given the urgent nature of the case, he called in for someone else to substitute for him on his patrol while he went back to the station. One of the first things he did as soon as he went back was to pull out manuals he had in his office about interstate criminal pursuit, the extradition process, protocols, et cetera. In fact, they had a separate section for Texas-New Mexico interstate crimes just like they had with other bordering states. But what Ramirez could not find an answer for was if this crime would be recognized under UCEA, or the Uniform Crime Extradition Act. He concluded that he needed someone at the highest level in the state to give him the authority to discuss UCEA with New Mexico so he could initiate the extradition procedure for Ava. In this case, given this was the first of its kind crime that they were pursuing someone for, he figured he needed the Texas AG to get involved. In the state of Texas, after Governor Fisher's administration had recently criminalized certain books and teachings of certain subjects in public schools, Ava's case was the first case where they were ready to charge someone, an educator to be precise, with serious criminal charges.

What his wife Camila made him promise kept ringing in Ramirez's ears.

"Honey, please promise me, if you ever find her, you won't harm her in any which way. Please."

Juana enjoyed having a meal outdoors on a beautiful day like today. Since she was going to meet her dad today, patio seating at a restaurant was the perfect way to enjoy the weather. While she was waiting for her father to join, she did what she always did—indulged in people watching. Alex was not a big fan of sitting outside, as he did not much care for the noisy ambience. But he agreed when Juana asked because it was not every day he got to have a meal with his daughter.

When he arrived at the restaurant, the waiter directed him to the table outside where Juana was already seated.

"Papa, so good to see you." She got up and gave her dad a tight hug. Since the shooting incident, she had been in touch with him multiple times a day and talking to him almost every night. But meeting in person was different. She felt guilty for not meeting her dad sooner. He sounded better on the phone compared to how he looked in person. Juana noticed that her dad had developed dark circles around his eyes. His walk was somewhat dreary, and he did not seem to have the spring in his step that she was so used to seeing. Alex kissed his daughter on her cheek before releasing her from his right hug.

They both sat down and ordered their lunch.

After ordered his salad, Alex paused for a second and then said, "I will have the same thing," as he pointed at the iced tea Juana was having. "It's a hot day!" he said and smiled at the waiter.

Juana and Alex looked at the consolidated list Alex had put together in a Google Sheet. According to Alex's research, the state Texas had witnessed fifty-two different incidents of hate crimes statewide since the time Derek Fisher called for a TEXIT referendum. These were fifty-two incidents that at least one local media outlet had reported: on TV or on their website or through their print media. In addition, Alex had also gathered that there were at least sixty-five to seventy more hate-related minor incidents throughout the state since Fisher called for a referendum, incidents that were not reported by the media but were covered by the public on social media platforms with some photo or video evidence. Alex had not done any fact-checking on these public reported incidents.

All the fifty-two incidents collated by Alex on the Google Sheet had a clear motive—race or religion-based hatred, resulting in a violent crime. These incidents had caused twenty-eight deaths and fourteen minor injuries, while the remaining ten were in critical conditions, still battling for their lives. The twenty-eight included Alex's four men. Juana was furious looking at the numbers, and she verified each of those fifty-two incidents by clicking on the links that Alex had attached on the Google Sheet.

"Good work, Papa!" She wiped a tear of her eyes. "What next?"

"Juana, my girl, you set me on this path. Without your motivation and this idea, I would have been lost. I would have taken a different route and failed miserably in my attempt to seek justice for my men. This has given me more purpose to what I want to do next. With just anger, I would end up nowhere. But now, I have a plan. Listen . . ." Alex started narrating his next steps in his plan to seek justice for the four men who worked for him and also to demand answers from Fisher for his failure to stand up for the minorities in the state.

Alex explained that he was in the process of building a broader Latino coalition across Texas by working with community leaders from each city, and the local community if possible. There was no centralized database of sorts to get this information from. So Alex had tasked a couple of high school students from his community to scour for information from every county and city in Texas. They had to build a database with the contact details of these community leaders. He thought he was almost seventy-five percent done with this work and he should have the first cut of the database with all the contact details within the next day or so.

"Then are you going to meet them all?" Juana was curious.

"That would be ideal. Wouldn't it?" Alex responded and continued that his plan at first was to establish a communication line with all of them. He understood not every person was going to be as passionate about fighting against Fisher as he was. So he wanted to spend a few days making calls individually to all of them, establish the first line of communication and trust with them, and then try to gauge their interest level in fighting for justice for the community as a whole. And more importantly, to hold Fisher accountable for instigating white supremacy mobs throughout the state, unchecked, and for being an active supporter of anti-minority and anti-white rhetoric, especially against the immigrant population in Texas who migrated from south of the border.

"I am going to build a team with whoever is interested. Then we are going to start an open campaign against these hate crimes. That's why I want only those who are passionate about this cause to join the fight first. Only those who will stay through with the fight till the end," Alex concluded.

"Wow. That's impressive, Papa. Let me know how I can be of help," Juana said.

When they parted after lunch that day with a quick hug, Juana asked her dad to be careful when Alex mentioned that he planned to meet Congresswoman Sima Daly with his new Latino coalition team after launching online and TV campaigns against these hate crimes.

"I will, Mi'jita! I will. Love you."

It was a hot summer day in Washington, DC, and even though the senator's office was air conditioned, Senator Dodson was sweating profusely, and his face was red with anger. He had just learned that Senator Brynes, as Senator Newell's proxy, met with the fifteen congressmen and women, and things did not look positive for the ratification at that moment based on Brynes's pitch to them. From his source, Dodson had learned that at least ten out of the fifteen were seriously considering the Newell deal.

The senator banged his fist on the desk and shouted, "I'll show him! I'll make him regret this!" He then picked up the phone and called his staff member, who would be his future campaign manager should he launch his presidential bid.

"Start putting together a plan for attack," he said. "I'm going to make sure that Senator Newell does not even think about this anymore."

The senator hung up the phone and began to plot his revenge. Little did he know that his secretary was on the phone at the same time with someone about a new bill that they were working on, and that she did not bother to mute her side of the phone when Dodson was speaking to the other staff member.

Congressman Williams just finished typing an email, which he was about to send to the secret group of Edward and Grace. He read it one more time before he clicked on send. The week's time he had given them both was almost up, and he wanted to remind them that they should be meeting him with more substantial proofs for their dirt on the Goose. He was checking with them both if Thursday evening would work. And instead of a restaurant or a bar, he invited them to his house.

The backyard pool at the congressman's house was a beautiful sight. The water was crystal clear, and the water was just cool enough to make one enjoy the hot summer evenings. The pool was surrounded by a deck with chairs and umbrellas. There was also a hot tub. The congressman's wife, Kimberly Williams, was very friendly, and she showed Edward and Grace where the drinks were in the backyard. A table had been converted into a temporary bar that had wine, beer, water, rum, bourbon, and some mixers along with a bucket of ice. Kimberly engaged with them in small conversations as she walked with them to the pool where her husband was swimming.

"What a beautiful house you have, congressman!" said Grace. "And your wife is lovely and very kind."

"Thank you. Welcome home. Please find a seat anywhere by the pool. I have four more laps to go. Will join you shortly," said Evan Williams, flipping back into the water.

Grace was admiring his physique and his broad shoulders. And Edward was admiring the congressman's perfect freestyle strokes and the speed and elegance with which he was navigating the water. Kimberly observed Grace looking at her husband's body and smiled.

"Have fun, y'all. I know he wants to talk business with you. So I will see you later," said Kimberly before walking back into the house.

As promised, after four laps, Evan got out of the pool, draped himself in a long white towel, put on his flip-flops, and walked towards the area where Edward and Grace were sitting. And then he remembered he needed a drink. So he walked back to the bar area and grabbed himself a can of Miller Lite. The sound of the fizz that came when he popped open the can quenched his thirst. He took a big swig. He walked back.

"Tell me guys. Tell me you got something," said Evan Williams.

It was Edward who started. After following the trail of the PAC he was talking about during their last meeting, his source was able to establish ample connections between the PAC donations and the timing of new ordinances that were enacted by the Dallas, Collin, and Denton counties, which effectively relaxed certain gambling rules. The PAC donations themselves were on public record and Edward had copies of the same. Edward's source was also able to establish the link between the PAC and the poker club that Fisher belonged to with proof. He had receipts. All that was left was to find some proof that linked Fisher directly to the club and potentially some financial statements of the club. Edward assured the congressman that he had his source working on getting the official membership database of the club. However, financial statements were going to be impossible to obtain.

"This is good, Edward. But I am afraid not good enough yet for me to tackle the Goose," Williams expressed his disappointment. He looked at Grace, hoping she had something more substantial.

"Congressman, trust me, we are close. I will get you the membership record within a day or two," Edward assured the congressman.

"We'll see," countered Williams.

"I have some good news, congressman," said Grace, pulling her phone out. She looked around and made sure there was no one within reasonable hearing distance. Then she opened the messenger app and opened a particular chat window where there was an audio recording.

"Listen," she said. Both Williams and Edward came closer to her phone.

The eighty-one-second audio clip was a conversation between Gloria Fisher and the Secret Service agent with whom she had a fling for three months before Derek found out. The conversation was sensuous, sexy, and explicit. The Secret Service agent was addressing her as "Gloria" and she was addressing him with a pet moniker, "BD." After listening to the clip, both Edward and Williams looked at each other with their dropped jaws.

Grace smiled at them both.

"This is good stuff, Grace." Williams was very appreciative, and he turned around and looked at Edward.

"Edward, I will wait for two more days for your proof. Just let me know through an email when you are ready." Williams felt he was closer to having that big conversation with Fisher than he ever thought he would be when he started this operation. There was a sense of joy rushing through his body.

"Before you ask, Edward and Grace, you will be rewarded for your work. No matter what happens to the presidency, you will get an advance in two days once I am satisfied with the proof you give me," said Williams. "In case the presidency happens, then I guess we don't have write the second check. You know our door will be open for you both. Needless to say, if the presidency doesn't happen, then your second installment will arrive soon."

When Edward and Grace left the congressman's house, they wanted to say goodbye to Kimberly. They could not find her. Evan sensed what they were trying to do. He picked his cellphone and called Kimberly. Within a few seconds, Kimberly came down and met them at the foyer area.

"We are letting your husband free. I know it must be annoying when you have business contacts coming home. It kind of blurs the separation between personal and professional lives. Sorry for being those intrusive guests tonight. Thank you for receiving us such a warmth," Grace said.

"You're welcome. You don't have to be sorry. I understand. It was great meeting you two. Hope we run into you guys around more often," Kimberly said.

"For that you have come to Austin," said Edward with a big laughter.

We all faced choices in life, some more difficult than others. But what would we do when the choice was between doing what was right and losing something important to us? On the one hand, we may have felt a strong sense of duty to do what was right, even if it meant sacrificing our own interests. On the other hand, we may have been reluctant to give up something that we have worked hard for or that was important to us. It could be a tough call to make, but ultimately, one must decide which was more important: doing the right thing or protecting our own interests. Whichever choice one made, one would have to live with the consequences.

Ava Walters knew that more than anyone else. She had thought over this during the entire time she had been holed up in that house in the middle of nowhere. When she did not have Juana for company and when her mind was not too exhausted to stay awake and indulge in self-introspection, she had thought about her choices over and over again.

The more she thought, the more she was convinced that if she changed her mind and surrendered to the Midland Police, she would forever regret her decision to do so. As painful as the consequences of her current choice were, she had something worth fighting for and maybe she could light the spark for a statewide protest by educators against these draconian attacks on education. Maybe she could become the face of the new teacher resistance.

Joanna's car pulled to the back of the house. It was past 10:00 PM. When Joanna walked in, Ava noticed that she did not look her normal self. For someone who worked ten-hour shifts, did some side gigs, and then drove an hour to this house in the middle of nowhere, Ava noticed that Joanna's mind was always energetic, and she was ever full of ideas even late at night. But the Joanna she saw tonight was not the same. Ava waited for Joanna to say something, but instead she just left the bag of food she brought with herself for Ava on the cot and went to sit on the beanbag in the corner. The beanbag had been a new addition to the house.

"Everything all right?" asked Ava.

"No. I got fired today." Joanna sounded like she was avoiding getting into details.

"What the fuck? Why?" Ava was curious nevertheless.

"You really want to know? It's because of you." Joanna blurted out something that she knew would be hurtful to Ava, something she did not mean at all from her very rational and reasonable heart.

Ava was silent. There was a sense of guilt that rushed through her body. She covered her face with both her arms. She wanted to cry but no longer was able. She was simply exhausted.

"I am sorry I said that. I didn't mean that. I shouldn't have. I'm such a bitch." Joanna walked towards the cot as if she wanted to give a hug to Ava.

Ava lifted her face and saw Joanna coming towards her. She got up and gave a very tight hug to Joanna. The two women stayed in that embracing position for a while. Ava was gently patting on Joanna's shoulders, and Joanna was doing the same, completely unaware of them doing that. Ava felt very grateful for all that Joanna had done, and she had already been thinking about leaving the place the moment she found out that the police had tracked down Joanna through Rosaline.

"You think they know who you are now?" Ava asked.

"I am absolutely sure they have me pinned. The manager couldn't even look into my eyes when he asked me to leave. I asked him why he was letting me go after working there for twelve years. I asked him seven or eight times. He just kept saying sorry and he couldn't give me a reason. Apparently, they were orders from his boss. Motherfuckers."

"I'm sorry," Ava said, hugging Joanna again.

"Don't be. I feel like I'm on this fight with you, Ava. I guess I've always been on this fight the moment I picked you up from that gas station. Just didn't realize. We are going to fight until your rights as a teacher are restored. Or until whatever heck that could happen next that will send this fight in the right direction." Joanna rattled out a battle cry, and continued, "It's just that my priority now is to find the next spot to move you to. And I don't have too many options. The only thing that's going to give us time to think about where to go next is the whole interstate crime mess and how they would spin this crime to extradite you from New Mexico."

"I hope Jason picks the story before that," Ava replied, and then as an afterthought added, "Wonder what they did to Rosaline!"

The price of freedom was eternal vigilance. In other words, if one wanted to maintain one's liberties, they must be ever vigilant against those who would take them away. This has always been as true of individuals as it is of societies. Each of us had a responsibility to stand up for what we believe in, even when it was unpopular or inconvenient to do so. This can require making sacrifices, such as giving up time or money or losing their careers or loved ones or putting themselves at risk. But if people were not prepared to make these sacrifices, then they could not hope to preserve their freedoms for future generations.

Ava Walters was putting herself at risk and had already made the biggest sacrifice of losing her loved ones. Now she was also risking the lives of her friends who really cared for her.

Dudley wanted to go see the woman they dropped off at the shelter the previous night as soon as he could. When Burl arrived at the hotel after his meeting with the commissioner, he asked him when they could go see the woman. Burl really had not thought about this, since he was occupied with his meeting with the commissioner in the morning and subsequently with the upcoming meeting with the governor, which was not in his original agenda at all. But when Dudley asked that question, he thought about it and responded in a way that did not quite satisfy Dudley. Burl wanted them to do some homework and come up with a plan to help the woman instead of just meeting her.

"How about we contact a women's support group or something?" Burl asked. "This is Austin. We should be able to find a few."

That's what they did. Dudley went online, searched for women's help and support groups and organizations in Austin, and called them one by one, until he found one organization who had someone picking up the phone who understood this woman's dire condition. She suggested that Dudley contact another shelter home that specialized in caring for women in potential legal distress like this woman, and once they were able to accommodate her there, then their organization could take her case up directly from that point. Dudley made a call immediately to the women's shelter and reserved spots for her and her daughter. He was relieved to hear that there was a trustworthy process in place, and he started to breathe easy.

Burl and Dudley decided to get lunch from a Chick-Fil-A that was not too far away from their hotel. After they finished their meal there, they packed two extra meals to go for the woman and her daughter. They arrived at the homeless shelter where they had dropped them off the previous night and parked their car along the curb, outside the main entrance. They went inside fearing to see a place filled with despair and desperation. Contrary to their expectation, what they saw was a place that was the opposite. The shelter was a place of hope and possibility. The people who resided there had faced challenges that Burl and Dudley couldn't have imagined, and yet they continued to fight for a better life. Most people there seemed resilient and determined, and they reminded Burl and Dudley that human beings were capable of overcoming anything. The staff members there were incredibly supportive.

Shelters like this could be a place where people came to get away from the outside world, a place where they could feel safe and secure. It could also be a place where people came to find themselves. When one was homeless, one was constantly moving, trying to find somewhere to sleep, somewhere to eat, somewhere to use the bathroom. They were always on the move, and it could be hard to find time to think about who they were and what they wanted in life. But when they walked into a homeless shelter, all those variables changed. For a few hours, they could just be. They could sit down, relax, and think about their lives and what they wanted to do with it. They could reflect on their pasts and learn from their mistakes. Though not everyone who walked into a homeless shelter could do this, some people could plan for their future and dream about what they want to achieve, during the time they spend inside a homeless shelter. In many ways, a homeless shelter could be a blank canvas; it's up to every individual to decide what they wanted to make of it.

When one of the staff members asked Dudley whom they were looking for, Dudley pointed at the woman and the daughter sitting in one corner. The woman was reading a magazine, which she probably picked from the shelter collection, while the girl was coloring a book with crayons. The staff member went to call the mom and daughter duo. As soon as she saw Dudley, she waved at him enthusiastically. She felt like she had just met one of her friends or a family member. When Dudley mentioned what the plan was, she thought about it for a while and agreed to it without asking too many questions.

"Thank you, for all this," she said. "You know if I had stayed here one more night, it would have become difficult to leave. It's really a safe place. With beautiful people. And there are many who do not have the promises of future like I do."

"Here's lunch." Burl handed over the Chick-Fil-A meal bags to them and turned towards the front door of the car. The mom and daughter opened the door, got into the back seat, and started eating. Dudley turned towards Burl and smiled. The two men sat in the front seat while the two women ate. Then they drove the women to the other shelter, which would set the pace for the woman's long road to justice and eventual restitution.

"Here's my number. You may call me anytime. They will let you make calls from here," said Dudley with moist eyes. Burl was feeling a little heavyhearted, too, but mostly he was proud of his friend Dudley and what he had done.

"Thank you," said the woman, who walked into the shelter with her daughter's right hand held firmly in hers.

The women's support group that Dudley spoke to earlier had already contacted this shelter, and they had set up their first interview with the woman for the next morning. When they heard that, Burl and Dudley knew they had done whatever the best thing was under the circumstances. Once again Burl looked at Dudley, and they both smiled at each other. They drove back to the hotel with a sense of satisfaction that was new, something they had not experienced before in their lives.

Burl and Dudley spent most of their Thursday driving around Austin, visiting Butler Park, and eating a couple of good meals. When they got back to the hotel in the evening, Burl decided to prepare notes for his meeting with Fisher. Since he did not know how long the meeting would last, he wanted to make use of his time effectively. He asked Dudley a couple of questions about his family farm as he prepared his notes. Dudley's father still was the primary caretaker of their farm, and Dudley was working with his family in the farm, just like most farming families in Lubbock County.

The hotel breakfast area on Friday morning was a bit busy even at 7:00 AM. And on days like today, it was in a place like the hotel breakfast lobby one got to see the see the best and the worst of humanity on display. On one side of the room, there were those who were bleary-eyed and barely awake, struggling to get through their morning coffee. On the other side, there were those who were well-rested and full of energy, chatting and laughing over pancakes and eggs.

Burl looked at Dudley and said, "In some ways, the breakfast area is a microcosm of the world outside. Isn't it? There are those who are struggling just to get through the day, and then there are those who seem to have everything going for them." He laughed.

"How true!", responded Dudley, clearing this throat.

When Burl Fogg arrived at the governor's office at 11:45 AM, the protocol to get in was a bit different from the one they followed at the commissioner's office. Once he entered and was asked to wait in the waiting lobby, he started to feel a bit nervous. He tried to recollect his first meeting with the commissioner of Texas Department of Agriculture. He recollected how nervous and anxious he felt before the meeting, and how quickly that feeling disappeared once he started talking. He forced that memory again and again almost like a pep talk. When it was his time to go in, the governor's executive assistant asked him to follow her into the office.

The governor's office was supposed to be more than just a room where someone held court and made deals. It was also a place that reflected the values and history of the state. When Burl walked in, he noticed how the Texas governor's office was adorned with portraits of past governors, including Sam Houston and Ann Richards. The desk in the office was made from an extinct wood called Texas ebony. And the window in the office looked out onto the State Capitol Building.

He thought to himself, *Wow. There's something special about being able to sit in that office and look out at the very place where laws are made.*

The governor greeted him, "You must be Mr. Fogg. When I was in college, I had a friend by name David Fogg. Hope you are not related to each other."

"Not that I know of, governor. But I would never know. We Foggs are known to get around a bit," said Burl with a forced laughter, as he shook his hands with the Governor of Texas.

"The commissioner tells me you have a cautiously critical opinion on our preparedness?" The governor asked the most difficult question first.

"No. It was nowhere near as cautious as you have been made to believe, governor," said Burl, brandishing a nervous smile.

"Listen. I do not want to waste your time and mine. What is that you want to tell me?" The governor was very direct.

For the next ten minutes, Burl went on a rant about what he had been observing elsewhere in the world. He told Fisher that in his observation, even the USDA was struggling to transfer the latest farming techniques and general knowledge about farming in general from around the world. He finally added that he had not seen any actions proactively taken by the Fisher Administration in days leading up to the referendum and after—actions that would build confidence in farmers like him about the future. Burl also explained how through its continued resistance towards the Union government that Texas agriculture had sadly fallen behind in technological advancements. By not cooperating with USDA, Texas had continuously missed out opportunities to enhance and improve some of the equipment, appliances, et cetera.

"What do you propose I do, Mr. Fogg?" Fisher, in his booming voice, interrupted Burl, almost dismissively. Fisher was already offended by the way Burl was directly accusing him for how poorly Texas had fallen behind. He was not going to let him continue with his pompous theory, he told himself. He also did not want Burl to contact any media outlet to share his views and opinions on how Texas was ill-prepared for TEXIT.

"Do you want to be my agriculture czar?" Fisher asked.

Interestingly, Burl had thought of this scenario. He somehow felt that Fisher, instead of asking questions about farming techniques, public policies on deregulation versus regulation, and then explaining why they were doing what they were doing, might go for the carrot treatment. Fisher was known for his abrasive approach when it came to negotiating. That was exactly Fished had done now—buying one's critics if one could and not giving an opportunity for the critic to pile on.

Burl was quick to respond. "No. Thank you, governor. It's an honor you would even consider making me an offer like this. Unfortunately, I will not be able to accept this offer. For personal reasons," Burl said.

"Then I have got only one thing to say to you, Mr. Fogg. You may leave now. I have my next meeting in five minutes," Fisher dismissed him.

Burl was not prepared for this sudden end to their meeting. A meeting that took a bizarre turn. He got up and asked, "So will we see you meeting more farmers from now on?"

Fisher's rage was growing by the second.

"I know my job, Mr. Fogg. I am pretty good at it. You had something to say. I let you say it. Have a blessed day!" And with that he too got up from his chair. When Burl came into the governor's office earlier, he wanted to talk about that woman he and Dudley had rescued. But now he was not going to be able to do so because the meeting had taken a rather unexpected twist and a not so happy ending.

"Mr. Governor, you have no idea what fire you have lit in the state. This politics of hatred you are playing with will only end in a huge disaster for the state after we become independent," Burl said in a loud voice before leaving the room. He had no idea what got through him and why he wanted to say that out loud. He found it hard to believe that the same Burl, who was a vocal supporter of Fisher during the gubernatorial elections, challenged the very man whom he supported, on his face, in a one-on-one meeting.

It was often said that the true measure of a person's character was what they did when no one was watching. This statement was especially true when it came to speaking out against someone in a position of power. It took courage to stand up to someone who had the ability to make one's life difficult, and all too often, people chose to remain silent rather than risk retaliation. And on that day, Burl stood up for something he believed in against someone who could and would make his life extremely difficult.

"After all, what good is being a Christian if you can't put your faith into action by helping those in need?" asked Gavin to Beth.

But helping others was not always easy. There were times when one may be tired or busy, there were times when one's principles, ideologies, and politics may come between them and the person they wanted to help, and there are times when they lacked the resources to help, and it was often tempting to just ignore the person who needed help.

In the case of Gavin Forbes, it was politics and his personal ideologies. He had been taught from his childhood that if someone did anything to a womb, he or she was not being a good Christian. He took it on its face value. He never questioned the merit behind that claim. He never tried to look at it from the person who was carrying the embryo and see if any situation would make him think of an alternative position. He never had to think of this from a medical practitioner's perspective either to see what he or she would do if their patient was in need of treatment. Because that was how faith worked.

As a devout Christian man, Gavin had always taken his beliefs very seriously. He had not read the Bible cover to cover but he attended church every Sunday without fail. But for the first time in his life, Gavin had started to question the rationale of his faith. It seemed to him that many of the things that he once took for granted were now open to interpretation. He wanted to meet every single preacher in the church and priests who taught him what being a bad Christian meant and ask them if they had changed their minds. He was torn between his own goodness and his faith. Beth, his wife, on the other hand, was a woman of reason. She called herself a devout Christian, too, and attended church every Sunday with Gavin. But when it came to making everyday decisions that got her through the day, she would never let her faith come in between. She never had that conflict.

Gavin and Beth were lying next to each other on their bed. Beth was reading a book and falling asleep. Gavin kept tossing and turning around with his eyes closed. Suddenly, he opened his eyes and turned towards Beth and said, "Honey, we need to help Lisa get out of Texas. Before you react, I know. I know. I've thought this through."

Beth closed her book, placed it on the side table, and looked at Gavin. She brought her left hand forward and brushed through his hair. And she held his left hand with her right. There were no further words exchanged between them that night. All Beth did was smile. It was the kind of smile that communicated a deep understanding and acceptance of who Gavin was, as well as a deep intimacy and closeness. They both lay silent. Beth kissed Gavin on his eyes and then on his lips.

Sometimes, the most profound moments were the ones where people said nothing at all. In the silence, they could truly listen to each other and connect on a deeper level. They could feel the warmth of the other person and savor the moment. There was a comfort in knowing that they did not need to fill the space with words—that simply being together was enough. In those quiet moments, they could feel the love between them more strongly than ever before. And in those quiet moments, Gavin could feel Beth's unconditional love for him and her unflinching support for what he was about to do.

The next morning, Gavin and Beth visited Lisa. They had messaged her earlier in the morning and informed her that they were coming over.

"It's almost an eerie coincidence that you guys said you were coming over to meet me and I received a call from Emily this morning," Lisa said as she opened the door to let them inside her house.

"Emily . . .?" Beth asked in an inquisitive tone.

"TWRA. Russell and Emily. That Emily," said Lisa.

Emily and Russell, who were on a mission now with Jason Greer, had remembered to carry a few critical files with them. Files containing details of the women they were working with before TWRA was clouded by legal issues and were forced to close their operations. Since there was no way for any of these women to contact them anymore—neither via phone nor email, Emily and Russell had been trying to contact these women one by one to check how they were doing and if they needed any further assistance.

Lisa handed over the envelope to Gavin, the envelope Emily and Russell had given her a few weeks ago when they visited her.

"It's just details of a few clinics. Out of state. And how to contact them, et cetera," Lisa said, then added, "Then there are also a bunch of instructions, pages from medical journals, et cetera. You know, some self-care stuff, if I decide to go through with this procedure."

"The reason we are here, Lisa, is exactly for this. Beth is in this with me. One hundred percent. I am going to help you get to this clinic, wherever. We are going to help you. We want to. You and I will leave any day you want to leave. Beth will be here, and she will take care of Lily. Lily needs her mom back—safe and healthy. You just let me know when you want to leave. Okay?" Gavin said in a shaky voice. He was surprised to see tears well up in his eyes.

Lisa became an emotional mess. She tried holding her tears for a few seconds, and then she bawled out loud. She was not prepared for Gavin becoming her guardian angel during a dire moment like this in her life. This was one of those times when Lisa had found herself in a situation where she genuinely needed help and was deeply touched when someone offered to assist her. She realized that Gavin's act of helping her was not just a token gesture but a true expression of care and concern. It came from his heart. She could tell how much thought he and Beth had given to this before deciding to do this for her. At least for that moment, Lisa was reminded that she was not alone in this world and that there were people who cared about her and Lily, and for that she was deeply grateful.

"This is too much to take in, Gavin. I am not going to insult you by just saying 'Thank you. Oh, gosh!'" Lisa wiped her tears.

"You pick the day and the place. I will be here," Gavin responded.

Lisa cleared her throat before she responded.

"I have already contacted all the clinics in this envelope. There are eleven clinics in New Mexico, and these would be the closest. But based on how dangerous my condition is, I think I would feel much safer at the one or two of the clinics in San Diego. They apparently have the capabilities and experience to take care of all health emergencies and risks that come with this," Lisa said.

"I have never been to San Diego," Gavin responded in jest.

"This is not a fun trip, Gavin," Beth scolded him playfully.

"I'm kidding. San Antonio to San Diego. Has a nice ring to it. Doesn't it?" he said smilingly.

The raindrops tapped against the windshield like the fingers of an impatient child, demanding attention. The windshield wipers swished back and forth, keeping time with the rhythm of the rain. In the front seat, a man and a woman sat quietly, lost in their own thoughts. In the back seat, another man kept staring out the window, his face pressed against the glass. He watched as the raindrops chased each other down the windowpane, racing to see who could reach the bottom first. Outside the parking lot of the hotel they were staying at was empty except for a few cars scattered here and there. The only sound was the soft patter of rain on pavement. It was a peaceful scene, one that was somehow both calming and chaotic at the same time.

The man in the back seat, Jason Greer, was scrolling through his emails on his phone. He saw that there was an email from an unrecognizable name.

It simply said *From: Joanna*. Usually, he ignored emails from unknown senders, if his automatic spam flagger on his email server did not flag any email as spam. Or at least he skipped reading them when he first saw them. He usually caught up on such emails later when he was more relaxed or when he was home after work and wanted some bedside reading. But today he had nothing else to do. He was waiting in the car for Russell in the front seat to receive a phone call and then to drive out for a meeting. It was not a fancy hotel they were staying at. A three-star hotel, about thirty-five miles to the north of Houston downtown, and they were able to get a decent deal for three nights.

He decided to read this email from Joanna. Every word in the email made him angrier. Jason was caught between feeling ashamed for not knowing such a blatant attack on a public school teacher was happening in Texas and the fact that the media had not covered it for more than a week since it became a police case.

You are our last hope. Please pick this fight up on our behalf!, Joanna had concluded in that email. Jason was enraged beyond words can describe. He wanted to publish this story right away, but how could he do that without visiting Midland at least once and fact-checking a few things before writing it? He had committed himself to spending at least three nights in Houston along with Russell Weston and Emily Chase in their search for the missing link between RapFuel and Fisher. He looked at the time on the phone. It was 10:15 PM. He decided to call Myra.

"Hey, Myra, Can you talk now?"

"Tell me you're okay and this is not a distress call, Jason." Myra sounded worried.

"I'm fine. This isn't about me. But I have a scoop on a huge story. It's huge. From Midland Texas. Can you check your email? I will call you in about fifteen minutes after you get to read it." He hung up the phone quickly.

In the front seat were Russell and Emily, listening to Jason's brief conversation with Myra. They understood that his mind was somewhere else at that moment. They did not want to pester him with questions. They continued to watch pellets of raindrops pat on the windshield with lesser intensity as time went by. Russell was growing impatient. His contact at RapFuel was supposed to call him and let him know where he wanted to meet them tonight. And he had not called yet.

At 10:30 PM, Jason took out his phone again, looked at Russell and Emily, and paused.

"Do you mind if I walk back to the patio to make this call? It's a little . . ." he asked them politely.

"We totally understand. We will signal you as soon as we get this call." Emily pointed to Russell's phone. The rain had slowed down a bit. Jason opened the rear seat and ran towards the main door of the hotel. The covered patio offered him the perfect shelter to stay dry while he called Myra.

"So did you read it?" he asked Myra.

"My God, Jason. This is an explosive story. I'm glad it landed with you. How are you going to manage? When can you go to Midland?" asked Myra.

"I don't know. It will be four days before I can get there if I stay committed to my work with Russell and Emily right now. Maybe three if we gather information faster than we estimated. Do you have someone who could do this for me?" Jason was in agony as his voice fluttered.

"I don't think I can trust anyone with the burden of something like this. Fuck it. You know what? I will go. I will go *tomorrow*. I'll gather all the facts needed. And if we are ready, we can publish the story in a couple of days. Do you still want to write it?" Myra asked Jason. She sounded like she was already as involved in this scandal as Jason was. Among the many authoritarian outreach laws that the Fisher government was indulging in, the laws banning books at public schools felt very personal to her. Her mother was a librarian at a public school. She worked for thirty-three years and loved every day of her work. Never complained. Not a bit.

"That would be wonderful, Myra. Thank you for stepping in. I will let Joanna know that we are picking her story up. So she doesn't take this to anyone else. And yes, I want to write this. I will get started on it already." Jason was very appreciative of Myra's gesture to step in to help him.

"This is personal for me, Jason. Be safe out there. I will call you tomorrow night." Myra hung up. The rain had picked up some intensity again and there was another new guest car that just pulled in front of the patio. A young couple got out of their car with their suitcases to check in. Jason nodded at the man, smiled at both, and then started jogging back towards their car.

As soon as he knocked on the car door, which Russell had locked, Emily saw him and unlocked the door to let him in. Jason stepped inside, settled down on the back seat, and started rubbing his wet hair as if that would dry them. Then Russell's phone rang. Their contact had confirmed that he would be able to meet them in another twenty minutes. He gave the address of a diner where he wanted to meet them. He told Russell that the diner was exactly twenty minutes from their hotel. Russell thanked him, looked back at Jason as if to indicate he should get ready, changed gears, and started backing out of the parking lot.

"We are on our way!"

It was a typical diner for Houston, Texas. The sign outside promised *Home Cooking*, and that was exactly what was served there, day in and day out. As soon as Jason stepped inside, the smell of frying onions and bacon immediately hit him. The small space was brightly lit with fluorescent lights, and the menus were plastered on the walls. The tables were occupied by families and working men, all of whom were tucking into hearty meals. Russell and Emily joined Jason inside shortly. It was 11:05 PM. But it felt like the diner was just starting to fill up. The air was thick with the dominant smell of frying bacon and coffee. The jukebox in the corner was playing Patsy Cline, and a couple was slow dancing in the middle of the room. The waitress, a tall woman with curly hair, was taking orders and cracking jokes with the patrons, all speaking loudly over the music and the chatter. The atmosphere was electric, and one could not help but smile.

The trio looked around to see how to spot their contact. Russell had never met Ralph before, and they had only spoken over the phone or through emails. They confirmed there was no table with just a single person sitting. So they asked the waitress to find them a table for four. Emily had started to feel hungry.

"I didn't have a good meal, you know." She smiled.

After they were seated, she ordered the chicken-fried steak, and it did not take long for her order to be served. She was not disappointed. Russell and Jason ordered some coffee, which they sipped slowly. Ralph walked into the diner and walked straight up to their table. He somehow recognized the trio without the waitress directing him here. He was cracking a joke to the waitress which none of them could hear, and he leaned forward and patted on her shoulder, before sitting down next to Jason.

"I am Ralph Penney! And I know who you all are!" he introduced himself quickly in a booming voice . "God, I love the chicken-fried steaks here. But I can't eat them now."

This was a typical night at any diner in Houston. It was a place where strangers became friends and acquaintances became annoying, and memories were made and scandals were broken.

Ralph Penney was an ebullient person in any environment and at any time. He appeared full of energy and was chatting nonstop. Emily was already finding his ceaseless energy annoying. She looked at Russell and rolled her eyes. Ralph did not seem to notice any of that. Since he was sitting right next to Jason on one side of the table, Jason could not really see Ralph's face as he was speaking. But he did notice Emily's reaction and smile.

Russell was the one who finally interrupted Ralph. He asked Ralph if he was going to order some food or coffee. Ralph told him he had already placed his order with the waitress, Sharron, and he was getting his regular. He was very particular to emphasize how familiar he was with the diner and how Sharron knew of his regular order without having to explain anything. He was almost proud of that.

"Shall we get down to business?" Russell asked Ralph.

"Of course, Russell. But what's the hurry?" Ralph let out a loud laughter.

"Well, Jason has to work on something tonight and we've been driving all day. We're exhausted. Besides, we may need to save our energy for tomorrow to go through all the data you are going to give us," Emily replied.

"Understood, ma'am. I have it all here." He handed over an envelope to Russell and Emily.

They thanked him for what he had done, and in a quick exchange of favor, they handed a small envelope to Ralph. "Just a small token of thanks from us," Emily said.

"You didn't have to do this. You know I'm doing this for my brother. His memory. May God bless his soul!" He bowed his head down and made a gesture of the cross on his chest. Jason quickly understood that there was a backstory. He speculated that perhaps Ralph's brother was killed in one of the RapFuel accidents and he was doing this to pay back in some remote manner.

The rest of the night—that is, twenty-five more minutes—belonged to Ralph Penney. He kept sharing story after story about this diner and the kind of strangers he had met here. And how many of them had become his good friends since. He believed that this diner had a magical power of making things happen.

"If you came here wishing for something, or like you are doing, on a mission to find the truth, I believe this place has something. I don't know what it is. But this diner will make it happen, y'all. Trust me. Keep the faith. Keep up the good work, y'all. And bring Abhinav's ass down!" Ralph spoke with the same energy he started the night with.

Jason, Russell, and Emily drove back to the hotel without speaking much in the car. They were all exhausted. When they parted at the hotel lobby to go to their respective rooms, they had agreed that they would meet at the lobby again for breakfast at 7:00 AM before starting to work on the data they had received.

As they started looking at the data next morning, Russell brought out his handwritten notes to guide. He had jotted down a few different data points he remembered from their earlier document that someone stole from their office. And Emily had taken her own notes as well to compare and reconcile. The idea was to get down to the data points they know were problem areas and work on them first. One of the first things Russell remembered was how RapFuel had overstated their oil and gas assets for multiple years. He remembered going through this with his team at TWRA, and he was looking for that section in the file that Ralph gave them. He pulled out a sheet and set it aside. What he remembered one of his accountant experts telling him was that RapFuel's inflated valuation had significant impact. They had inflated the value of their assets by more than $500 million, thereby turning a penny stock company into a NYSE-listed company with its stock reaching a high value of eighty-three dollars per share a year ago to trading at eighty dollars per share as of today.

"Wow! That's some scandalous scheme!"! exclaimed Jason.

"Wait till you hear this. Have you heard of royalty underpayment?" Emily asked.

"No," responded Jason.

"It's like this. Companies are supposed to pay a fee known as royalty for the public lands they have leased for drilling, right? This royalty is based on the reported market value of the oil they extract. Guess what. Companies like RapFuel underreport the value of the oil they extract. A large percentage of this fee goes to Native American tribes for different purposes. But yeah, RapFuel had done that consistently," Emily explained.

Russell sifted through the file and pulled out a few papers he thought were relevant for royalty underpayment. As the day progressed, Russell and Emily were able to use their memory and their notes to pull out relevant sections of the reports that Ralph had given them to substantiate a couple of more financial accounting frauds committed by RapFuel.

"I think that covers all the accounting frauds. There is also the falsification of safety permits for offshore drilling rigs and the illegal release of pollutants from ships in international waters that came up during the public trial. So those records are already out in the public. Right?" Jason asked Russell. He had never worked on a story like this. A story that involved a large oil company where he got to play a detective in unearthing a massive financial scandal to the tune of hundreds of millions of dollars. He was very excited to be doing what he was doing and wanted to do more.

"There is one last piece of the puzzle we need to find, or at least we need proof for its existence," Emily said, looking at her notes.

"And I just found that!" Russell exclaimed. He flipped through the file and pulled out two pages. He pointed at a specific section in one of those pages.

Jason Greer got hold of that paper from Russell and started reading. At first, he could not make heads or tails of the specific section Russell was pointing at. When Russell showed the other paper, Jason understood the explosive scandal they were sitting on.

"Is it who I think it is?" Jason asked.

"Yes,", came the response from Emily. According to the documents Jason was holding, it was clear that RapFuel was paying a company called Prairie, Inc., another Texas-based company where the payments that went out on a monthly basis were for suspicious expense items. Prairie, Inc. was sending invoices for items such as "special processing," "special handling," "legal handling," et cetera—all of which should have sounded an alarm and raised suspicion for any auditor. These were not large amounts individually, but together they added up to six-figure amounts every month.

Russell explained that Hubert Fisher was the owner of Prairie, Inc. It was the front for bribing officials in foreign governments such as Brazil, Colombia, India, Angola, Mexico, Nigeria, and a few more. Prairie, Inc. was bribing these officials to get preferential treatment to expedite the importation of goods from RapFuel, to circumvent local regulations if needed, and to get lower tax estimates. And Prairie, Inc. would in turn invoice RapFuel to get these bribery payments reimbursed with their service fee added on top through those suspicious service charges.

"Massive FCPA alarm. How come this hasn't come up until now?" Jason asked.

"For starters, Prairie, Inc. is not only providing these services to RapFuel alone but also to other US oil companies," Emily replied by stressing the word *services* using air quotes.

"Interesting. And this Hubert Fisher is . . . who I think it is?" asked Jason, pointing at the second page, which had the public company listing information for Prairie, Inc.

"Yes. Derek Fisher's younger brother," said Russell.

"Son of a holy gun! Goddammit!" Jason folded both his arms behind his head as if he were giving support to his neck.

Like most quality investigative reporters and journalists, Jason Greer was relentless in his pursuit of stories, and in his deep sense of justice. This combination of qualities was what that gave him a high on days like today. There was a sense of satisfaction which was hard to describe—the kind of satisfaction that came not just from getting the scoop or writing the story and putting it out for the public, but also from knowing that he could actually be making a difference to the society.

Congressman Evan Williams had called Governor Fisher's office as soon as he got the remaining proof from Edward Coll that linked the poker club with

Fisher directly. One of Edward's sources, who was also a poker player, was able to get a membership record of this private club, and there he was—member number twelve: Derek Fisher. Edward could not get hold of any financial records of the club. At least not yet. But as far as Evan Williams was concerned, this was enough. He had two solid proofs that could get Fisher cornered. He was hoping he would be able to close the negotiation with Fisher soon.

Fisher's office had given him an appointment for the very same day, because Williams had mentioned it was a critical issue, one that was TEXIT-pertinent. So when he walked into the governor's office at 2:00 PM, he was greeted with a sense of urgency, and he was told that the governor was waiting for him. He walked into his office.

"Why! Haven't spoken to you in a while congressman. I know you are busy in DC getting the votes for ratification. But to what do I owe the pleasure today? Or should I say fear?" Fisher welcomed Williams with a tight hug. The warmth of it had cooled Williams down, and the intensity with which he walked in to negotiate with Fisher had already been lowered just by that friendliness that Fisher showed in receiving him.

"I'm going to be honest, governor. I came here to make a deal with you on behalf of Senator Dodson. But after entering this office and seeing you, I've had a change of heart. I think I'm going to make a different deal with you now." Williams put Fisher in a state of deep suspense.

"Now you've got me all twisted, Evan, what do I do?" asked Fisher.

Williams went near the governor and whispered something in a very mumbling voice. The governor's face began to turn red. It was clear to Fisher that Williams meant business, and the governor knew that he had been exposed. By the time Williams finished mumbling in his ears, Fisher's face had completely turned red, and sweat bullets started trickling down behind his ears. This was a rare moment in his political career thus far that Derek Fisher, the master of political manipulation and the most successful populist leader of his generation, found himself in a corner with no easy way out. His mind was ticking fast as he took a deep breath. He looked deep into Williams's eyes. It was the kind of look that gave away nothing. Even if Williams had spent a few seconds staring into Fisher's eyes or reading his body language, of which he did neither, he could not have been able to tell if Fisher was angry with him or disappointed at his betrayal.

The governor was not the kind to give into extortion easily, and it was not a surprise that he was reluctant even in the middle of a threat like this to even think about agreeing to Williams's demands. But the stakes were too high. He told Williams that he needed a few days to think about what he had asked for. Williams readily agreed, and he walked out of the governor's office.

Outside, the afternoon sun beat down on the Austin cityscape, casting long shadows on the buildings. The heat was oppressive, and the air was thick with humidity. It seemed like it was the kind of day that made people angry even if they did not step outside, and it seemed to reflect the mood of the Governor of Texas that afternoon.

CHAPTER 13

THE SILENT ENEMY

Senator Newell was visiting Omaha, Nebraska with his friend and colleague from the state, Senator Brynes. Brynes was holding a political meeting of sorts in Omaha. He was not up for reelection, but he had created this routine of meeting with the most important donors from his state every quarter. And whenever he met with his donors, he always brought a member of Congress or the senator with him, someone representing a different state. Someone from his political party.

This was a way for him to engage his most influential donors with the problems other states faced. These meetings were also an opportunity for him to have his donors appreciate the challenges associated with getting a bill passed in Washington, DC and how getting a bill passed of his donors' liking involved not just his vote but also getting buy-ins from so many other people. And most importantly, when he wanted to include a certain provision in the bill that would benefit some of his donors, he also had to make sure they were not in direct conflict with the donors of some of the other senators or members of Congress he had to work with to get the bill passed. Brynes valued these interactions a lot. He believed that these interactions brought him much closer to his donors and made sure they did not treat him like someone they did favor to. Senator Brynes was born in Omaha and had been a resident of this other "Gateway to the West."

Omaha was a city with a rich cultural heritage. From its early days as a frontier settlement to its present-day status as a major Midwestern metropolis, Omaha had always been a place where people of different backgrounds and traditions came together. This diversity was reflected in the city's food, music, and art scene. Brynes was very proud of his city and had never failed to remind Newell that contrary to what many may think, Omaha was a more expensive city to live in when compared to Houston. He had been asking Newell to join him for one of these donor meetings, and in fact, they had had scheduled a couple of times in the past and ended up canceling these appearances due to last-minute conflicts in schedule for Senator Newell. But this time around, the timing of Newell's visit could not have been better.

Hot off the heels from the referendum for TEXIT, and with all the eyes on DC next for the ratification, most of the country was focused on Texas. News channels, talk shows, weekly newsreels—they all wanted to cover Texas. The Nebraskan news networks were no different. And who better to share his insights with his donors than one of the three important men of the moment, the senior senator from Texas? Brynes was very sure of a very heavy turnout for today's event.

Newell and Brynes drove directly from the Eppley Field airport to the hotel where this event was being held. It was an early evening event, followed by a cocktail hour. Newell was catching up on his emails on his phone in the car, while Brynes was on the phone with his local staff who were coordinating the event for him. The staff just shared with Brynes that the latest count of confirmed registered attendees was 110.

"One hundred ten?" Brynes asked, then looked at Newell and said, "I have never seen more than sixty to sixty-five. You are a superstar here."

Senator Newell just shrugged his shoulders.

As they drove through the streets of Omaha, Newell was reliving the last few weeks in his mind. How much life threw at him in the last few weeks, how much he caught of what was thrown at him, and how much he had missed, all leading to be here in this moment. He was playing out all the likely scenarios that could happen in the next few months.

"Congress does not ratify TEXIT. Which means it is the end. At least for now. Or Congress ratifies, but Article 49 does not pass. Or Congress ratifies, Article 49 gets delayed. More confusion. Or everything passes, and there is a presidential election which he contests and wins. Or . . ."

Senator Newell did not realize he fell asleep as his mind processed all of the above scenarios. He had not been catching much slumber of late. To be fair, no Texas politicians these days had been able to. They were about five minutes away from the venue when he woke up on his own. He noticed Brynes was still on the phone. He grabbed a bottle of water from the car cup holder and took a sip. The car slowly approached the hotel, and a host opened the door to receive him.

It was warm outside the hotel when the senators entered the ballroom where the event was being held. The meeting was set up in a lecture room style. There was a small stage with two chairs, one each for Brynes and Newell. And then an open floor with multiple rows. It definitely looked like there were more than 150 people in that room. Brynes waved at familiar faces as he walked in. So did Newell. And when they settled down on the stage, Brynes's event coordinator and his long-time senior staff member in the local Omaha office gave a quick welcome speech and welcomed them all. He said that there were four ushers around the hall available to hand over a microphone to them if they had a question, and they just had to raise their arms until they had an opportunity to get a microphone.

Brynes welcomed them all for joining and thanked them for a particularly overwhelming response for this event. He also thanked his long-term friend and an admirable colleague Newell for joining him today. The guests were initially patient and very polite with their questions. Then the mood started to slowly shift from being calm to mildly tense when Senator Newell, in response to a couple of questions, began to defend his pro-TEXIT position despite being considered a moderate conservative. The crowd wanted to ask more questions. But the ushers were not able to keep pace with the number of arms being raised. Restlessness was setting in, which then turned into mumbling and eventually some jeering. Senator Brynes was not prepared for a sudden change in mood. He turned to calm the crowd, but it was of no use. Suddenly a tall and well-built man, who was sitting quietly until then, got up from his seat, lunging forward with something hidden in his hand. He was in the first row and was already on stage before the security personnel standing at the back noticed him. He stretched towards Newell, revealing the object he held. It was a knife.

The senator tried to dodge, but the man caught him in the arm and a good part of his shoulder, and upper left chest, probably missing his heart only by a few inches. Security rushed forward and tackled the man to the ground. But not before he managed to stab Senator Newell seven times.

The senator lost his consciousness and fell on stage. The security personnel along with other staff there called for emergency help, and the senator was rushed to the hospital within five minutes. All the other guests were safely escorted to another room for questioning before being dismissed one by one. Initial questioning was going on at a methodical pace and it did not take long for the police to narrow down the suspect. With so many eyewitnesses around, the suspect was taken into police custody immediately. The suspect cooperated with the police during the time of arrest.

Back in his car, Senator Brynes was sitting in a state of shock. He was absolutely devasted by the sudden turn of events and was feeling guilty for being a central point for today's attack. He was praying that Newell would somehow pull through and that the injuries were not life threatening.

He received a call on his mobile phone. It was one of his staff members calling from the hospital.

"Sir, Senator Newell will make it. No damage to his heart. Serious but not life threatening," said the voice from the other end.

Brynes took a deep sigh of relief.

What doesn't kill you makes you stronger! he thought to himself.

Captain Ramirez was typing furiously on his computer in his office. The response he had received from the state AG was not what he was expecting. The AG's office had simply said that he should contact the local police station in New Mexico, where he suspected Ava to be hiding, and initiate extradition request with the state for a crime that had already been registered on the books as a "legitimate crime" for which New Mexico could extradite her. A crime like "an attempt to murder" or "first-degree arson" or any crime that would mark Ava a serious and potentially dangerous criminal. The AG's office basically recommended that Ramirez did not use the specific crime for which they were pursuing Ava Walters for in Texas, a crime for which proper criminal laws were not even written in the state of Texas yet.

"You've got to be fucking kidding me!" He let out a scream after reading that long email response from the Texas AG's office.

Officers sitting outside could hear him scream. Officer Ken had just come back to the station after another round of search at Rosaline's house. By now, she was getting used to him coming over in the evenings and spending time with her computer and phone. She knew that it was only a matter of time before they got to Ava, unless the story got some sort of political wind.

As he slowly settled down in his seat, Ken was thinking about what Rosaline asked him earlier today. She had asked him what the rationale was behind still holding Bradley in detention without any formal charges. She also reminded him that they were intentionally depriving a young child of valuable parental supervision, and if they were aware that they could be held directly responsible for any health risk that the child may experience. The more he thought about her question, the more he was convinced that the Midland Police perhaps crossed the line when they brought Bradley to the station and put him in detention, but what was beyond reason was how they did this even after knowing that there was a little girl who needed her father. He got up from his seat and walked towards Captain Ramirez's office. The door was open, but he could see Ramirez's face was flushed red.

"Excuse me, Captain. May I have a word?"

"Sure, Ken. What is it?"

"At this point, I think we should release Bradley and reunite the child with her father. We have our tracks laid for Ava. Bradley is not going to be able to help us anyways." Ken was cautious to explain his reasoning without pointing out the abrasive tactics used by Midland Police in the illogical and dangerous arrest of Bradley in the first place.

"You're right. Why don't you initiate the release? Just bring me any paperwork if there is any for me to sign," Ramirez told him.

"Are you okay, sir?" Ken wanted to make sure Captain Ramirez was all right, given he heard him scream just a few minutes ago.

Captain Ramirez explained what had transpired between him and the Texas AG. He shared his frustration with Ken about entering this dangerous territory of criminalizing public school teachers for doing their jobs.

"You know they will never be satisfied with this banning stuff? They will keep pushing. They will keep pushing. Until we have public schools teaching only propaganda books written and printed by the government. Like North Korea." Ramirez rang that pessimistic bell.

"You're overreacting, captain." Ken was not sure if he really agreed with Ramirez's assessment of the Fisher Administration's claws finding stronger grip over the public school system in the state.

"Well, no matter how I react, I have a job to do. That right now is to get Ava. Seems like the fastest way to do this is to charge her with a high crime that will make it easier for us to extradite her from New Mexico. You go and work on Bradley's release while I get on with this," Ramirez dismissed Ken back to his seat.

Officer Ken went back to fill the necessary paperwork for the release of Bradley Walters. He also filled an application form to be sent to CPS citing that the father of Eveline was now safe, and he presented no danger to the child, and in fact, it was recommended by the child's pediatrician that the child be reunited with her father as soon as possible for her health and psychological reasons. Within a few minutes, a tired looking Bradley walked out of the lockup. He was clearly in a state of stress thinking about Eveline. As soon as he saw Ken, the first thing he asked him was where she was. Ken explained that she was at a safe place, at a foster home, to be precise, and once CPS approved the release form, he would be able to go pick her up.

Far away in Atoka, outside the old home, was a car parked in an awkwardly crooked manner. Joanna, the driver, got out of the car, opened the door from outside, and entered the house. She had brought back all of Ava's electronic devices. She dropped them on the sleeping bag.

"You want the good news first or the good news first?" she asked Ava.

"Whatever…" replied Ava.

"Jason responded. He said they are going to do the story but need some time to do some fact-checks." Joanna raised her fist and said, "Yay!"

"Fair enough, I think. These fact-checks. Right?"

"And there's more good news for you. Bradley is home with Eveline. Rosaline is doing okay. But under constant police surveillance. Of course, that's how they know me. That friend of yours, I tell ya, she has got some balls, man. She somehow managed to sneak one message out to me from another device while her devices are still under surveillance." Joanna was all praise for Rosaline.

"Thank you. Thank you, Joanna, for that good news." Ava got out of her bean bag to come running towards Joanna to give her a hug.

"Now, there is more good news and bad news. Your computer and phone are here. But what use are they now? They're going to track us the moment we tether to the internet from wherever we are. That brings me to the bad news…" Joanna left her thoughts in a state of suspense.

"What?" Ava asked.

"We have to leave at dawn tomorrow. 5:00 AM. We are getting the hell outta Atoka. Don't ask me where. For your own safety." Joanna shrugged her shoulders and smiled.

Joanna had had a long day. She wanted to get some rest before their upcoming road trip. She was tired. She closed her eyes and tried to sleep. But it seemed impossible. Her mind would not stop racing, and her body would not relax. She kept tossing and turning, but it only made her more frustrated.

Every time she closed her eyes, she kept seeing the same thing: a never-ending pursuit for freedom.

About 320 miles to the northwest of Atoka, in Midland, Camila heard her husband's car pulling into their garage. She went to the kitchen, opened the refrigerator, got a bottle of Modelo, and poured it in a tall beer glass. She did not want to ask him about Ava's case, although that was the only thing playing in her mind the moment she realized her husband was home.

"We released the husband. He is safe with his daughter." Ramirez kissed Camila on her cheeks, and grabbed his beer from the table.

"And Ava?" Camila asked.

Captain Ramirez pointed his fingers towards the sky and touched his heart as if to say he had the faith in him that God would guide him to do the right thing.

After all, there was always a happy ending if one was willing to let one's mind write a story that would get one there.

Jason could not go back to sleep easily that night. They had uncovered so much data that day that he was beginning to write this explosive scandal that could shake up Texas in his head already. He was excited and so looking forward to work on this. But this was a story that needed confirmation from multiple sources and one that involved stringent verification before he could even give it to Myra. He was fully aware of that. But part of his mission—that was, going on a road trip with Russell and Emily—was to finish all the investigations he needed to from the ground. Some of the source verifications could be done later once he had the basic framework of the scandal he wanted to expose laid out. His head was churning with so many ideas on how to write this story. He wondered how Myra would react when he shared with her what he knew. He wondered how she would pitch this story to the managing editor for final approval, for a story like this could not get to see the light of day unless the boss approved.

Myra—his biggest supporter, critic, friend, and foe in *The Austin Star*. From the first day Jason stepped into his Myra's office, he was struck by her intelligence. She carried herself with the confidence of someone who was used to being in charge, and her voice commanded attention. Jason quickly learned that Myra was someone to be respected, and when she questioned his work, it just meant he needed to redo his work. Over time, he had developed a deep respect for her editorial skills as well. He admired her ability to always stay calm under pressure, as well as her brilliant ability to see a story not just for its content but for the context and the timing of publishing it, not to mention the consequences.

As their relationship grew, Jason became her most trusted journalist within a very short time. She started entrusting him with the most critical stories *The Austin Star* got leads for. With him proving his credentials through his incredible reporting style and his passionate investigative instincts in a short time, he became a star of his own right just as quickly and had earned enough trust with her to pick up stories and leads that he felt driven by. Which was why she even stepped in for him when Joanna sent the Ava lead to him.

It was 10:30 PM. Jason was waiting for a call from Myra. When he did not hear from her until 10:40 PM, he decided to text her. She responded right away and said she was with someone in relation to the story, and would call him back as soon as she was done. Jason was curious to know more about what she had managed to find in Midland and if the Ava story was a go or not. He turned on the television and started watching ESPN Classic playing an old Superbowl game. His eyes were on the TV, but his mind was on the work he would be doing with Russell and Emily the next day.

Myra called. "It's a go, Jason. I verified all names, incidents, and places. They check out. Even the dates. It's all kosher. So your source, that woman, what's her name again? Joanna. Yes. She's made our job easier. Start working on the story. I don't think we have had such a solid lead on a story with all Ts crossed and Is dotted. This is gold."

Jason was relieved to hear that.

The next morning, Russell, Emily, and Jason met at the hotel lobby for breakfast. Russell looked like a man possessed and full of energy. Emily just hated days like these when Russell was unusually hyper at 7:00 AM. It meant they were going to have a really long day when he would have 100 different ideas, all at the same time, all conflicting with each other, and some making no sense at all. But she had developed a knack for handling Russell on days like this, which was to never counterargue with him, even when he spouted those nonsensical ideas. He usually forgot those ideas the very next day.

"Where are we heading first?" Jason asked.

"We are going to meet a couple of folks—I mean, accountants from the environmental advocacy group. You know the group that sued RapFuel and won?" Emily was trying to set the day's agenda for Jason.

The first thing Jason noticed when driving through Houston was the heat. The city seemed to radiate heat, as if it had been cooked in a giant oven. The air shimmered with heat waves, and the pavement seemed to ripple. Even the buildings seemed to sweat, their glass windows reflecting the relentless sun.

But Houston was more than just hot. It was also a city of contrasts. Despite the heat, Jason noticed that the city was full of green space, with parks and trees lining the streets. The architecture was also varied, from towering skyscrapers to quaint bungalows. As they were driving through Houston, Jason got a sense of the city's energy and diversity. They arrived at the coffee shop in downtown Houston where they were meeting the accountants.

There were two accountants from the environmental advocacy group waiting for them at a corner booth. The trio joined them and quickly completed their introduction.

"Welcome to Houston, guys. Good to see our friends remembering us," said Curtis.

"How can we forget you, Curtis and Sean?" Russel responded immediately. There was a sense of long-lost familiarity and friendship in the tone. After exchanging quick pleasantries, they got on with their topic of discussion immediately.

"Like we had already mentioned in our email, when we were working on the documents for the trial, I was wondering if you guys remember what we found out about Harvey. There was a strange connection between Abhinav and Harvey if my memory serves me right," Emily asked Curtis and Sean.

"Of course. We *do* remember. At that time, what raised the red flag was that there were a few accounting entries involving payments to Harvey. We noticed that these payments were going out regularly for twelve months. These were, we believed at that time, some consulting payments that went out to him directly from RapFuel when he was working on Wall Street," Sean explained.

"He could have done some freelance consulting for them. Right? Nothing wrong with that," said Jason.

"Except these were huge amounts. Almost 100-to-200K every month." Curtis smiled. Russell looked at Jason to see how he would react after hearing these numbers. But Jason didn't react at all. He merely sipped his coffee and acted like he was looking for the real reveal.

"After the trial, we continued to follow the accounting paper trail of Harvey and Abhinav. This was totally not part of the case. But we just felt suspicious," Russell said. "We found evidence for insider trading involving Harvey and Abhinav. During the same period of twelve months, when he was receiving payments from RapFuel, we were able to establish both Harvey and Abhinav were involved in insider trading independently with their own portfolios. Curtis and Sean have proof of that. Right, guys?" Russell asked.

"Yes," came the response. "You may look at these documents for yourself." Curtis handed over a file to Jason.

Jason looked at Russell with a twinkle in his eyes and handed over the set of documents to him, who in Jason's opinion understood these accounting data better.

Russell had flipped through only a few pages when he shrieked out a

"Wow!" The trio already knew they had more explosive stuff to go after. But the reporter in Jason was already looking at it as an opportunity for an entirely new story, which would be an offshoot of the main scandal. This was the sort of filtering an experienced reporter would do automatically as soon as he saw a huge story. He shook his head in disbelief. Russell and Emily thanked Curtis and Sean profusely for their quick help, and they left the coffee shop after shaking hands with the trio.

Russell, Emily, and Jason glanced at one another. There was a long silence. They all knew what the other was thinking with just a glance. It was as if they could communicate through some unspoken language that only they understood. They had been working together for only three days and yet this was a moment when they did not even need to say anything out loud for the other person to understand. They could communicate through a simple exchange of looks. Russell and Emily, by virtue of having had the opportunity to work together for much longer, knew exactly what the other was thinking. Jason continued to shake his head. After a few minutes of silent celebration for getting hold of another important piece of evidence, they decided to leave the coffee shop.

Jason made a note to himself to ask his colleagues at *The Austin Star* and his other professionally connected sources from New York and Austin to run a thorough background check for Harvey immediately.

When they were driving back to the hotel, Jason started sending a bunch of emails, all of them to multiple contacts of his, requesting them to do a background check on Senator Harvey. The ask was very simple. Just do a basic background search and find out if there were any shady work-related routines and/or personal routines.

Before they could reach their hotel, Jason received three different emails in response to him asking them a favor. Jason could not wait to open them before they got back to the hotel. All these three emails were short ones, and they said the same thing. His sources told Jason that Harvey had a routine of going to a specific gay bar in Austin on Thursday nights and/or Friday nights, if and whenever he was in town. And if that was not proof enough, they all shared their intel from Harvey's New York days. Their numbers varied from five to eight, but all of Jason's sources said that they could confirm the fact that Harvey did have regular sexual relationships with at least five different men during his time in New York.

"I had a doubt. I always did. Now that I know this, I guess it has been quite obvious all the time." Jason smiled.

"What's obvious?" asked Emily.

"You won't believe what I just found out from my sources."

Emily was looking at all the twelve women in her file. These were the twelve women whom she had shortlisted as ones who needed more handholding than the rest either because of the seriousness of their specific pregnancies or because of a very basic support system that they lacked. She did not have photographs of these women. Russell and Emily had not had the opportunity to meet at least two of them. But they had seen their photos on their old phones when they used to text or call them. As she stared into each document, the image of the corresponding woman floated in the air, reminding her of the circumstances under which they had met each of them.

Emily decided to call Lisa first. Lisa did not pick her phone up. Emily assumed that since was calling from a different number, maybe she didn't recognize the same. So she kept trying. After the fourth attempt, Lisa picked up.

"Hello, is this Lisa? I am Emily. Emily Chase."

"Oh . . . hello. Is this your new number? I saw an unrecognizable Houston number, so I didn't pick up." Lisa was trying to explain why she didn't attend to the phone the first four times.

"No. This is not my new number. It's only temporary. Listen, Lisa, I want to make sure you are doing okay and have made a safe decision. As you know, they've made this a felony in Texas as of today. Huge fine, and they're saying doctors could get a life in prison if they provided abortion care. So you have really run out of luck if you're looking for any help within the state. What used to be remote chances are now almost none," explained Emily, trying to let Lisa know of how much worse the state laws against women's rights have become recently.

"I was not even going to try in Texas. Going out of state. Using your recommended list. I will share all the details after all this is done. Just for my own safety. A friend of mine is going to drive me. We leave tomorrow." Lisa was providing just enough information to Emily, but not a whole lot.

Lisa was not entirely sure if Emily had a gun pointed at her while she called her and if someone from the Fisher Administration was trying to get details of all the women trying to get abortions in the state, through her. Lisa felt guilty for not being able to trust even Emily at that point.

"I'm sorry. I don't want to put my life under risk. What if someone is listening to this conversation? Or what if you're being threatened to call me to get more details? I can't trust anyone, and it feels like the entire state is becoming more of a surveillance state. I'm sick of it," she said.

"I understand, Lisa. You take care. I'll call back to check in in a couple of weeks." Emily disconnected the call. She was relieved that Lisa had a plan and that she felt confident enough to handle this. She then began to contemplate if she could use her current proximity to Jason to push a story in *The Austin Star*—without naming names. And highlight the perils of Fisher Administration's attack on women's rights and health by quoting a few women on their journey to their own death beds, as they try to maneuver through these new misogynistic laws.

Before Burl Fogg could get back to Stansley after his disastrous meeting with the governor, he had been hearing some chatter about growing impatience among the farmers around the state. Since he was a member of a few different farmers associations, his group chat on his messaging app had been buzzing nonstop. Dudley was a bit annoyed by the buzzing noise that he even asked Burl if he could put his phone on a silence mode. When Burl and Dudley decided to take a break the next time, Burl opened his phone to see that he had missed multiple calls and there were two voice messages.

Burl was a member of the Texas Peanut Producers Board, National Grain Sorghum Producers Association, Texas Grain and Feed Association, and a couple more. The chatter among these groups over the past twenty-four hours had been that they were getting prepared for protests that their previous generations had to indulge in, in order to show their stance against some Reagan era policy changes.

Burl remembered his dad talking about these protests from the 1980s. As a staunch conservative, his dad always understood the problems as more of intermediary problems or ones that arose out of mismanagement by the middlemen, and never as issues that were caused by outrageous policy making at the top. When Burl grew up and had a better understanding of the protests from the 1980s, he invariably had a better appreciation of how the protests in the 1980s, in many ways, had redefined how farming was practiced in the US since then. Burl had understood that the Reagan era accentuated the farm crisis through deliberate federal policy changes. Some of the changes such as erosion of parity prices systemically, in combination with other deregulatory efforts, forced farmers to consolidate. Farmers with the means to consolidate were rewarded for growing monoculture commodities. Farm suicides in rural America used to be forty-five percent higher than the rest of the population in the country. Burl had stopped arguing with his father about this and let him have his own version of what caused the protests in the 1980s.

There was a voice message from the president of the Texas Peanut Producers Board. Burl, as the board's secretary, had become somewhat of a celebrity within the board, and the president wanted to ask Burl when he was coming back to Stansley. He said that there were growing concerns among the farmers not just in Lubbock County but elsewhere, too, that there was an impending disaster with how Fisher had been handling this.

When Burl arrived in Stansley, it was past 7:00 PM. He thanked Dudley for giving him company and dropped him off at his farm. He invited him over to his house for dinner the following day as a way of showing his gratitude. Dudley, in return, thanked him for being receptive to the idea of helping that woman and her daughter.

"If anything, I feel this trip was worth it just for that alone. It was like God sent us to help that woman and her daughter, man. So thank you, my friend. Thank you." Dudley gave Burl a tight hug before grabbing his bag from the trunk and walking in.

Burl got home and called the president of the Peanut Producers Board. The president wanted to know how his meeting with the commissioner went. And Burl just gave a terse response.

"How about we chat tomorrow? All I can say is that they are not listening. We need to be loud."

When he met the president of the Peanut Producers Board the next day, Burl was in a much more composed mood. He was very measured when he told him about his meeting with Fisher. The president, an ardent supporter of Fisher was in awe of Burl getting an opportunity to meet his hero in person, and in his office, at that.

"I bet the governor's office looked glamorous."

"Indeed. But I can't say the same thing about the meeting itself. Basically, I got kicked out for sharing my honest opinion," Burl started, then went onto sharing a minute-by-minute replay of that meeting.

"I'll be damned. Fisher did that to you? Are you sure?" the president kept asking.

After getting over the shock, the president shared his own involvement with multiple discussions with various local farmer groups in the last few weeks. He told Burl that the farmers were beginning to feel pissed.

"I've been thinking about this. Even before I learned about all this growing dissent across various groups, I was thinking how to excite these groups to come out and fight. We should channelize this anger, properly." Burl was speaking animatedly.

"And you propose?" said the president.

"I propose a rally in Austin." Burl raised his right arm and pumped in the air.

Political scandals were a fascinating phenomenon. They often involved complex issues of morality, ethics, and power. But at their core, they were about human psychology. Why did politicians cheat on their spouses? Why did they take bribes? Why did they lie? Why make back door deals? These were all questions that psychologists had been trying to answer for years. And while there were no easy answers, there were some psychological theories that could help explain why political scandals happened. For example, psychologist Abraham Maslow's "hierarchy of needs" suggested that people were motivated by a need for power and prestige. Once they achieved them, they wanted to hold onto them indefinitely. This need could lead people to engage in risky behaviors, such as affairs or bribery, in order to gain and consolidate status and power. Other psychologists have argued that political scandals were often the result of personality disorders, such as narcissism or paranoia.

Senator Dodson had always thought he was the most flamboyant politician that the state of Texas had ever produced. He considered himself to be more people-friendly than Newell ever was. Newell may be the more knowledgeable senator, but he considered himself to be more politically nuanced than Newell ever was. He considered himself to be more open to reaching across the aisle than Newell ever was. That was until Derek Fisher exploded into the Texas political scene and changed the average conservative Texan psyche. Dodson still had not been able to figure out how he missed the signs of what made

Fisher the populist he had become to be. He kept wondering, *Am I losing my grip on reading the pulse of the people? Am I spending too much time in DC that I don't know what's going on at the grassroots level in Texas conservative politics?*

His staff member interrupted his train of thought.

"Sir, you wanted to talk to Congressman Williams. We had been trying to reach him for a while and have finally managed to get him online. He's on line two. Please."

Senator Dodson, still had not been able to recognize the kind of growth Evan Williams has had in his political career. For him, Evan was always a twenty-three-year-old intern who had difficulties explaining the difference between the House of Representatives and the Senate. But what Dodson often conveniently forgot was that this happened twenty-two years ago. Evan Williams, since then, had quit Dodson's office and moved on to work for a senator from Louisiana before deciding to run for public office himself. He won his first ever contested election when he ran for the school board and then followed by running for the county board. He was currently serving his first term as a congressman at the US House of Representatives. But for Dodson, Williams still evoked a certain unflattering and unintelligible persona, which in turn kept Dodson awake late at night.

"Hey, Evan, how are you?" Dodson released line two on his phone and started talking.

"Well, senator. Really well," replied Evan Williams.

"Sweet! So what have Edward and Grace got to say about how well you are doing?" asked Dodson with a smirk. He wanted to know how much dirt they had managed to dig up on Fisher.

This was the moment when a younger and a more naïve Evan Williams would have gone back to narrating every minute of every meeting he has had with Edward and Grace to his mentor. And perhaps this was the moment a younger Williams would have let Dodson know of all the dirt Edward and Grace had dug up on Fisher already. But the Williams of today was a bit swifter and more nuanced. He had gained more and more insights onto himself. He was focused on the bigger picture and committed to getting there, as opposed to the younger Williams, who would rather finish tasks assigned to him. And most importantly, the Williams of today was more confident of his political career and his ability to chart his own path.

"No, senator. I am afraid not. Both had great openings into their respective stories, and I was optimistic at first, too. But they still have not been able to come up with substantial proofs to take these stories any further. I guess either I put too many hopes into thinking Edward and Grace would deliver the goods for us quickly. Or there are no goods at all," Williams lied openly to his political mentor.

Dodson did not know whether to be angry or disappointed. Was he being lied to? Or had he simply hoped for too much? With the congressional ratification on the line very soon, he needed Williams to be on his side more than ever, and if for any reason Williams had a doubt that Dodson had lost trust in him, he could become destructive of his own efforts that he had put in over the past few weeks. Dodson could not afford that.

"By the way, senator, I heard about the attack on Senator Newell. I'm glad he's doing okay. Do you know who was behind the attack?" asked Williams in a very empathetic tone.

"Yes. It was such an unfortunate event. No suspects yet. The police are still investigating the case, I am told. I am glad he is okay, though. God bless his soul," Dodson replied.

And before Dodson could finish, Williams started.

"So it did not originate from your office?"

"When . . . w-what? What are you talking about? Ridiculous," Dodson countered.

"That's good to know. Because whenever such things happen, based on the location where this happens, they would have named —five to six suspects right away. They haven't named anyone yet. You know, the media is always looking for scandals. With the story about you and Senator Newell at the restaurant still running hot on some gossip columns, I'm sure you know what to do to cover all the bases," said Williams.

"Hear you, son. If you find out who is behind the attack, please let me know," said Dodson.

"Of course, senator. I will be the first one to tell you if I hear anything about who the culprits are or if I hear about any relatable event," Williams responded.

Dodson hung up the phone and wiped the sweat beads from his forehead using a Kleenex sheet.

Race had always been in proximity to the surface in American political discourses. Not quite on the surface, so it was never talked about all the time. But it was always an inherent factor. Of late though, race and identity had become right, left, and center in American political discourses and campaigns. The "Southern Strategy" set in motion by the former Republican Party about fifty odd years ago was finally beginning to pay off. Politicians like Derek Fisher and his party of enablers were simply riding the wave set in motion.

Sima Daly did not consider herself to be a white nationalist. But she would never hesitate to use her identity to gain advantage in any situation. Just like Fisher, Sima would never mind using race and identity to generate a cataclysmic divide between the people of her constituency to intensify the passion of her grassroots supporters. In the end, the more passionate the voter was about fighting for a cause he or she believed in, the more likely he or she would turn up on election day to vote. It was all about getting people to show up. What the new breed of conservative politicians had done in Texas was to find out which light to fuse that in turn would generate the kind of passion they needed for a higher voter turnout. The kind of passion that was triggered not by a strong belief in a certain ideology or cause, but the kind of passion triggered by anger. Strong anger on something or someone or usually on a group of people who would come between them and their beliefs if not fought against.

Alex Pedroza was not paying attention to the cultural shift that was happening in Texas right under his nose. He had always been appreciative of what the state of Texas and the USA had done to him and immigrants like him, and how much more superior their lives were as a result. And for that, he would forever be grateful to this country and this beautiful state. When Alex was busy building his business, being a spokesperson for his community, being a father, and being a good husband, there had been an explicit cultural shift in the state politics. As a devout Catholic, he had always leaned conservative all his life thanks to the notion that he had been preached from early on in his life, that the other party was the party of Satan, while the Conservative Party was the only party that associated with Christianity. He was taught to be afraid of the other party. He was made to believe that the other party would get rid of Jesus from the vocabulary of the nation. As a firm believer, it was never a choice for him to vote for the other party. There were many like him. So the cultural shift based on race and identity had skipped him. He had bigger things to look out for.

When he looked back at the transition that had happened in the state politics, he was amused. Which explained why Alex did not blink an eye when Sima Daly approached him about writing a huge check as donation for his community hospital. He was too naïve and ill-informed to suspect any motive behind for him to refuse such a generous offer from a sitting congresswoman of the state.

Alex was on his way to Austin to meet Sima in her office. He knew the state congress was in session that week. Since the time he met with Juana, and the time since he started working on putting together a broader coalition of the Latino community leaders around Texas, he had been very encouraged with the kind of response he had received thus far. His database now included more than forty-five different individuals, of whom fifteen had spoken directly to him and thrown their weight unanimously behind him for his fight against the Fisher government's open support for white nationalism. Three out of those fifteen had promised him that they would come to Austin to meet Congresswoman Sima Daly. So Alex had called Sima's office a few days ago and had scheduled an appointment for Thursday at 2:30 PM. When the secretary asked him the reason for this request for meeting, he simply mentioned "Latino politics."

On Thursday, a few minutes before their appointment time, Alex and three other Latino community leaders—two from Austin and one from San Antonio—arrived at the State Capitol. After the security protocol, they were let in. Alex was a little nervous about the meeting. As he was walking along the main corridor, it felt like each step brought him closer to the marble hallway and the imposing wooden doors that stood at the end of it. Alex's shoes echoed against the tile, a sound which ricocheted through the hall and created a sense of foreboding in his mind. He could feel his heart racing as he tried to control his breathing and calm himself down. The door seemed to get larger as he got closer to it, and it took all his courage to raise his hand and knock.

After a short wait, they were let into the visitor lounge. Then began another long wait. It felt like an eternity for Alex, as his mind was restless, imagining the many directions the meeting ahead could go. Finally, the other door swung open, and they were confronted by the congresswoman herself. Sima was a tall woman with piercing blue eyes, and she received Alex with a sense of superficial warmth politicians in general were good at wearing at any given time. Alex had rehearsed what he wanted to say to the congresswoman, but he was also certain that he would not be able to stick to the script if Sima started saying things that took him on a detour. He was anxious.

"Good afternoon, gentlemen! It's so good to see you, Alex.' Sima smiled at Alex.

"Good afternoon, congresswoman!" boomed Alex.

Once they got through with the initial formalities, it came down to Alex kicking off the core conversational topic.

"Congresswoman, I am here to tell you we, the Latino community in Texas, are very disappointed with you and the Fisher government's nonstop attacks on non-whites. What you think are only campaign speeches have real world consequences. I have data to share with you. These attacks have become openly racial and discriminatory in the past few months. And no one from the administration has either condemned these attacks or called and spoken to the victims' families yet," said Alex, and he suddenly remembered that he had forgotten to introduce the three other leaders who were with him. So he continued, "This is Mike from San Antonio, Sebastian from Austin, and Gabriel from Austin."

"I'm sorry, Alex. I did hear about your employees. What a tragedy! But I had been caught up with so many things that it was impossible for me to find time to speak with you. That's just an excuse, I know." Sima was superficial in her response.

"We want you to stop this right now. The governor could get on stage and call off all these violent attacks and hate crimes," said Alex.

"Alex, we are not responsible for these hate crimes. The last I heard, the police are still investigating the attack on your employees, and they haven't named any suspects yet, right? So let's all take a moment and calm down a bit." Sima sensed the nervousness in the room and tried to appease the four men in front of her.

"Come on, congresswoman! You know it," said Sebastian.

"I'm sure you all know that Fisher's prescription for success has been to pay attention to what people are talking about on the streets and use that to create narratives. The governor never looks back at any of his old campaigns or walks back on what he has already said. What Fisher is saying on stage in campaign rallies are exactly what people want to hear. He or anyone in the administration has not said anything that called for attacks on your employees, did they? This is really a law enforcement issue, Alex," said Sima, once again lacking total empathy, and looking right through Alex.

"So that's it? Who is going to console that little girl who lost the only surviving parent she had? I've lost four of my precious employees to this hate crime, ma'am. What am I going to tell their families? What about the fifty-one other hate crimes reported by the state police?" Alex waved the printed document that contained the details of the fifty-two hate crimes reported by news media outlets. "Look at this. These all are on Fisher and you, congresswoman. Blood on your hands, and more to come."

"I can't promise anything else at this point, Alex. We have congressional ratification, then Article 49, et cetera, et cetera. We are busy. Why don't we circle back early next year and talk about how we can compensate you?" said Sima, hinting that they should leave.

"Next year, you say? You will hear from us much sooner than that, congresswoman. We are not going to let you get away without taking responsibility for all of these. Just wait and watch!" threatened Alex before leaving her office. Mike, Sebastian, and Gabriel quietly followed Alex out of the door. Sima walked behind them and slammed the door closed once she was able to confirm they had left.

She came back to her desk and screamed into thin air to relieve her frustration.

"Fuckkkkkk you, Alex!"

CHAPTER 14

HIDDEN AGENDAS

itting in his hospital bed, Senator Newell could not help but replay the events of the fateful day over and over again in his head. He had been speaking to a group of donors in Omaha the day before yesterday, when he was suddenly attacked on stage by a man sitting in the front row. This was an intimate setting where Brynes's team would have vetted every single person coming in. He remembered feeling a sharp pain in his arms and then being knocked to the ground. The next thing he knew, he was waking up in the hospital with a group of concerned doctors and nurses standing around him. Thankfully, the senator had been able to identify his attacker before losing consciousness completely, and the police quickly apprehended the suspect. Now the senator was on the road to recovery, but the incident had left him shaken. Looking down at his bandaged torso, he vowed to never take his safety for granted again.

The nurse walked in with her tray of medications and wound care supplies. The doctor was due for his visit after she left. Newell had a local newspaper in his hands. Senator Brynes was sitting on the side of his bed on a chair that seemed uncomfortable for a bottom-heavy man like Brynes. Brynes had apologized several times to Newell already and yet he felt obligated to stay there until Newell was released from the hospital. The news had shocked the country, and in particular, the party. Leaders from all over the country had called to check in on Newell and Brynes had patiently answered all the calls. He had kept a record of all those who called to check on Newell and the time they called. He knew Newell would have wanted that.

Both men sat silently without exchanging a word while the nurse finished her wound care procedure and gave the medicine cups to Newell. He swallowed them all quickly and drank a few sips of water that she gave him. She asked him if he needed anything else to eat. When he said no, she had to remind him that the next meal would be his lunch, and that was not going to be for another two hours. The nurse already knew that Newell did not appreciate the hospital food that was served to him for lunch. He would get a bowl of boiled vegetables along with a small cup of soup, which he absolutely loathed. He told the nurse that he remembered the lunch schedule and he was fine. The nurse left the two senators in silence and left the room.

"Any important calls?" Newell asked Brynes.

"You mean calls that were not asking about your well-being?" Bryson responded with a smile.

"You read my mind well," said Newell.

"Yes. There was a call from Marks and Vivienne. They did ask about your condition, but they also asked when they could talk to you about something else," said Brynes.

"Oh! Alan Marks. He's a state congressman from Texas. And Vivienne is the minority leader in the Texas senate. I would like to talk to them after lunch, maybe," Newell said

After the doctor did his routine checkup, he told Brynes who was still in the room that Newell's recovery had been very encouraging, and if he continued to improve at the current pace, they could have him discharged from the hospital in three to four days and have him shifted to home care in Houston for another two weeks before he could make a full recovery. Brynes thanked the doctor for all the care his team had been providing Senator Newell and for the optimistic estimate on his health.

The soup of the day was potato-leek. Newell could tolerate this soup much better than the barley soup he had the day before. He even enjoyed the boiled vegetables even though the bowl and the vegetable medley they served him looked identical to what was given the day before. He waited for the nurse to leave and then told Brynes that he was going to take a nap. Senator Brynes needed one, too. He had not gone home since Newell was admitted here. He went to his local office twice just to freshen up and connect with his staff members. His office building was only a few blocks away from the hospital. Else he had been spending all his time amid the hospital chaos. He decided to give himself a well-earned break now that he had heard the doctor give an optimistic outlook.

"I will see you tomorrow morning, senator. I'll sleep slightly better now that I know you are going to be okay," said Brynes, who then left.

Newell looked for his phone, which was on the side table by his bed. He scrolled through to see that he had sixty-four missed calls. He went to his contacts book and looked for Alan Marks's name, then clicked dial.

"Hello, Marks. Senator Newell here. Thank you for the call," said Newell.

"Good afternoon, senator. I know you prefer meeting in person. But under the circumstances it's best you don't travel to Austin to meet us." Marks paused, waiting for the joke to settle, and continued. "I am kidding, of course, sir. We could have traveled to Omaha but don't know if they would let us in to see you. So just wanted to pass on a quick update."

"Go ahead, Marks."

"This is Vivienne, sir. Relieved to hear you are doing better now." She had just joined the three-way call. Being from the opposite party, Vivienne had always minimized her direct interactions with Newell.

"I will keep this short," Marks began. "My team was working on some more updates to our report. And when we put together the progress that the state had made on trade agreements, or lack thereof, it is clear to us that Article 49 would find a major blockade in the state senate. Our party has only eighteen votes. Even if all of them vote yay, they still will need three from Vivienne's side. There are potentially five vulnerable senators on Vivienne's side who would vote yay otherwise. But trade agreements are a line they won't cross, and this report will raise a huge red flag in their books. So Vivienne thinks that getting four out of these five, if not all five, to say no would not be that difficult."

"Brilliant. Why did I not know this before?" asked Newell.

"With all due respect, sir, this was always our Plan B. To pull the trade agreement trigger. It's highly speculative. But it's easy to paint a dark future using this. It will open lots of debates when economists get to read this. But our focus is just the votes for now. Right?" said Vivienne.

"You're right, Vivienne. Thank you."

"You take care, senator. Can't wait to take you to the steakhouse I talked to you about," Marks signed off.

"You got it, Alan. I need to make that trip to Austin soon." Newell smiled as he hung up the phone.

Jason, Russell, and Emily had planned on spending one more day in Houston to talk to a few more sources to corroborate the two explosive stories they had managed to unearth in the past two days. It seemed like things were going as planned and they were ahead of their target date for collecting data.

When they got back to the hotel that night, the trio looked at one another, still processing the information they had just heard from Jason's sources. They sat down in the hotel bar and poured themselves a tall glass of cold beer each. None of them was judging Harvey for his sexual orientation. They were just surprised and shocked that something like this could go undetected so long in this day and age, especially in a party that had been openly homophobic. Not only had Harvey managed to keep this under the wraps from his party peers, but he had managed to win an election. Russell was the first one to call it a night. It was that kind of day. Jason remembered the story he had to finish writing. So he left after a few minutes. Emily reminded him that they had an early start the next day. They were going to meet another source, and it was going to be a long drive.

Jason got back to his room and opened his computer. He stared at the draft version he had been working on. The moment he started reading what he had written, he started to feel angry. There was a voice inside his mind that kept yelling, *How did we end up here? Penalizing teachers for doing their job? Have we hit rock bottom yet? Or are there more depths to plunge into?* There were journalists and reporters like Jason who did not get stories like this to work on regularly. This was more than a job for Jason. The more he got himself immersed in reporting what happened to Ava, the more in control he felt.

Jason sat on the makeshift work desk he had made the hotel table to be, typing rapidly on his laptop. He was on a roll; the words were flowing easily, and he had a clear vision for the article he was writing. He knew exactly how he wanted to frame this article. This was an important story, one that needed to be told and one that would determine the future of the children in Texas. He cared passionately about the issue at hand, and at that moment he did not care if his readers would be moved by his words or not. He cared about only one thing. Bringing justice for Ava.

He had been working on the article only for two days, but since the research part was made easy, he did not have to collect any data. Even though he was not involved in the research personally like the RapFuel stories he was currently working on, it was all coming together like he had been working on it from scratch. He was imagining himself to be standing in the middle of a classroom in that public school in Midland where Ava was teaching. He could feel a sense of urgency and anticipation building as he neared the end of his piece. This was one of those articles he did not even have the mindset to judge if it would be his best work or not. He simply wanted more people to know about the injustice being meted out to Ava Walters, a public school science teacher.

As he read over his final draft, he could not help but break smile. He was proud of what he had accomplished; he hoped that this article was going to make a difference in Ava's life and maybe in the lives of many public school teachers. A story like this came to him once in a blue moon, and it was exactly stories like this that inspired him to become a journalist in the first place. He could not wait to see it in print. But more importantly, he could not wait to see the reaction this story would evoke around the state and the country. He could not wait to see the pressure this would put on the Fisher Administration to do the right thing.

It was 1:25 AM when he finally completed his proof reading. He remembered he had to be ready by 7:00 AM for their long drive to meet two more sources. He sent the final draft of the article to Myra with a note, "I hope this article makes a difference. I hope we make a difference in Ava's life."

The hotel conference room was set up with a long table in the center, microphones at each seat, and no podium. The walls were hung with banners bearing the hotel's logo, and the bright overhead lights gave the room an antiseptic feel. The door opened and a group of reporters began to filter in, taking their places at the table. They all had a serious air about them, and the atmosphere in the room was calm. The press reporters who had come had no idea what this conference was about. Suddenly the lights above the stage dimmed and four men walked onto the stage. They took their seats. A man leaned up to the microphone placed in front of him and cleared his throat before beginning to speak. He looked around the room, making eye contact with each person in turn. His voice was calm and steady as he delivered his message, but there was an undercurrent of anger and grief that was palpable. The Dallas press had the first opportunity to break this story, which no one knew anything about.

The man who spoke was Alex Pedroza. The three other men on stage were Gabriel, Sebastian, and Mike. They were here on a mission. Juana, Alex's daughter, had coached them how to speak and what message to deliver for maximum effectiveness. She was standing at the back corner of the room. She was giving thumbs-up to her father as he spoke.

"Good morning! My name is Alex Pedroza. I am a small businessman. I own a landscaping company in Dallas and have been a lawful citizen of this country. I have been living in the great state of Texas since I was four years old. I love everything about Texas. Texans are my brothers and sisters. And I love them all. I am a devout Christian. Catholic. I have one daughter—Juana—standing at the back of this room. My wife, Maria, passed away a long time ago. God bless her soul. I have been involved with many charitable activities in my community. We are currently building a hospital. Governor Fisher extended his support to our community and promised he would do more for Latino communities throughout Texas. He even sent Congresswoman Sima Daly to personally check our community out and give us a generous donation for the hospital. While I was carried away by the generosity, I was clearly not paying attention to the hate politics Governor Fisher, Congresswoman Daly, and others in their party have been fomenting over the past couple of years. Everything peaked around TEXIT. We have people now in Texas who are ready to kill people like me because we are not white, and we do not look like them. In fact, that is exactly what happened to four of my own men, in Dallas, just a few weeks ago. They were shot dead by a madman for no reason except for the fact that they were Latinos. It has made me sad and angry. So I decided to confront Congresswoman Daly and asked her to condemn these actions by their supporters. She said they could not afford to do that until Article 49 is passed. She was very dismissive of our earnest request, and it is clear to me now that Congresswoman Daly just wants to use us for our votes and nothing more.

"I am not a politician and I do not understand votes, bills, and strategies. But what I do know is love for fellow human beings. I do not understand how it's okay to let fellow human beings kill each other. I do not understand Governor Fisher's and Congresswoman Daly's silence on hate induced violence. Do you know Texas has witnessed fifty-two different incidents of hate crimes statewide since the time Governor Fisher called for the TEXIT referendum? Fifty-two reported incidents. With twenty-eight deaths. These are all serious crimes. And then there are at least sixty-five to seventy more hate-related minor incidents since the referendum was called. But these incidents were never reported by the media. I spent the past few weeks looking at this. And I, along with my fellow Latino community leaders from around Texas, Gabriel, Sebastian, and Mike, went to meet Congresswoman Daly. She was unable to answer out questions and she asked us to get out. She didn't even show any regret or remorse. I, on behalf of all the minority communities from around Texas, hereby demand that Governor Fisher and Congresswoman Daly publicly condone the hate crimes being committed by white nationalist groups. We demand they issue an apology to all minorities around the state and assure us that they would direct the law enforcement officials of the state not turn a blind eye to future incidents of hate crimes. Thank you for coming to this press conference. This is our joint prepared statement. And that's all I have. We are not taking any questions right now. Thank you again for coming."

Alex read through this prepared statement without any interruption, pausing at the right moment, modulating his tone very little and showing great poise and control over what he was delivering. He tried to keep his emotions at bay and not show anger at all. The press reporters in the room were in a state of shock, and they were all typing notes as soon as Alex finished his prepared statement. A few official press photographers who were present were busy taking pictures when the four men on the stage quietly walked out through the back door.

"You did great, Papa," said Juana, hugging him. She was waiting for him in the waiting room that connected the conference room with a kitchen.

"Thank you, Mija. You helped me. It's you," Alex told her, hugging and kissing his daughter on her cheek. He looked a lot more relieved than he was before the press conference started.

Meanwhile, out there in the social media world, the Dallas press conference was already trending along with three names: Alex Pedroza, Derek Fisher, and Sima Daly.

The insider trading story that Jason, Emily, and Russell had uncovered in Houston were corroborated by two other sources they met the next day. The trio drove almost 100 miles to go to Beaumont, where they met a couple of investment advisors who used to work as Abhinav Agarwal's wife's personal financial planners. These advisors brought with them copies of some of the planning work they did for her and the portfolio they managed for her for almost three years. Russell and Emily had Ralph to thank for connecting these sources with them.

Jason was really energized seeing the evidence. And he was confident that they now had a story to go after. He could even start writing it now, as he had cross-checked all the basic verification requirements. But then, as per his protocol, he needed Myra's go-ahead before he could start writing it.

After they finished meeting with the sources, the trio decided to not take up any more research work for the day and instead focus on analyzing what they already had. They got back to the hotel early evening and went out for dinner at a nearby hibachi restaurant. It was the first evening in four days all of them had a few hours to really unwind. They all felt that they had accomplished everything they wanted to during their Houston stay.

Jason was waiting for Myra to respond to his email about this story. He did not share the details and was waiting for her to call.

"So I guess we are done here. We all need some time to go through these documents, data, and process them before we form conclusions. But for now, we will decompress," Russell said.

"I assume we can check out tomorrow as planned," Jason asked.

"Yes. We could. Listen, Jason, since this part of the work is done, I guess you don't need us for a while till you are ready with your story, right?" asked Emily.

"Why? Are you getting tired of my company? Is it my drinking habit? Or my loud snoring in the car when we go on long drives?" Jason was joking. They all laughed.

They split their dinner bill and went back to their hotel rooms for an early night. They had agreed to part ways the next morning. Russell and Emily would drive around Houston meeting their old friends and try to dig up more information on who was behind the TWRA attack, while Jason would drive back to Austin. They would meet again in Austin to debrief their two explosive stories and make sure everything was still kosher. That was the plan. Russell and Emily agreed that they were not interested in the gay-Harvey- story at all, so Jason could deal with it separately.

Jason received a call from Myra at 10:30 PM. It was short. But Myra was interested in Jason doing the Abhinav-Fisher story before the Abhinav-Harvey one. She wanted him to reach out to Abhinav first for his comments and reactions to what Jason was able to corroborate until now. Jason had agreed and promised Myra that he would call Abhinav the next day. So that's what he did after saying goodbyes to Russell and Emily.

The receptionist called Abhinav in his office to let him know that a reporter was online and that he mentioned that it was urgent. Abhinav asked her to put Jason through immediately. Abhinav had heard of Jason Greer. He had read a few of his articles, especially the profile piece he wrote on Richard Harvey. When they spoke, Jason kept it short. He said he had been working on a massive story linking Abhinav to Fisher. And that he wanted Abhinav to react or respond to some of his findings that had already been corroborated by a few sources. Jason said he would be emailing a few bullet points and Abhinav could either respond through email or if he preferred to respond via phone, Jason would be happy to call him again.

Within a few minutes, Abhinav received an email from Jason. He was nervous to open it at first. When he opened the attachment, he understood immediately what this was about.

It was human nature to dread certain situations. And yet, inevitably, there came a time when that very thing happened, and one was put in that situation. Whether it was being forced to confront a fear head-on or simply being caught in an unfavorable situation, there was no escaping the fact that sometimes the things one dreaded the most did happen. When that occurred, it could feel like the world was crashing down around somebody. Their heart raced, their palms sweated, and their mind went blank. It was an overwhelming feeling, one that could leave us feeling shaken and vulnerable.

In that moment, Abhinav was feeling shaken. He felt the most vulnerable that he had ever had.

The early night fell softly in Austin, like a shawl draping over the shoulders of a sleeping city. The air was still warm, scented with the perfumes of jasmine and honeysuckle. A few fireflies drifted lazily through the air, their gentle light a reminder that summer was not yet over in this part of the world. The streets were empty at this hour, but the city hummed with a low, steady energy. It was as if all of Austin was holding its breath, waiting for the night to really begin. Soon enough, the sounds of laughter and music would fill the air as people came out to enjoy the cooler temperatures and the festive atmosphere of the city streets. For now, though, all was quiet and peaceful, and the early night held Austin in its gentle embrace.

The gentle warm embrace of early night in Austin was a far cry from the humid wet hug of early night in Houston. This was Jason's first evening in Austin after his road trip to Houston. When he set out to go on this mission, his focus was about one thing—to dig more into the RapFuel accounting scandal and put together the story that he almost had once with him before someone sabotaged it. But he came home feeling more accomplished than what he set out to do. The Ava story was the most meaningful work he had done in a while. The RapFuel-Fisher story he was working on could become politically the most influential story of the decade. And finally, the Harvey story, if he ever chose to write about it, would be the most salacious story he would have ever written.

His phone buzzed. It was a text message from Lee Sung.

Time to talk?

Jason had been meaning to call Lee for a while. At least since the time *The New York Post* picked his scoop after Jason and Myra decided not to act on it soon enough. So he called Lee immediately.

"Hey, stranger! What's up? Miss our DC nights out, dude," Lee Sung greeted him.

"Same here, brother. There's lots to talk about. But I am in Texas. You know. We are buried deep in our own shit and stinky new stories every single day. But tell me more about what you are working on. What are you up to these days, man?" Jason wanted to know how his former colleague and friend was doing.

"Like you said, there's lots to talk about. But I wanted to talk about one big story I thought you may be interested in. Cause it involves Texas. You know your state senator, Richard Harvey? *The New York Post* is breaking a scandalous story tomorrow about him. I know exactly what it is. It's salacious, dude. Trust me." Lee wanted to say more but curtailed himself from revealing.

"Are you shitting me, Lee? No way. Do you know who's writing it? Or the sources?" Jason was caught by a whiff of surprise with what Lee just shared. He wanted to know how *The New York Post* picked this story up at around the same time he learned about it. He was just curious about the timing and not so worried about not breaking this story. He thought to himself, *I guess it's better it came from* The New York Post *and not from* The Austin Star*!*

"Vincent O'Gorman is writing it. No idea who the sources are. The way you are reacting, it sounds like you already know this. Wait. Is it one of those leads you decided you would just sit on because of vetting, due diligence, and all that shit, and let *The New York Post* take it?" Lee was both curious and sarcastic.

"I'm terribly sorry about what happened, Lee."

They talked for another couple of minutes before hanging up. Lee was surprised that Jason Greer would sit on a lead like this and not capitalize on the mass traffic his website could have gotten by being the first one to break this story, even if he did not have all the details and if the story was scanty in details.

It was midnight, and Jason was sitting in his dark bedroom, surrounded by mountains of pillows that he had propped up against the headboard. He was scrolling through his X (Twitter) feed, trying to distract himself from the fact that in less than seventy-two hours, a story that he was privy to but did not work on would be out. The scandalous story would reveal that Senator Richard Harvey was gay and had had affairs with multiple men. *The New York Post* story probably would even mention that he was still meeting men secretly at a specific gay bar in Austin.

Jason did not know why he was feeling anxious about this story getting published.

It was not just another Monday in Governor Fisher's office. There was an eerie calm all around. The governor had canceled all his morning meetings. He had invited two of his legal team members for an emergency meeting. And that was the only meeting he was going to have. Everything came to a grinding halt that morning when Derek Fisher opened that email from Jason Greer, senior reporter for *The Austin Star*. Based on a four-page document attached to the email, it was clear to Fisher that Jason had got down pretty much to the bottom of establishing connections between Prairie, Inc. and RapFuel and other oil companies.

It was public knowledge who Hubert Fisher was. Hubert was one of the founding partners of the grocery chain. He was more of the entrepreneurial kind out of the two brothers, but it was Derek Fisher who came up with the idea for the grocery chain. When Derek decided to enter politics after a successful stint as an entrepreneur, he let Hubert take over the chain. He promised the Texas public that he had nothing to do with that business anymore. Hubert Fisher continued to grow the grocery business while leading a life that hardly interfered with Derek Fisher's politics. The brothers and their families even avoided public appearances together, so there were no photos available for public to remember Hubert.

The document sent to Derek Fisher was the final version of the article Jason was going to publish. Jason, as per the protocol, had reached out to all three parties affected by the story and had asked for their comments. Before beginning to write the article, Jason, while he was still in Houston, had emailed Abhinav a few bullet points and wanted his comments. Abhinav pretty much froze looking at the detailed data Jason was able to gather and decided not to respond to that email.

After Jason got back to Austin, he started writing the most explosive political story of his career. A story that could put *The Austin Star* on the national map. Myra was working with Jason closely, helping him in every which way until he got the final draft ready. When he sent the final draft to the Fisher brothers and Abhinav on Sunday night, it was Abhinav who sent a response first. This time around, he did not ignore Jason's email. Abhinav's response was very short, and Jason received it within twenty minutes of sending that email. In his email response, Abhinav neither confirmed nor denied any of the facts being reported in the article. It was simply a condescending response asking Jason to mind his own business since he had no idea about the economics at stake for Texas when this story went public.

He even ended his email on a somewhat threatening note: *As your well-wisher, all I can hope for is that your newspaper gets to stay alive until we become independent. Who knows what will happen after?*

Derek Fisher saw the email first thing Monday morning and immediately summoned his legal team for discussions. The first challenge to him was how to prevent the story from getting published. If for whatever reason Fisher was unable to prevent *The Austin Star* from running the story, how could he do damage control, and what were the legal implications? These were the questions running through his mind. He wanted to meet Hubert at the earliest opportunity and to get him on the same page before either of them responded to Jason. After discussing various legal consequences and actions, Derek Fisher's advisory team concluded that the first thing that the governor should do was to request *The Austin Star* to give them some time to respond.

Derek Fisher personally drafted a short response.

Dear Jason and Myra, thank you for giving me the opportunity to comment on this article. As an affected party, I would be very appreciative if you could give me ten days' time to respond to the various misconstrued and assumed facts covered in the article.

The mansion was bustling with visitor activity. The afternoon sun shone through the windows, casting a warm glow on the floor-to-ceiling portraits of former governors that lined the walls. In the center of the private room, Fisher and his wife Gloria were sitting down and staring at their lunches. Governor Fisher was not in a good frame of mind to continue to meet people in his office that afternoon. He had been thinking about the consequences of the exposé. He had asked Hubert to drive to Austin as soon as he spoke to his legal team in the morning, and he just found out that Hubert would be arriving early evening. They needed to get on the same page first. But his mind was on Jason Greer. *How did this relatively inexperienced reporter have the balls in him to go for such a big exposé?* he kept wondering.

The TV at the center of the room was turned on. CNN cut their regular programming and took the viewers to a hotel conference room in Dallas. Fisher saw four Latino men sitting on a small stage and one gentleman addressing the press. Alex Pedroza was reading his prepared statement. Fisher thought Alex looked familiar. But he could not place him immediately, nor could he remember his meeting with the Latino community members in the Eagle Ford neighborhood in Dallas before the gubernatorial elections. He asked the butler to increase the volume. It took him a while to understand what was going on and what Alex was saying. The chyron at the bottom did not help. After Alex's statement, a CNN panel was reacting to the press conference, and in that segment, they gave a Cliff Notes version of Alex's statement. It felt like the day just got worse for the governor. He stopped eating and got up from his chair.

"Honey, I'm sorry. I have to make an important call." He kissed his wife on her cheek and walked to his private office upstairs.

He called his secretary and asked her to set up a conference call with Sima and Harvey right away. While he was waiting to get connected with the other two, Gloria gently knocked on his office room door and waved at him. He waved back at her and gestured her to come in. She walked near him and showed her phone to him. There was a X (Twitter) link for a *New York Post* article. He clicked on it.

The headline read: *Harvey's Secret Gay Life.*

Derek Fisher covered his face with his palm and took a deep breath. There was a beep at the other end of the phone. It was his receptionist. She said she was ready to connect him with the other two.

"A day from hell! Explain why it's all happening today!" Fisher screamed at Sima and Harvey.

There was silence. In a strange twist of fate, all three of them were in the news today for different reasons. Even though Alex's allegations on Derek Fisher and Sima Daly could be termed manageable, the Harvey exposé was the one that concerned Fisher the most. Fisher had no idea how in all these months he had known Harvey he did not guess he could be a gay man.

"Governor, if I may, mine is not a scandal. It's about me, the person. I just know the party base would reject me if they found out I am gay, and that's why I kept it away. I can go out and publicly admit my gayness any time. To be honest, I will be relieved of carrying this burden. I may not get reelected. So be it. Or maybe I will be able to convince enough people in the party base. The point is this should not be the scandal we need to focus on," Harvey said, sounding like a man who had thought through this.

Fisher decided not to share Jason's story linking him and the RapFuel-Prairie, Inc. scandal yet with Sima and Harvey. He thought about it and decided that he had a few more days to tackle that, and at that moment, these were of higher priority.

"Before you jump to any conclusion, Richard, we are here to help each other. So let's focus on damage control first. All right?" Fisher asked.

Both Sima and Harry nodded their heads in acknowledgment and replied "Agreed" in unison.

Then he continued, "Who knows Jason Greer? And how do we get to him?"

"Governor, I think he is the same reporter whom you gave your first interview to after assuming office. He got to break the news about TEXIT." Harvery responded.

Within minutes after the attack, #NewellStabbing was trending on social media. The attack quickly became the top story on all the major news networks. Pundits began speculating about the motive for the attack, and whether it was motivated by politics or mental illness. As the police had not released much information about the attacker, the conspiracy theory world was only rife with several theories. The motive for the attack remained a mystery to the outside world. However, one thing was certain: Since Newell was recovering well, after a few days of covering this, the news outlets were ready to move onto the next big story and push this to the sideline.

Evan Williams was convinced that the attack on Newell originated from his mentor Senator Dodson's office. He himself had personally witnessed several instances during his interactions with Dodson how the animosity towards Newell ran deep inside him. Even though Dodson had never openly called for violent attacks on Newell in Williams's presence, he had never been shy of letting Williams know that he would be happiest the day Newell retired from politics, and he would do anything to accelerate that process. His recent trifle with Newell over the potential leadership battle of independent Texas was common knowledge to the whole world now. Which was why when Williams spoke to Dodson earlier this week and Dodson feigned innocence on the attack, Williams could not entirely buy the innocence. Dodson did not sound very convincing when he reacted to Williams's speculative question, and he was merely surprised that Williams would ask that question directly to his face, or on the phone, to be precise.

Derek Fisher, who had been having own share of feud with Dodson on the leadership battle, also suspected that Dodson must have been behind the attack. He had no evidence, but it was more of a political gut instinct. Since his last meeting with Evan Williams, Fisher had spoken to Williams twice over the phone, and on both occasions, it was about the congressional ratification. That meeting between Fisher and Williamson had changed the dynamics between these two men. Williams had been communicating more with Fisher about his work on getting the fifteen votes for the ratification, while Dodson was only getting summary updates in the last few days.

Williams was in his DC office when Fisher called him. Derek wanted to know if Williams had connected with Dodson since their last meeting. As much as Fisher had a newfound trust on Williams in the recent past, he was fully aware that the Dodson-Williams relationship went a long way back. So Fisher was naturally worried if the dirt that Williams had on him had reached Dodson or not. Evan Williams comforted Fisher and told him that he had not shared any information with Dodson yet.

"Besides, governor, a little birdie told me that between *The New York Post* story and the press conference by what's his name—the Latino guy—you are already knee deep in dirt yourself. This dirt I have on you can wait," said Williams.

"That's a relief. Where are you with the ratification?" Fisher asked.

"That's a conversation for another day and not on the phone, governor." Williams tried to cut the governor short.

"But the vote is within a week?" Fisher was anxious.

"I'm working on it. Now, if there is nothing else, governor, I've more important work to do. Like making sure Texas's independence is guaranteed." Williams smiled and hung up.

The ratification votes, unlike votes for a typical bill, needed different sets of strategies. Williams worked through forming some coalitions with likeminded congressmen and women. But he could use not use media to generate public support for ratification unlike for a typical bill because the public support for ratification around the country was less than twenty percent. And finally, he had to find a creative way to use lobbyists, because not all of them were in favor of ratification themselves. In fact, there were many who were working against the ratification. Which was why what Williams had managed to accomplish to get it down to only fifteen votes was nothing short of remarkable. He was not going to give up at this stage. No matter how low the Newell-Brynes duo was willing to go to play the game, he was willing to go lower.

After he got wind of the Brynes meeting with the fifteen congressmen and women about illegal contracts for the next twenty years, Williams decided to match the offer in addition to the ten percent share on the offshore drilling he had already promised. Now, this was becoming a bribery of a huge magnitude. Worth anywhere between two to four billion US dollars. In the last two days, Williams had met with all fifteen of the undecided congressmembers one-on-one, pitched his latest offer, and watched their eyes open as wide as the Grand Canyon. He was getting a kick out of manipulating these men and women for votes. And by the time he met the fifteenth member, he was convinced he had them by their necks. Unless Newell and Brynes could think of something huge in the next four or five days, it was impossible to do better than what he had offered. It would be foolish on any of these fifteen members' part to not take Williams's offer and rely on an injured Newell to get better and deliver what he had promised them.

After pitching his offer to the fifteenth member, Congressman Evan Williams walked outside the Capitol Building to get some fresh air. The sky was deep blue, almost navy, and the sun was sneaking out a little. He could not help but feel hopeful as he looked up at the sky. Everything felt possible. He felt like anything he dreamed of at that moment could come true. He was so filled with hope that it felt like his heart might burst. He closed his eyes and made a wish, hoping that somehow, someway, it would come true. For that moment, everything was perfect. The world felt alive and full of possibility. Williams allowed himself to just be in that moment, surrounded by hope and possibility. It was a feeling Evan Williams would never want to forget.

CHAPTER 15

THE REDEMPTION

The air was thick with anticipation and the hum of conversation. The exhilaration of breaking a big story was palpable, and everyone felt a part of something larger. When a story like this was finally published, there was a sense of relief mixed with excitement. In moments like these, the newsroom was united by a shared sense of purpose. The mood was electric with excitement, as everyone knew that they were about to publish a story that would rock the government and possibly even the nation.

Myra and two of her editors were huddled around the conference table, poring over the final draft for the hundredth time and debating whether to add one caveat or not. And Jason Greer was pacing nervously outside the conference room. The publisher of *The Austin Star* himself was there, too. He was wondering whether they were about to unleash a journalistic bombshell. Everyone gave a thumbs-up.

Then, with a click of the mouse, it was done. When the final article went live, there was a collective sigh of relief in the newsroom. The final layout was approved for the print edition for the next morning. Now the waiting game began.

How much of an uproar would this story cause? Only time would tell. If this story reached as big as they all were hoping, this was the kind of story that people could remember for years for bringing policy changes. It was all thanks to a public school teacher who took her job seriously and decided she was not going to be a pawn in the hands of an authoritarian administration who came between her and her primary duty of educating her students. It was all due to a woman in New Mexico who decided to help this teacher after she escaped from the state law officials. Someone who took the time to give as many details to Jason Greer as possible and made the fact verification and corroboration tasks for Myra easy. It was all due to a journalist like Jason Greer who believed that his prime responsibility was to speak the truth against the power no matter what the consequences would be.

Jason Greer went back to his desk and launched *The Austin Star* website. He thumped on his desk to celebrate this moment. He yelled "Yes!" and pumped his fist in the air.

Then he kept staring at the front-page cover story.

MIDLAND PUBLIC SCHOOL TEACHER TARGETED BY
FISHER ADMINISTRATION FOR DOING HER JOB
By Jason Greer

It was a bombshell. The Ava article was explosive, to say the least. It detailed how the Governor of Texas had been systematically destroying public education in Texas before getting into the chronological details of what Ava did that resulted in a police chase. The story, first published by *The Austin Star*, had since been picked up by all the major news outlets, and within a matter of two days it had become the talk of the country.

The governor was furious, and he quickly began trying to discredit the article and its author by tweeting out denials. Derek Fisher was already in the middle of multiple crises, and this was a story that came out of nowhere without any warning. He was fuming in anger and wanted to act on the newspaper. He wanted to meet Jason Greer in person and punch him in his face.

However, Fisher's advisors soon stepped in and asked him to take a step back, as some damage had already been done, and his reputation had already been dented. For the time being. The more he dug himself into defending his position, the more it would have far-reaching consequences for the state's politics and for his own political future post-TEXIT. They advised him that he should keep his focus on the big picture and start working on damage control.

"You are toast on national media. Don't bother convincing them. Let's devise a plan to get Ava back to Texas. Do a photo opp. Then worry about the next steps. You have too much to clean on your plate right now, governor!" they told him.

Fisher nodded in agreement. He was after all a man with experience in handling pressure situations. But he was still seething in anger. He had already been raging over Jason for the past few days for the other story he was planning to publish and now this was a surprise he did not plan to deal with. He had called his AG, Walter Lodge, to come to his office for a meeting. Walter Lodge, whose office was in the next block, was there within a few minutes. In fact, since this news story broke, he was waiting in his office for a call from the governor for this meeting. Along with the AG was the commissioner of education.

Their meeting covered three different aspects of the Ava issue. The first one was legal—how to bring Ava back to Texas? And what kind of charges they should file on her? What charges should they relieve her from? Should they revoke her teaching license? And most importantly, should they codify this crime for future?

The second one was state education policy. Should they revisit the book banning and the broader public education policy in the state? The answer to which was no. What if other teachers emulated Ava's approach to teaching banned topics? Should Ava be allowed to teach after she came back to Texas?

The third one was media. How should they respond to the story? Should they wait till Ava was brought back to Texas? Should they issue a statement of regret of some sorts? Should they blame the entire situation on the woke mindset and the woke media? Should they use Christianity and Bible as their cover, and paint Ava and Bradley as anti-Christians? What was the general mood in the state like and would this crisis affect Fisher's overall ratings?

Governor Fisher insisted on his AG to initiate the extradition procedure right away. By then, news had trickled to Fisher that the AG had a delayed response to a request from Captain Ramirez from Midland Police about extradition. Fisher was not very happy with the AG. Meanwhile, all of them in the room agreed to one thing very quickly—that this was not the time to revisit the policy change that got them here in the first place, as this would have to go back to the legislature, and it was impossible for this to have any chance there.

Fisher's media counsel advised him that they should not sound apologetic in their response at all, and they should double down their attack on teachers like Ava who were not fit to teach the children of the state because they were poisonous and had a specific anti-Christian agenda. They also decided that this would be a great opportunity to go after the woke media houses like The Austin Star who had profited from peddling sad personal stories like these, when there were two sides to every sad story. They also concluded that they should attack the media houses for conveniently ignoring the trauma of the parents of the students who were force-taught satanic lessons by teachers like Ava.

When Fisher was done with his meeting, he was thoroughly exhausted. All he could think of was lying down in his couch and listening to some music. His secretary knocked on his door and reminded him that Senator Dodson would be visiting him in about fifteen minutes. Dodson was in Austin for a few days, and he had requested a short meeting with the governor.

"You look charged up for a man ready to be thrown into a gladiator cage, governor! How are you?" Dodson walked in with a wide grin.

"As you can see, the ceiling doesn't have any shit at all. It's all under control. I've been in worse situations." Fisher shook hands with Dodson and welcomed him. The last time these two men met in the governor's office, it was all bitter.

"I was in town. I saw *The Austin Star* story and decided to pay my respects to you and ask you if I could be of any help. That's all. I won't keep you long," admitted Dodson, pouring himself a cup of coffee.

Fisher carefully avoided getting into the details of any of the current scandals he and his close party associates may be facing. He assured Dodson that he was in control of all the stories and his team would start quashing all the attacks on him one by one soon. He told Dodson none of these stories were true and they all had been timed in such a way to cause maximum damage to him days before congressional ratification of Article 49.

"I won't be surprised if it's a woke national media secret network that's trying to bring down this TEXIT thing," Fisher said.

"Talking about Article 49, we are still living precariously. Williams says we are almost there. But I will believe it when we get there," said Dodson.

He had wanted to talk about the post-TEXIT presidential bid with Fisher. But that was before the latest Ava story broke. So he decided he did not want to get caught in a foul mood.

"Senator Dodson, before you leave, I should ask you this. How is Senator Newell doing? And do you have any idea who attacked him?" Fisher was trying to act curious, but he really wanted to poke Dodson.

"He's doing fine. Thank God. Recovering. Should be ready to travel in three to four weeks, they say. The police haven't released any suspect names," Dodson responded, carefully measuring every word that came out of his mouth.

"Thank God, indeed," Fisher responded and kept staring into Dodson's eyes. He was hoping he would be able to read guilt in his eyes, but all he was able to read was loathsome anger and disgust.

Dodson left on a much more polite note when compared to his last visit. But somewhere else in Austin, Evan Williams learned that Dodson had paid a visit to Fisher. He was neither angry nor upset that Dodson did not invite him for the meeting, although part of him felt disappointed. He was just anxious to know what they talked about. Williams was confident of the trust he had built with Fisher, but with the recent bout of scandals Fisher found himself in the middle of, Williams did not know what to make out of Fisher at this moment. Everyone had a breaking point beyond which their actions could become unpredictable. So as much as Williams was worried about where Fisher might fall politically after he came out of these scandals, and how unpredictable his actions could become, he decided to weigh the risks of poking into the hornet's nest now versus just waiting.

He remembered one of Dodson's frequent pieces of advice to him when Williams was his intern. Dodson would keep reminding him, "Patience is a virtue. In politics, somethings are best left untouched for a while."

That's exactly what Williams decided to do. To wait it out.

Congresswoman Sima Daly leaned back in her chair with a satisfied smile on her face. She had just finished planting the seed of a new conspiracy theory, and she knew that it would take root and grow quickly. Her social media team had been hard at work making this story go viral as quickly as they could. With any luck, it would blossom into a full-blown smear campaign against her new opponent—someone she never thought would consume so much of her time.

Alex Pedroza had been living rent-free in her mind the past few days. And the only way she could get back at him was to turn the tables against him. Make the community leader who claimed to be doing a lot for the community a villain. Paint Alex Pedroza as a selfish man who had been swindling the community money to grow his business. Sima's team had been careful to choose their target of the conspiracy theory carefully—someone who was already susceptible to believing in conspiracy theories. And she had been equally careful to plant the seed in fertile ground—a specific social media platform where fake news stories usually flourished. Now all she had to do was sit back and watch, as the conspiracy theory took on a life of its own. Before long, it would be all anyone would be talking about. And Alex's reputation would be ruined. He would be pushed into a weaker and more vulnerable position. Then it would be easier for her to take him on by attacking him directly through the mainstream media.

Downtown Houston was a bustling metropolis of high-rise office buildings, luxury hotels, and trendy restaurants. The streets on this day were teeming with pedestrians, and the ambience was alive and could be felt with the sound of car horns and sirens. The towering skyscrapers cast a long shadow over the city, and the bright lights of the skyline could be seen for miles. The coffee shop was busy for a weekday morning. But amid the hustle and bustle, there was a sense of calm. It was as if time had slowed down inside the coffee shop, and the only thing that mattered was the conversation happening at each table. At one table in particular, Russell and Emily were meeting with a source. They kept their voices low, leaning in close so as not to be overheard. The source looked nervously around the room, clearly uncomfortable with being in such a public place. But Russell and Emily were old pros in this, so they kept their calm and quickly reassured their source that they were in no danger. After all, this coffee shop was known for its discretion. The man opened his phone and showed a photo to them.

"That's Owen!" Emily said.

"His real name is Finn. Finn Burton," he replied to the source.

It was clear in that moment to Russell and Emily who stole the document they were planning on sending it to Jason Greer. Owen had been working as a volunteer at TWRA for more than four months. And looking back, nothing in their interaction with him was ever suspicious. Finn Burton, a.k.a. Owen, was a Houston native, and he was a contractor in the IT department at RapFuel. In some ways, his assignment in Austin was also a contract job. He was supposed to infiltrate into TWRA as a volunteer, earn the trust of Russell and Emily enough that they would trust him enough when they discussed confidential matters, and finally alert RapFuel corporate any time their names and data were being discussed or scrutinized. That's exactly what Owen did when Russell and Emily started working on RapFuel data. He waited for the right moment as per instructions and stole the document before it could be delivered to Jason Greer at *The Austin Star*.

"Bastard!" Russell was grinding his teeth.

After the source left the coffee shop, Russell opened the one-page printed document that he had given them. It was a copy of the email an anonymous sender had sent to the IRS complaining to them about certain financial frauds happening at TWRA. The email said they were attaching a document as proof. Since the source did not give them that attachment, they had no way of knowing the contents of the attachment. Then they remembered what the source said to them. This email was sent from a RapFuel computer in the office, and it originated from a specific IP address which he could remember even in his sleep.

"Abhinav Agarwal," he said before leaving.

"I won't put it past Abhinav to attach a fake document he painstakingly created as a proof of our supposed scam." Emily was disgusted. Russell acknowledged. Suddenly, Emily remembered something. She opened her handbag, picked up her temporary phone, and checked her email. There was a response from Lisa Barkley.

Hey, Emily, we've somehow made it to San Diego. There was a lot of trouble, and we were delayed. Can't get into details in this email. I'm doing okay. Some cramps and some vomiting. My friend, Gavin, is my angel. Got an appointment for day after tomorrow. Will update you soon. Thanks, Lisa.

The red Chevy Impala crept forward, its headlights barely piercing the darkness. The roads were empty at this time of night, and the only other vehicles were an occasional tow truck or a passenger car with a lone driver. In the passenger seat, a woman stared out the window, her eyes darting from side to side. Every shadow seemed to hold a lurking danger. Beside her, the driver wrapped her fingers around the steering wheel, her knuckles white. She kept her gaze fixed on the road ahead, her jaw clenched in determination. The moon cast a pale light over the landscape, and the women could just make out the outline of trees and bushes. There was no sound but the crunch of gravel beneath the tires. The car moved slowly, carefully, as if afraid to make a noise.

The women did not speak, but they did not need to. They sat in silence, each lost in her own thoughts. They both knew what was at stake and what was at risk. They exchanged a glance, and in that moment they both knew they were thinking the same thing: They had to get to safety before it was too late. The barren desert gave way to rolling hills and mysterious valleys, and the star-filled sky seemed to stretch on forever. Even the roads seemed to change, winding through canyons and past hidden lakes.

Every turn brought something new, and yet neither Ava nor Joanna couldn't care less to wonder what more secrets lay ahead on this land. They were both tired, scared, and running out of options. But they were also determined to make it to their destination alive. The journey was uncertain, long, and arduous, but eventually they needed to reach their destination safely.

And for now, that was all that mattered.

The nation's capital is a unique place. From the grandiose architecture of the Capitol Building to the lively energy of Georgetown, there is much to explore in Washington, DC. However, the city can also be fast-paced and stressful, and many residents find themselves longing for a slower way of life. For those who are considering a move from Washington, DC to Austin, there are a few things to make note of.

To begin with, Austin is known for its laid-back atmosphere. Although the city has been rapidly growing, it still has a small-town feel. Secondly, Austin enjoys a mild climate year-round, which can be a welcome change from the hot summers and cold winters of DC. Finally, housing costs in Austin are relatively affordable, especially compared to other major cities. With its vibrant culture and slower pace of life, Austin may not be a bad place for those looking to make a fresh start or for those looking for a short break in the pace.

Elizabeth Greensburg read the note she had received from Steve Riggs and smiled. Steve Riggs had a certain charm and suaveness, and Elizabeth always knew he could easily convince her to move to Austin, albeit for a short time. She read and reread the note. She folded and put it in the envelope before putting it in her bag. She looked around her office room and checked if she needed anything else. There were a few boxes stacked on the carpet, and they were filled with document folders, notebooks, a few desk accessories, but mostly books—books she may never need or read. She would keep coming to DC at least once every two weeks. So Elizabeth really did not need much from her office here. The new office room was as large as this one, but it had already been furnished. As she walked outside, she stopped one last time, and looked up and down before closing the door shut.

Elizabeth Greensburg was moving to Austin. She had already signed a lease agreement for a small office in downtown Austin. She had also rented an executive apartment not too far from her office location at almost fifty percent of what she would have paid for a similar size department in DC. If everything went as planned, she knew would need this office space for not more than two years before building the necessary working relationships locally to be able to manage the lobbying operations of GB, Inc. remotely from Washington, DC.

But moving to Austin also amounted to Elizabeth rekindling her flame for Steve. She had first noticed him even before she started working with him directly as his company's lobbyist. It was an instant and intense kind of attraction—the kind that made one's stomach flutter and heart race. She could barely think straight when she was around him, so she made sure to do her homework before every meeting. During the initial stages of their business relationship, she avoided meeting him personally whenever she could. It was not just that Steve was smart and successful, which she admired, but it was more than that. There was something in his eyes that made her want to trust him, even though she knew better than to let her personal feelings get involved in her work.

She tried to ignore her feelings, but it was impossible. Elizabeth knew she was treading dangerously close to the line between professional and personal, but she couldn't help it. She had never been this attracted to anyone before, and she didn't know how to deal with it for the longest time. She felt grateful that Steve Riggs didn't live in the same city as she did or anywhere close by. Otherwise, she knew she would have either lost his business by now or their relationship would have blossomed into something more personal making it impossible for her to be his lobbyist.

She never had to think about giving up on her crush and moving on because of the distance, but she knew things could become different once she moved to Austin. Perhaps Elizabeth Greensburg was looking forward to the newer challenges—both professionally and personally, and Austin could just give her that fresh start.

In the age of social media, anyone could become content creators, and anyone could create news, thereby blurring the lines between professional content creators and non-professional content creators, and likewise between mainstream journalists and citizen journalists. They all must compete on the same platforms that have somewhat equalized the entry points. The younger generations, who were growing up in this digital age, had certainly developed newer practices when it came to how they consumed news and newer attitudes on news itself. Things that were in stark contrast to how the previous generations behaved. For mainstream legacy media outlets to compete and survive in this environment, they had no choice but to have a deep social media presence. They need to keep reinventing tools to use social media platforms to both disseminate news and to market themselves. It was the latter that was becoming increasingly harder for some legacy media outlets, which were leading to failures eventually. But as long as mainstream media outlets stayed competitive, adopting robust and creative social media strategies, they could still find ways to reach the audience with their news. News that mattered. Social media had truly reduced the world to a global village.

The rise of social media meant that more and more people were being able to connect through common aspirations, desires, beliefs, interests, and even politics. People were more connected than ever in the history of mankind, and yet their connections seem to make them increasingly live in their own bubbles. As a result, facts have to compete with social media and create strong reactions on social media for them to stand out and not get drowned by misinformation or disinformation.

Mainstream media outlets did have a challenging responsibility for how to disseminate the news they are breaking to their target audience—somehow. The public, however, should have been constantly aware of the irreparable damages to societies that consuming news from social media could cause.

Which was why the job of an honest reporter or a journalist with professional integrity was even more important today. Stories they broke could still alter the political landscape. Exposés they investigated could still advance social justice and equality. Passionate reports they did could still hold politicians, business leaders, and other people in the public eye totally accountable. Honest reporters and journalists full of professional integrity like Jason Greer and Myra Bristow belonged to a breed that may have been dwindling in numbers. But they were as relevant as they were yesterday.

After Ava's story broke, *The Austin Star* office had been inundated with telephone calls for interviews with Jason Greer and Myra Bristow. It had gotten to a point that they disconnected their main landline so they could get work done. National media outlets and even a few global outlets like BBC had picked up the story and had started doing their versions and takes on the politics behind it all. Reporters from around the country had started descending in the capital and in Midland. Bradley and Eveline had to stay under the radar, and whenever they stepped out of the house, there were paparazzi waiting to get a photo. The Midland Police main precinct had cordoned off the main entrance to the parking lot because there were already half a dozen media house vehicles that had descended into the parking lot with cameras and long microphones. Captain Ramirez had given strict instructions to all his officers not to talk to the press even by mistake. For more than forty-eight hours now, it felt like the Ava story had taken over the news wave. According to the latest Gallup poll, more than sixty-two percent of Texans still supported the book bans and the steps Governor Fisher was taking in eliminating wokeness in public school education in the state of Texas.

Myra had asked Jason to take a few days off and stay away from the office. She wished if the frantic coverage was no longer about who reported and instead it became more about the facts reported in the article, then they may feel safe. Jason latched onto the opportunity and decided to travel to Utah and spend a few days visiting national parks in the state, and then spend a couple of days visiting his parents who lived in Salt Lake City. He was excited that he was finally going to take a break from work. His story on RapFuel would be the next big exposé, and before he started working on that huge story, he felt deserved enough to have had earned this break.

Ready to recharge. Thank you, was his last text message to Myra before he boarded his plane from Austin.

Right after that message to Myra, he sent a message to his friend in Salt Lake City. Jason told him that he was going to visit SLC, but this was going to be a surprise visit for his parents. He asked his friend if he would be available to pick him at the airport and drop him off at his parents since it would be a late arrival. He also wanted to check if this friend was available in SLC to meet with him when he was there.

The friend responded immediately, *I will be there whenever you ask me to. See you soon at the airport, bro.*

Jason felt relieved as soon as he saw that message. Memories from his middle school years came rushing to him. He had not seen his parents in more than two years.

Boarding the plane, Jason could feel his excitement bubbling inside him. It had been months of planning and waiting, but finally he was going to get a break. He tried hard not to think about the RapFuel story. The story that would expose the truth, bring some politicians down, change the future of the state, and make him a household name. He settled into his seat and closed his eyes, mentally preparing himself for the days ahead.

But first, the vacation.

The morning air was chill and fresh, with more than a hint of the autumnal colors to come. The sun was just peeking over the horizon, casting a pink and orange glow over the nation's capital. The city was slowly waking up. The streets were empty, except for a few early risers walking their dogs or jogging along the mall. Dew glistened on the grass, and one could see their breath in the air. It was October in Washington, DC, and nature was putting on a show. The trees were ablaze with color, from deep reds to vibrant oranges, albeit not in their full glory yet. It was a beautiful sight, and one that on one would ever tire of.

As the main streets started to grow busy with people rushing to work or running errands, there was a feeling of freshness in the air, an anticipation of something new to come. October was a month of change, and there was no better place to see it than at the nation's capital. Walking in the park was the best way to start any day, and it was just perfect to do so on this October morning.

Congressman Evan Williams was getting his walk in before he started the most crucial day in his congressional career.

At 9:30 AM, Evan Williams, like his 433 other colleagues and fellow Congress members of the United States of America, were present inside the chamber. It was already shaping up to be a long day. The representatives had started debating the TEXIT ratification bill, and it was expected to go on for hours. Williams was confident about the outcome, and yet he was very nervous.

He expected tempers to fray throughout the day as both sides got on a head-on collision of sorts. It was a good TV spectacle. Members of both parties were on their feet, shouting at each other. Some were red-faced with anger; others were close to tears. The vote was expected to be close, and everyone knew it. The aisles were filled with lobbyists and reporters, all eager to see how this would play out. There was tension in every nook and corner of the chamber.

The debates went on till 12:30 PM, when the speaker adjourned the House for a short lunch break. During the break, some members were getting up to pace the floor, while some others furiously scribbled notes before rushing to the cafeteria. Then there were those who were opening their social media apps on their phones and rapidly scrolling the screens for the latest coverage. There was a sense of anticipation in the air, as everyone knew that the vote was going to be close. The voting was scheduled for 4:30 PM. So the speaker had set aside two hours after lunch for further debates, cross-questioning, and responses. When the time came to vote, the representatives filed into the chamber and took their seats.

Exactly at 4:30 PM, the Speaker of the House banged his gavel on his desk and called for the vote and the representatives began to cast their ballots. Those who were watching it live on TV could see the tally almost real time. As the votes were tallied, it became increasingly clearer that the outcome was going to be very close.

At 5:30, the counting was complete. In the end, as most excepted, it was decided by a margin of just two votes. The representatives who had voted alongside the way the bill went let out a collective sigh of relief, while those who had voted on the other side started to file their way out of the chamber slowly.

The United States House of Representatives had just ratified TEXIT—the state of Texas's petition to leave the Union. And now it was entirely up to the state of Texas to put together an exit proposal and plan for the presidential approval.

The adrenaline rush had slowed down and Jason quickly fell asleep. The plane had not even moved out of the gate. The flight attendants were still walking down the aisle checking the cabins for any additional cargo space while making sure all the passengers were seated properly.

Jason suddenly woke up from his deep sleep as heard a voice from behind him. Someone was tapping on his shoulders. He looked up to see two federal air marshals making their way down the aisle towards him; this was not normal procedure. The third one was behind him trying to wake him up.

As they made their way closer, one of them spoke. "Sir, we need you to come with us immediately." Stunned with confusion arisen out of his sleep-derived grogginess and partly because this was a scenario he had not anticipated at all, he stood up from his seat without making a fuss. He pointed at his carry-on backpack and one of the officers grabbed it for him. Jason was wondering if they were going to bring out the handcuffs and publicly humiliate him for a few minutes as he walked to the front of the aircraft, but to his relief they did not. He followed the marshals off the plane without a question.

This must be the governor! Jason thought to himself.

His vacation plans were now officially derailed, as the mysterious circumstances of his removal had him completely stunned. As they brought him off the plane through a special staircase directly to the side of the plane, he saw two identical unmarked black cars waiting for them. He was pushed into the back seat of one of the cars. There was plenty of space for him and one air marshal to seat themselves comfortably in that space.

Jason had no idea where he was being escorted to.

The room was large and airy. It was on the second floor of the house. The walls were painted a pale blue, and the floors were covered in a plush carpet. There was a large window on one side of the room, and the bed was situated so that the senator could enjoy views of the garden outside. The room was furnished with a comfortable armchair and a small table, on which a vase of fresh flowers had been placed. A TV and a laptop had been set up so that the senator could stay informed and connected while he recuperated. There was also a phone beside the bed in case he needed to make any calls. There was a nurse attending to him, and she was staying with him in the room while the family was only a call away. Senator Newell's wife Cynthia had made sure that he had everything he needed to recover quickly and comfortably. It was the day after ratification. All news channels were covering what a thrilling vote it was at the US House of Representatives the previous day and how narrowly Congress managed to ratify TEXIT.

Senator Newell was sitting in his chair, lost in thought, when he heard a knock on the door. He slowly rose to his feet, but the nurse got up before he could make his way to the door. He did not have to wonder who could be coming to see him. In fact, he was expecting someone at this specific hour. When the nurse opened the door, he gave a big smile to Vanessa Glass, who had not seen him in a long time. Vanessa had called him two days before and asked if she could visit and check on him while he was recovering from his stabbing injury. She had brought a bouquet of daisies, something to bring more cheer to the room. The two exchanged greetings and spent a few minutes catching up on what they had been doing since they last saw each other in Galveston. Eventually, the conversation turned to politics—and specifically, the stabbing incident. The senator waved at the nurse, gesturing her to wait outside the room. She walked out.

The senator talked about his work in the Senate on various bills and then about the ratification. He did not tell Vanessa how much he worked behind the scenes to defeat the ratification bill. He did not tell her how relieved he was now that Congress had ratified it. He was always prepared for this eventuality, although he would have preferred the status quo. The stabbing incident changed his perspectives on things. He was determined more than ever to look past the ratification and to the future of Texas.

Vanessa did not understand the politics Newell was talking about, but she could feel the passion when he talked about ratification. Like Newell, she, too, had prepared herself to for the eventuality of an independent Texas. As an African American who belonged to eleven-point-eight percent of the state's population, she just did not know how to be a productive participant in an independent Texas. That changed after she met Senator Newell. So naturally she was shocked when she learned about the stabbing incident and was praying for his speedy recovery. And today, both Vanessa and Newell were talking about ratification in the most optimistic terms.

"I'm glad to see you back on your feet, senator," said Vanessa.

"Me, too." Newell smiled.

"Any idea who did this to you?" Vanessa was hesitant to ask this question, for she was afraid of reigniting some trauma in him, but she had to ask before she left.

"I really don't. In politics, it's never easy to know who your friend is and who your enemy is. Let the police do their job," Newell replied with the shrug of his shoulders. "Although I may have some suspicions." He smiled.

"It was nice of you to give me some time today and for letting me visit you, senator. I continue to pray for your speedy recovery. Now, if you will permit me, I do not want to be a bother any more than it is needed. I hope to see you soon again." Vanessa got up and bowed her head before walking towards the door. And then she stopped.

"One more thing, senator." She paused and looked at the senator for his reaction. Newell did not blink his eyes, and he had his mouth open as if he was going to say something. Perhaps he was waiting for this moment.

"It's a yes!" Vanessa blinked her eyes as she said it, smiled, and closed the door behind her.

Newell smiled, too. A wide smile that his face had not experienced in a long while.

He closed his eyes and looked back at the last few months of his life. From the time Fisher got elected through the tumultuous times of TEXIT referendum to the last few weeks of ratification craziness in Washington, DC, where the political drama never ended and there was always a fresh dose of political insanity every day. Despite the hardships and the setbacks, Newell knew he must keep going. Because he believed that there was something better waiting for him on the other side just like his father had often told him.

"Never to give up no matter how hard things got, son! It's like a good novel. Even if the novel has its fair share of twists and turns, you must keep reading it because you want to know how it ends. Don't you? The ending might not be what you are expecting, but remember, it's always worth it in the end."

His father's words echoed in his ears, and the anticipation that Senator Albert Newell had in flipping to the next chapter of the book was palpable.

He thought to himself, *It better have some good parts.*

ACKNOWLEDGEMENTS

Writing a book is a journey, and I am grateful for the countless individuals who have walked this path with me, providing support, encouragement, and inspiration along the way.

First and foremost, I would like to extend my deepest gratitude to my copyeditor, James Abbate, whose keen insights, and meticulous attention to detail elevated this book to new heights. Secondly, I would like to thank my designer David Ter-Avanesyan, who was my creative partner in giving the book its final shape.

To my beta readers, Emily Benoit, Tucker Lieberman, Kathy Brown, and Joe Walkers, their detailed feedback and constructive criticism were instrumental in shaping the narrative and refining the ideas within these pages. Their insights challenged me to grow as a writer, and I am deeply appreciative of their time and commitment.

I must also acknowledge the incredible circle of close friends from my alma mater, BITS Pilani, India, who have supported me in ways too numerous to count. I am also indebted beyond measure to Thorsten Gorny, my long-suffering interlocutor, for his wisdom and friendship. For too many years, these friends have been stoic readers of my unevolved writings and for their unwavering belief in me, I owe them all more than I can express here.

Family plays an indelible role in our lives, and I am fortunate to have the most remarkable family by my side. To my mom and my late dad, who took immense pride in my writing. My dad would have relished the opportunity to read my first book, but sadly, he left us in June 2023. To my loving wife, Kameshwari, who has been my first and my most devoted reader. Her early feedback and unending encouragement sustained me through many long days and nights of writing. I am eternally grateful for her guidance and patience.

I would be remiss not to mention my children, Nakul and Rachna, who provided moments of levity and love, even during the most intense writing sessions. To the two loyal canine members of our family, Tayga and Monk, who were my steadfast writing companions, as their presence brought warmth and solace to my workspace.

Lastly, I want to dedicate this book to my late grandfather, K.S. Ganapathy. He was a teacher, and a fervent reader, who kindled the spark in me to write and drew delight from watching me become a better writer through my adolescent years. My grandfather's belief in my abilities and his love for learning and literature continue to be a guiding light in my creative endeavors. This book is a tribute to his memory.

To all those mentioned here and to many others who have touched my life in myriad ways, thank you from the bottom of my heart. Your support has made this book a reality, and I am forever grateful.

9 7 9 8 9 8 9 2 4 3 5 1 8